Raves for Chr[...]

"Dodd delivers a high-octane, blo[...] suspense novel is a delicious concoction that readers will be hard-pressed not to consume in one gulp." —*Publishers Weekly*

"Warm characterizations and a caperlike plot make Dodd's hot contemporary romance a delight, and the cliff-hanger ending will leave readers eager for the sequel." —*Booklist*

"Dodd brings her unique sense of plotting, character, humor, and surprise to this wonderful tale. You'll relish every word, cherish each poignant moment and ingenious plot twist, sigh deeply, and eagerly await the sequel. Dodd is clever, witty, and sexy." —*Romantic Times*

"Dodd adds humor, sizzling sensuality, and a cast of truly delightful secondary characters to produce a story that will not disappoint." —*Library Journal*

"Strong and likable characters make this an enjoyable read. Ms. Dodd peppers the story with interesting secondary personalities, which adds to the reading pleasure." —The Best Reviews

"Sexy and witty, daring and delightful."
—*New York Times* bestselling author Teresa Medeiros

"A master romantic storyteller."
—*New York Times* bestselling author Kristin Hannah

"Christina Dodd keeps getting better and better."
—*New York Times* bestselling author Debbie Macomber

"Treat yourself to a fabulous book—anything by Christina Dodd!"
—*New York Times* bestselling author Jill Barnett

Other Books by Christina Dodd

CHRISTINA DODD

Dangerous Ladies

Trouble in High Heels

AND

Tongue in Chic

NEW AMERICAN LIBRARY

New American Library
Published by New American Library, a division of Penguin Group (USA) Inc., 375 Hudson Street,
New York, New York 10014, USA
Penguin Group (Canada), 90 Eglinton Avenue East, Suite 700, Toronto, Ontario M4P 2Y3,
Canada (a division of Pearson Penguin Canada Inc.)
Penguin Books Ltd., 80 Strand, London WC2R 0RL, England
Penguin Ireland, 25 St. Stephen's Green, Dublin 2, Ireland (a division of Penguin Books Ltd.)
Penguin Group (Australia), 250 Camberwell Road, Camberwell, Victoria 3124, Australia
(a division of Pearson Australia Group Pty. Ltd.)
Penguin Books India Pvt. Ltd., 11 Community Centre, Panchsheel Park,
New Delhi - 110 017, India
Penguin Group (NZ), 67 Apollo Drive, Rosedale, North Shore 0632, New Zealand
(a division of Pearson New Zealand Ltd.)
Penguin Books (South Africa) (Pty.) Ltd., 24 Sturdee Avenue, Rosebank, Johannesburg 2196,
South Africa

Penguin Books Ltd., Registered Offices:
80 Strand, London WC2R 0RL, England

Published by New American Library, a division of Penguin Group (USA) Inc. *Trouble in High Heels*
and *Tongue in Chic* were previously published in separate Signet editions.

First New American Library Trade Paperback Printing, October 2009
10 9 8 7 6 5 4 3 2 1

Set in Adobe Garamond
Designed by Jessica Shatan Heslin/Studio Shatan, Inc.

Printed in the United States of America

PUBLISHER'S NOTE
These are works of fiction. Names, characters, places, and incidents either are the product of the
author's imagination or are used fictitiously, and any resemblance to actual persons, living or dead,
business establishments, events, or locales is entirely coincidental.
    The publisher does not have any control over and does not assume any responsibility for author or
third-party Web sites or their content.

Dear Reader,

The way to fight a woman is with your hat. Grab it and run.

The guy who said that was a wise man. He knew what most men don't—women are powerful creatures who should be handled with care, or they can become very, very dangerous.

When I wrote *Trouble in High Heels*, I knew exactly how lawyer Brandi Michaels would react when she discovered her lousy, deceitful fiancé got his girlfriend pregnant, then had the guts to ask for her engagement ring back. I knew she would become as dangerous as a wounded lioness, pawn the ring, and use the money for a new gown and killer heels. Then she would go to a society party looking for revenge. And a fabulous revenge she would find . . . in Roberto Bartolini.

Roberto is an Italian count, sex in an Armani suit, Johnny Depp without the eyeliner. He has more than money, more than breeding, more than looks—he radiates power. Brandi considers him as challenging as Everest, and she's ready to scale his heights.

What Brandi doesn't know is that Roberto comes from a family of famous robbers; he's been accused of jewel theft; and he's in town to steal the magnificent Romanov Blaze, a priceless cursed diamond. Nor does she know that she's part of his defense team.

Brandi is in deep trouble.

When I wrote *Tongue in Chic*, I knew Natalie Meadow Szarvas was a different kind of dangerous lady—less sophisticated, more wholesome, but just as determined to complete her mission of recovering her grandmother's painting, even if it involved breaking and entering—and getting caught by the mansion's owner.

Though Meadow is a fast thinker, Devlin Fitzwilliam is a fast talker gifted with the face of a dark angel. In Meadow, he recognizes the opportunity for revenge against her family, but he'll soon discover the real reason he can't seem to let the rash, eccentric, laughing artist escape his control . . . or his heart.

Brandi and Meadow are the kind of dangerous ladies I love to write—intelligent, funny, willing to stand and fight for what they believe, and oh so surprised when love sweeps them off their feet.

I hope you enjoy this chance to enjoy two of my favorite novels in one volume, and remember—in the right circumstances, every lady is dangerous.

Warmly,
Christina Dodd
www.christinadodd.com
For the wild at heart!

Trouble in High Heels

For Scott.
When I write about love forever,
I write about you.

Acknowledgments

Some books come to fruition without struggle.

So I'm told.

My thanks to my editor, Kara Cesare, for holding my hand through the battle, and to Kara Welsh, for being so patient through disaster and flood. To my plot group, Lisa Kleypas, Connie Brockway, Susan Kay Law, and especially Susan Sizemore and Geralyn Dawson, who answered my panicked phone calls with brutal wisdom and witty banter. And to my agent, Mel Berger, thank you for being a sounding board, mentor, and friend.

1

Eleven-year-old Brandi sat in the open door of her bedroom with the floaty princess curtains and the pretty canopy bed, and listened to the sound of her mother's hysterical voice.

"But I don't know how to write a check."

"It's time you learned." Her father couldn't have sounded more disgusted.

"But you always did that for us."

"That's right." Daddy was sort of stomping as he packed. "I'd come home from a hard day's work at the office and I had to sit down and pay the utilities and the house payment and the credit cards and all the other bills. I had to make the reservations anytime we traveled and arrange to have someone mow the lawn. Taking care of you was a damned pain in the ass."

"But you wanted it that way!"

Daddy must have recognized the justice of her statement, because he sounded a little nicer. "It's not hard, Tiffany." Then he was back to impatience. "For Christ's sake, my secretary can do it."

"It's her, isn't it?" Mama's voice shook with suspicion. "It's Susan. That little slut is the one you're leaving me for."

"She's not a slut," he snapped. Then he took a long, audible breath. "And I'm leaving you because you don't do anything except . . . groom."

Brandi imagined her father waving his big hands at her thin, blond, immaculately coiffed and manicured mother.

"What do you want me to do? I can do whatever you want." Mama sounded panicked.

Brandi knew Mama *was* panicked, because Brandi was scared, too.

"You *can't* carry on an intelligent conversation. You *can't* discuss my business with me. The reason you always get picked for jury duty is because you don't know a damned thing about current events." He snorted. "A man like me needs an intellectual challenge, not an aging doormat."

Brandi had to know what was going to happen—to her parents, and to her.

Brandi's mother gasped. "I'm thirty-two!"

"As I said."

Why was he being so mean? Tiffany was beautiful. Everybody said so. All Brandi's friends at ballet envied her for having a mother who looked like a movie star. Brandi didn't think it was so hot having people talk to her all the time about Tiffany and ask if she was proud to have such a pretty mother, but she always smiled and nodded her head, because then they always said, "And you'll look just like her when you grow up!"

"You never wanted to talk to me about your business before." Mama's heels clicked on the hardwood floor as she followed Daddy around their bedroom. "You said you left Jane for me because she was always talking about that stuff when all you wanted was a peaceful home where you could relax."

Daddy grunted.

"Look around you. I've consulted feng shui experts and brought in decorators to make this a home that you could be proud of—"

"And I paid through the nose for that fool Japanese guy—"

"Indonesian!"

"And for some idiot decorator to change my curtains in my office four times a year." Daddy was getting hostile.

"Drapes. They're drapes. And you bring clients into that office, Gary, and we had to get them right!"

Brandi loved that when it came to something she really cared about, Mama got in Daddy's face.

"Besides, our house headlined in the Frontgate catalog—"

The spread in Frontgate catalog had been Mama's pride and joy, and had given her great cachet among her friends.

"That catalog brought you a lot of work. The Dugeren murder case and"—Mama's voice quavered—"that high-profile divorce case. . . ."

She was right.

So Daddy attacked from a different direction. "Do you think I don't notice the bills to the dermatologist and the plastic surgeon? Your discreet little visits for your facial buffs and your body peels?"

"What's wrong with that?" Honestly bewildered, Mama asked, "Don't you want me to be beautiful?"

"I want something more than an empty shell who smiles vacuously and babbles about how Vicky at tennis has to do something about the cellulite on her thighs! And your daughter's just as bad."

Brandi wanted to cover her ears, to not hear her own father disown her by saying *your daughter,* but it was like listening to a car wreck—the insults and the rejection commanded her attention as surely as the screech of brakes and the crumple of metal, and for one wild moment she wondered if she would come out alive.

"All that girl does—"

"Brandi." Mom took a deep breath, and Brandi pictured her squaring her shoulders. "Her name is Brandi."

"All Brandi does is take ballet and gymnastics and cheerleading classes. She's a mini-you. Why couldn't she be more like Kimberley?"

Kim was his first daughter, his daughter with Jane.

"Kimberley plays softball, and she does it damned well." His voice rang with pride. "She's got a sports scholarship to UT. She's going to be an engineer and make something of herself. Not like that kid of yours. Brandi is stupid."

Stupid. Daddy thought she was stupid. Brandi closed her eyes to try to contain the anguish, and when that didn't work she put her fist against her mouth and shoved, holding back her shriek.

She wasn't stupid. He was. *He was.* She wanted to go down to her parents' bedroom, stomp her foot, shout and rail at her father for throwing her and her mother away as if they were trash.

But Brandi didn't make scenes. Brandi followed the rules in the hope that being good would somehow make everything okay.

Everything was not okay, but if she just tried a little harder . . .

"She is not stupid!" Mama said.

"How would *you* know?"

Brandi gasped. How could he be so cruel to Mama?

"She's your daughter as much as Kimberley. She's smart, too. She's never had anything but straight As, even in math." Mama didn't pay a bit of attention to Daddy's insult to her, but leaped into the fray to defend Brandi.

Of course, Mama's strengths weren't taught in school. She was really good at making their house pretty and knowing the right thing to wear and smiling at men so they got flustered and turned red.

"Brandi's probably going to be some kind of freaking English major and a drain on my wallet for the rest of my life." He sounded so disgusted, as if being good in English were a waste.

"She's the best in her class in gymnastics and ballet."

"A bunch of skinny little girls in tights!"

Brandi gritted her teeth. She wasn't skinny or little anymore. She had a figure, and at five-foot-ten she was an inch taller than Mama and four inches taller than any of the rest of the girls in her class. But around the house Daddy hardly glanced at Brandi, and he had never bothered to come to her recitals.

"Kimberley plays real sports," he said. "Competitive sports."

In a prissy tone, Mom said, "If you ask me, Kimberley is a lesbian."

With a soft groan, Brandi dropped her forehead against the wall. It was true. Of course it was true. Kim had told Brandi herself. But Daddy was homophobic, and he sure didn't want to know that his sports-inclined daughter was gay. Mama had just messed up big by telling him.

Daddy shouted, "Why, you jealous little—"

Mama gave a little cry of fright.

He was going to hit Mama.

Brandi started to her feet, picking up her beloved ceramic dragon to use as a weapon.

She heard the sound of glass shattering.

Heart pounding, she ran into the hallway, dragon upraised.

In a guttural tone Daddy said, "For Christ's sake, Tiffany, don't be stupid."

"I'm not stupid!" Mama stomped her foot. "I just think things like manners and pleasure are important, and you shouldn't have broken that vase."

Brandi skidded to a stop.

Mama continued, "It took me months to find the right vase for that table!"

Slowly Brandi lowered the dragon. She crept back toward her room. If they knew she was listening they'd make her shut her door, and no matter how her stomach churned, she had to know whether her daddy had destroyed their lives.

"That's the problem," Daddy said. "You always cared more about vases and manners than about ideas or work—or me."

"That's not true!" Mama whimpered like a kicked puppy.

It *was* true, but to Brandi's childish eyes, it had seemed that that was all he required of her mother. Only in the last year had he grown restless and contemptuous.

Mama's quiet sobbing must have made Daddy uncomfortable, for he tried cajoling her. "C'mon, Tiff, you'll be all right without me. Jane is doing just fine."

"B-but J-Jane had a prenuptial agreement. Y-you didn't want me t-to get one."

"That was your mistake."

Brandi recognized that tone in her father's voice. Guilt was hotly prodding him—and he blamed Mom.

"Y-you said . . . you said you'd take care of me forever."

"For shit's sake, would you stop blubbering? It's disgusting." He slammed his suitcase closed. "I'll have my lawyer call your lawyer."

"I don't have a lawyer!"

"Get one." Daddy's heels slapped the polished hardwood floor as he walked down the hallway.

Brandi tensed as she waited to see if he would stop to hug her before he left.

But he passed without a glance in her direction.

Brandi swallowed her disappointment. She knew how. She'd done it for years.

Mama ran past her and after him, crying with ever more desperation. "I don't have a job. How will I support Brandi? We'll starve!" She caught him as he opened the door, grabbed at his arm, and tried to hold him back.

Even Brandi recognized high drama at its best.

Quietly she shut herself into her bedroom and left them to it.

Her stomach hurt, roiling with distress. She absently rubbed the pain and looked around her bedroom. Mama had decorated it with white-and-gold furniture and pink-and-gold upholstery. When Brandi was young she had felt as though she were living in a Barbie dream house, and she'd loved it.

Now that she was older she felt as if she were living in a Barbie dream house, and she wanted it changed. But she hadn't wanted to hurt Mama's feelings, so she'd added a few touches herself. A stained-glass window done in shades of blue that looked like her favorite print in *The Hobbit*. Her shiny green dragon with sparkling gems for eyes. Three black-and-white posters of the Hadrien Boys from England. But peering through the stained glass, running her fingertips over the dragon's scales, and looking at the boys did nothing to ease the ache in her chest. In her heart.

She opened the window and looked out at the soft green unfurling in the trees. Nashville was beautiful in the spring. Their huge yard was tiered and landscaped and usually the sight made Brandi feel warm and secure. Today it wasn't working. Nothing was working.

Downstairs she heard the front door slam so hard it shook the house.

Her throat hurt, so she took big breaths of fresh air, desperate to hold back . . . no, not tears. She wasn't going to cry.

She was going to fix this. Somehow she had to do something that would make it better.

Walking to her painted desk, she pulled out a tablet, one engraved with her name, and at the top she wrote, *Things to Learn.* She drew a line beneath the words and numbered down the lines, and wrote:

How to Take Care of My Mother.
1. Learn how to write checks.
2. Find out what a utility is.
3. Figure out how to make the house payment.

Then she tore that list off, set it carefully to the side, and on the top of the clean sheet, wrote:

How to Take Care of Myself.
1. Learn how to write checks.
2. Get scholarships so I can go to school.
3. Play baseball.

She frowned at that one and chewed on the end of her pen. No, that wouldn't do. She wasn't good at baseball; to Kim's annoyance Brandi ducked when the ball came in her direction.

Brandi crossed off *Play baseball* and replaced it with *Become a lawyer.*

She didn't know exactly what a lawyer did—a girl who attended ballet, gymnastics, and cheerleading classes in every spare moment learned remarkably little about the real world, especially when her father never talked to her about his job—but she knew he made a lot of money. And her father had required her mother to look beautiful and Brandi to be charming when Mr. Charles McGrath and his wife visited, and Mr. McGrath was an important Chicago lawyer.

That was what she wanted. She wanted to be important. She wanted the power to make her father behave, and the ability to get her mother a prenuptial agreement.

Whatever that was.

Learn how to make a prenuptial agreement.

2

*I*f Brandi's caller ID had been working, she would never have picked up the phone.

But it wasn't, and she did, and that just figured, because it had been one hell of a week.

Not that Brandi hadn't expected it. Anybody with a lick of sense could predict that moving from Nashville to Chicago in the dead of winter would be difficult, and Brandi prided herself on her good sense.

But she'd picked the coldest winter Chicago had seen for a century, which made the pipes in her apartment building freeze for the first time ever, which meant that her movers had had nothing to drink—not that that had stopped them from using her toilet, which for the lack of water didn't flush and probably wouldn't for weeks, and using it with such typical male abandon that she didn't dare sit on it even in the most dire circumstances because there was no way to clean the seat. And one guy caught her talking to herself while she tried to wipe the seat with a wadded-up Kleenex out of her purse, and the son of a bitch had the gall to inch away as if she were crazy.

She didn't think much of men right now, and the movers' back-pedaling only increased her ire—and her sense of isolation.

She didn't know anybody in this town except Alan and Mr. McGrath—for years now she'd called him by the honorary title of Uncle Charles—but where were they while she crammed her entire life into a one-bedroom apartment?

In a lovely piece of irony, the icy roads had sent the truck carrying her new sofa and armchair careening into an empty Marble Slab Ice Cream Shop. The deliverymen wrestled the furniture up to her fourth-floor apartment by tilting it sideways in the freight elevator, a maneuver that made her cover her eyes and pray to the gods of furniture placement.

Her entreaties must have worked, because they planted the sofa and the chair in front of the small propane fireplace, put the otto-man between them, and moved her end tables into place.

Surely her luck had turned. The sofa wasn't damaged. The colors and fabrics were exactly the way she had ordered them. They would fit perfectly in the new apartment she and Alan would move into when they married. It was only later that night, when she stopped unpacking long enough to drop into the chair, put her feet up on the ottoman, and look, really look at the furniture, that she realized the sofa was eighteen inches too short.

She'd received the love seat, not the full-size sofa she'd ordered.

She spent the whole night on her hastily made bed, worrying about making the phone call to Amy, her salesperson at Samuel's Furniture.

That, at least, went well. Amy was apologetic, behaving just as well as Brandi could have hoped, but the fact was that she had to wait another six weeks until the actual furniture she'd ordered arrived, and for a few minutes it seemed as if that sucked more than anything else that had happened in this horrific, endless week.

Until the phone call she picked up because she thought, honestly thought, that Alan was calling to tell her he was coming over at last.

Instead, it was her mother.

"Well? How did the move go?" As always, Tiffany sounded like a cheerleader bolstering her team's spirits before the big game.

Brandi stared around at the endless parade of boxes. Empty boxes piled catawampus against the wall. Flattened boxes stacked by the door. Boxes, far too many boxes, still taped shut and scratched with black Magic Marker from her last two moves. An endless supply of boxes, no stereo system in sight, and pizza for dinner again. "Well, I've been unpacking for a day and a half and I haven't seen Alan. Not once."

"Now, sweetheart, I'm sure he's busy. After all, he is a physician." Mother's Tennessee accent sounded soft and tender.

Brandi didn't know why she'd bothered to complain. It was pure exhaustion and loneliness that made her give in to her irritation and criticize her fiancé to, of all people, her mother. "He's not a physician. He's a resident."

"That poor boy. I saw on *60 Minutes* how those hospital administrators work their residents ninety-six hours at a time. And you said he was brilliant. Remember? You told me he was the top of his class and all eyes were on him."

For once Brandi wished her mother would take her side. About anything. "He hasn't called, either. He may have e-mailed, but I don't get connected to the Internet until next week."

"I hope you didn't call him. A nagging woman is an unpleasant creature." Tiffany was the personification of 1950s Southern womanhood.

"Yes, Mother, I know, although if he'd remember me long enough to do as he promised, I wouldn't be seized by this overwhelming desire to nag him." Brandi scratched her nails against the grain of the fabric on the couch, watched as the brocade rose in four welts, and wondered which one of them she wanted to scratch—her mother or her fiancé. "But I'd like to point out that I'm a lawyer who relocated from a lovely, soft, *warm* city to be close to my fiancé. I'm about to start my first full-time job at a major Chicago law firm, and *I'm* going to be working all the time. He could at least call to see if I've frozen to the side of the Dumpster taking out my trash."

Mother's voice took on that pious tone that made Brandi want to shriek. "To keep her man, a woman always has to give one hundred and ten percent."

"How did that work out for you?"

The sound of her mother's shocked inhalation brought Brandi to her senses. She loved her mother, she really did, but Mother had been Daddy's first trophy wife, and he'd left her and the quietly anguished eleven-year-old Brandi for his twenty-three-year-old secretary and a new baby, a son guaranteed to give him what he needed—a football-uniformed mirror image of his youthful self.

Except, of course, Brandi's half brother was now thirteen and supremely uninterested in sports. Instead Quentin was a brilliant computer programmer.

Brandi felt sorry for Quentin; she knew what it was like dealing with a panicked mother who was losing that dewy glow of youth, a father who didn't bother to hide his disappointment in his child, and their rapidly disintegrating marriage.

"I'm sorry, Mother. I'm a bitch."

"No, you're not."

"I'm pretty sure I am." Not always a bad thing, in Brandi's opinion. "Let's face it, with his current troubles Daddy has proved he doesn't know what he wants. Not in a wife. Not in his kids."

"Your father is a good man."

Brandi smiled bitterly and stroked the slick scales of her treasured old dragon. No matter how much Daddy screwed Tiffany over, she never said a nasty word about him. When Brandi was a teenager she might have been conflicted if Mother had badmouthed him, but those days were long gone.

Daddy was not a good man. He was self-centered, abusive, and manipulative, and no one knew that better than Brandi.

"When you get off the phone with me, call him. He'll want to hear that you got there safely."

"Oh, Mother. He'll barely remember I moved."

"And tomorrow's his birthday."

"Oh. I forgot." He'd probably forgotten, too, but Tiffany kept up the pretense that he was a normal man who celebrated special occasions, probably because that way Brandi was forced to communicate with him on a semiregular basis.

When Brandi thought of talking to him, of the chance that he would yell at her, or, worse, of the possibility that he wouldn't have time to speak to her, her stomach hurt. She always put it off as long as possible.

That was why she'd gotten engaged to Alan. He might not be a man of fire and passion, but he was steady and dependable—or he had been until she needed him.

And Mother was right about that, too. He probably had a whopper of an excuse. But Brandi—who'd broken a fingernail down to the quick, whose deodorant had failed hours ago, who was dehydrated and didn't dare drink her bottled water because she couldn't flush— wasn't in the mood to hear it right now.

"Alan'll be by soon." Mother used a conciliatory tone. "Maybe he'll come tonight to take you out to dinner."

"I don't want him to take me out. I want him to help me unpack." Yep. Definitely bitchy.

"No, go out! You should seize every chance for a good time right now, while you're young." About this, Tiffany sounded fierce.

And that made Brandi squirm with guilt. The reason Tiffany hadn't been out there kicking up her heels was because she'd been trying—not succeeding, but trying—to make a living for Brandi. "Mother, you're not exactly old. You're not even fifty. *You* could get out there and have a good time."

"Men my age want women your age, and men who want women my age are too old to have a good time. In every way." Tiffany's voice was droll. "But actually, I've been thinking. . . ."

"What?"

Tiffany hesitated.

"What?" It wasn't like her mother to be coy. Quite the opposite.

"I wish *I* could be there to help you!" Tiffany burst out. "I miss you!"

Brandi would have sworn that wasn't what Tiffany intended to say. But she was too tired, too dirty, too disheveled to dig for the truth. "I haven't lived at home for seven years. You can't miss me that much."

"I know, but it's different with you so far away. When you were at Vanderbilt you were right across town, and I thought if you needed me, I could get to you right away. Now . . ."

"I'm okay, Tiffany. Really. I'm good at taking care of myself." *A lot better than you are at taking care of yourself.*

"I know. You are capable. I'm proud of you." But Tiffany sounded fretful. "I just wish Alan were there. He's so reliable."

Except now. "Tomorrow night he's going to take me to a party at Uncle Charles's." And if he did this disappearing act and didn't show for that, she didn't care what excuse he came up with; she was going to kill him.

"A party?" Tiffany inhaled with excitement. "At Charles's home? Oh, that is a showcase. He recently had the foyer remodeled. Do you know that when they stripped the paint off the curved stairway, they found that underneath it's solid mahogany? Can you imagine? I wish I could see it! Do you like Charles?"

Her mother's leaps from one subject to another made Brandi blink. "Sure. I've liked Uncle Charles since he used his legal expertise to wring child support out of Daddy."

"Your father was confused by that woman he married."

"So we're hoping he's pussy-whipped instead of morally corrupt?"

"Don't use that term, Brandi. It sounds bitter, and that's not at all attractive in a young woman."

"Yes, ma'am." Interesting that when Tiffany got motherly, Brandi felt more secure.

"Tell me all about the party."

"It's a charity ball to raise money for the museum. There'll be a silent auction, and during the entertainment—by the way, Uncle Charles got Elton John—I'm sitting at the McGrath and Lindoberth corporate table." Of course she was. She might be new, but she'd earned straight As out of Vanderbilt Law, and that was no small feat. Even without Uncle Charles's influence she would have been interviewed, and she'd aced that. She'd won this job fair and square. She was good, and she knew it.

"What are you wearing?" Tiffany asked.

Uh-oh. "That black sheath I bought for parties at law school."

Tiffany didn't say, *Oh, but you bought it at Ann Taylor,* or, *But that's two years old.* Instead she said, "Darling, black? That's so New York. Show those Chicago lawyers how good a Southern girl can look!"

"I look awful in pink." Brandi slithered down to sit on her backbone.

"Wear red. Men adore red."

"I don't care what men adore," Brandi snapped, then took a long breath. Tiffany had never changed her mind. She'd lived through fourteen years of miserable existence, and she still thought a man was a woman's best friend—a man and the gifts she could get from him.

"But the sheath doesn't show off your figure."

"Thank God. Do you know how hard it is to dress for business with a chest like mine?"

"Women pay good money every day for a chest like yours. Marilyn Monroe made a fortune with a chest like yours. With a figure like yours!" Tiffany laughed, the kind of throaty purr that said she knew a lot about how men and women played.

Unwillingly, Brandi laughed, too. It was true. If she hadn't become a lawyer, she could have been a Las Vegas showgirl. She was all hourglass figure. During interviews she'd mashed down her bosom so the women wouldn't immediately hate her and the guys would look at her face. "I can't afford a new dress right now. This move cost a fortune."

"I thought Charles paid for the move."

"The firm paid for the move," Brandi corrected. "But I bought furniture"—furniture that was the wrong damned size—"and paid first and last month's rent on the apartment. And starting this month I'm paying Daddy back for my student loans."

"Your daddy would want you to have a new dress."

My God. Tiffany was like a dog with a bone. She never let go.

"Your daddy likes pretty young girls to have pretty things."

"Only if the pretty young girl is his secretary and he's screwing her." Before Tiffany could object, Brandi added, "Besides, with Alan there I don't need to worry about catching a man."

"No, but you need to make sure his gaze is riveted to you and he never leaves your side for fear that the other men will whisk you off."

Brandi laughed again, but wryly. "Alan's stable. He's professional. He knows he can depend on me. He's just not the jealous type."

"Given the right incentive, every man is that type."

No use arguing. Tiffany did know her men.

"But I don't want that type. I consider marriage a meshing of equals, a . . . a calm in the midst of the storm of modern life." Brandi's modern life—a life whose touchstones were good sense, moderation in all things, and a logical progression toward her goals of not being like her mother, proving her father wrong, paying back her debts, and being a model citizen.

She wanted nothing about *Desperate Housewives* to taint her.

"Good heavens," Mother said blankly. "You don't mean that you and Alan are calm in bed?"

"No, don't be ridiculous." Although since Alan had entered medical school he was brief and businesslike, and lately, on the infrequent weekends he managed to get time off, too tired to perform at all. "We have our moments. But there's no shrieking fights or huge dramas."

"You're annoyed with him now, but you're not going to shriek at him?"

"How often have you seen me shriek?"

"Never." In a tone that indicated total cluelessness, Mother said, "You were almost frighteningly calm, even as a child."

Because her parents were playing out the big dramas. "When I see Alan I'm going to explain that he needs to be more sensitive to my needs." Brandi injected humor into her voice. "You can't have it both ways, Tiffany. I can't be sensible enough to know that he probably is too busy to remember that I moved this week *and* cherish such a huge passion for him I can't survive without his very presence."

"No, I . . . no, I suppose not. It's just that those first few years when your father and I got together in bed we erupted into flames—"

Brandi pulled the phone away from her ear. "Ew, Mother, don't tell me that!"

"It seems so early in your relationship to be so cavalier." Tiffany's voice brightened. "And that's why you need a new dress!"

Brandi sighed deeply. "I'll think about it." For about three seconds.

"Get your hair highlighted, too, honey. You've gone a kind of mousy brown."

"I'd call it dishwater blond." Brandi fingered the split ends—Tiffany would have a spasm.

"Dishwater blond is just as attractive as it sounds. Get highlights."

Someone beeped in. Thank God. "Tiffany, I've got to get this." She cut off her mother and answered with a snap, "Hello?"

"Brandi? It's Alan."

"Yes, Alan, I know your voice. Let me hang up on Mother." She switched to her cajoling tone. "Alan, promise you'll hold on."

"I'll hold on." He sounded sullen.

Great. It would be one of *those* conversations. But she couldn't take the chance he'd ditch her and later say it was a medical emergency. He'd done it before and this time she really did need to talk to him.

She clicked back to her mother.

"Speak of the devil, there he is! Let me take this call, Mother. I'll talk to you later!" When she wasn't so tired and could control her irritation a little better.

She cut Tiffany off in the middle of her good-byes and said to Alan, "Where have you been? I've been worried about you!" Which sounded better than *I've been irritated at you.*

"I'm in Las Vegas." His normally flat Massachusetts accent vibrated with some violent emotion.

"Las Vegas?" She was so dumb. She didn't suspect a thing. "What happened? Is someone sick or something?"

"Sick? Is that your best guess?" So much for the calm in the storm. Alan was shouting.

"I—"

"My girlfriend's pregnant. I just got married. And this is *all your fault.*"

3

*B*randi stood with the phone held loosely in her fingers, staring at the apartment she'd rented and paid too much for so she could be close to the medical center and Alan, and tried to absorb the message.

She was a smart woman. She was a lawyer. Words were her weapons and her tools. But she couldn't comprehend him. There was—there had to be—some kind of mistake.

"Alan, are you drunk?"

"A little bit. I needed some liquid courage before I called you. Can you blame me?"

Blame him? She didn't even know him. "I don't understand. Y-you've got a girlfriend?"

"Not anymore. Now she's my wife. I tell you, none of this would have happened if you'd moved to Chicago when I did." That made even less sense than anything else he'd said.

"But I got accepted to Vanderbilt Law and you got accepted to University of Chicago. How could I come with you and get my degree?"

"For shit's sake, I'm going to be a doctor. Do you think I couldn't support you?"

"I think it wasn't about you supporting me. I think it was about me being fulfilled in my work. You *said* you understood." The numbness was wearing off. Alan was married. Married.

"Oh, blah, blah."

"You've been sleeping with someone on the side." Married with a baby on the way. Alan. The guy who used a condom and insisted she use contraceptive foam all at the same time.

"On the side, on the back, on the front . . ." He lowered his voice like he didn't want to be overheard. "Listen, this isn't what I wanted either, but she's pregnant. I have to marry her, or I'm a jerk."

"That ship has sailed," she said with a bite in her voice.

Obviously he didn't like that. His voice got sharper and he dug deeper with his nasty little insinuations. "And another thing. If you'd been a little less of a cold fish, I wouldn't have been such an easy catch."

Yes, the numbness was wearing off, and temper was starting to stir. "This is crap. You're not blaming me because you couldn't keep your zipper closed!"

"I sure as hell am."

"Let me rephrase that. I'm not accepting the blame." She tightened her fingers around the receiver as if it were Alan's neck.

"Alannnn." Through the phone Brandi heard the high, satisfied tones of a woman who'd just gotten her way.

"Is that *her*?" Brandi asked.

"Yeah. That's Fawn." Alan didn't sound any happier than Brandi. But Brandi took damned little comfort from that.

"Alannn, don't forget . . ." The bitch must have covered the receiver, for all Brandi could hear was a low murmur.

Then Alan abruptly spoke into the receiver, dropping the imitation of an injured party and sounding just like he always did when he spoke to Brandi—like a doctor giving advice on how to shed excess pounds.

Why hadn't she realized that before? Why hadn't she realized that he wasn't too tired to make love to her; he was uninterested . . . and getting satisfaction elsewhere?

"Brandi, I need my ring back."

"Your ring?" Brandi was back to not understanding.

"I'm a resident. I can't afford another diamond, so you need to give me my ring back." When she didn't reply, he said impatiently, "My engagement ring."

Brandi glanced at her finger. She'd removed it to protect the diamond while she unpacked. Because it was precious to her. Because it represented careful planning and logical life decisions and true love and all that crap.

She curled her hand into a fist. "Alannnn." If she did say so herself, she did a pretty good imitation of Fawn. "It's not *your* ring. It's *my* ring. And let me give you a little legal advice. In a situation like this, possession is nine-tenths of the law."

She hung up. She hung up softly, without a hint of the ire that roiled in her belly, but she did hang up.

Still holding the cordless, she hurried into the bathroom.

The phone started ringing. And ringing. And ringing. She had to find her answering machine and hook it up. Alan needed something to talk to.

Opening the medicine cabinet, she stared at the shelf where the diamond nestled in its black velvet box. Protected and cherished. She knew her diamonds—when you had a mother who was a trophy wife, you learned these things—and this was a good diamond. Alan had insisted on taking out a loan to get her just the right stone, just the right setting. A marquise-cut, one-carat, pure white diamond that blinked with bits of ancient blue sky and new yellow sun. The platinum setting displayed its simple grandeur.

At the time she had thought he realized how much she wanted it. Now she wondered if it had been nothing more than a symbol of his own good taste. It sure wasn't a symbol of his good sense.

Abruptly irritated with the constant chime of the phone, she answered, then cut Alan off, then opened the line again. She hesitated, her finger over Tiffany's number.

Telling her this, tonight, seemed like an admission that Tiffany was right. Tiffany said no man was interested in a sensible, intelligent, well-organized lawyer with the ability to support herself and be fulfilled in her work. Tiffany said every man wanted a high-maintenance wife dependent on his approval. In fact, that bastard Everyman wanted Marilyn Monroe in a red silk dress.

Brandi's finger smashed down on the autodial. She counted the rings, then heard her sister's voice say, "I can't come to the phone right now. . . ."

Of course not. It was Thursday night. Kim was a coach, and there had to be some kind of game at Smith. Volleyball or softball or whatever-ball season it was.

"Please, Kim, call me as soon as you can." Brandi hesitated, not sure what else to say. Finally, she worked up, "I sort of need you," and hung up.

Had her voice trembled? She hoped not. Kim would think she'd been crying, and she'd never been so far from crying. All this churning in her gut was a combination of rage, humiliation and, well, humiliation.

Yanking the ring from the box, she tossed it like garbage at the toilet.

Luckily, the lid was down and it bounced off and skittered across the tile floor.

Yes, she was mad, but not so mad that she tossed a flawless diamond ring down the tubes.

Besides, even if she succeeded in hitting the bowl, she couldn't flush. The pipes were frozen.

She chased the glittering, glorious symbol of her romantic folly into the corner by the tub. Picking it up, she cradled it in her palm . . . and smiled, a Machiavellian smile that, if he'd seen it, would have made Alan sweat.

No, it was better, so much better, if she made use of the ring—to make herself happy.

As Brandi walked along, huddling close to the buildings in an attempt to avoid Chicago's blistering cold wind, her cell phone gave a series of sharp rings. She wanted to ignore the summons; answering would involve peeling off her glove, digging into the capacious pocket of her black London Fog, and pushing up her wool hat to put the phone to her ear—all activities guaranteed to turn her already flash-frozen flesh into a solid Popsicle.

But that was Kim's ring tone, and after a night spent awake and fuming, Brandi needed to talk to *somebody*. It took her a minute of frantic fumbling before she managed to pull out her cell and flip it open.

"What is wrong?" Kim's deep voice demanded an immediate response.

"Wait a minute; I'm going inside." Brandi opened the door of Honest Abe's Pawnshop, the one her landlord had recommended as the most reputable in the area.

The heat hit her cheeks and she moaned with joy.

"Why are you making that noise?" Kim sounded even more coachlike and commanding.

"It's cold outside. It's warm in here." In the last twelve hours, Brandi had gone through anguish, embarrassment, and rage and now had reached the moment where she relished imparting her news just to hear Kim's reaction. "I'm pawning my engagement ring."

"Why?"

"Alan jilted me."

"You're shitting!" Kim shouted. "*Alan* did?"

It was a small shop, crammed with large goods against the wall and small goods inside the glass counter, and everything had a fluorescent tag on it with the price written in black Magic Marker. Brandi smiled at the Asian man behind the cash register and at the two handsome young men lounging by the gun counter.

This was almost fun.

Well, except for the fact she had to go to a major charity function tonight . . . alone. But she had a plan. Man, oh, man, did she have a plan.

"Mr. Nguyen?" she said to the man behind the counter.

"Yes." The owner was short with black, black hair, dark eyes, and beautiful golden skin.

She placed the black velvet box on the counter. "Eric Lerner at my apartment building said you were honest and would give me a fair price."

"I appreciate the business. Thank Eric for me," Mr. Nguyen said.

"So how much?" She pushed the box toward the pawnshop owner. Into the phone she said, "Alan got his girlfriend pregnant and had to marry her in a quickie Vegas wedding."

"Was Elvis involved?" Kim shot back.

"Dunno."

"Wait, wait, wait," Kim said. "That bloodless little weenie Alan got a girl pregnant and had to get married?"

Now Kim had surprised Brandi. "Didn't you like him?"

"You know how doctors always have this cachet, this intensity, this certainty that makes you pay attention to their every word?"

"Yeah."

"Alan would have made a good accountant."

Brandi gave a spurt of laughter.

The pawnshop owner wasn't really old, maybe in his sixties, but he had that palsy that some people get. His fingers were shaking as he placed the jeweler's glass in his eye and peered at the diamond.

"You don't sound particularly brokenhearted." Kim sounded cautious.

"I'm sure brokenhearted will come later. Right now I'm just furious. I guess it's the prospect of pawning my diamond and knowing that Alan will have to pay through the nose to get it back."

"Hmm. Well. That's good."

Brandi knew Kim had made some judgment, the sense of which escaped her, but she didn't care. As long as she got her revenge. Because no matter what they taught in ethics class in law school, revenge tasted really good.

"A fabulous diamond in a popular setting," Mr. Nguyen said.

"You can easily resell it," Brandi agreed.

In her ear, Kim asked, "What did Tiffany say about Alan and his new wife?"

"I haven't exactly told her."

"You didn't tell your mother?" Kim sounded incredulous.

"I can't. She's going to say, 'I told you so. I told you you have to cater to a man. I told you you couldn't act as if your career is as important as his. I told you to be a Stepford wife.'"

"I think you're doing your mom a disservice." As usual when they talked about Tiffany, Kim sounded calm and wise.

"Last night when I hadn't heard a word from him since I moved, she was defending him." And while that had riled Brandi last night, today it made her furious.

"Last night you intended to marry him and she wanted desperately to make sure *your* marriage worked, so she counseled you the best she knew how."

"I suppose." Kim could be right. Probably was right. But Brandi wasn't in the mood to be fair.

"Have you talked to our father?" Kim used the deeply mocking tone she always used when she talked about Daddy.

"About Alan? I don't *think* so." Brandi ladled on the sarcasm.

"No, for his birthday."

"Damn. I forgot again." And Tiffany had reminded her.

"Don't blame you. I girded my loins and made the call. Bastard didn't even bother to pick up, so I left a message."

"Aren't you lucky?"

"That's what I tell myself."

Mr. Nguyen was staring at the diamond as if deep in thought and tapping his chin.

"I have the paperwork," Brandi told him. She'd searched half the night for the sheet that rated the diamond's clarity and flawlessness.

He barely glanced at it. "Okay, I'll give you eight thousand."

"Dollars?" Brandi was stunned. Alan had paid ten thousand; he'd made sure she saw the bill of sale. In fact, he'd demanded she *appreciate* the bill of sale.

The asshole.

As Tiffany's jewelry had had to be sold to support them, Brandi had gained experience with pawnshop owners. They never paid more than twenty-five percent of appraised value, and *then* they acted as if they were doing you a favor. And they never, ever appraised the jewelry wrong.

Haggling was a fine art in a pawnshop, and Brandi had been prepared to bargain. But maybe while she'd had her head down studying in law school, diamonds had taken a hike in value. Hastily she said, "Sure. Eight thousand. It's a deal."

"That's good," Kim said appreciatively.

Mr. Nguyen slipped the diamond into a box and slid it into the case. "A pretty girl like you needs jewels to decorate your neck and ears. Yesterday I got in diamond earrings—"

"I don't care if I never see another diamond as long as I live." Brandi had never meant anything as much in her life.

"Who are you and what have you done with my sister?" Kim gasped in simulated dismay.

"Shaddup," Brandi said into the phone.

"Sapphires to match your beautiful eyes." Mr. Nguyen smiled at her, but he had white lines around his mouth and a birthmark on his cheek . . . or a bruise.

She glanced at the two guys. They'd moved to the computer counter. They were chatting in low voices, seemingly focused on the array of iPods in the case. They weren't standing close, and they seemed unconcerned about her transaction, but both had their scarves wrapped over the tops of their heads and over their mouths. A niggling unease worked its way up her spine. It almost looked as if they were trying to disguise themselves.

"Kim, hold on a minute. . . ." She leaned across the counter. "Sapphires might be just what I need." In a lower voice, she said, "Do you need help?"

"What's happening?" Kim spoke softly in her ear.

Mr. Nguyen smiled even more broadly as he placed a small white box on the counter. "No. I'm hiring no one right now. It's too cold and business is not good."

"What's wrong?" Kim repeated.

"Nothing. I think." Brandi picked up the box and asked Mr. Nguyen, "Those guys aren't bothering you?"

"They're in the neighborhood all the time. They came in to get warm and to see what I have in electronics." He shrugged. "They're hackers."

"Hackers?" That wasn't good.

"Maybe I said that wrong. They're computer geeks." Leaning across, he flipped open the lid.

What met Brandi's eyes made her catch her breath. Held upright on the tiny white velvet showcase, the sapphires blinked in a glorious shade of blue.

"Whoa." They must have been a carat each, set in yellow gold. Brandi forgot how to haggle, how to play hard to get. She was almost salivating on the counter when she said, "Gorgeous."

"I swear to God, Brandi, if you don't talk to me . . ." Kim sounded pissed.

"Sorry. I got distracted. There are these sapphires—"

"Good ones?" Kim liked her jewelry and had been a willing student when Tiffany taught the girls how to tell the real from the dross. "No, wait! You can't divert me. Is there something wrong in that place?"

Brandi glanced at the guys again. They were pointing down at an antique tiara and laughing. They looked youthful and carefree, and one laughed hard enough to start coughing. He sounded sick, like he had bronchitis, and the other pounded on his back. Brandi supposed the scarves might be because they were cold or ill. She didn't know why Mr. Nguyen wouldn't tell her if there was a problem.

And the sapphires drew her gaze like hot coals. "Everything's fine. Now let me look at these stones." Brandi accepted Mr. Nguyen's offer of his jeweler's glass. She wiped it carefully, then held it to her eye. "Cornflower blue," she pronounced.

"From Kashmir," Mr. Nguyen said.

"From Kashmir," Kim echoed. "The best."

"One has an inclusion partially covered by the prong. The other has a blemish. I think they're real."

"They are real! Ask around. I have a good reputation. I don't rip off anyone!" Mr. Nguyen was obviously indignant. "One thousand!"

"Apiece?" she asked, incredulous about the price.

"For the pair!"

The sapphires were real, with the flaws only genuine stones contained. They were cornflower blue, the most desirable shade. He wanted only a thousand, and just as pawnbrokers were known for buying low, they were also reputed to sell high.

Kim reflected Brandi's suspicion. "A thousand for the pair? Why?"

"It is my birthday, and a Vietnamese tradition to treat the first guest with honor on that day." Mr. Nguyen, who so far had been speaking and acting like an American born and raised, bowed like an Asian.

Caught by surprise, Brandi bowed back. "Happy birthday."

With a return to his businesslike demeanor, Mr. Nguyen said, "So I owe you seven thousand dollars—that's the eight for the ring minus the thousand for the sapphires, I'll cut you a check and wrap the earrings for you."

"Yes. Thank you." Into the phone Brandi said, "Maybe my luck has changed."

"I'll say!" Kim's enthusiasm was contagious. "What's the plan now?"

"What makes you think I have a plan?"

"Honey, you're a lawyer. You don't take a shit without a plan."

"Hey! That's not true. I can be spontaneous!" Sometimes. Once in a while. Occasionally.

"Yeah, yeah. You and your master lists and your daily lists and your daily planner and your PDA."

"You are such a bitch."

"Yes, I know, and what you are is the antithesis of *spontaneous*." Kim sounded wry, amused, and not at all offended.

After the divorce, Kim had been the older sister who helped Brandi through the trauma of losing her father, of seeing her mother fall apart, of eventually losing their house and of dealing with the slow, difficult drift down into poverty. Kim had been the one who insisted Brandi look forward and see that someday she would be able to take control of her own life and no longer be driven by circumstances.

Brandi scrutinized Mr. Nguyen as he slid the earrings into the holes in the display insert. He affixed the backs to the posts; then, noticing the way she watched him, he smiled and lifted the insert out of the box. "Do you want to wear them?" He held it out.

She did. They were so beautiful, and sapphires were reputed to bring good luck. Or bad luck; she couldn't remember. At this point, who cared? She would survive. She would prosper. She would make that son of a bitch Alan sorry.

She leaned over the mirror and inserted first one post, then the other into her pierced ears. "My God, Kim. They're fabulous." They *were* the same color as her eyes. Smiling into her reflection, she groped for the display insert and handed it back to Mr. Nguyen. She heard the click as he shut the case, and tore herself away from the enthralling sight of her ears in those gorgeous earrings. Straightening up, she accepted the small velvet box from Mr. Nguyen and stuck it into her pocket.

"Who do I make the check out to?" Mr. Nguyen asked quietly.

"Brandi Lynn Michaels." B-R-A-N-D-I L-Y-N-N . . ." Brandi spelled each name slowly and carefully.

"The plan," Kim demanded.

"I don't have any water at my house. I'm dirty and I'm tired of peeing in a frozen toilet. I'm taking this money. I'm going to a five-star hotel."

"Okay, I'll buy that." But Kim sounded cautious, as if she heard something awry in Brandi's tone.

"I'm getting myself a suite on the concierge level. I'm going to bathe in a huge tub; then I'm going down to the shops on the Miracle Mile and I am buying myself the best dress ever. Red. I'm going to buy red, one that shows off my cleavage."

"If I had your cleavage I'd show it off all the time," Kim said.

"With touches of blue so I can wear my sapphires." She smiled as she contemplated her next move. "I'm going to buy great underwear. Fancy, lacy panties and a bra that would make a statue drool."

The guys at the end of the counter stopped laughing and stared at her. Stared as if they were memorizing her figure.

She must have been talking a little too loud.

She didn't care. "Great shoes. I'm going to wear the highest heels, the most impractical fuck-me shoes ever created."

She accept the engraved check Mr. Nguyen handed her. It was for the right amount, and she shook it at him and beamed. "I'll be back!"

"Go on now." He made a shooing motion at her. His hands were really shaking now.

"Are you sick?" Brandi asked.

"Yes. Sick. You should go. Go!"

"Thanks. It's been great doing business with you." She headed for the door.

"I'm not going to like the next part of your plan, am I?" Kim asked.

"You always told me I was old before my time."

"Now I *know* I'm not going to like this."

Brandi stepped outside. The blast of cold air felt as if it scoured the flesh off her face. "You always said I should do something wild while I was still young."

"*Now* you listen to me?" Kim moaned.

"I'm going to have a massage and a pedicure and a manicure and get dressed in all my glory." Brandi pulled her scarf close around her ears. "And I'm going to a huge, prestigious charity party at Charles McGrath's home."

"Don't do this," Kim warned.

"I'm going to pick up a man."

"This is not right," Kim said.

"And I'm going to have one fabulous night of sex to remember for the rest of my life."

4

As the cab drove Brandi deeper into Kenilworth's wooded streets, a pang of guilt struck her. With its old-fashioned lampposts, its huge estates, and the mansions set back among the trees, Kenilworth was the epitome of the classic old-money neighborhood. "Wow," she murmured. "Mother would love this."

"What?" As he'd been doing since he picked her up from the Tirra Spa on West Erie, the driver glanced in his rearview mirror, then apparently decided he didn't care about restraint or public safety, and stared.

Not that she didn't appreciate the proof that the spa makeup artist and hairstylist had both been brilliant, but she truly didn't want to hike the miles to Uncle Charles's house because the driver had hit a lamppost. Not in stiletto heels. "Look out!" she said.

He whipped his head around and stared into the evening shadows. "What?"

"Oh. I thought I saw a dog." Not true, but at least he was peering forward again.

"A . . . dog?" He swerved, his already awful driving exacerbated by her warning. "These people in here are so rich they'll get your license taken away for hitting their dog. Can you imagine?"

Yes, she could imagine very easily. To take her mind off the peril she faced with every screeching turn, she took out her phone and cradled it in her hand.

She still hadn't called her father. And she had to. And if she did it right now, he would probably be at dinner and wouldn't answer, and if by bad luck he did, she could be on the phone only until she got to the party.

Part of any plan for calling her father always included an impending reason to hang up and the good possibility that she could leave a message.

"Are you warm enough?" The cabby's hand crept toward the heat to turn it off.

"Barely." Tiny gold straps curled around her feet and up her ankles, and she used her bare, red-polished toes as the excuse to demand warmth. Actually, with her London Fog buttoned and belted, she was comfortable, but she wasn't about to admit that. The heater had two speeds, full-blast and off, and when it was off the windows frosted over so quickly the driver couldn't see.

Not that that seemed to worry him.

Closing her eyes for a moment, she took a few calming breaths and punched Daddy's number.

He answered. *Bad luck.*

"Daddy, it's Brandi." She kept her voice cheerful and warm, a direct contrast to the cold roiling in her belly.

"Oh. Brandi. What do you need?"

She'd obviously caught him in the middle of something. He had that I'm-too-busy-to-bother tone going. "I don't need anything, Daddy. I called to wish you happy birthday."

"Yeah. Thanks."

Keep the conversation rolling, Brandi. "What are you doing to celebrate?"

"I'm working."

"Oh. Well." What a surprise. When she was a kid, he'd missed more birthday parties—hers, his, Tiffany's—than he'd made. "I arrived in Chicago safely."

"You did, huh?" She heard him shuffling papers. "How's the job going?"

"I haven't started yet. I start on Monday."

He grunted. "That'll be interesting. I'll bet they've never had a ballerina working at McGrath and Lindoberth before."

"I haven't taken ballet lessons since I was thirteen." When Tiffany had run out of the alimony money and they'd had to make a choice between ballet and eating.

"Bullshit. You took it in college. Stupid thing to do. Why didn't you take a sport? That would have taught you some backbone, some competitive spirit."

"Dance isn't stupid, Daddy." Of course, it wasn't dance that he considered stupid. It was her, and he took every chance to make sure she knew it.

She didn't know why she cared; she knew it wasn't true. Yet when he used that cold, lashing tone, he took her back to that moment fourteen years ago when he'd walked out on her and her mother, and all the anguish she'd felt rushed back and she shivered with the pain of an abandoned child.

"Yeah. How's McGrath?"

"I'll see Uncle Charles tonight. Shall I give him your regards?"

"Sure. The old coot doesn't like me, but what the hell. It's always good to keep up connections." Someone spoke to him. A woman. His secretary, maybe, or his newest lover, or both. "Listen, Brandi, I'm busy. Call me back after you've started the job and let me know whether you're putting that damned expensive law degree to use."

Sometimes she just wanted to wring his fat neck. "Daddy, *you* convinced me to borrow the money from you rather than use a student loan. You said it made sense because you wouldn't charge me interest."

"I didn't say I didn't want to get paid," he shot back.

"I'll pay you," she said softly.

"You bet you will."

The driver said, "Hey, is this where I turn in?"

He veered so suddenly that her shoulder hit the door. "I hope to God." She had never meant anything so devoutly. She wanted out of this cab. She wanted off this phone call. And not necessarily in that order. She spoke into the receiver. "Daddy, I have to go. Talk to you later."

But he'd already hung up.

The cab passed through the open iron gate and tore up Uncle Charles's long, softly lit driveway at thirty miles an hour.

Viciously she shoved her phone into her bag. She could feel her cheeks burning. Damn her father. He always made her feel like some kind of shiftless no-account mooch. She should never have borrowed the law school money from him. Even when she'd done it, she knew it was the wrong thing, that he had offered it only so he would keep the power to manipulate her. But like the sucker she always was about him, she hoped that this time he'd offered because he'd realized, at last, that he cared about her.

Sucker.

The driver slammed on his brakes ten feet past the wide, curving stairway that led to the front door. "Thirty-seven twenty-five," he said, pointing at the meter.

"Back up to the door." She articulated each word in tones so clear they rang like struck lead crystal. She was in no mood to take shit from any man, much less a cabdriver who tried to cheat her by going the wrong way and then kill her with his ineptitude.

He started to object, but he looked in the rearview mirror one last time, and something of her simmering rage must have shown through her still mask, for he slammed it in reverse and got her to the right spot.

A man in a long, dark coat and dark hat decorated with an escutcheon waited to assist her. Was he . . . a footman?

He was.

He opened the door.

A blast of cold air hit her.

He extended his gloved hand. "Welcome, Miss . . . ?"

"Miss Michaels. Miss Brandi Michaels."

He touched his gloved hand to his hat. "Miss Michaels, Mr. McGrath asked that I extend a special welcome to you. He's looking forward to seeing you."

"Thank you." Oh, yes, Tiffany would *definitely* enjoy this.

Brandi handed him her brand-new Louis Vuitton duffel bag and shoved two twenties at the cabdriver. "Keep the change."

"Hey, that's only three bucks tip. I got you here in a hurry!"

"And I wanted to be late." Taking the footman's hand, she lifted herself out of the warm cab and into the frigid Chicago winter.

In these shoes she was over six feet tall—five inches taller than the footman and two inches taller than Alan. Not that she cared about *that*, but for the first time in four years she didn't have to cater to some man's ego.

She looked up at the well-lit exterior of the stone English Tudor home.

The house spread its wings wide in both directions. Its conical towers rose four stories, and the stones were arranged in fantastic patterns, with half-timber work and roofs and gables that swooped and rose to delight her eyes.

She knew Uncle Charles's history; he'd bought the house for his wife—they'd delighted in decorating and entertaining—and when she'd passed away over ten years ago, he'd mourned sincerely. He'd called to talk to Tiffany occasionally; he seemed to feel she understood, and in some ways Brandi supposed she did. After all, death was a kind of abandonment, too.

"Go on in, Miss Michaels," the footman advised. "It's thirty below and the wind's starting to kick up."

She shuddered at the report and hurried up the steps. A tall, burly man with a shaved head and frosty blue eyes surrounded by pale eyelashes held the wide door open for her. She sighed in delight as the heat of the foyer enveloped her.

"May I see your invitation, please?"

Brandi glanced at his name tag. Jerry. Security. And everything a security man should be: He was muscled, his suit was black, his shirt was white, his tie was gray. Two black men and one Asian woman, all dressed precisely like him and with similar impassive expressions, stood in the foyer waiting to welcome other guests.

That, more than anything, told Brandi how many important people were attending this event to raise money for the Art Institute of Chicago. Uncle Charles feared party crashers, and wanted no violent incidents involving his very wealthy clients and friends.

Brandi stood, poised and calm, while Jerry examined her invitation, the guest list, and her face.

Behind her, a well-groomed older Hispanic couple stepped into the door and were treated to the same scrutiny by another security man.

"Miss Michaels, would you mind if I went through your, er, satchel?" Jerry indicated her bag.

"Feel free." She handed him her duffel.

The other couple shed their coats and watched curiously as her guard placed her bag on the elegantly fragile Queen Anne table against the wall and popped the latch.

This place was beautiful. Everything was big, tall, expansive—the shining parquet floor, the Old World portraits of stiffly posed, bewigged nobles, the wood-paneled walls. As she admired the newly discovered mahogany on the curved stairway, the crystal chandelier sparkling two stories above her head, and the carved Chinese rugs, her toes curled. The house was as glamorous as Tiffany had hoped.

She made note of the details to tell her mother—the mother she had yet to inform of her broken engagement.

Of course, Brandi had spent the day luxuriating in a much-needed bath, massage, manicure and pedicure, spray tan, haircut and -style, the biggest shopping spree in which she'd ever indulged. . . . It was amazing how quickly one could spend seven thousand dollars when one was determined.

Oh, and she'd spent time arguing with Kim about the execution of her plan. Kim, who'd become surprisingly stodgy when it came to her younger sister's morals.

Who'd had time to call Tiffany?

The faint sound of choking brought her attention back to Jerry.

His broad shoulders stiffened. A slow, bright red crept up his pale skin from his necktie to his receding hairline.

Good. She hoped he was embarrassed. She understood the need for him to search her bag, but she didn't have to like it.

He swallowed as he lifted the brief, thin scrap of silk and lace that would cover her breasts so erotically. She knew it would; she'd tried it on in the shop, as well as the other various sheer undergarments and bits of hedonistic sleepwear.

He tried to refrain from looking at her, but he lost the battle. His brown gaze darted over her bosom.

He saw nothing but a woman huddled in her black London Fog. As much as she would have liked to appear swathed in a gossamer cape, she refused to go out in this godforsaken Chicago deep freeze without her heaviest coat—and even it wasn't heavy enough.

He pulled his hand free of the bag as if escaping some fatally baited trap. "Okay. Do you want to, um, check the bag? I mean, do you want to check it so you don't have to carry it? You know, get a check tag so you can have it when you leave?"

"That would be delightful." She kept her voice pitched at that tone she'd heard her mother use so many times when she wanted a man to do something for her. "Jerry, would you take care of that for me?"

"Yeah." He pulled at the collar that circled his linebacker-size neck.

"And my coat, too?" She fluttered her eyelashes, the ones with the mascara the makeup artist had promised was like tar.

"Oh, yeah," he said.

When the other guards coughed and shuffled, he realized how he'd been manipulated. Looking stern, he said, "The checkroom is right over there. . . ."

She smiled into his eyes.

In disgust he said, "Oh, never mind. Just give me the coat. I'll do it."

She unbelted the coat. Unbuttoned it. Taking a deep breath, she slid it off her shoulders and down her arms.

The silence in the foyer was profound.

She looked around. Jerry's mouth was hanging open. One black security guy had his arm braced against the wall. The other had taken a step forward. The Asian security guard was smiling as if she'd just had a vision—Brandi hadn't realized she was a lesbian, but obviously she was. And of the Hispanic guests, the husband looked enthralled and the wife furious.

So Mother was right. A red dress worked.

A long, silk, sleeveless scarlet dress with, as Mr. Arturo said, "Two really elegant design features, darling, and both of them hold up the bodice."

Of course she was wearing underwear—a thong—and her stiletto heels, and a crystal blue bracelet and those sapphire earrings, those great sapphire earrings. But she hadn't been absolutely sure whether she'd achieved the effect she sought.

Until now.

Yes, it appeared this dress, this body, and these shoes could stun every race, every economic strata, and both sexes. In any language, she called that success.

Unfortunately none of these men were candidates for her plan.

She'd made a list of her requirements.

She wanted a man who was handsome, mature, rich, discreet, and most important of all, from out of town. That way, with any luck, she would never see him again.

Even if she did, she was determined not to care. Nobody cared about their honor or their reputation anymore—witness Alan—so she sure as hell didn't, either.

A large arch led to a broad hall, and from beyond Brandi heard the chatter of men's and women's voices and the clink of glasses. She strolled through and into the reception.

The crowded room was painted a creamy gold, with one wall of bookcases rising to the tall ceiling. A log fire blazed in the immense stone fireplace on the far wall. Large, gilt-framed mirrors reflected the beautiful people who mingled, smiling, holding champagne glasses, and posing for photos. The men were in tuxedos, the women in black and sometimes a subdued blue. She was the only one in scarlet.

Good. Let them notice her. Let them all notice her.

As she stood in the doorway, conversations faded first nearby, then rippling out from the epicenter that was *her.*

She took a long, slow breath that allowed her breasts to swell above the low neckline and eased the breathlessness that came with knowing that she stood here alone when she should have been on the arm of her fiancé. Alone because she'd been a fool. Because she had believed she could write a grocery list of the qualities she required in a man and check them off as if he were a hothouse cucumber.

She took another long breath and smiled, a smile that glittered and beckoned, a smile she hoped would disguise her rage and project sexual readiness to all the eligible men in the room.

And it must have worked, for a dozen tailored suits started in her direction—then halted when Uncle Charles broke free of the crowd with his hands outstretched.

Her smile became one of genuine pleasure, and she took his hands.

Charles McGrath was a dapper seventy years old with a shining bald head, sagging jowls, and a glorious smile. Years of criminal law hadn't dimmed his enthusiasm for life, and the spring in his step and his frank appreciation for beauty attracted both friends and women. He was a bit of a chauvinist—he'd been amazed that Brandi could succeed so well in law school, and then that she wanted to work after marriage. But he had gamely subdued his male protective instinct and assigned her to Vivian Pelikan, one of the nation's foremost—and most ruthless—criminal lawyers.

Now he spread her arms wide and looked at her with a twinkle in his brown eyes. "You are stunning. Forgive me for saying so—I know no young woman should be compared to another woman—but you'll permit an old man a little reminiscence."

"Of course." She already knew what he was going to say.

"You remind me of the first time I saw your mother. She was eighteen and the most glorious creature I had ever seen. I would have swooped in, but I was married at the time and had foolish ideas of fidelity."

"Good for you." She must have been a little fierce, for he looked taken aback. She stepped forward and pressed her cheek to his. More quietly, she said, "I mean, that's rare these days."

He misunderstood. Of course he did. He didn't know about Alan.

"Your father's a fool. To leave a treasure like Tiffany for another woman—" He broke off. "But none of that tonight. You *do* look stunning. Who would have thought when I first met you at the age of three pirouetting around your father's office in a leotard and tutu that you would grow so tall and so beautiful?"

"Oh, yes. Ballerina Brandi." The memories that gave Uncle Charles such pleasure made her want to writhe. "I danced up until the time the boys complained they couldn't lift me because I was taller than them." That wasn't strictly the truth, but this was neither the time nor the place for her more truthful and bitter reminiscences.

Uncle Charles threw back his head and laughed aloud. "Now you have the revenge. What happens to this magnificent dress if you let out your breath?"

"Your party gets a lot more interesting."

"Breathe in," he advised. "I'm too old to handle a stampede in my house. Now where's your fiancé? I expected to see him."

She gave the response she'd been practicing, the one that said so much and so little. "You know he's a resident."

"He'll be sorry he missed you looking like this!"

"He already is sorry." *A sorry, deceitful son of a bitch.* "He just doesn't know it yet." Time to change the subject. "Uncle Charles, I haven't been to your home before. It's stunning!"

"Thank you." Uncle Charles tucked her hand into his arm and walked her into the crowd. "It's a work in progress, but it's so big. Most days I rattle around here all alone. I miss having a special someone in the house."

"I'm sorry." She hesitated, then presumed on an old family friendship. "Perhaps it's time to find someone else."

"I think you're right. Now have you viewed my coup d'état?" He beamed and steered Brandi toward the far wall.

Spotlights were focused on some exhibit.

"What is it?" she asked.

"You'll see." Uncle Charles worked his way inward, carrying Brandi along in his wake. "Excuse me."

"It's gorgeous, Charles." A contemporary of Uncle Charles's clapped him on his shoulder.

"Thanks, Mel," Uncle Charles said. "I didn't know if I was going to get it until the last minute."

"Wow! That was freaking wonderful. Great job, Mr. McGrath." Eyes shining, a young woman grabbed Uncle Charles's hand, shook it hard, then wiggled her way toward the bar.

He looked after her and shook his head, smiling. "I have no idea who that was."

The crowd grew more tightly packed, the comments more numerous.

"Beautiful exhibit, Charles."

"Extraordinary to see it up so close."

At last he and Brandi reached the front. A velvet cord held the guests back from a glass case surrounded by spotlights, and inside the case was a necklace, the kind of necklace that would make any sane woman's heart beat more quickly.

Brandi was very sane.

Set in antique platinum and surrounded by white diamonds, massive in their own right, was the most immense sparkling blue stone Brandi had ever seen.

"It doesn't even look real," she said in awe. "What is it?"

"Oh, it's real, all right," Uncle Charles said. "That's the largest blue diamond in the Russian royal jewels. That, my dear, is the Romanov Blaze."

5

"The Romanov Blaze is part of the traveling exhibition currently on exhibit at the Chicago Museum," Uncle Charles told an awed Brandi. "It was given to Empress Alexandra by Czar Nicholas when she told him she was pregnant with their fifth child. It's reputed to be bad luck, and indeed, seven months later Crown Prince Alexis was born with hemophilia."

"Which helped bring about the fall of the royal family," Brandi whispered.

Everyone in the crowd was whispering as if they were in church, as if the presence of such beauty required reverence.

The diamond's cold beauty and dreaded curse mesmerized and beckoned.

But four burly men who looked like Jerry stood on each corner of the exhibit, and she didn't have a doubt that if she, or anyone here, made a move toward that jewel all hell would break loose.

"It's extraordinary, Charles." A middle-aged woman in an elegant black sleeveless gown and her own glittering stones couldn't keep her gaze off the Romanov Blaze. "How much is it worth?"

Uncle Charles tucked his thumbs into his lapels. "Colleen, in its present incarnation, with the weight of its history behind it, it's priceless. If it were stolen and cut into a few smaller stones, it could be worth forty million, more or less."

"Surely no one would cut that magnificent diamond!" Colleen protested.

"It can't be sold as is except to a collector, and the chances of being caught with it are too great. If it's cut, it's not easy to identify, and there's a market for stones of this purity."

Brandi was impressed. Uncle Charles knew his stuff.

He turned back to Brandi and lowered his voice. "Security was a bear, but at the last minute I managed to bring in enough guards to satisfy the Russians and the museum. Even with that, I had to tell the museum directors the Blaze would double the donations to support the exhibits. Those people know this stuff; I don't know what got into them to think of refusing."

The grim edge to his mouth told her more clearly than his words how poorly Uncle Charles had taken their rejection, and she suspected he'd bludgeoned them with the threat that he would withdraw his support unless they yielded. This was a side of Uncle Charles she never saw, but she knew must exist.

His guests sucked up to him. The museum and the Russians had capitulated to his demands. He was, after all, a very powerful man, and used to getting his own way.

"Might as well leave room in front for the newcomers." Taking Brandi's arm, he led her out of the crowd and signaled to the man they'd met on the way in. "Brandi, have you met Mel Colvin, one of our senior partners?"

"No, we haven't met," Brandi said. "But I've admired his work on Nolan versus Chiklas."

"How kind of you!" Mel smiled broadly and took her hand. "Charlie, you old rascal, is this the lady you were telling me about?"

"No! We've hired Brandi to work criminal law." Uncle Charles glared at Mel.

"Oh. Oh! Good to meet you, young lady." As if he'd lost interest, Mel gave her fingers a perfunctory squeeze, leaving Brandi confused by his sudden change in mood, and turned back to Uncle Charles. "But is the lady you told me about coming?"

"Not tonight. Not yet." Uncle Charles quickly turned Brandi to another guest, a petite, toned, attractive female in a full-length black Vera Wang knockoff. "This is Shawna Miller, McGrath and Lindoberth's able head receptionist."

Shawna shook Brandi's hand, but the chill she projected rivaled the deep freeze outside. She did *not* approve of Brandi. "That dress you're wearing would be fabulous at, say, the Academy Awards!" Shawna said.

Meaning, of course, that it was a bad choice for a charity dinner hosted by a law firm.

But Tiffany had imparted many lessons to her unwilling daughter, including how to handle short, hostile women.

Brandi leaned close to Shawna's ear and in a whisper advised, "Try ABS next time. They make divine knockoffs at a reasonable price."

She had to give Uncle Charles credit: He recognized undercurrents when he saw them, and before Shawna could give vent to her swelling fury, he dove into the fray. "Have some champagne." He handed Brandi a glass from a passing tray, then directed her to an attractive, older, African-American woman. "You know Vivian Pelikan."

"Indeed I do. It's always an honor, Mrs. Pelikan." Vivian Pelikan was one of the first black women to break through the glass ceiling and become a senior law partner, and she'd done it solely with sheer brilliance and drive. She wore her graying hair cropped short, and her lively brown eyes danced; she'd obviously heard the exchange between Shawna and Brandi.

Mrs. Pelikan shook Brandi's hand. "You've come just in time, Miss Michaels. We're starting an exciting new case on Monday, and I've put you on the team."

"I look forward to that," Brandi said. "It's an honor to work with you."

"Let me introduce my husband, an architect with Humphreys and Harper."

"How good to meet you, Mr. Pelikan."

"Mr. Harper," he corrected, but he smiled and introduced her to his partner, Mr. Humphreys, who fit all her criteria for a lover except that a) he lived in Chicago and b) he looked like a bug-eyed frog.

Brandi's wild, flaming affair would be conducted with the bedroom lights blazing, and for that she needed a man who lifted weights, who had a dusting of dark hair on tanned skin, and whose chest hadn't descended into his drawers. So she smiled, allowed Uncle Charles to mention her fiancé, and when he had moved off to welcome more arrivals, she continued to work her way deeper into the crowd, searching for the jewel of a lover hidden somewhere among the tuxedos and metrosexuals.

She met a lot of fellow employees at the law firm. Tip Joel, Glenn Silverstein, Sanjin Patel. Sanjin had been friendly until she'd made it clear she wasn't interested in an affair with a coworker. Tip and Glenn had taken one look at her and decided she'd traded on her sexuality or her family friendship with Uncle Charles or both to get her position in the firm.

When she went in to work, they would learn. They were men. Men like Alan. She'd crush them like bugs beneath her pointed heels.

She moved with the ebb and flow of the pack into the next room, a large reception hall where the caterer was setting up the buffet. The huge mirrors on the walls reflected the china, the silver, the dancing motions of the waiters as they waltzed through the crowd offering hors d'oeuvres. A bar was set up in each corner, and there Brandi lingered, searching for the Man.

She met a lot of lawyers and businessmen from across the city and the country. Something was wrong with each one. They were local, they were unattractive, and if they were handsome, then they were married. . . .

Most of them were married, and seemed very willing to sleep with her regardless. The deceitful bastards.

After two hours of serious searching, she found herself leaning an elbow on the bar, sipping her second glass of champagne and morosely conversing with Gwynne Durant, a junior lawyer from the firm whose physician husband was at this moment delivering a baby. Gwynne thought she and Brandi were alone for the same reason, and felt sorry for them both.

Brandi didn't disabuse her. Gwynne would find out the truth soon enough. Everyone would find out that Alan had been sleeping with Fawn, got her pregnant, and got married while engaged to Brandi. Brandi could hardly wait for the snickering to start.

Feeling vaguely ill, she put down the champagne and stared as the golden bubbles detached themselves from the side of the glass, rose, and popped.

Her feet hurt, and for what? For nothing. Among all the wealthiest, most handsome, most educated men in Chicago, she could find no one to help her forget Alan. To forget his deceit, her humiliation, the incredible disappointment.

She smiled bitterly as she listened to Gwynne's rambling commentary on marriage to a doctor and the sacrifices she'd made for his career, and reflected that Kim would be relieved to hear that Brandi would spend the night alone huddled under a comforter in a chaste bedroom in Uncle Charles's house.

"They're starting the buffet," Gwynne said. "I had hoped Stan would get here in time to eat with me. I know it's not a big deal, but it's nice to have a guy to stand with you so you don't look like the world's biggest loser— *Oh, my God.* It's the count!"

Gwynne's tone made Brandi straighten away from the bar. "The count?"

"Roberto Bartolini. He's an Italian count."

"You mean like Count Chocula?" *A count. C'mon.*

"No. How can you look at that man and think children's cereal? All I can think is slow hands and hot sweat."

Brandi had been disappointed so often tonight, she couldn't work up the energy to turn and take a look. She just hunched a shoulder and took another sip of her drink.

But Gwynne burbled on. "I heard him talk on the news. He has this voice like Sean Connery, only Italian. He has only the faintest accent"— Gwynne measured his accent between her thumb and forefinger—"but you know he's not American because of the words he uses."

"Italian words?" Brandi asked sarcastically.

"No, English words, but . . . you know . . . *long* words."

"Like spaghetti?" *Wow.* Sarcasm was becoming a way of life.

"*No.* Flattering words. Words you don't hear every day. Like magnificent. And postmodernism. And . . . I don't know . . . ancestry. He uses words like an artist uses a brush."

"All right. Fine." Gwynne was in such an ecstasy of awe, amusement and genuine panting lust, Brandi took a chance, swiveled on one her of stiletto heels—and froze.

The crowd had parted, and there he was—sex in an Armani suit. Roberto Bartolini was tall, at least six-four, with shoulders that made ballerina Brandi imagine how easily he would lift her, spin with her, hold her. . . .

"See? What did I tell you?" Gwynne fiercely poked Brandi in the ribs.

He was Johnny Depp without the eyeliner. Like a pirate, he stood and surveyed the room from beneath dark, hooded eyes that looked amused and unsurprised by the interest he roused. His shoulder-length dark hair was swept back from his tanned face, leaving the stark compilation of features unadorned and glorious, like a harsh and savage mountain range. His mouth was a wide slash; his lips were full, firm, supple, the kind that made Brandi, and every other woman in the room, shiver with anticipation.

More than that, he carried himself like a man who knew his worth and was certain of his welcome. He had more than money, more than breeding, more than looks.

He radiated charisma. And power.

"Is he married?" Brandi demanded.

"No, but what difference does that make? You're engaged. I'm married. We can only look at the menu; we can't order off it."

That's what you think.

"Not that I'm complaining or anything. I mean, Stan's a good guy, but he can't compete with Roberto Bartolini. Look at him. He's rich. He's foreign. He's a world traveler, and he just got in from Italy."

Uncle Charles walked toward Roberto with his hand outstretched, pleasure in every step.

With slight smile, Roberto shook his hand, and Brandi caught her breath at another glorious aspect of Mount—or rather, *Count*—Bartolini.

Gwynne moved closer and wiggled as she prepared to impart the most important piece of information. "And *get this*—"

"Sh." Brandi laid her hand on Gwynne's arm. "Be quiet and let me enjoy the view." And soak in the fact that fate had, for once, played fair with Brandi.

He was the one. He was the Matterhorn and she was going to scale him.

Placing her glass on the bar, she stood the way they'd taught her in ballet class: arms softly curved, back straight, chest out. Her scarlet gown glowed like a jewel among the black fashions. She glittered with rage and the need for revenge. And she looked at Roberto Bartolini. Compelled him to look back at her.

His head turned as if he heard her summons. He sought her in the crowd.

She knew he would see her.

The instant he focused on her, a thrill shot up her spine.

He took in the sight of her quickly, then with lingering appreciation.

Then he looked into her eyes.

Gwynne's babbling faded from Brandi's consciousness. She brought air into her lungs. Her heart pumped. Her sexuality stirred. She was, for the first time in her life, a creature of instinct, concentrating on one thing and one thing only—the satisfaction of her own body. And without words, this man with his smoky sensuality and smoldering eyes promised he would give it to her.

Noticing nothing, Uncle Charles stepped between them and waved a hand toward the diamond's display case.

Roberto's response was all that a host could wish, but he stepped aside so once again he could see all of her.

She smiled at him, a faint, feminine taunt.

"Love 'em and leave 'em . . . reputation in the 'love 'em' part is terrific." The volume control on Gwynne's voice must have been broken, because Brandi could hear only a few phrases.

"Yes," Brandi breathed. "I know." Deliberately she turned and strolled slowly toward the corridor that led to the private living quarters. She paused in the doorway. How long, she wondered, would it take him to find her?

6

Roberto wondered what the woman wanted.

He wondered if he would give it to her.

If it was what he was hoping, he would. Who could resist a magnificent creature like that? Her hair was caught in a loose chignon at the back of her head, and strands of bright gold brushed her cheeks and kissed her rosy lips. Her scarlet gown stood out among the sleek sophisticates with their everlasting, dreary black. Her body made him catch his breath—all long, long legs, rounded hips, narrow waist, and a bosom that would have made Botticelli weep with joy. From this distance, Roberto couldn't discern the color of her eyes, but the expression in them challenged him. Beckoned him.

"Thank you for coming, Roberto."

Roberto jerked his attention to Charles McGrath, the head of his law team.

"Your presence will add a most interesting element to the mix here." Charles's eyes twinkled with mischief.

"No, thank *you* for having me. Not all men would have the courage to court such notoriety."

Charles laughed. "The promise of meeting you and your notoriety got many of these guests here and their wallets opened."

"For such a good cause, I am honored to be of assistance." Roberto liked the older man. Charles McGrath was a remarkable combination of kindness and ruthlessness, shrewdness and hospitality. Certainly he knew how to summon stunning women to his parties.

"Shall I let her at you?" Charles asked.

For a moment Roberto thought Charles meant the lady in red. But no, a female in her late thirties stood not far away, staring at him in the manner of a ravenous crocodile.

"Of course. I'm here to meet your guests." Roberto glanced again at the lady in red and allowed himself a moment of cold logic.

Fate was not usually so kind as to offer, without strings, an anonymous woman of beauty for his delectation. So the strings must be there. Invisible, but there nonetheless. "As you have instructed me, I must be careful what I say to reporters. How will I recognize them?"

"All of them are wearing their press identification badges," Charles said.

"Ahhh." The lady in red had not been wearing a badge.

"The badges are big, they're white, and they're obvious. I personally made sure of that, and made it clear the consequences to their newsgroup should anyone remove them. The women aren't happy about that—they complain the badges ruin the cut of their gowns—but I say that's the price of doing the job." Charles lowered his voice. "I know I'm an old curmudgeon, but I liked the days when men had the tough jobs and women were more decorative."

"Ah, didn't we all? Now so many of them insist on using their brains for things other than pleasing their men. It is a disgrace." Roberto chuckled, amused by his own chauvinism.

But Charles didn't chuckle. He nodded. He was, like Roberto's father in Italy, of a different generation.

With an eye to the magnificent creature in the red gown, Roberto said, "But I do beg your pardon. I may have to retire early. I fear I suffer from jet lag."

"Of course. An hour of genial conversation should do it."

"I'll make the hour count." Roberto exchanged a smile with

Charles. He glanced toward the lady in red and saw her disappear into the depths of the house. He took a step after her.

Then the best of Chicago society rushed him. They did so elegantly, of course, with more class than the paparazzi, but still they rushed.

Charles introduced Amanda Potter, one of Chicago's leading architects. She flashed her smile and her bosom. "Mr. Bartolini, I'm so pleased. I've never had the pleasure of meeting a real . . . Italian count before."

The woman was too old to successfully carry off *coy*, but Roberto bowed over the hand she extended to him—the hand sporting a ring with a handsome emerald in a white-gold setting.

"What a striking stone." He touched it lightly. "From Colombia and, of course, two point one carats."

She gasped in amazement. "That's . . . that's absolutely right."

While the crowd murmured, Roberto allowed his gaze to touch each face and then each jewel. Some guests stepped back. Most pressed forward.

A party trick. He performed nothing but a party trick, but it impressed them.

And when his duty was done, he would follow that gorgeous lady in red.

More women greeted him with flutters and flattery. Men shook his hand and expressed their admiration. The press followed, cameras at ready. Everyone wanted to pose with him for photos.

Charles steered him toward the right people, introducing him to the mayor of Chicago, two senators, and the fashionista who hosted a reality television show teaching American women proper fashion sense.

He did not like her. She despised her audience. She was insolent and rude.

But she liked him. She fawned on him, putting her stamp of approval on him. "Mr. Bartolini, you look fabulous in that suit. Armani, isn't it?"

For *this* he was not pursuing the woman in scarlet? "I don't know. I don't pay any attention to names. It's so bourgeois, don't you think?" He smiled into her eyes, mocking her pretensions.

She drew back. She didn't like him anymore, and she attacked like the beast she was. "So, Mr. Bartolini—or should I call you Count?"

"Mr. Bartolini will do."

"Are you going to go look at the Romanov Blaze?"

"The Romanov Blaze?" He cast a deliberately bewildered glance around him. "What is that?"

As he intended, the crowd laughed. He walked toward the display case, away from that dreadful female, and he found himself anticipating his first glimpse of one of the grandest diamonds in history. He enjoyed seeing the guards tense as he approached, and quickly assessed the security they'd rigged up. Very impressive. Lasers and pressure pads, not to mention the heavyset, cold-eyed guards. He acknowledged them with respectful nods—his grandfather had taught him to show respect to those assigned to futile missions.

They nodded back, hulking men who itched to tackle him on any pretext.

And there it was, glittering beneath the spotlights—the Romanov Blaze. It sparkled with hypnotic splendor, and for one moment he forgot his surroundings and smiled to see such beauty.

But while he admired the diamond, it was cold and hard . . . unlike his magnificent creature. He wanted the woman in scarlet.

He had given Charles and his guests fifteen minutes. Fifteen minutes of being suave, continental, mysterious, everything they wanted and expected.

Now he excused himself and walked down the hall after the mystery wrapped in scarlet silk. He glanced into one doorway after another until he saw her, gleaming like a ruby in the dim setting of McGrath's library. She stood by the fireplace. She gazed into the flames, a faint smile on her lips, and in profile he could see the different facets of her beauty. In the firelight, her pale skin glowed like burnished gold. She'd taken off her shoes, yet she was still tall, the

kind of woman with whom he could dance—among other things—
and still look in her face. Her hand clasped the mantel, and her
upraised arm proved she took her health seriously, lifting weights to
sculpt her bare shoulders. The silk gown caressed her body, outlining
the lift of her breasts and her bottom.

His eyes had not misled him. She was, indeed, a magnificent
creature.

Turning her head, she observed him with such amusement it was
clear she had known he stood there, and posed for him. And she
wore only a thong beneath that silky gown—or if he were lucky,
nothing at all. One-carat sapphires at her ears, yet her eyes contained
a warmer blue flash than any cold stone.

"Glorious," he said.

"Thank you." She knew what he meant and acknowledged it
without false humility.

Stepping into the room, he shut the door behind him. "I think
you want to talk to me."

She glanced down at the floor as if she sought the right words.
Then she straightened her shoulders, turned fully to face him, and
lifted her chin.

She looked, suddenly, less like the dream he'd been seeking all
his life and more like a professional. A professor, or more likely a
lawyer.

Or FBI?

Yes, of course. An agent from the FBI.

Abruptly his pleasure in the encounter cooled. Tucking his hand
into his jacket pocket, he waited.

"For tonight, I would like to sleep with you," she said.

Roberto's hand clenched into a fist inside his pocket, and the
flare of excitement lit again. Not FBI. Not unless they'd significantly
changed their tactics.

"I have my reasons. I don't expect you to inquire about them. But
I need . . . a night . . . a man . . . I need *you.* I've never done this before, so you don't need to worry about wearing a number or being a

notch on my belt. You don't have to worry that I intend any kind of entrapment. My purpose is solely for my own pleasure. And yours, of course, I hope." She waited for a response with a stillness that betrayed fierce emotions tumbling beneath the surface.

Not FBI.

A groupie?

Possible.

The first spy placed by the Fosseras?

A theory worthy of note.

Or perhaps she was a gift from fate to offset the ruin of his good name.

She grew discomfited by his silence. Looking down, she searched out her shoes and donned them one at a time. "But before I continue, perhaps I should ask whether you're interested."

"Interested?" There wasn't a straight man in Chicago who wouldn't give his right arm to stand where Roberto was standing now. The crackle of the flames and the faint sound of her breathing broke the silence in the library. He strolled toward her, and when she lifted her head and shook the golden strands of hair away from her face, he smiled with all his charm. Lifting his hand, he let it hover an inch away from her chin. "May I?"

He had thought she would relax toward him. Instead, like a spinster schoolteacher allowing a liberty, she gave a stiff nod.

Ah. Not experienced. Not a groupie.

She smelled good, like a flower that bloomed in the night. Like a woman with secrets. Slowly he slid his fingers under her chin toward her right ear, taking pleasure in that first, all-important contact with her skin. The texture was as velvety as it looked, and warm with the heat of the fire and the heat of her need. He touched her earring, a gorgeous sapphire, then caressed her lobe, tucking her hair back. Like a cat, she turned her cheek into his hand.

A sensuous creature who liked to be stroked.

She watched him from the most amazing cornflower-blue eyes, her expression solemn, as if he were her teacher and she an earnest student. She had a way about her that nourished his ego—an ego his mother regularly told him needed no feeding.

Leaning over, he kissed her lightly, a brief brush of the lips. He wanted the slightest taste, an exchange of breath, to see if they were compatible . . . and with that, he wanted more. He pressed his finger on her full lower lip. "Are you worried that your lipstick will smear?"

"The makeup artist promised that when all the rest of me has turned to dust, the lipstick and the mascara will be left."

He grinned. She was funny.

But she didn't grin back. She was stating a fact. She pressed her hand to his chest—a touch firm with determination. "I would like a kiss. A real kiss. I want to know if it will be as good as I think, or if good sex is a myth fostered by movies and fed by loneliness."

A deliberate challenge? Perhaps. And perhaps she was ingenuous. Certainly love had cheated her somehow.

He still grinned as he leaned toward her again and gave her what she wanted. Lips parted, tongues meeting, sliding . . . for the first time in years, a mere kiss took the world away. He closed his eyes to better savor the taste of her—champagne first, then as he explored, her own flavor. Sweet brown sugar melted on uncertain yearning. Cool cream poured over warm desire.

She was like a grand cru wine from the vineyards of Bordeaux—expensive and worth every sip.

He forgot deliberation. He forgot restraint. He pulled her close, crushing the delicate material of her dress, craving the slide of silk against her bare skin. His other hand slid beneath the nape of her neck to hold her in place. He bent her back, holding her weight against him, and experienced her through his mouth, through his body, through the scent of her and her hold on his lapel.

A primitive part of him clawed to be free, to shove her skirt up, to push her down on the floor, to take her quickly, with all the need thrumming in his veins.

Some remnant of the gentleman he had once been made him

release her, steady her with a hand on her elbow, and ask huskily, "Does that answer your question?"

She stood looking at him, blue eyes wide, fingers pressed to her lips. "Not a myth," she whispered.

"No." He wanted to laugh, but the effort of freeing her had strained something chivalrous inside him and he didn't dare push the issue. "No, good sex is not an illusion, but what's between us isn't good sex. It's more like a force of nature . . . or a trick fate has played on us both."

"Funny. I thought . . . *fate* . . . I thought that when I saw you."

"We are agreed. This is fate." How pleased his grandfather would be to know that Roberto proved himself half Contini after all! Wild. Reckless. Incorrigible. "So we'll spend the night together. You don't have to tell me why. I don't have to pretend to love you. And in the morning we'll part, never to see each other again." He'd never been rash before. Why now?

Ah, yes. Because his life had tilted sideways and everything he had known, everything he had been, had been knocked askew.

"All right. It's a deal." She extended her hand to shake his.

When he took it, he realized she trembled. He hoped not from nerves; he hoped from suppressed desire. Lifting her hand to his lips, he pressed a lingering kiss on the palm, then closed her fingers on it.

"But I don't want to be seen leaving together." For a woman who had been thoroughly kissed, she showed a practical streak.

For that matter, so did he. "I have to stay longer. To do less would be ungrateful to Mr. McGrath. So I'll call my driver. He'll pick you up when you step out the door. I'll tell the concierge at my hotel that you're coming." He handed her his passkey.

She looked down at the card in her hand. "Aren't you worried I'll steal something?"

With all the people who were watching him? "That is the last thing I'm worried about."

"Somehow I can't imagine that you're a trusting soul."

And she was a discerning soul. "Tonight I will trust you with myself."

She inclined her head, not because she believed him, but because she accepted his right to prevaricate. She strolled toward the door, each motion of her body beneath the scarlet gown an enticement. "Don't change your clothes," he said.

She turned back in surprise. "But I bought the most gorgeous negligee."

Suspicion—some would call it good sense—rose in him again. "For me?"

"Yes. Well . . ." She shrugged. "For the man I found tonight. Luckily, it *is* you. The negligee is a cream silk with lace inserts here and—"

"I want to remove your gown," he whispered huskily. At his own instructions, desire hit him hard and low. The thought of seeking out the zipper of that enticing dress, sliding it down, seeing what was beneath it . . . He took a step toward her.

She saw his craving and chuckled, low and warm. "Remember, Roberto, you must stay at the party for another hour."

He did have to. He was in Chicago for one reason. No woman, however attractive, could change that.

"At midnight, you can turn into a pumpkin." Again she strolled toward the door.

He remembered what he didn't yet know, and called, "What's your name?"

She leaned against the door frame, her body a beckoning silhouette, and smiled. "Brandi. I'm Brandi."

"Brandi?"

"Yes?"

"You go to my head."

Gwynne and a weary-looking man in a rumpled suit had engaged Uncle Charles in conversation. Gwynne's husband. Gwynne leaned against him, holding his hand, secure now that he was there, and Brandi worked her way across the floor toward them.

Gwynne and Stan turned away as Brandi approached. Gwynne tried to stop, but Stan tugged her toward the buffet table, and she gave Brandi a helpless wave and followed.

Brandi had Roberto on her mind, so when Gwynne looked back with pity in her eyes, Brandi didn't know what to think. Pity? For the woman about to spend the night with Roberto Bartolini? With a dismissive shrug, Brandi said, "Uncle Charles, I'm going to take my leave. I know I was going to stay, but the move . . . I have so much to do before Monday. . . ." She tried to arrange her expression to weariness, and not show the guests, and certainly not Uncle Charles, that she'd just experienced the kiss of a lifetime. When she thought of it, of Roberto, she wanted to put her hand over heart to feel it race and know, at last, that she was alive.

To her surprise, Uncle Charles didn't object. "I'll walk you to the foyer."

She was so relieved, she didn't notice the somber cast to his eyes. She got her things from the checkroom, and as he helped her into her coat, he said, "I was just talking to Stan Durant. You know he works at University Hospital."

"Yes." She buttoned her coat and wished Roberto were departing with her. Of course, they couldn't leave together, but it felt odd going to an assignation by herself.

"Stan says there are rumors flying around the hospital that your fiancé . . . that Alan . . ."

Uncle Charles had succeeded in capturing Brandi's attention.

". . . married some female in a Las Vegas wedding."

Busted! Busted, and now Uncle Charles was going to figure out why she was leaving, too. She probably had guilt written all over her face. "I . . . I didn't want to tell you. . . ."

"Dear, dear girl." He straightened her collar. "You were so brave to come here tonight when your heart is breaking."

"Breaking. Yes." Maybe guilt looked like suffering. Certainly she

didn't feel as if her heart were breaking. More like she couldn't wait
to make love with Roberto Bartolini.

"I'll let you go without another word"—Uncle Charles took her
hand—"but promise you'll come to me if I can do anything to mend
your grief."

"If I think of something, you'll be the first to know." Or not.
Uncle Charles would never find out how she mended her grief; on
that she was determined.

"Let me bring my car around for you."

"No!" She swallowed. "I mean, I've made arrangements for a car.
But thank you; you've been very kind."

He held her in place and looked into her eyes. "Promise you won't
be like your mother and let one bad apple spoil the whole crop. That
lovely woman should have remarried years ago, and she won't take a
chance and trust another man."

He was comparing her situation to her mother's. It was inevitable,
she supposed, but how she hated it! "I won't. Good night, Uncle
Charles." She kissed his papery cheek and picked up her bag.

"Your car's waiting, Miss Michaels." Jerry opened the door.

A blast of frigid wind took her breath away. She gasped, then hurried out. A long black limousine stood at the bottom of the steps.
The driver stood holding the door. He must be freezing. As she slid
in, he tipped his hat, then shut the door and hurried around the
car.

A dim overhead light illuminated the interior of black leather and
polished wood. The clean, new-car smell intoxicated her. She sank
back and let the seat heater thaw her bones.

"I'm Newby, miss. I'll have you to the hotel in about a half hour."
The driver had a British accent, and just like in the movies, he wore
a billed cap. "Can I get anything for you before we start? A drink?
Something to read? A phone or computer? We have satellite connection if you'd like to check your e-mail or surf the Net."

She was impressed. Of course she was impressed. "No, thank you,
I'm going to sit back and enjoy myself."

"During the drive, if you desire anything, let me know."

"I will, thank you."

"There's a button right there to summon me." He rolled up the window between the seats, put the car in gear, and, unlike her cabbie, drove her smoothly down the road.

The luxury and the lack of reality enfolded her. She was on her way to an assignation with the man of her dreams, the assignation she'd successfully arranged for herself. Perhaps she had a career in labor negotiations. She'd made a bargain . . . but when Roberto had taken her hand, when he'd kissed her, he made it feel like more than a bargain.

Fate had given her just what she asked for.

Why did she choose this minute to remember that Fate always required payment for her services?

7

The concierge didn't flinch when Brandi requested iced champagne, a bowl of fruit, and three dozen white candles. He asked only, "Scented or unscented? In jars? On stands?"

"Not scented, and a few in jars if necessary, but mostly I think simple pillar candles will do. Bring them in and place them . . ." She surveyed her temporary domain. Roberto occupied a corner suite on the top floor of the fifty-eight-story Resolution Hotel on Michigan Avenue.

She didn't like being up so high. Heights made her queasy. But as long as she didn't look out the window, everything was fine. More than fine. The ceilings in the sitting room and the bedroom soared two stories, and skylights showed the stars glittering bright and cold in the black of eternity. In the sitting room, the gas fireplace bathed the walls in a flickering golden glow.

Roberto's laptop, a marvel of technology with its custom case, sat on the antique desk. In fact, all the furniture looked antique, yet the seats were comfortable and included a backless sofa upholstered with a striped satin fabric and standing on clawed feet. "I think I'd like you to place them there on the table." She gestured toward that sofa.

"Behind the fainting couch?" the concierge asked.

"Yes. Exactly there. I'll distribute them. I'll need them in the next half hour."

"Of course." He bowed his way out.

Brandi waited until he'd shut the door before picking up her bag and tearing into the bathroom. She had her ablutions all planned out, and in less than forty-five minutes she had showered, shampooed, and slipped back into her scarlet dress and her gold shoes. She dried her hair and clipped it atop her head. She dabbed her neck and wrists with sandalwood- and orange-scented perfumes. She lit the candles and posed on the fainting couch, reclining on her side, her head propped up in her hand, the flames flickering around her, bathing her with sultry intent. She was confident she'd done everything to make this her night of sensual debauchery with the sexiest man in Chicago—a man of her choice.

Then Roberto walked in, and she realized she could control everything tonight . . . except him. In her carefully plotted scheme of revenge, he was the unknown element.

He stopped short at the sight of her. His hands flexed. His eyes narrowed.

A pirate.

He looked like a pirate.

He moved into the room, discarding his bow tie and jacket, and he didn't swagger, but he did . . . stalk. And he looked hungry.

Suddenly she felt less like a seductress and more like a maiden to be ravished.

But he sounded mild enough. "Do you like your accommodations?"

"I've never seen anything so lovely in my life. The view . . ." She gestured at the two gigantic corner windows where the lights of Chicago spread out like candles on a cake, and beyond that Lake Michigan was a dark blot in the icy night.

"Good." His already deep voice deepened more. "I want you to be happy."

"I am happy." She sat up a little straighter. "Very happy. That bathroom is the epitome of decadence. I could perform the solo from *Swan Lake* right there between the tub and the vanity." She was chatting, and all because her heart was beating faster.

This was what she wanted, wasn't it? The chance to make love with a man every woman dreamed of?

Of course it was, but she hadn't taken into account that women dreamed of dangerous men. Surely an Italian count with a reputation for great sex wasn't dangerous, but right now, in the dark, knowing that soon their bodies would meld, he *seemed* dangerous.

In fact, now that she thought about it, he'd seemed dangerous at the party, but her own fury had insulated her from apprehension.

Now, torn between trepidation and a rapidly increasing awe, she chewed her lip and watched as he unbuttoned his shirt.

Clothed, he gave the impression of being tall and healthy, but his suit hid the cascade of muscled ribs, the ridged belly, the bulging arms. This man took working out to an art, and that surprised her. Most men who exercised to such a state of fitness worshipped their own bodies and had no time to admire a woman.

All Roberto's attention was fixed on her. It was almost intimidating to be the focus of so much attention. Intimidating . . . and exciting.

"On the way here, I convinced myself that my eyes had deceived me. I told myself there was no way you could be as magnificent as I remembered. But you . . . with your golden hair piled high on your head and the red silk caressing your glorious curves"—he smiled, and dimples pressed deep into his cheeks—"and those frivolous gold sandals, you look like a Roman feast."

"Do I?" Odd how easily her cold feet warmed under the sunshine of his praise.

He returned her to the time when she was eighteen, at college, and just learning of her potent sexual appeal. Tiffany had told her that youth was the greatest aphrodisiac of all, but until Brandi saw the senior frat boys sauntering toward her, one by one trying desperately to impress her, she hadn't realized how right her mother could be.

Then she'd met Alan, the sensible choice, and she'd done the right thing. She'd accepted his proposal. She'd been with him for four years, and somehow during that time the thrill of knowing she could smile and turn a man into a willing slave had vanished, leaving behind a female prosaic and almost weary.

Now Roberto caressed her with his deep voice, and called her magnificent, and she believed him.

Recalling her plans for seduction, she slithered back on the couch and stretched, her arms a graceful arch over her head, her breasts almost—almost!—slipping free of their restraint.

His harsh inhalation was a balm to her soul.

She released the clip that held her hair in place, and shook her head. The newly highlighted strands tumbled around her shoulders.

She barely saw him move, yet suddenly he was kneeling at her side.

"You're a Roman feast, and you convince me I'm a conquering gladiator." The warm, rich timbre of his voice had changed. He sounded guttural with desperation. With need. Catching her head in his broad hands, he held her still for his kiss—a kiss of rough desire, of tender desperation.

Where had he learned to kiss like this, with just the right pressure of his lips on hers, with a tongue that stroked the cavern of her mouth so expertly she felt a growing warmth between her legs? He lifted his lips, and she pressed her thighs together, trying to preserve the sensation.

But he was only moving up to kiss her eyelids, then over to suck her earlobe, then bite it with a gentle nip that made her gasp and struggle briefly.

"Did I injure you?" he murmured. When she didn't answer right away, he drew back and wet his finger on his tongue, then slid it along her lower lip. "Darling, you have to instruct me. I never want to harm you. To tease you, to titillate you, to make you cry aloud with ecstasy. But hurt you, never."

"No. No, you didn't hurt me." Yet the sudden change from pure slick recklessness to the sharp edge of his teeth reminded her to be wary. She didn't know this man. He was big, far taller and broader than she had remembered. And the way he watched her, as if he were a predator and she his prey . . .

Yet when he said, "I only want to take you to the brink of pleasurable insanity," she learned she trusted him to take care of her—her body and her feelings—far more than she had trusted Alan for a long, long time. And she realized, also, that Roberto's voice, his accent, his words, and his care for her created warm havoc in her body.

Grasping the edges of his shirt, she pulled him up to her and kissed him. Kissed him as she had never had the nerve—or the interest?—to kiss Alan. She captured Roberto's tongue and sucked on it, needing the taste of him in her mouth, needing the intrusion of his body into hers. When she finally let him go, she asked, "*That* brink of pleasurable insanity?"

He ripped the remaining buttons off his shirt. Actually ripped them.

They bounced across the floor. He gestured at them, at himself. "You make me a beast."

"I do, don't I?" And how pleased that made her! She pushed his shirt off his shoulders, down his arms . . . everywhere she touched his skin flushed and burned with fever.

He shook himself free of the shirt and cupped his hands over her bare shoulders. "I savor the silk of your skin, the strength of your arms."

She looked at him: at his face, his chest, his waist. In awe, she whispered, "You are so beautiful."

"Beautiful? Me?" He chuckled in resonant amusement. "Men are not beautiful."

"You're beautiful like a statue, like art, like"—she looked up at the skylight—"like the stars in the midnight sky. You're so much more than I expected . . . but you're everything I deserve."

"I like that you have such expectations, and that I fulfill them. Most American women, they can't say what they wish." His Italian accent was strong and tender. "They haven't the words, or they're too shy to use them. I always pitied them for that deficiency. But you . . . you speak to me and I am mad with passion. Do you want a madman?"

"I want *you*." In a leisurely gesture, she stroked the straining neckline of her dress. "I want you to undress me." *My God.* She was actually purring.

"I know a few things about undressing a woman, and somewhere on this gown there must be a zipper." His gaze roamed over her, but he wasn't looking at the dress. He was looking at *her*.

"Somewhere there is." She trailed one finger down his breastbone and over the ridges of his stomach.

His erection pressed against his zipper, and he sucked in his breath, still and waiting.

But not yet. Not yet. She smiled a Mona Lisa smile, and walked her finger back up to touch his lips.

"You're a tease. I hope I survive the night," he said hoarsely. "And if I don't, well . . . what a superb way to die."

"A man with a sense of humor. More than that, a man with a sense of humor about *sex*." Tilting her head back, she laughed aloud with joy. "I didn't know such an animal existed."

"What kind of animals have you known?"

Oh, no. They weren't going to have this discussion. Not now. "The zipper," she reminded him.

"The zipper," he repeated. He explored the back seam on her dress, trying to find the elusive pull.

"It isn't there. Of course not. I'm desperate, and the damned zipper is hidden." Hooking his finger in the neckline, he tugged lightly. "I don't want to tear your dress."

"It doesn't matter. I won't ever wear it again." She had never meant anything as much as she meant that, and she smiled at the success of her plan to chop Alan from her life in a grand—and expensive— gesture.

"You smirk like a cat with a canary feather drooping from its mouth." Taking her chin, he held it until she looked at him. "About whom are you thinking?"

So. She had to tell him something. "My ex-fiancé."

"Ah. That explains . . . so much." He projected charm, demand . . . seduction. "Think of me instead."

"That's very easy to do." She gave in to curiosity, and her hands dropped to his belt. She unbuckled it, then tugged it free of the belt loops. Taking her time, she loosened the button, then dragged the zipper down.

Her knuckles dragged across his erection, and she felt his heat through two layers of cloth.

When their flesh touched, she was alive as she had never been in her life. . . . What would it be like to experience that heat inside her? The anticipation was so great that every inch of her felt exposed, nervy, anxious . . . craving.

He watched her from beneath lowered lids, and again that sensation of danger lapped at her. He wanted her so badly his breath raised and lowered his chest in painful increments. He had red along his cheekbones, and his hand hovered over the top of hers as if he wanted to grab it and force her compliance right now. Yet still he waited, a powerful man yielding to her wishes.

Flirting with danger, she discovered, had a piquancy of its own.

His pants sagged on his hips, and she slid her fingers inside the waistband of his shorts. Her fingertips brushed lower and lower, not really seeking . . . tormenting. When at last she brushed the tip of his erection, he braced himself against the sofa and closed his eyes to better absorb the pleasure.

Watching him accept her servicing was a potent aphrodisiac. In a breathy voice, she said, "I think you'd better locate my zipper pretty soon or *I'll* tear my dress off."

"I thought you'd never ask." He ran his fingertips over her neckline, barely touching her skin, leaving a thread of sizzling flesh behind. He found the zipper on the side, and it slithered down with a faint hiss.

She was so tight with tension, so sensitive with euphoria, the slick silk seemed to abrade her skin. Her nipples ached and she could barely breathe.

He slid the material off her breasts like a man unwrapping his most anticipated Christmas present.

The cool air whispered across her nipples. With a faint sense of dread, she watched Roberto's expression. After all, Alan had complained about her breasts—they were too abundant, the nipples were too large, too rosy, too sensitive. . . .

Roberto groaned aloud, and dipped his head to lick her as if she presented him with flawless diamonds set in pure gold.

His tongue, rough and expert, created sensations so intense her fingertips tingled with the need to stroke him.

Placing her palm on the side of his head, she turned his face up to hers. His skin burned beneath her hand.

He had a fever, and she'd given it to him.

She was young. She was beautiful. She had gifts men would kill for. That Roberto would kill for. Turning his head, he kissed her fingers and banished the cold that had possessed her since she landed in Chicago. He made her heart dance, her blood warm. His perfect body exuded power, and she controlled that power.

She exulted in her supremacy. "Watch," she said.

With her hands on her hips, she slinked out of the silk dress.

He observed, his lips slightly parted, as she revealed her body to him.

She kicked the dress away.

He groaned aloud. "*Bella, bella!* You are . . . so beautiful. So beautiful!"

She had brought a flush to his cheeks, a flame to his dark eyes.

And except for a lacy bit of a thong and her stiletto heels, she was naked, more naked than she'd been in her whole life. She wanted to cover herself with her hands, but how ridiculous was that? The die was cast.

He stood. With a grin that bared his straight, white teeth, he dropped his pants to the floor and stepped out of them.

She waited, breathless with anticipation. Tickling her brain was the memory of her first sight of him at the party. Would she be as amazed now?

He pulled down his underwear.

The answer was simple, succinct . . . and anything but short. He was a big man, and nothing about him disappointed. His belly rippled with muscle, his hips were tight, his thighs bulged like those of a man who rode and rode hard. . . . She took a long breath and wondered if she could bear it if he rode her hard.

Or if she could bear it if he didn't.

"Tell me, *cara.* Tell me if I please you."

His glorious voice and exotic accent masked, for an instant, the meaning of his words. Then she realized—he wanted *her* approval. This magnificent man didn't assume anything about her. He was taking the time to find out, and to have him at her mercy intoxicated her.

She placed her index finger on her tongue, then slid it, wet and warm, down the ridge of his thigh. "You please me very much."

Without art or deliberation, he shed his shoes and socks. He slid her thong down her legs without disturbing her shoes, then held the tiny, lacy thing in the air and examined it with a smile that both mocked and worshipped its brevity.

Dropping it, he placed his knee between her legs, bent over her, touched her throat, slid his fingers down her breastbone and her belly. He swirled his thumb around her navel, then kissed it . . . and thrust his tongue inside.

The spark he sent through her made her arch off the couch.

And he laughed softly. She almost thought he laughed in Italian.

Scooping her legs up in his arms, he went down on her.

The first brazen touch of his tongue made her fight him. She wasn't used to such intimacy . . . or the concentrated rush of passion that hit her like a runaway train.

But he paid no attention to her struggles, holding her for his ministrations until she fought not for freedom, but for passion. His tongue shredded her composure, left her without masks, without defenses, teetering on the edge of control. He pushed, and orgasm ripped through her.

She writhed. He encouraged. And she soared beyond restraint, in the freedom of knowing her joy pleased him, enthralled him.

When she finally finished, she found him on top of her. He let her feel his weight, and she reveled in it.

Everything was so different than it had been with Alan. Alan sulked if she made suggestions, backed away from acts he considered disgusting, defined by anything that gave her pleasure. Roberto was bigger, broader, taller, tougher . . . she didn't worry about breaking him. She could say nothing, do nothing that would hurt his ego. He was so sure of himself. . . .

She wanted to be sure like him.

Taking his shoulders, she looked into his eyes. In her most commanding tone, she said, "On the bottom, mister."

He laughed, a short, pained gasp of amusement. Slipping his hands underneath her, he flipped them.

Suddenly she found herself dominating a man who gladly gave up supremacy. She lifted herself above him, looked down at him, saw him watching her from beneath lowered lids. He smiled, a slight, challenging smile, and she responded with all her competitive spirit. She placed one stiletto on the floor, then the other.

"Don't hurt yourself," he said.

It was a taunt, a challenge.

She smiled back at him. "Don't worry. I was in ballet and gymnastics. I'm very . . . limber."

He closed his eyes as if absorbing the implicit promise into his mind and his body. When he opened them, she could see the painful anticipation that held him in thrall. And she proceeded to show him a side of herself she never knew existed.

8

*B*randi's cell phone rang, a silly little tune, waking Roberto from a pleasurably exhausted doze to the full light of morning. Late morning, by the looks of the sunshine beaming in through the skylights.

She lifted her head off his shoulder and looked toward her purse with an expression that was a mixture of helpless affection and annoyance. Touching Roberto's chin, she smiled wryly. "I have to get this." Sliding out from under the covers, she grabbed her phone and flipped it open. "Hi, Tiffany. I know, I should have called you with a report on the party." She was talking fast, making excuses to someone who had the right to know.

Tiffany . . . she hadn't mentioned a Tiffany.

Of course, the two of them hadn't done a lot of talking.

Interested, Roberto lifted himself up on one elbow.

Brandi stood bathed in the sun, gloriously naked and unselfconscious. Strands of gold hair tumbled around her shoulders. Her breasts were superb, with full pink nipples that had almost hummed when he touched them. She was tall, not some tiny fragile thing he had to worry about crushing, with legs that wrapped around his waist and a body that lifted to his, demanding her due.

"Good for Uncle Charles," Brandi said. "Yes, it was fabulous. Important people, lots of reporters, *great* clothes. It was worth moving to Chicago for, even with the frozen pipes and no Internet."

He lifted his eyebrows. She'd just arrived in Chicago? "I wish you could have been there. You would have loved it." She listened. "Did he? Well, Uncle Charles is right. If I do say so myself, I was gorgeous."

Roberto lifted his thumb to her.

She grinned back at him. Whereas last night she had been unsure in her sexuality, today she was confident.

He had done that.

"No, Alan was busy." Brandi turned toward the window.

Alan. The ex-fiancé. Roberto didn't know what the hell difficulty Alan had had realizing what a treasure he possessed, but Roberto was grateful to the idiot. If not for him, Roberto wouldn't have spent a night of decadent pleasure in Brandi's arms.

He looked at her left hand, the hand that held the phone. There was a pale mark and an indentation where she'd taken off a ring. So the engagement had only recently terminated. Yesterday, perhaps? That would explain so much.

She looked out across Lake Michigan, then glanced down. Down the fifty-eight stories to the ground. She stared as if mesmerized, then suddenly, hastily, she paled and backed away.

Roberto recognized the symptoms. His mother was like that— not really afraid of heights, but not willing to look down. She had gone up in the Tower of Pisa, but the whole time she had kept her hand on her heart and her eyes on the horizon.

Brandi unzipped her bag. "I didn't stay at Uncle Charles's. I was tired and I left early."

So whoever this Tiffany was, Brandi wouldn't confide in her. Didn't tell her where she'd spent the night, or with whom.

"But I wish you could have seen the Romanov Blaze." She rummaged in the bag. "It's so *big*. I never heard for sure, but I think it's probably fifty carats—"

Brandi had a good eye. Forty-eight point eight carats.

"—with a sparkle and a purity that would tear your heart out. It's a beautiful clear color, violet almost, with a fire in its heart." She pulled out a thin, long strip of sheer rose-colored material. "No wonder it's called the Blaze." She slipped one arm into it, then the other.

Roberto realized she was putting on her robe . . . if that transparent wrap with lace inserts could be called a robe. The winter sunshine beamed down on her from the skylights, penetrating the material, hinting at her outline and giving her skin a rosy glow.

Or was the glow the result of his lovemaking?

"Uncle Charles has a great house. The refinished foyer is gorgeous." She walked into the sitting room and lowered her voice.

Roberto had good ears and a healthy interest in hearing her end of the conversation.

"Say . . . Mother? Did Uncle Charles tell you anything about me?"

Mother? Roberto sat straight up. She had had to answer her mother's call, of course. That was good. But she called her mother by her first name?

"No?" Brandi kept her voice perky. "I was just trying to get a feel for how he really felt about hiring me."

Hiring her? Roberto leaped out of bed and walked to the doorway. This woman who looked like a model or a socialite or, for God's sake, a high-priced call girl, *worked* for Charles McGrath?

As a secretary. Please, as a secretary.

"There seemed to be some resentment among his employees about me." Another pause, and while she stood beside the desk, she caressed his laptop with one elegantly polished finger. "Well, because they think I got the job because we know him or because of my looks, or both. Yes, I know, Mother. I don't undervalue myself." Her voice contained a snap that surprised him.

If he had ever spoken to his mother in such a tone, she would have smacked the back of his head.

"Graduating magna cum laude from Vanderbilt Law was enough

to get me into all the top firms," Brandi said. "But the other employees don't have to be fair, do they? Especially when they haven't worked with me yet."

She was an attorney. A newly hired attorney with the best grades from one of the top law schools in the United States.

But . . . but . . . her sapphires were large and real, and her gown was couture. She had said she would never wear it again. That kind of careless disdain for something so expensive always signified that there was money in the family.

Not that a wealthy background precluded her own success, but wealth coupled with her looks meant she shouldn't have that drive to get to the top . . . and he was being a presumptuous ass. He'd had the advantages of a privileged background and a handsome face, and in his thirty-two years, he'd done well for himself. Very well for himself.

And when life had brought a reversal of fortune, he had done what he must to find his way back. Right now he was paying the price, but it would be worth it.

Yet Brandi worked for McGrath and Lindoberth.

He looked away from her. He had to look away from her. He needed to think, and that was impossible when she stood silhouetted against the windows and all her peaks and valleys called to him.

Had she known who he was when she beckoned him? She'd known his name. Of course she had to know the cause of his celebrity. His picture had been in all the papers.

But apparently she'd just moved to Chicago. If she'd been unpacking, if she'd had no water, if she had no Internet, it was possible she hadn't heard about him. Perhaps the gossip at the party hadn't reached her ears. Assuming that was all true, and that she wanted her job at McGrath and Lindoberth, then last night had been a hell of a miscalculation—on both their parts.

Should he tell her?

What good would that do?

The damage had been done.

They couldn't go back.

So why not enjoy themselves and pay the piper when the time came?

Was he making this decision out of logic or desire? As she said good-bye and shut the phone, he slowly paced toward her. It didn't matter. Nothing mattered . . . as long as he could have her one more time.

He caught her around the waist from the back. "I would like to extend my invitation to remain here for the weekend."

He felt her spine straighten. She was going to say no.

But he had powers this *piccola tesora* could barely imagine.

He opened her robe, then ran his hands down her thighs and up to linger on the golden fluff of hair that barely concealed her lips.

She caught her breath.

Bending his knees, he pressed himself against her, and whispered in her ear, "I haven't shown you what I can do with my . . . tongue."

"Yes . . ." She cleared her throat. "Yes, you have."

"There's more. So much"—he slid his tongue along the shell of her ear—"more."

She wasn't easy. She tried to think about it. About her resolve to take only one night for herself. "I have to unpack," she said faintly.

"So you can go to your cold apartment with the frozen pipes and work to finish unpacking—the unpacking that you can easily do next week—or you can spend the time with me being warm and bathed and pampered . . . and loved." He opened her to his fingers and tenderly explored her, touching all the right places, making her melt against him. "I can show you such pleasure as you've never imagined. You'll be insensible with joy. You won't be able to stop smiling. Come, *cara*, be mine for one more day."

Her phone rang again, a series of sharp rings. She still held the phone in her hand, but she looked at it as if she didn't understand what she should do. Then she shook her head as if coming out of a daze and lifted it to her ear.

Accidenti! He had almost had her.

"Hi, Kim. Everything's fine. Yes, I did." She listened. "I know you didn't, but you were wrong. It was everything I could have wished. In fact"—she cast a long, even look over her shoulder at him, a look that teased and revealed—"I'm going to have to call you back on Monday, because I'm spending the rest of the weekend with him."

As Brandi walked down the hall toward her new apartment, she couldn't wipe the smile off her face. It was Sunday. Sunday night. She had spent the entire weekend in the arms of a man who made her forget what's-his-name. Roberto had everything any woman could ever desire—smoky sensuality, sexy accent, great cheekbones, muscular body, slow hands—and best of all, she would never see him again.

Her smile slipped.

She would never see him again.

But that was what she wanted. She sighed only because he'd introduced her to decadent pleasures she'd scarcely imagined, and she knew she would miss watching with hungry eyes as he strode from the bathroom to the bedroom to the sitting room.

She fumbled to insert her key in the lock.

Clothed, he was glorious. Naked, he was—

Before she succeeded, the door swung open on its hinges.

For a long, long moment, she stared, not understanding. She had locked the door. She knew she had. Yet she examined the lock. It was smashed.

Someone had broken into her apartment.

Stunned, she pushed the door open and stared, hands limp at her sides.

The cushions on her new sofa had been tossed. Papers were strewn everywhere. The boxes she'd left packed were opened and dumped. The glasses she had put in the cupboard were shattered on the floor. Across the cream-colored wall, red paint dripped a message—DIE BITCH.

And her dragon . . . she whimpered and rushed inside. She knelt beside the green shards and touched the sharp edges with tender fingers. All these years, she'd kept her dragon pristine with nary a chip on him. She'd dragged him from the home where she'd lived with her parents through a series of smaller and smaller apartments, then to the college dorm, then to the law school . . . and now someone had come in and broken him.

She stared around at the mess with disbelieving eyes. She'd been robbed.

And how dumb was she to be inside? The criminal might still be here.

She rushed back into the hallway and called 911.

9

"*I* might point out, Miss Michaels, that it's not a good idea to be late the first day of work." Mrs. Pelikan stood at the head of the conference table, her team assembled before her, and reproved Brandi as she slipped in the door.

"It's okay when Mr. McGrath is your family's best friend." Sanjin Patel smirked.

Brandi considered how pleasant he'd been Friday night when he'd been hoping to get into her pants, and supposed that a firm smack across his handsome chops was out of the question. "I apologize, Mrs. Pelikan. My apartment was vandalized. The police left about midnight. The locksmith left at one. I had to clean enough to get to the bed, so I didn't crash until three. This morning I did call with a message." Which she'd given to Shawna Miller knowing full well it would never be passed on.

"You could have e-mailed," Sanjin said.

"They smashed my laptop." They didn't steal it. They smashed it.

"I'm sorry." Mrs. Pelikan sounded sincere. "Not a good introduction to our fair city."

Your fair, freezing-ass-cold city.

"What did the police say?"

"They said the security in the building is actually very good. The apartment manager was completely apologetic." So apologetic he'd arranged to let her insurance agent in today to take pictures of the damage and was paying for a crew to clean up the mess. Eric did *not* want to give his other tenants reason to worry. "He gave the police the video from the cameras at the doors. They're going to study it and see if they recognize the perp, but usually in cases like this, one of the tenants was being 'nice' and let him in."

"What was stolen?" Mrs. Pelikan asked.

"Nothing appears to be missing. It looks like an act of pure vandalism." Somehow, that made the situation worse. To think someone attacked her things, slashed her new, wrong-size couch, dumped her drawers and the boxes she hadn't yet unpacked, for no reason except spite seemed vindictive and far too personal.

Last night after everyone left, Brandi had tried to sleep, but every time she had drifted off, she jerked awake. Then she lay in the darkness, her eyes wide, waiting to hear the soft sound of a footfall or see a dark form move across the window.

"You could have stayed home, Miss Michaels." Mrs. Pelikan frowned as she looked Brandi over. "Perhaps it would be better if you *went* home."

Obviously Brandi hadn't done a good job with the concealer on the circles beneath her eyes. "Of course, thank you, Mrs. Pelikan. But I have been looking forward to working with you and your team, and I didn't want to miss the chance to be in on the ground floor of this exciting new case." She stood there, clutching her briefcase in sweaty palms and hoping she maintained some semblance of professionalism, while she sounded like a major suck-up.

But she couldn't bear the idea that on her first day everyone was sniggering at her, gossiping about her behavior at the party, taking the opportunity to make snotty comments about her connection to Uncle Charles. So she'd dragged herself up, put on her best booby-mashing bra, dressed in her most conservative, least wrinkled black suit, and indulged in a cab to get her to McGrath and Lindoberth as quickly as she could. At least now Sanjin could make his snotty comments to her face.

"Good." Mrs. Pelikan turned crisp and businesslike. "You know everyone here. Tip Joel, Glenn Silverstein, Diana Klim . . ."

Brandi wished she were back in the suite with Roberto, safe and warm and loved.

Not loved, exactly, but certainly cherished. Although he'd made no attempt to find out her last name or where she lived. He'd been content to let her walk out of his life forever . . . and that was right. That was just what she had wanted. In fact, a weekend had been far more than she'd wanted, and his indifference—for that was what it was—had kept her from calling him when she'd discovered the break-in. Thank God she still had her dignity.

Instead she had this room of coworkers who stared at their organizers, their notebooks, or their Palm Pilots. Anything to avoid looking at her and murmuring pleasantries.

Maybe that was the way they greeted people in Chicago, but Brandi was from Nashville. In Nashville, good manners were the standard, not the exception, and she wasn't going to let them get away with it.

She marched up to Tip. "Tip, Friday night I thought you were fighting a bit of a cold. I hope you're feeling better."

Tip was an old lawyer, probably not the best because he was sixty and not a partner, but he knew how to play the game. He shook her hand. "I'm better, thanks."

"Diana, how good to meet you again," Brandi said. "I hope you'll give me the name of your hairdresser. The guy who cut mine slaughtered it."

Actually he'd been an artist, but Diana was thirty-something, married, with highlights that shouted "Beauty School" and a cut that accentuated her plump cheeks. A little flattery wouldn't go amiss there, and didn't. Diana's brown eyes lit up, and she said, "Sure, I can do that."

Glenn cleared his throat.

"Later," Diana added.

"Sanjin—" Brandi offered her hand, but she didn't think Southern charm would get far with him. Never mind a woman scorned—he was single, intelligent, from India, and didn't like the fact she hadn't been interested in a man who worked at her firm.

He touched her hand and inclined his head with a chill that told her she'd made an enemy.

"Miss Michaels, if you're done with the chitchat?" Mrs. Pelikan managed to sound severe and look as if she knew exactly what Brandi was doing. "Glenn is the team leader on your first case, so you'll be working for him."

Brandi saw Glenn nod pontifically and knew she faced trouble. He was fifty, balding, and fighting it with a bad comb-over. Friday night after he'd slavered over her like a rabid dog, she'd spent ten minutes joking with his wife about old fools. Perhaps it hadn't been wise, but in her opinion a man who was willing to cheat on his wife should be put down and then neutered, and not necessarily in that order.

"Glenn, why don't you outline our case for Brandi?" Mrs. Pelikan sat down and crossed her arms over her chest.

Brandi opened her notebook and held her pen at the ready.

"I'll try to be succinct, since everyone here already knows the details and our client will be in soon." Glenn rose and spoke directly to Brandi while everyone else looked disgusted. "He has dual citizenship, American and Italian. The FBI claims he's a jewel thief. They assert his specialty is diamonds, big diamonds, and that he's stolen from museums and private citizens in New York City, San Francisco, and Houston. The CIA also has an interest in him, claiming he's committed similar crimes in Rome, Bombay, and London. But the FBI landed him first."

Brandi nodded.

"Would you like to take notes, Miss Michaels?" Glenn looked pointedly at the blank notebook in front of her.

Everyone in here already hated her, so she told them the truth. "I have a photographic memory, Mr. Silverstein, but I will take notes when necessary to verify the details." She smiled toothily at him.

Glenn took a long, patient breath that clearly expressed his doubt. "The FBI has videos of our client in two of those locations prior to a robbery, and most important, an audiotape of him speaking to the owner of the jewel a mere hour before the robbery took place. He's renowned for romancing females before he allegedly steals their finest pieces—"

"Their finest pieces?" Tip gave a snort.

Brandi endeavored to keep a straight face.

"And this woman, Mrs. Vandermere, says she saw him take her eight-carat diamond necklace before he left for the night. The FBI is prosecuting on circumstantial evidence and one woman's accusations." Glenn swayed like a cobra preparing to strike. "They might be able to make it stick . . . if our client were poor. But he's not. He can afford the best defense, and that's us."

"Of course," Brandi said.

"He's independently wealthy and a respected businessman." Diana smiled with reminiscent pleasure. "The fact that he's an Italian count doesn't hurt, either."

The hair on the back of Brandi's neck stood up. She drove her pen tip into her notebook. The top page tore, but she barely noticed. Wildly she looked from one attorney to another. "What's his name?"

"Don't you ever read the papers?" Sanjin asked.

"His name!" Brandi rapped her knuckles on the table.

Her fierce demand took even Glenn aback. "It's Bartolini," he said. "Roberto Bartolini."

10

"Surely you saw Mr. Bartolini." Mrs. Pelikan observed Brandi's horrified expression from sharp brown eyes. "He was at Mr. McGrath's party."

"She left early. She'd already filed us away in her photographic memory." Sanjin's voice held a wealth of spite.

The door opened. Mrs. Pelikan's secretary stepped inside and in a breathless voice announced, "He's here."

Before Brandi could collect her composure or lift her jaw off the floor, Roberto strode in.

He looked delicious even with his clothes on.

No wonder he hadn't asked her last name. She'd told him where she worked. Whom she worked for.

The silky black hair she had so loved to run her fingers through had been trimmed into a businesslike cut.

He knew she'd be on his case. He knew he'd meet her again.

His dark gaze swept the room, lingered on Diana. . . .

She had to recuse herself.

Oh, God. Oh, no. She had to recuse herself . . . and she had to tell them why.

He looked at Mrs. Pelikan. Glenn.

Brandi wanted to fall off her chair and hide under the table.

Dear God. She was going to be fired from her first job. Her father would snort about how useless she was and how she would never pay him back for college. And . . . and maybe she wouldn't, because she had committed the cardinal sin: She'd had an affair with a client.

Distantly she realized introductions were being performed.

"Mr. Bartolini, I think you've met everyone here," Mrs. Pelikan was saying. "Glenn, Sanjin, Diana, Tip . . ."

They were standing up as their names were called.

Roberto shook hands with each one.

"I don't think you met Brandi Michaels?" Mrs. Pelikan asked.

"Miss Michaels." The smile he offered her was polite, admiring, and basically that of a man who was meeting an attractive woman for the first time. "How good to meet you."

She was insulted. After their weekend together, he dared pretend he didn't know her?

No, wait. She was pleased, because this gave her a moment to think what she should do. Recuse herself, obviously. At Vanderbilt she'd taken Ethics and the Law. It had to be done.

Someone poked her in the back. Glenn. He glared and indicated she should stand.

She scrambled to her feet. "Mr. Bartolini, I look forward to working with you."

She didn't know where that had come from. She wasn't going to work with him. She was going to recuse herself. The fact that it would be unpleasant and grossly embarrassing and the end of her career and she'd have to work at McDonald's for the rest of her life serving Happy Meals made no difference.

Interesting that he was offering her the choice, keeping their relationship a secret. Was he ashamed of her?

No, it wasn't that. He hadn't known she was a lawyer at his firm until she told him. She remembered how he'd scrutinized her—as if he weren't sure what to think.

Someone poked her in the back again.

Glenn. Everyone was seated now.

Roberto sat at the head of the table with Mrs. Pelikan, listening as she explained their defense plan.

Brandi sat, too, and tried to think what to do. Regardless of whether Roberto gave her the chance to avoid telling the truth, she had to. If their relationship ever became known, it would jeopardize his defense. But she didn't have to blurt it out here. Not with Sanjin shooting her the evil eye. After the meeting was over, she would follow Mrs. Pelikan into her office—

Sanjin's voice jerked her attention back to the meeting. "I say we send Brandi. She needs to meet the judges in the city, anyway, and her inexperience won't matter, because what can go wrong with this sort of meeting?"

She glanced around. In her turmoil she'd missed something very important. "I'd be glad to do whatever needs to be done." An innocuous statement.

"Fine," Mrs. Pelikan said. "Tip, you and Diana see what else you can dig out of your sources at the FBI. Sanjin, the research—it's all yours."

Sanjin's face fell. *That* served the little weasel right.

"Glenn, you're with me. Brandi, you go with Mr. Bartolini to meet Judge Knight. It should be simple enough. He's a pushover for a pretty face." Mrs. Pelikan stood up and nodded briskly.

The whole team stood up and nodded briskly.

Brandi imitated them, but . . . she had to go with Roberto to meet a judge? How had that happened?

That's right. She'd been distracted by the plan for the ethical and required murder of her own career before it had even had the chance to draw breath.

Everyone seemed to be waiting for her to lead the way out, so she did, with Roberto close on her heels. The team split for their offices.

Brandi started after Mrs. Pelikan.

Roberto caught her arm. "Where are you going?"

"To tell her—"

"You can do that later. Nothing will be harmed if you go with me to a meeting with Judge Knight. You heard Mrs. Pelikan. He likes a pretty face, and he's not disposed to like me at all, so you'll be my protection."

She looked down at his hand. The last time that hand had been on her, she'd been kissing him good-bye, and that kiss had ended on the floor before the fire in the hotel bedroom. She looked up at him. The last time she'd been this close, she'd buried her nose in his chest and smelled the clean, fresh scent of him as if it were an aphrodisiac.

Now she could smell the scent of him again, and she didn't know whether to run into his arms or away.

But he seemed oblivious to her flight-or-fight reaction. He let her go and in a sensible tone asked, "Where's your coat?"

"In my cubicle."

"You'll need it. It's cold out there."

"Ya think?" That was sarcastic. But she hadn't insisted she go to Mrs. Pelikan. That would have been the right thing to do. Yet she was scared, and Roberto was right. Wasn't he? It wouldn't do any harm to go with him to charm a judge.

She let him help her on with her coat. She put on her gloves in the elevator. She didn't look at him. Didn't look at the people who got on with them. Didn't even glare at the woman who did a double take and checked him out.

But she did think it would be fortunate if the elevator dropped all forty stories to the ground and ended Brandi's cowardice and indecision—and while it was at it, finished off that slut who winked at him.

Roberto's limousine stood illegally parked at the curb, and Newby stepped out. He doffed his hat to her and opened the door.

A witness. Newby was a witness that she and Roberto had had an affair. The concierge at Roberto's hotel was another witness. So was anybody who'd seen her walk into the hotel. Oh, and Jerry, the bodyguard at Uncle Charles's, had seen the car she had slid into.

Putting her hand to her face, she imagined their depositions in the case disbarring her.

"It's okay." Roberto took her arm and herded her toward the car. "You're making it too complicated."

"I don't think I am."

He shoved her inside the car and followed her in.

"I think it's very clear-cut. I am just too much of a coward—"

He grabbed her shoulders and spun her to face him. "You are not a coward. Of all the things I learned about you this weekend, that is the number one truth. Please do me the favor of not disparaging yourself in such a manner again."

She'd forgotten. During their weekend of overwhelming, completely fabulous monkey sex, she'd found herself liking Roberto. Rallying her defenses, she said, "Well. Thank you. But you're a jewel thief, so how good a judge of character can you be?"

"First—I am not a jewel thief until a jury convicts me."

Which, as his lawyer, she knew.

"Second, a jewel thief must be a very good judge of character." He leaned across her.

She shrank back from his warmth, his scent, the pressure of his body against hers.

Taking her seat belt, he buckled it for her. "It's almost more important than being able to hold myself by my fingertips on a ledge five stories over the street."

The car started, and she stared at him in horror and fascination. "Hold yourself by your fingertips on a ledge five stories over the street? You could be killed!" She flinched at the idea of this beautiful man plummeting toward the pavement. . . .

Unbidden, a memory popped into her head . . . Roberto, unbuttoning his shirt, revealing that rippling, muscled chest . . . No *wonder* he had such a buff body. Hanging by his fingertips required conditioning, practice. . . . "No. Wait." Remembering that, and what followed, was the last thing she should do. "You just admitted to being a jewel thief. Don't ever say that to anyone else. *Ever.*"

"What have I done, sweet Brandi, to make you think I am foolish?" His accent was rich and full in a way she had never heard it . . . except when they made love. Then each word he murmured in her ear was opulent with the tones of Italy, and when his body moved on hers, she could forget Chicago, the cold, her furniture, her ditz of a mother, her bastard of a father, and that son of a bitch who had spent their engagement screwing another woman. This weekend had been the best of her life . . . and this Monday was the worst day *ever*.

"I don't think you're foolish." That was the last thing she thought about him. "I think you're immoral. Why didn't you tell me who you were?"

"What did you think I did for a living?"

"I don't know. You're an Italian count!"

His mouth twisted wryly. "*Count* doesn't pay as well as it used to."

"No, I suppose it doesn't come with a salary." What *had* she been thinking?

"You knew my name. You didn't seem to know what I was accused of, but I saw no reason why that would matter to us."

Oh, fine. He was just like Alan. He was shifting the blame to her.

He continued, "Not until you were speaking to your mother and mentioned going to work for Charles McGrath did I realize we had committed a legal impropriety."

"Oh." He wasn't blaming her. He wasn't blaming either one of them. How refreshing. "Then it was too late."

"Exactly."

"Wait. That was Saturday morning." She remembered the conversation with Tiffany very well, for immediately afterward he'd come to her and proposed they stay together, and she'd melted all over him like hot fudge on ice cream.

He smiled at her, his dark eyes alive with amusement, his lips quirked knowingly, and waited for her to come to the same conclusion he had.

"Okay, so the damage was done," she admitted begrudgingly. "Couldn't you have told me?"

"And have you call Charles McGrath and tell him you had to quit? I think not. Besides"—he leaned forward and whispered—"I wanted to sleep with you."

He sounded just like he did when they made love. *Oh, no.* She looked down at her lap as she knit her gloved fingers together. She needed to concentrate. She could *not* jump his bones. "Look. I didn't have the nerve to tell Mrs. Pelikan the truth right away"—her voice trembled and she steadied it—"but I won't jeopardize this case. When we get back, I will do what's right and recuse myself and . . . and take the consequences."

It was good for her peace of mind that she didn't see the expression on his face.

"Now why are we going to meet a judge?" she asked.

"Weren't you paying attention?"

She turned and glared at Roberto.

"Okay!" He lifted his hands as if trying to stop a punch. "Judge Knight wants to meet me. He's been assigned my case. My instructions are to be earnest, to remind him of my reputation as an international businessman with ties to Chicago"—his voice hardened—"and to ease his case of the ass."

"This shouldn't be difficult. You're very charming. I'm charming, also." She practiced a Southern belle smile at Roberto. "We should be out of there in half an hour."

11

"How could you have said those things to Judge Knight?" Brandi stalked down the broad corridors of the courthouse toward the door.

"He's too sensitive." Roberto strolled beside her, his hands in his pockets, his collar unbuttoned, his tie loose around his neck.

"You told him the American justice system was a farce. You told him the FBI can't tie their shoes without reading the instructions. You as good as told him you were guilty and should have been caught years ago except that the CIA was a bunch of incompetents." She was hissing. She knew she was. But she couldn't stop. "This has been the most mortifying three hours of my life."

"But at least we get to stay together." They were nearing the outer doors.

She struggled to stick her arms in her London Fog.

He caught her collar and helped her into the sleeves.

"What is Mrs. Pelikan going to say when she finds out you've been remanded into my custody? She's going to fire me. I don't have to worry about recusing myself, because"—Brandi's voice rose—"she's going to fire me!"

People walking down the corridor stared.

Roberto shrugged at the police manning security and indicated he didn't know what she was carrying on about. "See? You didn't want to explain why you had to recuse yourself, so everything came out for the best."

"For the best? I've screwed up the first thing she asked me to— Wait!" Suspicion struck, and she stopped cold.

Roberto jerked her clear of oncoming traffic.

"What did you say?" she asked.

"I said, 'Everything came out for the best.'" He slid into his overcoat.

"No, before that. You said, 'At least we get to stay together.'" Her voice rose with her indignation. "Did you do this on purpose?"

"*Cara.*" He faced her. Put his hands on her arms. "You really do think I'm stupid. I adore you, but I wouldn't risk a lifetime in jail for a few weeks in your custody. That doesn't make sense."

"No." She calmed. "No, it doesn't. But neither does what you did in there." She pointed back at the judge's chambers.

"He's an American judge. I'm an Italian count." Roberto slouched against the wall. "He was insolent. I reminded him of his place."

Roberto's snobbery reminded her all too clearly that they had nothing in common. Nothing. "You certainly did. While you were out of the room visiting the men's room, Judge Knight told me that he grew up on the streets of Chicago to become the most respected official in the city."

"To impress a pretty girl, I'm sure he exaggerates." Roberto dismissed the judge's claim with an airy gesture.

She buckled her belt so tight she could barely breathe. Or maybe it was rage that constricted her chest. "He thinks he has the right to interrogate a man of your privilege who has turned to crime."

"He does not have that right." Roberto wasn't joking.

And to think she used to admire arrogance in a man.

She pulled her gloves out of her pocket. The white velvet case from the pawnshop came tumbling out with them.

He picked up the case and handed it to her. "I hope there's nothing valuable inside."

"No, I'm wearing the earrings." She shoved it back in her pocket, put on her gloves and her hat, and headed out the doors.

He followed.

When they stepped outside, the frigid wind whipped at her. The limo. The limo was heaven. She headed toward it.

He didn't. He stopped on the courthouse steps and looked up and down the street. His gaze lingered on two guys huddled next to the huge monument Picasso had presented to the city.

They were dressed up like polar bears with hats, mittens, boots, scarves over their faces, yet they had to be freezing their keisters off.

Then Roberto said the stupidest thing she'd ever heard. He said, "Let's walk."

"Walk?" Her lips were already numb. "Are you *insane*?"

"You already think so. I might as well confirm your opinion." He draped his scarf around her neck and over her ears, and smiled at her pinched crankiness. "Come. Let's tell Newby. He can follow us in the car."

"The office is miles from here!" The soft cashmere wrapped her in his warmth, his scent, his self-assurance.

"We're not going back to the office. We're going to a restaurant. I haven't eaten."

She glared at him.

"It's not far," he assured her. "Only a few blocks."

She wanted so badly to tell him that she would watch him walk from the car, but Judge Knight had been furious at his treatment at Roberto's hands, and his anger had spilled over to McGrath and Lindoberth, and specifically on Brandi. He'd been very detailed about what would happen to her and her budding career if she misplaced Roberto, so she didn't have the nerve to leave him. Not in front of the courthouse. Probably not until the case was over. "All right. We'll walk."

Roberto spoke to Newby, then joined her, setting a brisk pace down the sidewalk.

She marched along with her head down, muttering, "I hate this.

This isn't winter. Winter is hot chocolate and marshmallows. Winter is snow lightly falling on a hill. Winter is sledding. It's too damned frigid to snow. It's too damned glacial to do anything except freeze to death walking through Chicago."

"Here. Let me keep you warm." Roberto wrapped his arm around her.

She knocked him away.

He didn't look offended. Worse, he didn't look cold.

Only a few people cared enough to fight the wind and walk the streets. For the most part, pedestrians waited for summer and warm weather—even those two guys at the statue had apparently decided it was too bitter to stay out on the plaza, because they were trudging along about a block back. One of them was coughing—something must be going around.

"Why did you move here if you hate winter so badly?" Roberto asked. "It's not as if Chicago hides its reputation. It *is* the Windy City."

"Fiancé." He needn't think she was over that stunt he'd pulled in the courthouse. Her rage was the only thing that kept her from freezing.

"You moved here to get away from him?"

"I moved here because he lives here." She knew where the questioning was going, and she didn't want to tell him the truth. Finding a gorgeous Italian lover had removed the sting of Alan's rejection. Discovering her gorgeous Italian lover was a jewel thief had created a whole different range of humiliation. "How much farther to the restaurant?"

"A block." He glanced back at the car, then glanced back again. "Newby's right behind us with the car. You can get in."

She glanced behind them, too. Newby was cruising along at the same speed they were, blocking traffic without any apparent thought to the other drivers' convenience. "No. As soon as I turned my back, you'd make a dash for it."

Roberto laughed at her. Actually laughed at her. "If I wanted to make a dash for it, how would you stop me? Hang on to my ankle to slow me down?"

"You'd be surprised," she said darkly. Actually, ballerina Brandi could kick him right in the back of the head, but he didn't need to know that. She might need to do it sometime. Or at least, she might want to. "Where is this restaurant?" The only place she could see was a good ol' American greasy spoon with fluorescent lights that flashed advertisements for Budweiser and Old Milwaukee.

"That's it," Roberto said. "The Stuffed Dog."

The greasy spoon it was. "That doesn't look like your kind of place." Not the kind of place a full-of-himself Italian count would frequent.

"You'd be surprised. So . . . you moved here last week and you're no longer engaged this week?"

Wow. He was sort of like a boomerang, flying out, then coming back to the same spot. "That's right."

"Who broke it off?"

She timed her answer so that he was opening the door when she replied, "His wife."

The place had black-and-white linoleum on the floor, padded booths, and stuffed animals—poodles, chows, German shepherds, golden retrievers, yellow Labs—hanging on the walls wrapped in cellophane. The chairs didn't match, the table legs were metal, the tops were lacquered wood, the lunch counter was chipped, and the aromas were divine.

Brandi hadn't eaten since last night when she left Roberto. At the onslaught of mouthwatering aromas, a sudden loud complaint from her stomach told the grizzled waitress about it.

"Sit down, honey, before you fall down." She waved them toward a booth, then did a double take and stared at Roberto. "Say, aren't you that guy? The one in the paper? The guy who stole all those great jewels from those society women?"

He was in the paper? Everybody knew about him?

"The jewels were gifts." He bent all his attention to the plump, worn-out waitress and flashed her a smile.

She put her hand to her chest. She blushed. Blushed for probably the first time in forty years. Fervently she smiled back. "I'd believe it."

Yeah, his smile lit up the restaurant. It seduced a simper out of a woman wearing orthopedic shoes, a burn on her left arm, and an expression that said she'd seen it all and it hadn't impressed her. For sure it could seduce jewels out of any woman.

Roberto looked toward the back corner, toward the long table where men sat huddled over their plates, smoking, eating, and talking. No other customers sat around them.

Because of the smoke, Brandi supposed.

"I see friends of mine back there," Roberto said. "We'll join them."

The waitress started to object, then took a long look at Roberto. "It's your funeral."

Brandi recognized the feeling that she'd been played for a sucker. She ought to—she had been often enough in the last three days. "Are *they* why you wanted to eat here?"

"*They're* famous for their hot dogs."

Which was no answer at all. "What kind of friends are these?" she asked.

"Old friends of the family."

They'd already been spotted. At the sight of Roberto and Brandi advancing on them, the men rose to their feet. In fact, she was going to be the only woman here, and the way they were looking at her, as if she were a . . . a moll, made her feel out of place.

Some guy of around fifty-five with broad shoulders and a rotund belly stepped out from behind a plate of two hot dogs and a huge mound of fries. He advanced on them, arms wide. "Bobby! Bobby Bartolini! How good to see you. You're all grown up!" His Italian accent was stronger than Roberto's, and his voice rumbled in his large frame.

Brandi's eyebrows rose. If he dared called Roberto "Bobby," then these people *were* old friends of the family. But other than him and another guy at his right hand, they were all about Roberto's age. About thirty, various heights, and in good shape, with muscular arms sticking out from rolled-up shirtsleeves.

"Mossimo Fossera, what a pleasant surprise." Roberto embraced him heartily. "Who would have thought I would meet you here, now?"

Yeah, right. They'd come in here to meet them.

"We Fosseras hang out here a lot," Mossimo said.

Roberto patted Mossimo's belly. "As I can see. Greg, is that you, man?" He shook hands with a guy almost as handsome as he was. "Dante, hey. You still going out with that gorgeous girl, Fiorenza?"

Dante beamed. "No, I stopped going out with her . . . when I married her."

The men laughed.

Dante and Roberto exchanged fake punches.

"Fico, hey, your complexion finally cleared up. Ricky, when did you lose all that hair? Danny, great tattoo. Son of a bitch must have hurt like hell." Roberto had lost the faint Italian accent and sounded like any American man. He acted like an American man, too, all con and horseshit—although maybe Alan had made her a little prejudiced against the gender.

"What's this?" Mossimo talked to Roberto and indicated her with his head.

"Brandi, let me take your coat." Roberto unwound his scarf from around her face.

"Whoa." The exclamation slipped from Fico as if he were unaware.

Roberto slid her London Fog off her shoulders and hung it on the coatrack.

The men stared without subtlety, making Brandi all too aware that her booby-smashing bra and conservative suit weren't hiding her figure as well as she'd hoped.

Slipping his hand around her waist, Roberto pulled her close against him. "*This* is Brandi Michaels. *This* is my lawyer."

Much cackling and jabbing of elbows followed the introduction: "Hey . . ." "Yeah, sure." "Leave it to Roberto, heh?" "That's a new name for it. Your lawyer."

The men denigrated Brandi right to her face and laughed as if she weren't there. As if she were some superficial blonde.

As if she were her mother.

She smacked Roberto hard in the ribs with her elbow, and when his breath *oof*ed out of him, she stepped forward and offered her hand to Mossimo. "My name is Brandi Michaels. I work for McGrath and Lindoberth, and not only am I his lawyer; he's been remanded into my custody."

The younger men stopped chortling and gaped at one another as if they didn't know how to respond.

Mossimo bowed over her hand. "I should have expected Bobbie to have the best-looking lawyer in the business." Like Popeye, he talked out of the side of his mouth. She was surprised he wasn't eating spinach and popping biceps. "Sit down, Miss Michaels."

Danny pulled out a chair.

She seated herself, and Roberto shoved his way in next to her. Right next to her, almost on her lap, like some guy protecting his territory. She was tempted to elbow him again, but the waitress slapped menus on the table before her and Roberto, then stood with her pad at the ready.

A single glance told Brandi what she wanted. "A Coke and a garlic kielbasa." Garlic sounded like just the thing to ward off vampires . . . and Italian lovers.

"Grilled onions and sauerkraut?" the waitress asked.

"Oh, yes." Brandi smiled sweetly at Roberto. "And fries. Lots of fries."

"I'll have the same," he said.

The way he looked at her, she got the feeling that he wouldn't care if she smelled like garlic and sauerkraut, which was bad for her plan to stay away from him—and way too flattering.

"So, Bobby, how's your grandfather?" Mossimo grinned, a lopsided grin that matched the way he talked. "Sergio doesn't get out much. I haven't seen him for a long time."

"For a man who's eighty-one, he's good. A few aches, a few pains. When the weather's cold, his hand hurts." Roberto tapped his forehead. "But the mind's still sharp."

"Good. Good. As for the hand"—Mossimo pulled a long face—"it was too bad, but it had to be done."

The conversation died as the men looked at one another, then looked at her.

You'd think they never dined with a woman.

"Are you from Chicago, Miss Michaels?" Mossimo asked.

"No, I just moved here." No one said anything, and she added inanely, "It's cold."

The Fosseras shuffled their feet under the table. Roberto leaned back in his chair, apparently relaxed, his thumbs tucked into his pockets, and not at all interested in upholding his end of the conversation.

Why had he insisted on dining with these people if he didn't want to talk to them?

Yet Tiffany had instilled in Brandi her womanly duty, so she asked, "Have you lived here all your life, Mr. Fossera?"

"I was born in Italy, but I came here with my brother Ricky when I was eleven. These kids were all born here." Mossimo shut his mouth as if he'd inadvertently revealed state secrets.

Carrying on a conversation with these guys was the heaviest social burden she'd ever had, and when her phone rang, she gratefully pulled it out of her purse.

Then she looked at the number, and she wasn't grateful anymore. "Excuse me; I have to take this. It's McGrath and Lindoberth." Pushing her chair back, she walked away from the table.

She heard the buzz of conversation behind her as she left, but what those guys were saying *about* her wasn't nearly as important as what McGrath and Lindoberth was about to say *to* her. Taking a breath, she answered.

It was Glenn, and the tone of his voice froze Brandi as surely as did the weather. "What happened?"

"I was going to call you. We had a little trouble with Judge Knight." *Euphemistically speaking.*

"I just got off the phone with Judge Knight, and that's not what he told me."

Brandi should have anticipated that. She would have if she hadn't just suffered through Roberto's transformations: from Roberto the charming to Roberto the jewel thief to Roberto the aristocrat to Roberto the common jerk. Her brain was confused. "The judge took exception to a few things Mr. Bartolini said."

"Miss Michaels, in deference to your inexperience, I gave you the easiest job on the case—getting Mr. Bartolini down to meet Judge Knight so the judge would be predisposed to his case. And you failed."

What a balding, pompous windbag! She would take credit for being stupid and sleeping with a stranger—although not to Glenn—but she wasn't taking the fall for Roberto's behavior. "Mr. Silverstein, I am hardly capable of directing Mr. Bartolini's conversation, and in fact, if Judge Knight told you everything, he told you that I kept him from immediately putting Mr. Bartolini in jail."

"Instead you got him remanded into your custody. Every woman here would kill to be in your position." Glenn's voice rose. "Do you think I'm a fool, Miss Michaels?"

She wished he wouldn't ask leading questions. Not when she was this tired, this hungry, and this irritated with men in general and Roberto in particular. "Mr. Silverstein, let me relieve your mind. I'm having lunch in a hot-dog place that I froze my rear off getting to because Mr. Bartolini wanted to walk. I am now stuck with Mr. Bartolini's company when I should be home trying to reorganize my vandalized apartment. And in case you haven't heard the gossip, my fiancé just married another woman." It did her heart good to use Alan just once to deflect trouble.

"Um, yeah, I did hear that. But that's really no excuse." Glenn didn't sound quite as forceful, though, probably because he was one of those guys who hated it when women cried.

If only he knew how far she was from tears.

Her phone beeped. She checked the number and said, "Excuse me, Mr. Silverstein; I have to take this. It's my landlord—hopefully with the news that they caught the man who vandalized my apartment." With a wicked glee, she put Glenn on hold.

"Miss Michaels?" Eric sounded brisk and efficient. "The insurance man has come and gone, and he took pictures of the destruction. The cleaners are done. I personally supervised them. The broken glass is vacuumed up. Your belongings, the ones that were unharmed, were put away—I know that not everything is in the right spot, but you can return and feel that you don't have to immediately unpack. I had the cleaners put into boxes things that I thought you'd want to distribute yourself. They're stacked on the wall between your bedroom and the living room. The crew cleaned the carpets—"

"The carpets?" What had been wrong with the carpets?

"Yes, there was an odor. We ascertained that the vandals—"

"Vandals? There was more than one?" She rubbed her forehead.

"The video shows two men. They were wrapped up with scarves and hats; there's no way to tell who they are."

"How did they get in?"

"It looked like they broke in somehow."

She took a long, frightened breath.

"But probably someone let them in. We're upgrading the security at the front. I'm so sorry, Miss Michaels; this has never happened before, and it won't happen again." He really did sound sorry.

She wrapped her arm around her waist and shivered. She supposed someday she'd feel secure again. "I appreciate that, Eric. About the carpet?"

"The vandals relieved themselves in the living room, so we cleaned all the carpets."

She changed her mind. She would never feel secure in that apartment. And she was never walking barefoot in there again.

Eric continued, "The painters have covered all the graffiti on the wall. Your clothes went to the dry cleaner's. The place looks great, and I took the liberty of replacing your mattress with a new one. Same brand, same style, and the cleaning crew made the bed. You can sleep here tonight without any worries." He was really putting himself out, trying to make sure she didn't take legal action against him or his corporation.

If he knew how bad her fortune had been lately, he'd take legal action against her for moving in and bringing all that lousy luck with her.

She glanced over at the long table where Roberto sat surrounded by men who looked like thugs. They were bent forward. Their voices rose, but she couldn't understand a word. In fact . . . Oh. They were speaking Italian.

"Thank you, Eric. I appreciate your help. I'll let you know if I choose to remain or if I've suffered too much anguish and wish to move."

"I certainly understand if you do want to move. Don't worry about breaking the lease." Eric sounded so hearty and approving she wondered if he *did* know about her bad luck.

"Thank you." She looked at the screen on her phone. To her surprise, Glenn had stayed on the other line. She thought he would have hung up in a huff. So she hit the line talking. "I just discovered my carpets had to be cleaned because the vandals peed on them. The police have no idea who they are. And the landlord would be happy if I moved. Now Mr. Silverstein—do you really believe I'm in the mood to be swept off my feet by an Italian hunk with no morals and light fingers? And would you be accusing a man, even a gay man, of dereliction of duty for saving Mr. Bartolini from jail?"

"Miss Michaels, I didn't mean—"

"No, don't apologize. Just remember that gender-based discrimination suits are difficult to defend." She hoped her kind-voiced reprimand would drive Glenn into a foaming-at-the-mouth fit. "I do have to put things away in my apartment again tonight. Can I depend on you to babysit Mr. Bartolini for me? I pay ten dollars an hour!"

12

At the table, the men heard Brandi's voice get more forceful.

"She's fiery, that one. She must be a handful." Mossimo turned heavy-lidded eyes on Roberto and switched to Italian. "So why did you bring her to our meeting?"

"I had no choice. She's my lawyer. We had trouble at the courthouse." And she was eye-popping, absolutely gorgeous and charming. She'd distracted the men and upset the Fosseras' strategy to bully Roberto. Of course, Mossimo was going to get his own way, but Roberto enjoyed derailing his strategy, if only a little.

"That's why you're late?" As if Mossimo had the right to demand an accounting of Roberto's time.

"I knew you'd wait for me." Roberto tipped his chair back, returned Mossimo's stare, and waited to see if Mossimo had taken the bait.

Mossimo gave a sideways grimace that doubled as an ingratiating smile. "We had a problem with our inside man. The feds got him on income-tax evasion."

"Classic maneuver on their part. Wasn't he smart enough to . . . No, I guess not." Roberto wanted to laugh at the frustration on Mossimo's face. His inside man had been his son, Mark. Roberto had just dissed him, and Mossimo needed Roberto too badly to take offense.

Oh, yes. Mossimo had definitely taken the bait.

"But you have other inside men." Roberto waved a careless hand at the men seated around him.

"Yes, of course, but not of his caliber." Mossimo winked in a heavy-handed attempt at coyness and lowered his voice to almost a whisper. "Not for a job like this one."

"Tell me about it." Roberto didn't expect Mossimo to talk. Not yet. Not until the terms had been broached.

But he lit up a cigarette. The ring on his little finger winked at Roberto. With seeming candor, he said, "There is a diamond at the museum. It's fifty carats or so, sort of blue, sort of purple, very famous. It needs to be liberated."

"The Romanov Blaze." Roberto glanced at Brandi. She was still talking, but with less temper and more of a steely-eyed determination that boded ill for the person on the other end. She was paying them no heed. And he was glad, for he couldn't understand what game Mossimo was playing. What trump did Mossimo hold to give up his information so quickly?

"You know of it."

"Every aficionado worth his salt has heard about the Romanov Blaze. It's one of the top ten diamonds in the world." Roberto knew damned good and well that Mossimo had known nothing about the Blaze before it arrived in Chicago and he saw a way to make a profit off it. Nonno called Mossimo a thug; for sure he was a peasant who understood nothing about the finer things in life.

And Mossimo knew it, too. That was one of the reasons he hated Nonno so much. He always felt inferior—because he was.

Roberto rubbed a little salt into the wound, reminding Mossimo that Roberto traveled in the highest circles of society. "I saw it Saturday night at McGrath's fund-raiser at his house. Surely if the stone needs to be liberated, it should have been liberated while on the road between the museum and a private home."

"Better the night before it leaves to visit the next city. When it's packed up, it will be easy to transport."

"Very good. Very clever." Mossimo was shrewd, so Roberto played the innocent. "But what has this to do with me?"

"You're an inside man."

"I haven't been convicted yet."

"A technicality." Mossimo laughed and coughed, then stubbed out his cigarette in his plate. "Your grandfather was the best in the business."

"Until you took him out of the business," Roberto said without heat. He had no reason to be angry. Not when revenge was within his grip.

"It was time for a change. Believe me, I hated to push him out. But he was old. He was getting soft. It had to be done. Yet I think"—Mossimo shook his finger at Roberto—"he must have taught you all he knew."

Roberto sliced a glance at Brandi, talking low and fast, giving Glenn Silverstein the facts and taking no shit. "My lawyer won't be busy forever. Get to the point."

"For this job, I want you to be my inside man."

Roberto laughed loudly enough to make Brandi pull the phone away from her ear and stare.

Mossimo was unfazed. "It wouldn't be so bad, would it, to get a slice of that diamond?"

"I don't need the money." Roberto kept an eye on Brandi.

Her cheeks were flushed, her eyes hot, and she was snapping into the phone.

"You're a count. A really important man in Italy."

"In a few other places, too." Roberto realized he was enjoying himself.

"Yeah. In a few other places, too." Mossimo bared his yellow-stained teeth in what passed for a smile. "You never need the money, but you're stealing stones all over Europe and Asia. For a man like you, it's the challenge. The thrill. And think about it—taking down an important museum. You'll be famous among our kind."

Roberto toyed with the idea of denying he was one of their kind. But he didn't want to make Mossimo so mad he lost his temper. Roberto had seen the results of that. So he said, "I'll be dead. The security for that diamond is state-of-the-art. I'll be fried before I go two inches."

"You've looked it over."

Roberto shrugged noncommittally.

"So . . . it's a job that's going to get done with or without you." Mossimo talked faster as Brandi finished her conversation.

"Without me. I'm already going up on trial. Only a fool would do another job now."

"A fool with a grandfather."

"Ah. So that's it." Did Mossimo really think Roberto would fail to protect his own grandfather?

But Mossimo knew how Roberto's mind worked. "He's old. He's not leaving his house or his neighborhood, and he's not going to let you put a guard on him. If you don't cooperate, sooner or later we'll get him."

The waitress headed toward the table with their food.

"Sooner or later, Mossimo, someone's going to get pissed and take you out." Roberto's voice was so reflective it took a few minutes before the other Fosseras realized what he'd said.

Ricky and Danny stood up so violently their chairs hit the wall.

The waitress veered off and caught Brandi by the arm as she started toward them.

"Calmly. Calmly." Mossimo waved his men back into their seats. "There's no reason for threats. We're all friends here. We can work this out."

The stick and then kindness. Mossimo's grip on Chicago's lucrative jewel-robbery franchise was slipping, and he was desperate enough to try anything, no matter how risky, to keep control. Just as Roberto had hoped.

"We go way back, our families do. In Bernina for centuries the Fosseras and the Continis robbed together." Mossimo intertwined his fingers and showed Roberto. "A joining now is tradition."

"Not quite." Roberto put his hand palm down on the table. "The Fosseras don't know shit about being in charge."

Ricky and Danny stood up again.

So did Roberto. He placed his other palm on the table and leaned toward Mossimo. "Like having two of your guys follow me. That's stupid, and I want it to stop."

"I don't have my men following you." Mossimo managed to fake astonishment.

Before anyone saw him move, Roberto grabbed Mossimo's wrist and twisted it sideways. "Get them off my tail."

A collective growl rose from the Fosseras.

Cold metal touched Roberto's neck.

He let his gaze linger on the ring that decorated Mossimo's little finger. It was old, so old the design in the gold setting had worn off. The stone set into it, a flawed emerald with perfect deep green color, was not cut, but rounded and polished. That ring . . .

He hadn't wanted to seem eager to accept the job, but he hadn't expected the violent upsurge of emotion he experienced at the sight of his grandfather's ring. He wanted to wring Mossimo's neck. Instead he'd gone for his wrist. Without looking around, Roberto said, "Tell that son of a bitch to take that pistol off me or the doctors will have to cut the ring off your broken finger. It would be justice, yes?"

Mossimo's round face grew damp with pain and sweat. "Put the gun away. *Diavolo,* Danny, put it away before the cops see you. We don't need this kind of exposure!"

From the corner of his eye, Roberto saw Danny slide the gun under his shirt. *Yes.* "Now, Mossimo—get those men off my tail."

"I don't have men on your tail. You want me to take out whoever it is? I can do that." Mossimo was in real pain, so maybe he was telling the truth.

And maybe he was a lying sack of shit.

Roberto looked into Mossimo's mean little eyes, challenging him, letting him know that he had threatened an adversary to be respected.

"I am so sorry for the unfair accusation. I should have known you, an old friend of the family, would not stoop to so dishonorable a practice." He released him. "So I'll take care of those two men."

"I can help you," Mossimo said.

"No help needed." Roberto smiled with all his teeth, and turned to Brandi.

She had hung up her phone, and now stared at him with wide, astonished eyes.

Well, of course. She'd thought he was a dilettante, an Italian count with light fingers, not a man capable of serving a generous helping of violence.

He tossed her her coat. "Put that on," he ordered.

She did, and her fingers were trembling as she belted it around her waist.

He gave the hovering waitress a tip, told her, "Put those kielbasas in bags," and said to Mossimo, "Thanks for the lunch."

"What about the job?" Mossimo sat nursing his wrist, and he'd lost that fake geniality. He looked like what he was—a mean, petty thief without skill or finesse.

"I'll be in touch."

13

Roberto caught Brandi's arm gently but firmly and shoved her toward the door.

She was torn. She wanted to unequivocally state that she didn't appreciate being pushed around. At the same time she wanted out of that restaurant before someone got hurt. Like her. Or Roberto. "What was that all about?" she whispered.

"A disagreement about who would pay for the meal." Roberto grabbed the lunch sacks from the waitress.

"Do guns always come out when you guys disagree?" She glanced behind her. Everyone at the Fossera table was on their feet, watching with narrowed eyes as she and Roberto strode for the door.

She faced forward again, the skin between her shoulder blades itching. Or maybe the sensation was cold sweat trickling down her spine.

"How did the conversation go with McGrath and Lindoberth?" Roberto asked conversationally.

"The conversation with . . . Oh! With Glenn Silverstein." How could Roberto sound so normal when bullets could right now be winging their way toward them? "He wants me to check in every two hours."

Roberto shouldered his way outside. "Does he? What does he think that's going to accomplish?"

"That it's going to be a pain in my rear, which I believe is his goal." The cold air felt good after the stifling atmosphere—or maybe that was just relief. She took a long breath.

The car was nowhere in sight.

"Now where are we going to walk?" she asked sarcastically.

Roberto flipped open his phone and said, "Newby, we're ready."

She sidled away from the restaurant windows. Guns. Those people had had guns. Her father had a hunting rifle. Other than that, her whole experience with guns was watching Steven Seagal movies with Alan, and that only under protest. She knew she was naive, but she'd never seen a pistol used to threaten someone. Someone she knew. Someone like Roberto.

She glanced sideways at him.

Yet he looked unfazed, and she realized that during that whole scene, he'd exuded authority. Those men could have beaten him up, could have killed him, yet he'd been the one who had been in control of the situation.

Who *was* he? A jewel thief? A gangster? Or just a count?

He walked her to the entrance of the next building. Pushing her against the wall out of the wind, he handed her the bags. "Stay here." And he took off running—running like a man competing in a track meet instead of an Italian count/jewel thief in business clothes.

More to the point, those two guys who'd followed them from the courthouse were loitering at the corner, and when they saw Roberto flying toward them, they ran, too. Ran like they were guilty of something.

Roberto skidded around the corner.

He was out of sight.

Shit. She'd lost him already!

Brandi ran, too. The wind took her breath away. Her heart pounded with the cold, the activity, the fear he'd escaped her custody.

She rounded the corner. Roberto and the two men were nowhere in sight. She stared, feeling helpless and foolish . . . and alarmed for Roberto's safety.

Why? Why should she be worried about him? She should be worried about herself having to go back to Judge Knight and admit she'd lost Roberto Bartolini. McGrath and Lindoberth wouldn't be any too happy, either.

But she was worried that Roberto had gotten himself into trouble. Into *more* trouble. That he'd be hurt.

She was such a fool. She'd been clueless about Alan. She didn't know what was wrong between Roberto and the Fosseras. And Roberto . . . every time she thought she got a handle on his personality, he changed it.

Worse than any of that . . . mixed into her distress was the knowledge that the kielbasas smelled incredibly good.

How could she be thinking of food at a time like this?

Obviously the only thing she was good at was eating.

And, um, sex. She knew she was good at that. At one point over the weekend she'd reduced Roberto to begging.

She walked farther down the street, trying to keep warm, searching for him, hoping . . .

He came back around the corner at a run. "What are you doing here?" Again he grabbed her by the arm. He hustled her back to the corner. As Newby pulled up in the limo, Roberto shoved her toward the car.

"Would you stop pushing me?" She tried to shove back.

"I'm guiding you." He didn't wait for Newby to come around and open the door. He did it himself and "guided" her inside. He dropped into the seat beside her, shut the door, and Newby took off, all in one smooth motion. "Damn it, Brandi, I told you to stay put."

"I'm lousy at following directions." And sick and tired of being told what to do, shoved around, and generally made a scapegoat.

There must have been something about the set of her mouth that warned him he was in danger, for he said only, "Hm. Yes. I'll remember that." He took the sack out of her hand. "Good girl. You've still got the dogs."

"I'm glad I can do something right. I can't walk by myself, I get reamed out by Glenn for not keeping you 'under control'"—she made quotation marks with her fingers—"those men don't believe I'm a lawyer, I sl—" She shut her mouth. She must be tired. She'd almost referred to their weekend together, a topic of conversation she preferred not to pursue.

"You get peevish when you're hungry," he observed.

"I do not." Although the odor of the sausage, the onions, the sauerkraut was almost unbearably seductive, and that, coupled with her relief at being safe, at having Roberto safe, resulted in a huge belly growl.

Pulling a tray out of a hidden compartment in the side of the limo, he placed it on her lap. He ripped open the bag and handed her one of the warm, wrapped dogs. "Here, eat."

"Look. You have to tell me what's going on." She unwrapped the kielbasa with fingers that shook. "Who were those men?"

"The ones in the restaurant or the ones I was chasing?"

"The ones you were chasing."

"I don't know. I want to talk to them so I can find out why they keep showing up where we are."

She had to admire his skills in answering an interrogation. He didn't give away any more than he had to. "Do they have guns, too?" Then she bit into the kielbasa. She lost her train of thought. "That is so *good,*" she said through a mouthful.

He smiled at her. Smiled at her the way he had that night, that weekend, as if she were the most wonderful woman in the world.

Self-conscious, she reached for a napkin and met his fingers as he handed one to her.

Why would eating a hot dog make her think of sex with him? *Well, duh.*

She rushed into speech. "Who do you *think* could be following you?"

"Just about anybody." He bit into his dog, too, and chewed reflectively. "The FBI, the police, reporters. I thought it was the Fosseras, but Mossimo says no. Of course, he lies like a rug."

So those guys could have guns. She knew she wasn't going to like the answer, but she asked anyway. "Why would the Fosseras follow you?"

"Professional curiosity."

Like a shock of electricity, she realized what he meant. "They're jewel thieves?"

"Mossimo runs the largest operation in the world right from his house."

"I could get in trouble for letting you anywhere near a criminal. Near a firearm!" The idea made her almost faint.

"I doubt Judge Knight would be angry if I got shot." Roberto grinned unrepentantly. "After this morning he's rooting for it."

"No, really. You were breaking that man's wrist." He had looked like he knew what he was doing, too. "They pulled a gun on you. That was not your everyday, run-of-the-mill lunch date."

"Perhaps not for you. Don't worry, *cara*; I won't let the ugliness touch you." He popped the top on a Coke and handed it to her.

"Why does there have to be ugliness?" She drank, and the sugar hit her system in a welcome rush.

"With the Fosseras, there is always ugliness." He took another bite. "I should have asked for deli mustard."

He was not taking her cross-examination seriously. "You have been remanded into my custody. If you'll recall, Judge Knight told you the penalties for screwing up, and he told me the penalties if you screw up, and I wish—"

"If I answer your questions, will you answer mine?" Roberto passed her the bag with the fries.

Instantly she was on her guard. "What questions?" The fries were those floppy, yellow, undercooked things, and she passed them back.

"Your fiancé has a wife?"

How badly did she want to know Roberto's secrets? "Only one." He didn't laugh.

And really, what did it matter if he found out now or later? *Everybody* was going to find out sooner or later. That bastard Sanjin was going to find out—had probably heard from sleazeball Glenn. Yup, *if* she didn't have a year's lease on her poor trashed apartment, and *if* she didn't fully realize that quitting her first full-time position would screw up her résumé big-time, and *if* she hadn't had Roberto remanded into her custody, she'd leave McGrath and Lindoberth and go home to Nashville. Right now, the thought of having Tiffany hug her, stroke her hair, and call her "poor baby" sounded like heaven.

Brandi's hand crept toward her purse, toward her cell phone.

But no. She couldn't talk to her mother. Not here. Not now. Not with Roberto watching her and waiting for his answer.

"Alan got his girlfriend pregnant and had to marry her." She wiped her hands on the paper napkin.

"Ah." Roberto didn't act surprised, as though men did that all the time.

The bastards.

He looked her over, reflecting on some piece of information to which she wasn't privy. At last he passed judgment. "At least you didn't love him."

"I did, too!" She did, too!

"No, you didn't. You're not devastated; you're irritated."

"Because *you're* irritating!" And obnoxious.

"You haven't thought about your ex-fiancé all day. A woman whose heart is broken thinks of nothing else."

"Who died and made you the love expert?" Just because she'd jumped Roberto's bones without a thought of tomorrow, he acted like he knew stuff about her. Stuff she didn't know.

"Do you have questions you want to ask me," Roberto said, "or do you want to fight?"

"I don't fight."

He had the nerve to smile enigmatically.

She *didn't* fight. She was sensible and rational. So she grabbed at her fraying self-discipline and *focused.* "Yes. Yes, I've got questions. About the Fosseras—why did you go there?"

"They asked me to meet them." He didn't seem to care that the fries were underdone. He ate them with good appetite.

"Why? Why would you be so foolish as to go and meet people like that when you're awaiting trial?"

"No one says no to Mossimo."

Roberto's flat tone sent a chill down her spine. "Is he dangerous?"

"Very dangerous."

"Then why don't you turn him in to the police?"

"There are several reasons. First, the police aren't likely to take anything *I* say seriously. If you'll recall, I'm up for trial for stealing, and the police will believe it's a rivalry or a setup, or figure if he kills me, it's good riddance. Second, he hasn't done anything wrong that anyone has caught him at. He would take an investigation amiss and kill the person who started it." Roberto leaned close and looked into her eyes, and his were dark and stern. "Do you understand? You are not to speak to the police about Mossimo or the Fosseras. They don't care that you're young and pretty and a woman. They will kill you."

She didn't know what to say. She didn't know what to think. The stuff he was talking about . . . who was he? The passionate lover? The charming jewel thief? The imperious aristocrat? Or this grim-faced, intimidating man who . . . who perhaps was far too familiar with killing?

She hated being at such a disadvantage. Somehow she had to investigate him. If only she had her laptop. She glanced around the car. "Where's the computer?"

"What computer?"

"The computer Newby said was in the car."

"You wish to send an e-mail to the police?" Roberto sounded polite and unyielding.

"No . . ." But she couldn't tell him why she wanted a computer, that she wanted to know all the details about him, his life, his occupation, his famous love affairs, and his infamous larceny.

"Sending an e-mail wouldn't get the information to the proper authorities," he said.

He was right.

But since the moment she'd left him less than twenty-four hours ago, her life had been chaos, and now she was danger? Yes, she believed that, but who was she most in danger from? From the Fosseras, or from him? "I have to do what I think is best."

"Please remember, Brandi Michaels, that you are my lawyer, and any information about my movements or our conversations is off the record."

"I doubt if Judge Knight would look at it that way." Although he probably would; judges and lawyers usually took a firm stance on lawyer-client confidentiality.

"Then it's a good thing I've been remanded into your custody so I can keep an eye on you." Roberto sounded quite pleasant.

Yet a chill slid down her spine. He wasn't threatening her with violence; rather it seemed he relished far too much their unremitting closeness. "What did the Fosseras *want*?"

"My head on a platter."

"What would that profit them?"

"You catch on very quickly." Then the exasperating man ate some limp fries.

"They want you to work for them, don't they?" She *did* catch on quickly. Putting her hand on his shoulder, she squeezed it and said, "Roberto, they want you to steal something, and if you get caught again you'll be in prison for the rest of your life, and the most talented law team won't be able to stop that." And she couldn't bear the idea.

"I swear to you, I am not going to do anything to put your job in jeopardy, and I am not going to do a job for the Fosseras." His deep voice vibrated with sincerity, and his dark eyes pledged much, much more.

"I depend on your word because . . . Wait!" The limo slowly

cruised through the narrow streets of an old-fashioned neighborhood. "Where are you taking me?" And why did her heart leap at the thought that Roberto was dragging her to his lair to have his way with her one more time?

"I thought you'd enjoy meeting my grandfather."

"Oh." How deflating. He wasn't dragging her to his lair.

How flattering. He wanted her to meet his family.

How stupid. This wasn't about her meeting his family. It wasn't even about his being remanded to her custody and having to stay close. This was about his convenience and his convenience only. He couldn't be bothered to take her back where she belonged. She was so insignificant he just dragged her along like extra weight.

Her teeth snapping, she ate the rest of the kielbasa. And enjoyed it, too, damn it.

"You'll like my grandfather. Nonno's a good man, a little eccentric, but if you can't be eccentric at his age, what's the point of living?" Roberto finished his dog, too, and the whole double batch of fries.

"And?" She waited for the other shoe to drop.

"He's a jewel thief."

Ah. The other shoe. Heck, a boot. "Why would you think I'd like him, then? I like honest people. People with some moral responsibility, who don't steal things for fun." She was deliberately offensive.

But Roberto only grinned. "He didn't do it for fun. It was the family business. The Continis—"

"Continis?"

"My mother's family are the Continis. They've been stealing from the rich for generations. We're from Northern Italy, up by the mountain passes. We used to rob travelers when they were weak from making the descent."

"How heroic," she said sarcastically.

"Poverty teaches you to take what you can."

She could hardly argue that. She knew very well what poverty did to a person. It helped you develop galloping ambition and made success not an option, but an imperative.

"Nonno's a legend. He's got the fastest hands you can imagine. He'll warn you he's going to do it, then take your wallet, your watch, your earrings, your handkerchief, your keys. I've seen him take the driver's license out of a woman's wallet inside her zippered purse and close the zipper on the way out."

"So he's a pickpocket."

"No, that's too easy for him. No challenge at all." Roberto grinned proudly. "He's an international jewel thief. When he was younger he was the inside man, the guy who went in and actually picked up the jewels. He was the man who disarmed the alarm before the alarm knew anyone was there. He could walk across a wired floor and never trip it. He was a ghost, the man hired for the big heists, and eventually the man who planned the big heists."

She hated herself for asking, but she had to know. "Is that what *you* do?"

"I hate to buck tradition," he said mildly.

She glanced at his hands—long, broad, capable of bringing a woman to ecstasy. . . . "You're good at stealing things."

"Yes, I am. But, Brandi . . ." His severe tone made her look up into his eyes.

Then she was sorry she did. For the first time since those nights in his hotel room, he focused on her with real sensual intent. "I never took anything from you that you weren't willing to give."

"If you'll recall, I'm the one who made the offer." She sounded sensible, but she blushed bright red.

Not that she thought he'd forgotten their weekend, but he'd made no moves on her. Until now, he hadn't made a single intimate comment. It seemed he was willing to pretend their relationship was and always had been totally professional. She'd been a little annoyed that he could so easily ignore what had passed between them, but she was grateful, too. Fending him off would have been awkward—especially since she thought she might succumb.

Of course, it wasn't as if they'd been together for a long time. She'd only officially met him this morning. It just *seemed* longer.

But she had to clear the air. "Look, you've got it figured out. I was angry at Alan. I wanted revenge, and I took it with you. You're probably feeling used and abused, and I'm sorry. I know I shouldn't have done it, but I made sacrifices for him and he . . . he just blamed me because I hadn't done enough. I was pissed. Do you understand? Asking you for sex was revenge, pure and simple."

Taking her hand between both of his, Roberto raised it to his lips and kissed it as if the smell of sauerkraut, onions, and garlic sausage couldn't offend him . . . as long as the aroma was on *her* skin. "You gorgeous creature, you can use me as often as you wish."

14

When Roberto called her a *gorgeous creature* in that Italian accent, Brandi was ready to attack him with scented candles and fresh flowers and . . . Oh, man, what did men like? With a '56 Chevy Nomad which had, so she'd heard, a really big backseat that folded down.

He kissed her hand again, then said briskly, "Here we are."

As he helped her out of the car, Brandi looked around. They were in a working-class neighborhood with two-story brick houses set close to the street. Tall stairs ascended from the sidewalk to the doors. From behind her lace curtains an old woman peered at the limo and at Roberto and Brandi.

"That's Mrs. Charlton." Roberto waved cheerfully. Taking Brandi's arm, he steadied her as she climbed the stairs. "Don't slip on that patch of ice."

The elderly man who let them in looked like a caricature of every Italian grandfather ever photographed. Deep wrinkles cut his cheeks and forehead. His thin white hair stood on end and waved in the breeze. His brown eyes twinkled. He was perhaps five-nine and, unlike Roberto, of a slender build.

"Hurry. Come in. It's colder than a witch's tit out there!" He shut the door behind them, closing them into a dim, narrow foyer with doors that opened into other rooms and a stairway leading up to the second level. He tossed their coats on a chair. With a broad smile that bared strong white teeth, he turned to his grandson, wrapped him in his arms, and gave him a bear hug.

Heartily, Roberto hugged him back. They kissed cheeks with such affection tears sprang to Brandi's eyes.

Man, she did need to call her mother. She was lonely for family.

"Who's this gorgeous creature?" Roberto's grandfather beamed at her.

Another *gorgeous creature* in a rich Italian accent. She could get used to this.

"This is Miss Brandi Michaels, my attorney." Roberto sounded proud.

She could get used to that, too.

"Brandi, this is my *nonno*, Sergio Contini."

"Eh, Brandi. What an intoxicating name!" Mr. Contini threw his arms around her and kissed both her cheeks, too. "What a beautiful woman you are. And so tall! Welcome to my home."

"Thank you, Mr. Contini." He smelled of soap and wine, he felt strong and wiry, and his accent was exactly like Roberto's. She'd bet he had the ladies lining up.

"Call me Nonno." The phone started ringing, an insistent summons. He ignored it, took her arm, and led her into a parlor decorated with brown brocade drapes, black-and-white photos, and tan lace doilies. "So how did you meet my Roberto?"

"We met at a party"—an understatement—"but we're working together on his case." She glanced at the cordless phone beside the gold recliner. It still rang.

Nonno still ignored it. "That's right; he said you were his attorney."

"One of his attorneys," she assured him. "He has a competent team at McGrath and Lindoberth."

The phone still rang.

"He's in trouble, my boy." Nonno glared sternly at Roberto, then broke into a grin. "But he'll get himself out."

"Nonno." Roberto's voice held a warning.

"No, no. I'm discreet. I say nothing."

The phone continued its pealing.

Finally Roberto asked, "Nonno, are you going to get that?"

"It's Mrs. Charlton, the old snoop. She'll give it another five rings and quit. Thank God it's cold or she'd be over here to meet our gorgeous little attorney." Nonno smiled at her. "Sit." With his hand on her shoulder, he pushed her onto a brown sofa so old the cushions slumped.

Apparently all the men in this family were into "guiding."

As he predicted, the phone finally stopped its incessant ringing.

"Wine?" He was already pouring three glasses from a cut-glass decanter.

All around her she noted touches of wealth interspersed with a general shabbiness. Cut glass and a slumping couch. A plethora of leather-bound books and an old-fashioned heat register that rattled in an unsteady rhythm. An oil painting by Marc Chagall that could be an original and a matted green shag carpet. The room was comfortable, yet neglected in the way of a place well lived-in and well loved.

Roberto sank down on the other side of the sofa and stretched back as if, for the first time since she'd met him, he could relax.

Nonno handed her the wine, and she noticed his hand. The skin was scarred and the fingers stiff, as if he couldn't bend them. An accident? Was that why he'd retired?

Nonno waited while she took a sip. "Do you like it?"

"It's wonderful." Red, rich, smooth, warming her belly and leaving the taste of blackberries on her tongue. She'd better not drink too much or she'd succumb to her exhaustion right here on the saggy old couch. Like Roberto, the warmth and the comfort of Nonno's home had already relaxed her.

"Have a cookie." Nonno passed a plate.

She nibbled on one. The scent of vanilla and the buttery taste of almonds filled her head, intoxicating her with the richness of flavor, the crumbly texture, the perfection that made her want to take the plate and shove every cookie in her mouth. "That is the most divine thing I've ever tasted. Who made them?"

"I did. I'm retired, my wife has passed on, so I keep myself busy." Obviously pleased, Nonno passed Roberto a glass, took his own wine, and sat in the recliner before the television. He reclined the chair, hooked the heels of his worn boots under the leg rest, and beamed at them. "My boy. He'd be okay in the business. He moves well and has the good hands." He wiggled the fingers on his good hand, then smiled slyly at her. "You know this?"

She blushed.

"Nonno." Roberto bent a reproving glare on the old man.

Unfazed, Nonno beamed at the two of them. "Roberto's too tall, too broad to be one of the really great jewel thieves. We professionals need to be able to hide in small spaces, to slip in and out of bedrooms unseen. But his mother didn't listen to me when she fell in love, huh?"

"Is the count tall, too?" Amused, she turned to look at Roberto.

He sat absolutely still, his eyes cold, fixed on his grandfather with an intensity that sucked the air from the small room.

Nonno threw up his hand as if warding off a blow. "Roberto, I tell you, I don't know!"

Still Roberto stared.

And still Nonno spoke. "I don't. You are my beloved grandson. I would tell you if I did."

Roberto gave an abrupt nod. "All right. I believe you."

What had happened? What had she said? Or rather . . . what had Nonno said?

Before her eyes, Roberto returned to his comfortable self. "We ran into the Fosseras today. Mossimo sends his regards."

"May he burn in hell." Nonno lifted his glass to Roberto, who returned the salute. Leaning forward with an intensity that caught Brandi by surprise, he asked, "Did you see the ring?"

"He wears it on his little finger."

Trouble in High Heels

"He dares." Nonno's mouth tightened.

Brandi remembered the ring Mossimo wore—it had been small, the gold rich and old, but the color of the emerald had been exquisite. Apparently it was the object of some rivalry, and she experienced the sensation of being caught between the proverbial rock and a hard spot. With her parents she had experience standing there, and it was never the best place to be.

"He flaunted the ring at me." Roberto smiled unpleasantly. "I taught him to be more cautious in the future."

"Where did you learn to do that?" she asked. "That move with the wrist, I mean."

"The count is a very wealthy man. My grandfather's business is stealing jewels." Roberto sipped his wine. "When I was a boy it was deemed a good idea that I have an elementary knowledge of self-defense."

She had come to know a little about Roberto's character, so she said, "How elementary?"

"Smart girl." Nonno nodded at her. "He has his fourth-degree black belt in jujitsu and a second-degree in karate."

"Wow."

"But you, Roberto. You challenged Mossimo?" Nonno leaned his head back against the cushion and looked at his grandson, his dark eyes glittering from beneath drooping lids. "I thought you were going to play the cowering pussy."

"I found the role was not to my taste."

Nonno gave a bark of laughter. "You've made your task all the more difficult."

"What is life but one difficulty after another to be overcome?" Roberto extended his hand in a gesture so essentially Italian, Brandi felt as if she'd been transported to the boot itself.

"So true." Nonno smiled fondly at his grandson. "Sitting on the couch beside you, Brandi, you see my only grandchild, the only child of my only child. We Continis, we steal, but only from the rich."

Her mouth quirked into an irrepressible smile.

"Yes, yes, it is true! We are the Italian Robin Hoods. We help the poor, we stand for justice, and for generations we are known for our passion for life, our impetuous decisions, our dancing, our drinking, our daring . . . our loving." He lifted his glass in a salute to his ancestors. "But Roberto was such a solemn little boy, and he grew up to be a somber, responsible man, and I was proud—of course I was proud! But I thought the Contini blood had at last succumbed to civilization. But no. It was only simmering in my boy's veins, waiting for the right circumstances to transform him into a man as mad and impetuous as the founder of our family, as old Cirocco!"

Brandi's frustration with Roberto made her sharp and bitter, and exhaustion stripped her tact away. "So he's a somber, responsible jewel thief? I don't think so!" Then she bit her tongue. No matter how disappointed Roberto had made her, she had no right to take it out on a pleasant old man who loved his grandson and served her wine and cookies.

"You'll break my *nonno*'s heart talking that way about our family vocation." Roberto chuckled indulgently and touched the lobe of her ear with his finger.

She jerked her head away. "Apparently you aren't very good at your family vocation or you wouldn't be facing trial."

Nonno cackled and slapped his knee. "She's got you there!"

Obviously he was not at all offended, so Brandi warmed to her theme. "You should leave the illegal activity to professionals like Mossimo."

Nonno stopped laughing. In a reproachful tone he asked, "But Roberto, did you not warn the charming and beautiful Brandi about him?"

"Yes. She says she'll do what she thinks is right."

Both men turned to look at her as if she weren't very bright.

Nonno clicked his tongue in reproval.

"Nonno, I was hoping you would show Brandi your party tricks."

Nonno considered his grandson, then nodded slowly. "Yes, of

course." To her he said, "Of course, I'm feeble and not as quick as I used to be. You'll excuse an old man for his clumsiness, yes?"

Brandi recognized that she was being set up, but what could she do? She had to play along. "What do you want me to do?"

"Stand up." Nonno got to his feet and, with his hands on her shoulders, guided her to a place by the window. "So. Here you have the best light so you can observe me. You should wear your watch." He handed her a serviceable, leather-banded Timex.

She stared at it. It looked just like hers.

It *was* hers.

"Put it on," Nonno said.

"But it was on." And he'd picked it off her wrist while moving her into place.

Roberto grinned.

"Wow, Nonno." She buckled the watch on her wrist. "You *are* good."

"I'm flattered, but you have no one to compare me with, do you? No." He handed her the ring her mother had given her for graduation.

"How did you do that?" He'd taken it right off her finger!

"Watch the watch," Roberto advised.

She glanced at her wrist. Her watch was gone.

Nonno handed it to her again. "They're slippery devils," he said cheerfully. "Here. You lost your keys."

They'd been in her jacket pocket.

"And your cell phone."

In her other pocket.

"Watch the watch," Roberto said again.

It was gone. Again. Her head was whirling. "How do you do this?" she asked again. She put her cell phone and her keys back into her pockets. She strapped on her watch without much hope that it would stay there.

"It's nothing," Nonno said modestly. "You should have seen me before."

"Before what?"

"Before this." Nonno lifted his ruined hand and showed it to her, front and back. "It's my right hand. I'm right-handed. I'm not nearly as good with my left hand."

"What happened?" she asked.

Nonno's genial smile disappeared and he looked grim. Outraged. "Mossimo happened."

"What do you mean, Mossimo happened?" She leaned toward him, frightened and ill, remembering how Roberto had twisted Mossimo's wrist, not understanding how such a move could create such damage. "How could he . . . ?"

Roberto told her what she didn't want to know. "He used a ball-peen hammer to break every bone in Nonno's hand."

15

Brandi backed away, away from the image. A hammer, rusted hard steel, smashing again and again on the fragile bones of a man's hand . . .

"He wanted my business," Nonno continued. "I didn't intend to give it to him. But a man in the hospital can no longer lead his team, and a master thief with a hand like this can never work again."

"His men cried when they saw Nonno's hand. In his field, there was never anyone like Nonno before. There never will be again. He was an artist. Breaking his hand was like smashing the Romanov Blaze." Roberto watched her, his elbows on his knees, his hands clasped together.

She knew now why he'd started this. It wasn't a party trick; it was the best way to illustrate how dangerous the Fosseras could be. Not just killers, but men who enjoyed their work . . .

She surrendered, as Nonno and Roberto had known she would. "All right. I won't go to the police about them."

"Promise?" Nonno gave her back her watch, her ring, her keys, and her cell phone.

"I promise. I get it!" She sank down on the couch, her knees weak from the thought of such violence, such pain. "I'm not stupid!" But she flinched.

Was her father right? Was she stupid? She had landed herself in a stupid situation with professional thieves as allies and more professional thieves possibly threatening her life, and the lawyers who should have been her allies were her enemies, and one of the most prominent judges in Chicago scorned her for the company she kept. She rubbed the pain over her right eye and tried to ignore her father's derisive voice as it echoed in her head. *Brandi is stupid.*

She wasn't. She knew she wasn't. She was successful in school, and her friends valued her good sense.

But at times like this, when she was tired and in turmoil, it was almost easier to believe her father.

She attributed the familiar churning in her gut to worry about the situation. "Roberto, if you don't work for Mossimo, will he take a ball-peen hammer to you?"

"Don't worry about Roberto. He can handle himself. He isn't the thief I am, but he's one hundred times smarter." Nonno tapped his forehead and winked. "Well, not one hundred times, but he's a smart boy."

Roberto laughed. "Nonno, are you still dating Carmine?"

"No, she got possessive, you know?" Nonno flopped down in his chair in disgust. "Like when I took Tessa golfing, Carmine got mad. I've got no time for that."

By the change in conversation, Brandi knew they were satisfied with her promise. She leaned her head back on the couch and tried not to think about a hammer crushing Nonno's hand, or the guns and brutality, or her apartment being ransacked, or her precarious job. . . .

"Mama says you should marry again," Roberto said.

"Your mama should mind her own business," Nonno answered.

"She says she will when you do."

Roberto's voice sounded far away. She turned her head and looked at him. He was so handsome. Even his profile was gorgeous. He made her heart contract and the hair on her arms prickle, and when she remembered how deliciously they had made love . . . Whoa! She lifted her head. Of all the things she shouldn't think of, that was number one. Never, never should she reminisce about that night, that weekend. . . .

What were they talking about? It sounded like relatives now . . . in fact, she couldn't understand a word. Had her hearing failed her?

No. She smiled. They were speaking Italian.

She was warm, she was full, she hadn't had enough sleep last night . . . she was in trouble and she knew it. Tiffany wouldn't approve of her going to sleep on a visit, but she would close her eyes for a few minutes . . . just a few minutes. . . .

Nonno nodded at Brandi and smiled. "She's out."

"I knew she was going down for the count." Roberto stood up and looked down on Brandi, hunched into one corner, her chin settled on her chest. He moved her sideways so she was reclining. Nonno slid a pillow under her head while Roberto lifted her feet onto the sofa. She murmured and frowned, her nose wrinkling as if her dreams weren't pleasant.

Well, of course not. How could they be? She'd had one shock after another. Altogether, it had been one hell of a day.

"Get her cell, Nonno. We don't want her to wake up."

Nonno plucked the phone out of her pocket.

Roberto took the afghan Nonno offered and tucked it around her. He liked seeing her here, asleep in his Nonno's home, her golden hair spread across the dark upholstered pillow. He tucked a strand behind her ear, then turned to go with Nonno.

Nonno was watching him, hands on hips.

"You look like an Italian fishwife," Roberto said softly.

"Yeah. Sure." Nonno took the decanter and an extra bottle of wine and headed for the kitchen.

Roberto shut the door behind them. They settled down at the old table, glasses between them.

"So who is she?" Nonno demanded.

"A girl I met."

"A nice girl. What are you doing with her?"

His *nonno* could be damned cutting when he chose. "She picked me up. I let her. Then when I found out she was my lawyer?" Roberto spread his hands in a typical Italian gesture of resignation. "What was I to do?"

"You're crazy, bringing her along on a job."

"I'm not doing the job yet, and you should have seen the Fosseras when I introduced her. They didn't know what to make of her—or me." Roberto laughed softly and poured the two glasses full. The men clinked them and drank. "They didn't know whether to believe she was my lawyer. They couldn't take their eyes off her. I won't put her in danger, Nonno, but I'm going to use her to blind them to what's really going on."

"What is really going on?"

"We'll know soon enough." Roberto glanced at the back door, then at his watch.

It was gone. "Give it back." He held out his hand, offering his grandfather a handful of change.

Nonno groped in his pocket, and a smile blossomed on his face. "Hey, boy, you're getting good. I didn't know you'd been in there."

"I've been practicing."

"Damned straight." Nonno handed over Roberto's watch. "For a job like this, you have to be the best. Tell me again why the girl is involved?"

Roberto took a breath that made him aware of his expanding lungs, of his swelling chest, of the blood pumping in his veins, of an excitement he barely understood and had never experienced before. "I want this job to go down perfectly. I want revenge for your hand. I want to show the world what I can do. I want those bastards who hold my feet to the fire to realize who they're dealing with. And I want her with me. I want her at my side."

Nonno nodded his head, a slow bob of acknowledgment. "Boy, for so many years you buried the Contini deep in your soul. But I see it now. You're as crazy as the rest of us."

"I don't like to be pushed into a corner."

"No. And I like the girl." Nonno bent a dark glare at Roberto. "Are you sure she's who she says she is?"

"No. Not sure. She could be a plant, from the Fosseras or the FBI, most likely." Anything was possible.

"Yeah." Nonno rubbed his chin. "According to gossip, Mossimo's in trouble."

"Why in trouble?"

"He's got no skills. All he's ever been good for is planning these jobs and bullying people to pull them off. And it's been a long time since he's successfully delivered a big payoff. Rumor is that the younger men are getting restless, starting to branch off on their own, setting up their own protection rackets, making trouble on the streets—fights and robberies. Big family. Big trouble. None of them have been caught yet, but I think maybe there might jockeying to see who replaces him."

"Fascinating." Roberto thought of the men around Mossimo's table today. Which of them would take Mossimo's place? Greg? Dante?

No. Fico, the man with the acne scars and the sharp, intelligent eyes. He'd watched the action between Mossimo and Roberto without emotion, as if he had no vested interest in who won and who lost.

"Mossimo's *got* to force you to work for him and *got* to pull this job off or he's going into retirement whether he likes it or not," Nonno said. "Make sure you have a care for the girl. Mossimo is in a corner, and a cornered beast is dangerous."

"I won't let anything happen to Brandi." Roberto would tie her up before he allowed her to step into harm's way. And he would kill before he allowed anyone to hurt her. "Anything else I should know?"

Nonno grinned. "I got the museum plans."

"I never had a doubt." Roberto grinned back.

"But they cost me a bundle." Nonno fetched a clean, crisp roll of blueprints from behind the chipped, green ceramic bread box.

"I'll pay you back." As Nonno unrolled them, Roberto stood and put his full glass on one end to anchor it.

Nonno put his glass on the other. "Ack, no. This is the most fun I've had since I landed in the hospital with this hand."

Their heads almost touched as they discussed the points of entry and exit, what they knew about security, the likely traps they didn't know . . . what the Fosseras had planned and how to thwart them. It was a war council, and it was missing only one of its generals.

A knock sounded on the back door.

Roberto picked up the plans and stashed them in the pantry. Walking to the bread box, he flipped it open and took out the loaded pistol Nonno kept there.

Nonno went to the door between the kitchen and the living room and checked on Brandi. He nodded at Roberto and shut the door again.

Roberto looked through the peephole at the two men standing there. Their collars were pulled up, their hats pulled down, but their faces were bare and they looked straight ahead, knowing they had to be identified before he'd let them in.

Not that they couldn't shoot their way in if they chose.

He disengaged the alarm, clicked the lock on the door, and held it open while silently they slipped inside.

Nonno stood beside the table, his lip curled, his back stiff with rejection.

Roberto locked the door behind them and reset the alarm. "Did anyone see you come in?"

"No. They're watching the house, but they didn't see us." The older man shed his coat and hat without consciousness.

The younger man kept his coat on, staring at Roberto as if he were a criminal. Which, Roberto supposed, he was.

No one shook hands.

The older man seated himself at the table. He gestured to the younger man. "Get out the museum plans and sit down."

Reluctantly, the young man pulled his laptop out of his briefcase.

He opened it and the plans for the Art Institute were there—and they looked almost identical to Nonno's plans.

Almost. But not completely.

Roberto leaned forward and immediately identified the changes. Interesting—and more challenging.

"I never thought I'd be working with the likes of you," Nonno said to the strangers.

The older guy looked at Nonno. "I'm not thrilled about this myself. Now let's get to work. We've got a jewel robbery to plan."

16

$\mathcal{B}$randi opened her eyes. She didn't know where she was.

Where was she?

She drew in a sharp, panicked breath.

Then, in a gush of memory, the truth was upon her.

Roberto. This was his grandfather's house—Nonno's house. His grandfather had suffered such a grievous injury by men she'd met today. And she dared not go to the police.

Her apartment had been vandalized, her treasured dragon broken.

Her first day on the job had turned into a nightmare.

She was in an unfamiliar town. She had nowhere to turn. No one could help her except Roberto, and he was a jewel thief—or worse.

Slowly she sat up and looked around. She was alone in the living room. The light in the corner had been turned on, the curtains closed. She'd been prone on the couch. Asleep. When had she gone to sleep?

Had she heard men's voices in the kitchen?

Where was Roberto?

She leaped up so fast her head spun. She dashed through the door into the kitchen, and stood swaying against the wall, staring.

Roberto stood at the stove. He had his white sleeves rolled to his elbows, wore a ruffled white apron, and stirred a pot with a wooden spoon. Nonno was looking into a pot and arguing with Roberto about the contents.

Head rush. She'd gotten up too fast. Gotten up too fast . . . and seen Roberto. Both could cause a head rush.

Only Roberto made her feel as if it would never stop.

Both men looked up, bemused, at her entrance.

"You all right?" Roberto placed the dripping spoon down on the red Formica counter and took a step toward her.

No. She didn't want him to touch her. She'd pitch over onto her face for sure. "I'm good." She looked him over. "Nice apron."

"My grandmother's." He winked at her and went back to stirring the concoction. Puffs of steam rose from the pot carrying the aromas of garlic, onion, olive oil, and basil.

"Ah. She's awake, our little sleeping beauty." Nonno waltzed over to her, smiling, mellow . . . slightly tipsy. Tickling her cheek with his ruined fingers, he said, "We're fixing dinner for you, *cara*."

"Thank you, Nonno." She smiled at the old man and thought, *Roberto cooks?* "It smells great."

"It's an old family sauce recipe. We put it on our homemade polenta, and the angels sing with joy." Roberto kissed his fingers.

She wanted to snatch the kiss out of the air, but she'd made enough of a fool of herself today. Instead she looked around the narrow, old-fashioned kitchen. The table in the middle of the kitchen was set with a red-and-white-checked tablecloth, three plates with silverware, and a large salad in a wooden bowl. Three places were set. . . .

A sleep-drugged memory surfaced, vague and uncertain. "Is someone else here?"

"Someone else?" Nonno lifted his brows, but innocence sat ill on his wrinkled face.

"While I was sleeping, I thought I heard men talking."

"We were talking." Roberto gestured between him and his grandfather. "We haven't seen each other for months. We had much to catch up on."

"Okay. I guess that was it." Although it seemed she'd heard different voices . . . it must have been a dream. She pushed the hair out of her face. "What time is it?"

"Seven o'clock. You slept four hours."

"Oh, no." She groped in her pocket. "I didn't call McGrath and Lindoberth and report in."

"I did it. Your phone's by your place setting." Roberto indicated the cell on the table. "Do you like mushrooms? Because we worship mushrooms, and if you don't like them, you're going to have to have bottled marinara."

"Love mushrooms," Brandi said automatically. "Who did you talk to?"

Roberto smiled a rather crisp smile. "I spoke to Glenn and cleared up a few of his misapprehensions about who's in charge in the monkey cage."

"Oh, no." She groped toward her chair and sat down. Glenn wouldn't forgive her for that.

"I assure you, *cara*, this was a fight about what I expect from him. It had nothing to do with you." Roberto comprehended too much.

"He won't care." She cradled her head in her hands. "He'll take it out on his subordinates."

"But you won't be seeing him."

"What do you mean?" She lifted her head.

"I won't spend my days sitting in your offices, no matter how luxurious they are." He tasted the sauce, then offered the spoon to Nonno. "More parsley?"

"And a little more salt," Nonno said.

To her, Roberto said, "We are chained together by Judge Knight's ruling, are we not? All the time? Day and night, night and day?"

Somehow the details of Judge Knight's actions had previously escaped her. She'd been too exhausted, suffered too many shocks today to figure out all the ramifications, but now her brain was working.

Sluggishly, but it was coming up to speed. "I *have* to be in the office. I just started work."

"I have work, too," he said. "I'm the head of a large corporation."

"You're a jewel thief!"

"It's a sideline."

"Damn it!" She slapped the table. The dishes danced. "Who are you really?"

"Exactly who you think I am," he shot back.

"I doubt if you could be that wicked." Her voice rose.

"I'm fixing the polenta right now." Nonno poured olive oil into a skillet and lit the burner.

"Where are we going to sleep?" she asked. "Huh?"

"I'm going to sleep at my hotel." Roberto had the gall to sound calm.

"I don't want to sleep at your hotel. I have to go to my apartment. I just moved in. I have things I need to do." Things she needed to put away—again—after the break-in this weekend. A break-in that wouldn't have happened if she'd been home instead of lolling around in indolent luxury making love to Roberto.

"All right. You sleep at your apartment and I'll sleep at my hotel."

"You'll run and I'll be holding the bag!"

"I already gave you my word that I would do nothing to harm your career." Now Roberto had the gall to sound insulted.

"Little Brandi, bring me the plates," Nonno said.

She stacked them and put them on the counter. "I can't believe we're going to have to sleep together. What was Judge Knight thinking?"

The two men exchanged glances.

She pointed her finger at them. "Not like that. I am not sleeping with Roberto. Never again."

"Aha!" Nonno cuffed Roberto on the side of the head. "What were you doing? Brandi's a nice girl."

Shit. She couldn't even blame her exhaustion for her slip; she'd had a four-hour nap.

But she could blame it on her proximity to Roberto. He obviously blew the circuits in her brain or she wouldn't make those kinds of mistakes.

"She is a nice girl, and she'll be nicer when we feed her." Roberto looked meaningfully at Nonno. "Trust me. I know this."

"She has a temperament like Nonna, then." Nonno nodded wisely. "Dear Brandi, would you serve the salad?"

She narrowed her eyes and would have railed at them, but the smell of frying polenta mixed with the scent of the sauce and she was suddenly ravenous. She shook the glass jar filled with oil and vinegar and poured the dressing on the greens, then tossed them with the plastic salad tongs. Nonno put the plates on the table and seated himself on the end. Roberto removed the apron and seated himself on one side. She sat on the other side.

Nonno extended his hands to them both.

She placed her hand in his, then stared at Roberto's broad palm extended across the table.

She didn't want to touch him. It was as simple as that. Hearing his warm, slightly accented voice was bad enough, but when she touched him, she forgot the trouble he'd made for her, his dubious honesty, and his unsavory profession, and remembered, in the hidden recesses of her body, how he felt beside her, inside her, on top of her. Touching him made her *want*, a want she didn't know if she could resist.

Roberto was no man for a woman with her feet planted firmly on the ground and her eyes on the goal. For a woman like her.

But the men were waiting for her to close the prayer circle, so reluctantly she placed her hand in Roberto's.

There. That wasn't so bad. She could deal. . . .

Nonno said the traditional Catholic blessing, and ended with, "Dear Lord, we implore your support with our ventures. Amen."

Both Nonno and Roberto squeezed her hand.

"Amen," Brandi murmured, surprised at the addition.

Taking her first bite, she barely restrained a moan of joy. This wasn't food; this was ambrosia. She took another bite, looked up, and realized the men were watching her. "It's good," she said.

They grinned, exchanged high fives, and settled down to eat.

Brandi had finished her first slice of polenta when Roberto announced, "I also spoke with your sister."

Brandi put down her fork. "You spoke to Kim?"

"She called and I answered your phone."

"Why didn't you come and get me?"

"You were sound asleep. Don't worry; we had a good talk."

"I'll bet." Today was one disaster after another. "What did you tell her?"

"That I would care for you."

"Oh, no." Brandi could imagine how Kim had responded to *that*. Kim was not the kind of woman who trusted a man to do what he promised.

Come to think of it, neither was Brandi.

"She wants you to call her." He caught Brandi's hand when she would have risen. "Show some respect for our cooking. You can call her after dinner."

"I am not grumpy when I'm hungry," she said in irritation.

"No, dear." Nonno sounded absolutely placid. Looking up, he caught Brandi glaring at him in outrage. "I'm sorry! For a minute you sounded just like my wife."

Roberto bent his head to try and hide his grin.

He wasn't trying hard enough.

"I think you two should spend the night here," Nonno suggested.

She wanted some time alone to try to figure out how her life plan had gone so awry. So she smiled and patted his hand. "Thank you, Nonno, but I don't have any clothes. I don't have a toothbrush. And after my meals today, I really need a toothbrush."

"I still have drawers of Mariabella's clothes up in her bedroom. Mariabella's my daughter. She's Roberto's mother. She wouldn't mind at all if you stayed." Nonno smiled coaxingly. "I'll make the bed and Roberto will go down to the corner for a toothbrush."

Brandi was delighted to see Roberto look truly pained. "Oh, man. Nonno, it's cold out there!"

"Wimp." With a single word Nonno dismissed his grandson.

"You've got a driver!" Brandi said.

"I'm not calling Newby to drive me a block." Roberto finished his meal.

She smiled. This would teach him to make her walk all over Chicago in this weather. "Revenge is sweet."

"So you'll stay," Nonno said.

She really didn't want to. But her bed in her apartment was a new mattress paid for by the apartment manager. She wanted to go home—but not back to that place. She didn't want to smell the new paint and know the hateful message hidden beneath it, and see the couch with the cushions gone, and feel the damp carpet and hope the cleaners got every horrible thing out. Even with Roberto in the house, she would remember.

As she hesitated, Nonno sighed hugely. "I'm a lonely old man. So lonely. I would enjoy the company. Of course, you young people probably don't want to hang around with a feeble old man like me. . . ."

"Nonno, you're pulling my chain," she said.

"Why, yes." His eyes twinkled. "Yes, I am. Thank you for noticing."

She couldn't resist him. "I'd be delighted to stay."

Looking resigned, Roberto stood up and went to get his coat.

"Just for tonight!" she said.

"Of course, little Brandi." Nonno patted her hand. "Roberto, while you're at the store, pick up some eggs for the morning."

"Yes, Nonno." Roberto pulled on his leather gloves. "Anything else?"

"Milk," Nonno said. "And maybe some Bisquick."

"Yes, Nonno." He took a dark knit hat and pulled it over his ears. He should have looked nerdy.

Instead he looked boyish and sexy, and Brandi wanted to wrap his scarf around his neck, give him a kiss, and tell him to hurry. So she said, "About the toothbrush—soft bristles, compact head."

He looked at her. Just looked at her. He didn't smile, but his eyes were fond, as if seeing her sit with his grandfather satisfied something within him. "Soft bristles, compact head," he repeated, and headed for the door.

It opened and shut, leaving the two at the table smiling at each other.

"He's a nice boy. But he's spoiled." Nonno nodded wisely.

"He sure is." *Spoiled and breathtaking.* When he gazed at her like that, she forgot all his crimes and remembered only his charms.

"It's girls like you who spoil him. It's not good for you two to spend the night alone together." Nonno shook his head. "Things happen."

Things happen? They sure did, especially around Roberto.

"I know. I know. You young people are always sleeping with each other back and forth and you think old guys like me are out-of-date, but I'm telling you, my own daughter learned the hard way that men are louses who take their pleasure without a thought to the consequences!" Nonno's voice rose and his dark eyes sparkled with fury. "I had to send Mariabella to Italy to have her baby."

"Roberto?" Brandi had thought he was the son of a count.

"Yes, Roberto. He was born on the wrong side of the blankets. Then she married the count and he made all things right."

"Oh." She was confused and irritated. She needed to know more about Roberto. "But the count is his father?"

"In every way," Nonno assured her. "You stay here and drink a little more wine. I'll make up the beds."

"Actually, Nonno, do you have a computer I can use?" she asked impulsively.

"Of course. Roberto bought me a brand-new computer for my birthday. Come on, I'll show you."

Roberto walked down the dark street, his head bent against the wind, as cold and uncomfortable as Brandi obviously hoped. The porch lights provided spots of light; the stars were far away and brittle-looking in the blackness of space.

Yet he smiled—she'd been so wickedly thrilled at the idea of sending him out into the cold.

She was not a woman with whom a man trifled. She was intelligent, she was quick-witted, she was passionate—and so, of course, she was vindictive. The last trait was not a permanent part of her character, but when a woman had offered a riches of femininity such as she had offered to her fool of a fiancé and had them rejected, she would seek revenge on the whole gender.

Roberto understood. He only hoped she understood that, when the time was right, he would take her to his bed again.

Come to think of it . . . he hoped she didn't. She was a strong-willed woman, and if she realized his intentions, her resistance would strengthen. He liked leading her on, giving her support in her new job while kindling the fires of her body. When their current situation was resolved, he would sate himself—and her.

His fists clenched in his pockets.

Yet waiting was proving more difficult than he anticipated. Seeing her asleep on his *nonno*'s couch, sweet and defenseless, had touched a tender chord within him and a fierce chord within him. He didn't understand this *need* to possess a woman with whom he'd indulged himself only a day ago.

Yet he would control that need. After all, Nonno was right: Roberto had always been the sober, responsible one in the family, and—

Behind him, someone coughed. Coughed as if he didn't want to, but couldn't hold it back.

Roberto's steps didn't slow. Nothing about him indicated that he'd heard. Instead he waited until he reached the darkest spot on the street and slid into the shadows beside the garbage cans.

The guy following him bumbled along, coughing up a lung.

The guy was really sick.

When Roberto knocked him off his feet he was careful not to kill him.

The boy struggled, punching wildly.

Roberto sat on his chest, pressing him into the icy concrete. "What are you doing? Why are you following me?"

The guy wheezed. "Not."

"Yes, you are. You and that other guy. What did you do, divide up the duties?"

"Had to." The kid started coughing again.

Roberto would have bet the FBI had put a tail on him, but the FBI didn't put their agents into the field with pneumonia. "You're with the Fosseras."

"Not!" The guy struggled frantically.

Roberto leaned close. "Bullshit." *Per Diana!* He wanted to put his hands around the guy's throat and interrogate him, but the kid was literally gasping for breath. Roberto would be lucky if he didn't die while he sat on him. Standing, he fumbled for his phone. "I'm going to call you an ambulance."

"No!" The guy stumbled to his feet and stood swaying. Then he took off down the street, weaving as he ran.

Shaking his head, Roberto watched him go. He was no threat. He would be lucky to live through the night.

Who the hell would send this loser to trail Roberto? Not Mossimo. Not the FBI.

So who?

17

*B*randi sat at Nonno's tiny desk in his bedroom and stared in disbelief at the photo of a distinguished-looking Roberto on the nineteen-inch computer screen.

> Roberto Bartolini, CEO of Bartolini Importers, speaks at the stockholders' meeting to report profits are up seven percent. . . . The acquisition of Washington State's prizewinning Squirrel Run Winery is expected to add value to an already innovative company. . . .

She flipped away from the business news and to another page.

> Count Roberto Bartolini, respected Italian-American businessman and heir to the ancient Bartolini estates in Tuscany, escorts Nobel Prize winner Nina Johnsten to the ball in her honor. . . .

Looking proud and happy, he stood back and allowed Nina Johnsten to take her bows, and he showed so much pride she might have been a supermodel instead of a woman about ninety years old and half his height.

Brandi shoved her hair off her forehead and went looking for the dirt.

> Count Roberto Bartolini, known for his high-profile affairs as well as his discreet refusal to discuss his women, adds another notch to his belt with Chinese-American actress Sara Wong. . . .

"Wow." Brandi stared at the photo of Roberto with the tall, golden-skinned, dark-haired Asian woman. They were the most beautiful couple she'd ever seen . . . except for the picture of Roberto with English heiress Brownie Burbank. They were also the most beautiful couple she'd ever seen. And Roberto with German opera singer Leah Camberg. He had a way of making every woman more beautiful than she could be by herself.

Brandi looked down at her wrinkled suit. Except probably for her. Somehow she thought that, after today, she was the worse for wear.

But as much as she wanted to, she didn't dare linger over the photos of his various lovers. Nonno was making her bed, then coming back for her, and she needed to find out at what turn Roberto's life had gone wrong.

She found the stats in the most recent articles.

> Count Roberto Bartolini, respected international businessman, has been accused of stealing his lover's jewelry. . . . Mrs. Gloria Vandermere claims he took her eight-carat diamond after spending the night in her mansion. . . . "He's good, but not eight-carat-diamond's worth of good," she is quoted as saying. When asked, Count Bartolini shrugged and said, "I'm a businessman, not a gigolo," but the still-discreet Italian nobleman refused to address the matter of whether he slept with Mrs. Vandermere. Count Bartolini is a descendant of American Italians on his mother's side, and his grandfather Sergio Contini was allegedly the head of a

ring of jewel thieves in Chicago, but no whisper of dishonesty has ever before tainted his name. . . .

Brandi erased the browser's history, turned off the computer, and sat loose-fisted in the ergonomic desk chair. If anything, her investigation had confused her more.

Roberto had never before been accused of a crime. He was rich, he was respected, he was a businessman, he was a lover. . . . Had he hidden his hobby from the press until the moment when he took one chance too many? Was this an aberration in character? Or was Mrs. Vandermere nothing but a disgruntled former lover?

Nonno tapped on the door. "All right, little Brandi, your room is ready."

At once she was on her feet and moving toward Nonno. She couldn't think of this right now. She now knew what the world knew about Roberto, and she was more confused than ever.

Nonno led her down the hall and opened the door to Mariabella's bedroom. "Here you are. The heat is on, but it's a little chilly still." He waved at the maple dresser. "Mariabella's pajamas are in there. She left a robe in the closet. Don't be shy; use what you need. Mariabella is a sweet girl. She'd want to share."

"Thank you, Nonno."

"The bath's at the end of the hall. You can spend as much time in there as you want—Mariabella always did. Hours and hours." He cackled as if he were telling an old family joke.

Driven by impulse, Brandi kissed his cheek.

He patted hers. "I've enjoyed having a beautiful young woman visit, even if she is with my rascal of a grandson."

Downstairs, the door opened and closed.

"He's returned at last." Nonno headed back down the stairs. "I'll get your toothbrush."

"Thank you, Nonno." Brandi stepped inside the bedroom and felt as if she'd stepped back into the seventies. The carpet was lavender. The wallpaper and the bedspread were sprinkled with lavender flowers. A yellowing poster of Genesis featuring a young Phil Collins with hair that was a little longer but still thin was pinned on the ceiling. The heat register creaked and rumbled. Despite the chill, the room welcomed her with the generous warmth of a daughter of Nonno's, a mother of Roberto's. Brandi didn't hesitate to search the drawers for sleepwear. She found pajamas first and grimaced. Not surprisingly, Mariabella was shorter than Brandi—shorter by at least six inches. Of course, Nonno wouldn't think of that, and Brandi wouldn't hurt him by mentioning it. Instead she dug deeper to find a flannel nightgown. She pulled it over her head. It hit her at midshin.

She looked at herself in the mirror. Her arms stuck out. Her ankles stuck out. She looked like a gangly giraffe, and she felt sort of like Alice in Wonderland falling down the rabbit hole. All her perceptions were twisting, stretching, shrinking, and she didn't know which way was up.

She took out her PDA and opened it to her master list of qualities required in a man. She read them through. *Honest, dependable, goal-oriented, sober . . .*

Roberto was none of those.

It didn't matter. Or rather it shouldn't matter, because she didn't have Roberto. Shouldn't want to have him.

But . . . her stylus hovered over ERASE ALL.

Her cell phone rang. It was Kim, and with relief, Brandi put away her PDA and answered the phone.

"What are you up to?" Her half sister's voice blared in Brandi's ear. "Your mother keeps calling trying to pry information out of me. I'm pretending I know nothing—and you know how good I am at acting. Lucky for me, I can't figure out what you *are* doing. When I called earlier, that guy answered the phone."

"Did you think it was Alan?" Brandi buttoned the flowered nightgown.

"No, I did not think it was Alan. He didn't sound like a wimp who got spooked talking to a lesbian, so I knew it was the new guy.

The new guy! The one you were supposed to leave after one night. Then after the weekend. What's going on?" Kim's voice got louder and louder. "Are you *crazy?*"

"I'm not crazy." Brandi moved to the window and squinted up at the night sky, trying to see the moon or the stars . . . or God. She had a few words she'd like to say to God. "But someone out there has it in for me."

"Whiner."

"Bitch," Brandi answered absently. "My apartment was vandalized."

"What? When?" One thing Brandi could always depend on—Kim responded fiercely to a threat to her younger sister.

"Last night. Then I went to my first day of work and my Italian lover was the defendant in my first case."

"The guy on the phone?"

"The very one." Brandi took the pins out of her hair. "Then the judge remanded him into my custody. Now I'm at his grandfather's, where I'll spend the night, and we're arguing about where we're going to spend the rest of the nights until the court case is over."

"He wants to spend them all in your bed, huh?"

"Nooo." Brandi got her brush out of her purse.

"C'mon! He'd have to be blind and an idiot not to be interested!" Kim sounded absolutely incredulous.

"Alan was neither blind nor an idiot, and he wasn't interested." Brandi brushed hard enough to pull her hair out by the roots.

"No, he was a self-absorbed son of a bitch who wanted all the guys to envy him for the babe he was dating, but hated that you were taller than him, smarter than him, and infinitely more interesting."

"Hey, thanks!" Kim was a gruff woman not given to compliments, and Brandi treasured this one.

"He was an abuser," Kim said flatly.

"He never hit me!" Brandi tossed the brush aside.

"He didn't have to. He made you feel bad about yourself. Now you've got another one who got what he wanted from you and is ready to toss you aside."

Brandi thought about the way Roberto looked at her when he thought she wasn't looking. "Not . . . exactly."

"Aha!" Kim sounded triumphant. "I knew it. I knew you were kidding me. The guy who answered the phone has the voice of a lover."

Amused, Brandi asked, "What, my dear lesbian sister, do you know about the voice of a man who is a lover?"

"You're not the only one who had an adventure this weekend." Beneath Kim's prim tone, Brandi heard suppressed excitement.

"Wait a minute. Wait. Wait. Wait." Brandi wanted to get this straight. "Are you saying you've found someone?"

"It's not impossible!"

"It is when someone's as picky as you are," Brandi retorted.

Kim laughed, a deep, satisfied laugh. "Yeah, well, she's special."

"What's her name?"

"We were talking about you."

"What's her name?"

"So this guy is interested in you?"

"I'll tell you when you tell me her name." Brandi grinned into the resulting silence. Kim could be stubborn. But not as stubborn as Brandi.

"Her name is Sarah."

"The vice principal you thought hated you?"

"I answered your question; now you answer mine." But Kim was laughing.

She sounded so happy, Brandi's heart warmed. Heck, if not for Kim, the events of the past fourteen years would have prostrated Brandi, but Kim faced the prejudices against lesbians and their father's scathing complaints to become a successful coach, and with an example like that before her, Brandi had to achieve her goals. She owed Kim a lot. "What was the question?"

"You going to be okay?" Kim asked gruffly.

"Sure. What else can happen?"

"Well . . ."

At that single word, Brandi's antennae quivered with suspicion. "What? Kim, what?"

"I just want you to know . . . I might have said too much to your mother."

"What?" *Oh, no.* "What do you mean, too much?"

"She was questioning me. She confused me. I didn't know what to say, so she started guessing stuff and— Hey, I gotta go. The pool tournament is tonight and it's my turn."

"Don't you dare hang up on me! Kim! Don't you dare!" But the connection was dead. "Shit!" Now she had to call Tiffany. "Shit." But this time she was considerably less heated.

She should have called sooner. She knew it. There was no use blaming Kim because she'd tried to cover for Brandi and failed. It was just that this had gotten so complicated, much more than a simple jilting, and Tiffany would be so distressed—distressed because Brandi had been hurt, and more distressed that Brandi hadn't run to her mother for comfort.

But it had been years since Brandi had considered Tiffany capable of giving her anything, especially comfort.

Brandi's attitude didn't help their relationship, but what was she supposed to do? She'd tried to fake it, and all that had gotten her was hurt looks.

Taking a breath, she dialed her mother's home number. It rang and rang; then Tiffany's answering machine picked up. "I'm sorry I'm not home to receive your call. . . ." Brandi dialed her mother's cell. It rang and rang; then the voice mail picked up. "I'm sorry I'm not on the cell phone right now. . . ."

Where was she? At the movies? Somewhere with bad cell service?

Brandi tried Kim again, but of course she didn't pick up.

Nonno knocked.

Brandi put her phone in her purse. She slipped on the maroon velvet robe with the hem that exposed the ruffled hem of the nightgown. Walking to the door, she opened it two inches and peeked out.

It wasn't Nonno who inexorably pushed the door open; it was Roberto. He pushed her backward until he could look her over, and his smile blossomed.

Damn him. He didn't look amused. He looked . . . he looked the way he had when she'd finally put on the lacy nightgown and paraded enticingly before him. His black hair was tousled as if he'd just removed a cap. Tousled, with a lock that hung over his forehead that enticed her to push it back. His brown eyes held a kindling flame, and his lips . . . his lips were so very talented.

Not the best moment to think of that.

She fell back a step.

He followed.

She touched the buttons at her throat to make sure they were fastened. They were. She swallowed and asked, "Toothbrush?"

"Here." He pulled the plastic package out of his shirt pocket and handed it over. "I risked life and limb getting it for you. I deserve a reward."

"I risked life and limb going to lunch with you, so I'd say we're even." She cockily flipped the toothbrush into the air.

"So we both deserve a reward."

"None of that!" She waltzed backward, but somehow it seemed he was as good a dancer as she was, for she found herself wrapped in his arms. Driven by an inner rhythm, he moved her backward until, with a shock of pleasure, she felt his heated body before her and the cool wall at her back.

Burying his head in her hair, he inhaled as if the scent of her intoxicated him.

"Your grandfather would not like this." But *she* did. Oh, she did.

"I'm not doing anything except holding you." Roberto's voice caressed her.

"And sniffing me." Her body curved, settling into his as if it recognized its home.

He chuckled, a warm breath against her forehead. "I love the way you smell. Nonno would understand that."

Closing her eyes, she inhaled in her turn, but carefully, so Roberto wouldn't notice. He smelled like fresh air and rich passion, but something was missing . . . the scent of her on his skin.

"Besides, you like the way I smell, too."

Damn. He'd caught her. "Nonno warned me against men like you."

"Did he?" He touched her cheek with his lips. "He should know. He *is* a man like me. Besides, who do you think sent me up with the toothbrush?"

Lifting her head, she frowned into his face. "Why would he do that?"

"He likes you. He wants me to settle down."

"Settle down?" Her breath caught. "Like marriage?"

"It's his fondest wish to hold his great-grandchild before he dies."

"You're damned calm about this!" In fact, Roberto was still holding her so that every inch of their bodies touched.

My God. Marriage. Who did Nonno think she was? For that matter, who did Roberto think she was?

"Nonno knows we respect him too much to go too far in his house." As he spoke, Roberto slipped his knee between hers and pressed until she rode it in a slow rhythm.

She hated the thrill that slid up her spine. "A good matchmaker knows the first and most important element of bringing people together is a common background and common values."

"Like you had with Alan?"

"What a despicable thing to say." She dug her fingernails into his shoulders. "I told you that in confidence, not so you could fling my failure into my face!"

"It's not a failure." Roberto smiled, a slow, warm lift of his lips. "If you loved him, then it would be a failure."

He made her madder than Alan ever had. Ever could. "But I don't love you, either, and I'm not marrying a jewel thief."

"I haven't asked you." And Roberto kissed her.

Her hurt—if it was hurt—melted under the talented application of his lips and his passion, and the slow, relentless rise of her own desire.

How had this happened? At least in the matter of their affair, they'd behaved sensibly all day. He hadn't pressed her. She hadn't said too much. She'd been able to fool herself into believing they could work out their situation without squabbling. Now she knew the truth. Whether acknowledged or not, the passion between them irrevocably simmered and, with the slightest touch, came to a boil. She balanced on the edge of orgasm. . . . If he would only stop the motion of his knee, she could hold herself back. . . .

He didn't, and she couldn't.

He muffled her cries of fulfillment in his shirt against his chest, and held her when she had finished and melted against the wall. When her knees could support her weight, he let her go. Leaning down, he picked something up off the floor. Taking her hand, he placed it in her palm and closed her fingers around it. His velvet voice whispered across her cheek. "Good night, *cara.*"

She stared after him in a daze as he walked out the door. Looking down at her hand, she saw her toothbrush . . . with the imprint of each of her fingers in the plastic packaging.

18

As Brandi led him down the corridor to her apartment, Roberto stalked after her and wondered if she could feel his heat at her back.

"The place is a mess." She jingled her keys as she walked. "I moved in last week."

She displayed a charming skittishness, pretending that her explosive climax of last night had never happened.

And how dared she? Why wasn't she looking at him with adoration? Why didn't she demand the chance to wrap her long legs around his hips and ride him until they both burned to cinders?

"What is the number of your apartment?" *Three eleven, three twelve . . .*

"Three nineteen. Why?"

Because I'm keeping track of the numbers on the doors as we pass. Once we're inside, I'll press you against the wall and kiss you until you again fall apart in my hand. Then I'll take you to the floor and make passionate love to you until at last I am satisfied.

She must have read his mind, for her voice trembled slightly. "While I was gone this weekend, these guys came and—"

"Ah. Yes. *This* weekend."

"What?" She glanced behind her and jumped to see him shadowing close on her heels.

"Now we are going to discuss this weekend." *Three fifteen, three sixteen . . . Only three more doors . . .*

"N-no. No, we're not. Remember? Yesterday we agreed that if our relationship as lawyer and client was to work, we'd have to, um"—she turned and walked backward as if that somehow would stop him from leaping on her unaware—"concentrate on being professionals."

"I don't remember agreeing to that." But he did remember her riding his leg last night, and the soft cries she made as she came.

Memories like that had kept him awake far into the night . . . and gave him a hard-on big enough to warrant a line at the Navy Pier amusement park. He'd been confident he could taunt and tease her until she clawed his back in desire, and it was a tough realization that, where she was concerned, he had no restraint. He wanted her as desperately as he intended her to want him.

She'd turned the tables—and she hadn't even tried.

She stopped and glared at him. "Well, you did."

"Did what?"

"You agreed that we should act like professionals."

He was in no mood to be reasonable. "Are you trying to challenge me?"

"I'm *trying* to behave like a rational human being."

"Because I am definitely rising to the challenge."

He was pleased to see he'd left her speechless. With his hand in the small of her back, he turned her and propelled her toward her apartment.

"I am so tired of you guys pushing me around!" She hurried to get out of his grasp.

You guys? Jealousy caught at his throat. He caught up with a single step. "What *guys* are those?"

"You and your grandfather."

"Ah." His relief was huge, out of proportion, and another blow to the fragile structure of his self-control. Taking her keys from her fingers, he inserted them in the lock.

On the other side of the door, someone jerked it open.

Brandi screamed and leaped backward, slamming into his chest, knocking the air out of him.

A tall blond woman stood in the doorway. A tall, blond, toned woman who looked like a slightly—very slightly—older version of Brandi.

He recognized her. *Tiffany.*

"Mother!" Brandi quivered as her rush of tension dissolved.

"Darling, are you all right?" Tiffany held out her arms.

Brandi walked right into them and laid her head on her shoulder.

Roberto's drive to sexual satisfaction died an instant death. This was *not* the time.

"Why didn't you call me?" Tiffany walked backward, holding Brandi in her embrace. She gestured for Roberto to follow.

Roberto shut the door behind him, fascinated to see Brandi's display of weakness and her collapse into her mother's arms.

"I knew something was wrong—a mother's intuition, I guess—and don't yell at her, but I nagged Kim until she told me what happened." Tiffany rubbed Brandi's back in a slow, comforting circle. "Alan's a fool, darling, and you deserve better!"

Brandi lifted her head. Her eyes were slightly teary and she dabbed at her nose with the back of her hand. "I know. I'm not crying about him; it's just been a rough week."

"Well, don't you worry about anything anymore." Tiffany's voice was low and vibrant, with a dollop of a Southern accent and pure sex appeal. "I'm here to take care of you."

"Oh. Yeah." As if Tiffany had said the magic words, Brandi straightened her shoulders and stepped away from her mother. "Sure."

Despite Roberto's callous dismissal, he knew Alan's rebuff had hurt Brandi. She'd been told she wasn't good enough, and while Roberto took pride in his part in restoring her self-esteem, nothing could take the place of a mother's succor. Obviously Brandi loved her mother; why didn't she take what Tiffany offered?

And Brandi's rebuff clearly hurt Tiffany. She dropped her gaze and put her fingers to her trembling lips. For one unguarded second, she was the picture of dejection.

Then she recovered. Looking up, she smiled at him and extended her hand. "I'm Brandi's mother, Tiffany Michaels."

Taking it in both of his, he cherished it, offering his comfort and appreciation. Bending, he kissed her fingers. "I'm delighted to meet you, Mrs. Michaels."

"Tiffany, please." The color came back into her cheeks as she warmed herself in his masculine admiration.

"You must call me Roberto."

"Mother, this is Roberto Bartolini. He's my client at McGrath and Lindoberth." Brandi gave them a disgusted glance, then went into the kitchen visible over the half wall.

"I'm delighted to meet you, too, Mr. Bartolini." Tiffany briefly tightened her grip, a gesture of thanks.

Up close, he could see the faint lines around her eyes and mouth, and the skin on her hands was thin and marked by slight spots. She had to be in her mid-forties, yet she was a beautiful, vibrant female who understood the art of flirtation as few American women did. And she liked him. He would bet she liked his entire gender . . . except Alan.

He observed Brandi as she moved around the kitchen. Grabbing a Kleenex, she blew her nose, then stood indecisively. With a sudden display of determination, she opened the trash, flung the Kleenex in, and slammed the lid back down. Very violent for such a soft, inoffensive bit of paper.

He glanced at Tiffany. She watched Brandi, too, two lines between her finely tweezed brows, and the lines looked settled there, as if she worried more than seemed reasonable about such a sensible, studious daughter.

"Roberto, are you taking care of my little girl?" Tiffany asked.

"No, Mother, he's my client at McGrath and Lindoberth," Brandi called.

"I'm taking very good care of your little girl." He ignored the irritated flash of Brandi's sapphire-blue eyes. "And she's taking care of me."

Tiffany's gaze cooled. She took her hand back and stepped away. "That must be true, since you spent the night with Brandi." She was a mother demanding the explanation she considered her due.

"Tiffany!" Obviously appalled, Brandi came to the door. "What do you think you're doing?"

"Sh." Roberto went to her and put his finger on her lips. "This is your mother. She has the right to know where you spend your nights and with whom." *And,* his gaze warned her, *we do have something to hide.* "Tiffany, we spent the night at my grandfather's."

"At your grandfather's? Really? That's all right, then." Tiffany brightened. "Sometimes women do stupid things after a bad breakup, like get involved again right away, and I would hate to think you're Brandi's stupid thing."

If Tiffany had glanced at Brandi right then, she would have seen the truth. Brandi's pale cheeks and stricken eyes betrayed her, and he stepped between the two women. "I don't think Brandi could ever be stupid. Your daughter is a very skilled lawyer," he said, giving Brandi a moment to collect herself.

"I know. Isn't she wonderful?" Tiffany glowed with pride. "Do you know she said her first word at six months? *Cat.* She didn't say it right, of course, just *cka,* but she knew what it meant. My mother actually worried about her. Said that bright girls didn't stand a chance in this world, but Brandi proved her wrong. Proved everyone wrong!"

Brandi interrupted the intriguing glimpse into her past. "Let's sit down." She stepped around him and gestured him toward the chair.

Roberto seated himself, but he wasn't about to let the conversation drop. "Brandi has had a lot to prove to a lot of people, then?"

"Oh, yes." Tiffany tucked her arm through Brandi's. "As soon as she could walk she could dance, so she was wonderful at gymnastics and ballet. My husband only saw that; he never noticed that she got straight As in school, so when she graduated magna cum laude with a prelaw degree, he had to sit up and take notice!"

"Come on, Mother, let's sit on my new sofa. I think the color works well in here, don't you?"

Distracted, Tiffany sank down beside her daughter. "It does, but, darling, do you realize one cushion is slashed?"

Brandi had slept with him, but she didn't want him to really know her. She didn't want him to hear about her past. Because he was a jewel thief? Or because she wore masks she never discarded and kept secrets she wanted no one to know?

"Yes, I've taken care of the problem with the cushion." Brandi bit her lip as if she were accountable for something, although Roberto couldn't imagine what. "How did you get here, Mother?"

"I took a cab."

"From Nashville?" Brandi's sarcasm startled him.

"From the airport! The cabdriver was so pleasant, he pointed out the sights of Chicago, and he only charged me half the price on the meter. Wasn't that sweet?"

Roberto didn't doubt for a minute that Tiffany could charm a surly cabbie into digging into his own pocket to pay her fee.

"But . . . what about your job at the real estate office?"

"I quit my job."

"Mother . . ." Brandi sounded weary, as if she'd heard this too many times before.

"That disgusting man tried to sleep with me." Tiffany's heart-shaped mouth trembled. "I was being nice to his clients, and he seemed to think that meant I wanted to get in his pants."

"All right, Mother. All right." Brandi awkwardly patted her mother's arm. "I know it happens. Look at you. How could it not?"

"I don't ask for it!"

"I never said you did!"

"Your father said—"

"Oh, my father is a big fat jerk."

The exchange told Roberto far more about the family dynamics than a mere explanation could. Rising, he asked, "I'd like a drink of water. Would anybody like something?" When Brandi would have also stood, he said, "Let me do it. You want to catch up with your mother's news."

As he walked into her tiny kitchen, Brandi braced herself. She could almost have predicted what her mother would say and the tone of her voice.

"Darling, about Alan . . ." Her mother, who was never at a loss, seemed unsure what condolence to offer.

And obscurely, that made Brandi feel guilty. "I'm sorry; I should have called you when it happened, but—"

"You didn't want to talk about it. I understand."

Did she? When Tiffany had been dumped by Brandi's father, she'd talked about it endlessly with her friends, with her mother, with any stranger who would listen. Brandi had hated having everyone know their business, having everyone pity them, then watching their friends drift away because they didn't want to hear about it and know that at any time it could happen to them.

But that didn't excuse Brandi's neglect. She would have felt better if Tiffany were yelling.

Roberto dropped a glass on the floor and it shattered with a sharp, sudden sound.

Brandi jumped.

"Sorry!" he called. "Don't worry. I can find the broom."

"*That* is one gorgeous man," Tiffany murmured as he rummaged around in the closet. "What a wonderful accent. He's Italian?"

Brandi needed to nip this blossoming mutual admiration in the bud. "Yes, and he's a jewel thief."

"How romantic!"

Of course, Tiffany would think that. "No, Mother, it's not romantic. He's a criminal, and there's a chance—a very good chance—he'll go to prison for the next twenty years."

"He doesn't look like any criminal I've ever seen. He's rich. That suit is Armani."

They heard the tinkling sound as he swept up the glass and tossed it in the trash.

"Even better, he knows his way around the kitchen," Tiffany added.

Something about Tiffany brought out the worst in Brandi. She always seemed to need her mother's shallow character confirmed, and she couldn't resist saying, "He's a count, too."

"Yummy!" Tiffany drawled the word with a Southern accent thick as caramel sauce.

"He's yummy because he's got a title?"

"No, he's yummy because he's sexy and rich and handsome. The title is just like whipped cream on chocolate zinfandel mousse. What a husband he would be!"

"Husband!" Brandi turned on her mother. "Why did you say that?"

Tiffany widened her lovely blue eyes. "That's the way I think, darling."

"So did his grandfather!" What was it with these people? Nonno and Tiffany didn't even know each other. Years separated them. They lived miles apart. Yet they had the same one-track minds! "I don't want a husband. I tried that, and you know how well it worked out."

"Roberto definitely doesn't match any of the requirements on your list," Tiffany agreed.

Brandi flinched. Alan had met all her requirements. . . . Was Tiffany being sarcastic? No, impossible. Sarcasm required a subtlety Tiffany didn't possess.

Besides, Tiffany wasn't looking at her. She was looking at Roberto. "There is nothing the least sensible about him, hm?"

Brandi made the mistake of glancing in the kitchen as he stretched up to get down some paper napkins, and her mouth dried. Husband? She didn't want to think about him like that. As if he were a man who was available and attainable. Because she'd already sampled him, she knew that he wanted her, and if she started thinking about forever she would make such a fool of herself—and there'd been far too much of that lately. "Conjugal prison visits are *so* much fun."

"Darling, you know he won't go to jail," Tiffany said with inborn wisdom. "Wealthy people never do."

Brandi wished she could come up with a pithy retort, but she didn't know the details of his case. Her first week at work, and she'd logged about an hour at the office working on the case. This morning she'd called Glenn's office, but Mrs. Pelikan had picked up the phone.

She'd sounded brisk and instructive. *On Mr. McGrath's instruction, we've restructured the team. You now report directly to me, and your job, Miss Michaels, is to keep tabs on Mr. Bartolini. Don't let him out of your sight.*

Do you believe he intends to leave the country?

Don't let him out of your sight, Mrs. Pelikan had repeated. She didn't have to explain herself to Brandi, and she didn't.

Brandi glanced at Roberto. *Don't let him out of your sight.* Too bad the instructions made her happy. "Mother, a husband at risk for a criminal record is definitely not on my list."

Tiffany glanced at Roberto as he filled up the glasses. "*Was* he your stupid thing?"

Her mother had an instinct about men and women that couldn't be denied.

"He's been remanded into my custody." A serviceable half-truth. "That's why I stayed at his grandfather's last night, and we've been arguing about where we're going to spend tonight. I want to stay here." Then realization dawned. They couldn't stay here. There was a bed and a couch with a slashed cushion, and she'd planned to give Roberto the bed because he wouldn't fit on the short couch—well, neither would she, but she figured she'd just put up with the discomfort to have her own way.

Now that Tiffany had arrived, her plan was not viable.

"So." With a charming smile, Roberto handed the ladies their glasses. "We go to my hotel."

"I'll sleep here," Tiffany said, "but can I trust you two alone?"

"Mother, you can't stay in the apartment!" Brandi still smelled the soap the landlord had used to clean the carpet, and the paint that covered the graffiti was a slightly different shade. She had never loved this place; it had been a temporary and convenient location to rest her head until she married Alan.

Now everything about it gave her the willies. No way would she leave her mother in an apartment that had been vandalized. If anything happened to Tiffany, she would never forgive herself. And she would be . . . so isolated.

My God. She shifted uncomfortably. She imagined a tragic end for her mother and all she could think about was herself. She was going to hell for sure.

Yet she desperately wanted to avoid Roberto's luxurious, memory-laden suite.

"Of course Tiffany will go with us to the hotel," Roberto said.

"That's a horrible idea!" Brandi said. Having her mother stay there in the suite where she and Roberto had made love? On every piece of furniture, on the floor, against the wall, in each bathroom? That was just . . . icky.

"There's plenty of space, two bedrooms and two baths—"

"Two bedrooms?" Brandi didn't want to contradict him—Tiffany didn't need to know she'd been in his suite—but in his fifty-eighth-story suite, there had been only one huge bedroom.

"Two bedrooms," Roberto confirmed. "I already called the hotel and told them I needed to move to a more family-appropriate suite. Newby is packing for me now. We're on the fourth floor, Brandi, in deference to your fear of heights."

"I don't have a fear of heights." How had he known? "They just make me a little . . . uncomfortable."

"Me, too. Thank you, Roberto, for letting us stay with you." Tiffany touched his arm. "That's so sweet."

"It's not sweet," Brandi said. "It's a bad idea."

"Do you have a better one?" Roberto asked.

She didn't. Of course she didn't.

So the other two ignored her.

"I just unpacked and I haven't spread out at all," Tiffany said. "Brandi, do you want me to pack for you?"

They were conspiring against her. "I can do it," Brandi snapped.

"Make sure you bring all your"—he waved his hand in circles over his body—"fancy dresses. I have many invitations. Many important people want to meet the notorious Italian jewel thief, and it would honor me to have you on my arm."

"The only"—Brandi imitated his gesture—"fancy dress I have is old and black, so I imagine we're not going to accept your invitations."

"No!" Tiffany bounced in her seat. "We wear the same size, and I brought dresses with me!"

Incredulous, Brandi turned on her mother. "Dresses? You brought dresses?"

"Charles invited me to a party while I'm here." Tiffany watched her own hands as she smoothed them across her legs. "I can't go in some crummy old gown."

"That's nice of Uncle Charles, but you only need one dress!"

"Darling, when I left Nashville I didn't know which dress I'd want!"

Brandi worried that her mother had begun to make sense to her. She worried that her life had veered out of control and she would never get it back. And as Tiffany and Roberto rose together and headed toward her bedroom, chatting about their social schedule, Brandi worried that her lover and her mother had far too much in common.

After all, if they combined their forces, there was no telling what magnificent folly Brandi might find herself driven to commit.

But no matter what else happened, she was not going to go to any dinners or parties with Roberto. He knew too many shady men. He had too many shady connections.

She was going to put her foot down, and tell Roberto they were staying safely hidden in the hotel suite until she delivered him to trial.

19

When Tiffany opened the bedroom door and Brandi stepped out, Roberto caught his breath in instant and painful masculine awareness.

In makeup done by a professional and a red dress that shouted *Take me,* Brandi was the epitome of allure.

But in cosmetics applied by the loving hands of her mother and clad in a blue velvet gown cut in the medieval style, she looked sexy, classy, vulnerable, and as if she needed only his embrace to be complete—although perhaps his libidinous imagination had produced that last bit.

He could no more resist taking her hand between his and kissing it than he could resist the sweep of events that carried him along. "*Cara,* you are the most beautiful thing I've ever seen."

"Yeah, thanks." Brandi's blue eyes glittered with the same cold frost as the sapphires in her ears. Snatching her hand away, she stalked away from him. She wore gold wedge heels that made her legs look a mile long from thigh to toe, and a gold belt that sat low on her waist and clanged softly while she challenged him with the sway of her hips. "Let's get this show on the road."

He lifted his eyebrows at Tiffany, who shrugged and mouthed, *She's sulking.*

Well. He supposed Brandi had the right—for a while. She'd lost the battle to stay in tonight. If he could, he would have indulged her, but he had no choice. His course had been set before he met her. He was seeking the truth about his past, and this operation was his way to find it.

She stood with the door of the coat closet open, staring into its depths with a frown. "Where's my coat?"

Ah. The tricky part.

With a nod at him, Tiffany picked the thickly quilted winter-white velvet coat off the chair and hurried after her. "Here, darling, wear this."

"What is it?" Brandi frowned as she examined the warmest Gucci he'd been able to find.

"It's mine," Tiffany said. "I knew it was cold up here, so I bought it before I caught the plane."

Brandi's frown grew thunderous. "But you can't afford this!"

"It's all right, darling," Tiffany said airily. "I got it on clearance from bluefly.com."

"Mother, you can't afford this coat whether it's on clearance or not. And it's white! How impractical can you be?"

Tiffany glanced at him as if apologizing for her daughter's bad manners. "But it's pretty, isn't it?"

"You can't afford this dress, or the other dresses, and you can't declare bankruptcy again." Brandi was truly distressed. "You have to cut up those credit cards!"

When had the roles of mother and daughter been reversed? Roberto thought their relationship had been askew for a very long time.

But in this instance, he'd bought the coat—he was tired of seeing Brandi shiver in the black London Fog—and he wouldn't allow Tiffany to suffer for his actions. Before Brandi could scold anymore, he said, "Brandi, thank your mother for her generosity in allowing you to borrow such a gorgeous garment."

Brandi turned on him in a heavy swish of skirts and a wave of indignation. But when she caught sight of his grim reproof, she stopped. She thought. Her innate good manners took over. "Thank you, Tiffany." She stroked the velvet. "It's fabulous, and I'll take good care of it."

"I know you will, darling. It gives me such pleasure to know you're going out. It's been far too long since you've had a good time." Tiffany beamed.

She was a kind and lovely woman, and why she wasn't decorating the arm of a rich man, Roberto didn't understand.

As Roberto helped Brandi into the coat, Brandi asked, "Mother, what are you going to do tonight?"

"Nothing. Watch a little TV. Read a little. I started a good book on the plane." Tiffany yawned and patted her mouth. "I'm a little tired from traveling. Maybe I'll just go to bed. How late will you be?"

"Don't wait up." Roberto bundled up in his own coat and scarf. "We've got three parties tonight."

"Three." Brandi pulled on her gloves and kissed her mother on the cheek. "I can't wait."

He flicked his finger against her cheek. "Sarcastic little witch."

They went out the door arguing.

Tiffany went to the window and observed as Roberto handed Brandi into the limo. She waited until they drove away, and she waited a little longer.

Then she returned to the bathroom, to the makeup spread out on the counters and the stylish emerald-green dress hanging behind the door.

By the time the car arrived to pick her up, she looked almost as good as her daughter. In fact—she inspected herself and the excited glow that lit her from within—maybe better, because she was happy, as she hadn't been for a long, long time.

⌒

The lights of Chicago cast alternating stripes of color and shadow in the back of the limo, but whatever the illumination, Brandi was beautiful—and offended. She looked away from Roberto and out the window, her proud chin tilted up, her neck a tempting length.

But she couldn't ignore him all night. He wouldn't allow it. Unerringly, he found her gloved hand. "Allow me to tell you what we will do tonight."

She swiveled to face him, her blond beauty cool and indifferent. "Since I have no choice, I really don't care."

"Indulge me." Peeling off her glove, he kissed her fingers. "First we'll go to dinner at Howard Patterson's. He's well-known for bringing in the finest chefs from around the world, and tonight he promises French provincial cuisine."

"Good idea. Feed me first. That'll improve my temperament."

"So true, although I think champagne also improves your temperament. Anyone's temperament, for that matter." He pressed his lips to her open palm.

She inclined her head. "How gracious of you."

She had the sharp bite of an asp and the brilliant wit of a dilettante, and the combination made him dodge and laugh, for he knew that she hid another guise behind the mask of sophistication. She was a passionate hedonist and a tender woman who had become a lawyer to set the world to rights.

God knew she was working hard enough to try to fix him. And while there had been a lot of women in Roberto's life, none of them had ever tried to save his sinful soul.

"After we eat and improve our temperaments, we're going to a party given by Mossimo." Roberto caressed the pad beneath her thumb.

"BYOG?" She pretended to be indifferent, but her heartbeat increased with each stroke.

"BYOG?" Roberto frowned. Seldom did his English fail him. "What is that?"

"Bring your own gun."

"Ah." He chuckled. "Yes, I'm sure there'll be enough firepower to start a small war. However, I will be unarmed."

Her hand convulsed in his. "I don't know that that comforts me."

"Trust me. I'll protect you."

"I know *that.* I was more worried that you'd do something stupid."

She was insulting, yet beneath her disparagement lurked an unthinking confidence that he would secure her safety, and that made him puff up like a strutting peacock. "I suppose it is forbidden to kiss your lips and ruin your glorious lipstick?"

"I'm wearing the lipstick that will remain on earth when all the glaciers have melted."

He leaned toward her.

And ran into her free hand. "However, there is another reason why kissing me is forbidden." She spaced her words for maximum impact. "I don't want you to."

"Champagne," he murmured, knowing how very much it would annoy her. "Much champagne."

She lifted her glossy, perfect lips in a delicate snarl. "Tell me the rest of the plan—we're going to Mossimo's?"

"Ah. Yes. I have to make an appearance, but I promise it won't be for long."

"I can't wait."

If Mossimo were smart, he'd stop worrying about Roberto and start worrying about Brandi. Roberto suspected she could take him down with a few well-chosen words. "I've saved the best news for last."

"I'll bet." Sarcasm, but she didn't take her hand out of his.

"Every year, Mrs. John C. Tobias gives a benefit ball for the symphony and a contingent of musicians plays for the dancing. It's a night made for grace and beauty. It's a night made for you, my Brandi, and I can't wait to take you in my arms to lead you onto the dance floor."

If his graceful sentiment impressed her, she hid it behind an impassive frost.

"Then, after we've waltzed together, you'll get your way."

"Get my way?"

"We'll return to the suite and stay there," he said in spurious innocence.

She stared at him in outrage—an outrage that slowly dissolved into mirth. Leaning back against the leather seat, she laughed loud and long.

He watched her, loving that she could laugh at herself without restraint.

"And tomorrow we'll do things your way again?" she asked.

"That's fair. At night you get your way. In the day, I get mine."

"You really are a case, Roberto."

"A case of what?" he asked cautiously.

"I'll let you know when I figure it out." She took her hand away from him. "We're here."

The limo inched up to the portico of the New England–style home, and the doorman ushered them inside. They greeted Howard and Joni Patterson, who insisted that Roberto appraise Howard's newest acquisition, a two-carat diamond tie clip created in the 1920s.

Roberto told them the jewel was worth only thirty-six thousand, but the setting put the value much higher. Howard was ecstatic, and in a little more than two hours Roberto and Brandi ate, charmed half of Chicago society, and excused themselves to go to the rival party.

"I have to go," Roberto told Joni Patterson. "To ignore a chance to dance with Brandi would be a crime against nature."

"Damn that Tobias woman!" Joni said. "Why she has to have her party on the same night I have mine, I never will know, but I certainly understand about the dancing. The two of you are made to dance together!"

As they descended the stairs toward the portico, Roberto pointed out, "We're becoming quite the well-known couple."

"Wait until your trial," Brandi advised, "when we tell everyone I followed you around under court order."

"I wonder how many people will believe that?"

"All of them," she said crisply. "I'll make sure of it."

The dinner hadn't softened her ire quite as much as he'd hoped.

"I see you didn't tell Howard that we were leaving their lovely dinner to first go visit the Fosseras," she said.

"Sometimes I show a regrettable tendency toward lying."

"I suspected that."

"But not to you, my Brandi." Leaning close, he whispered in her ear, "Never to you."

He was delighted to note she hesitated before roundly saying, "And I've got a bridge I want to sell you."

Against all logic, she wanted to believe him.

When they pulled up to the Knights of Columbus hall, Brandi's mouth dropped. "Come on! The Fosseras can't afford a nice place for their parties?"

"They can." Roberto watched as Newby carefully parked the limo in a way that guaranteed them a quick getaway . . . if they should need one. "But their nice places are for their wives."

"You mean it's a guy party?"

"Not at all. But I don't believe we'll meet any wives here tonight."

"They're partying with prostitutes? And we're going in?"

"Don't be ridiculous. I wouldn't expose you to prostitutes." He helped her out of the car. "They're with their mistresses."

20

The big room had been professionally decorated and the food professionally catered. The band that played could have performed in the best nightclub in the city. But the Fosseras had still held their party at a Knights of Columbus hall rife with cigar smoke and the faint scent of gym clothes.

Roberto counted the number of Fosseras over by the bar—twenty-two—and paid particular attention to the number of exits, including the windows. He noted the clump of females standing together near the dance floor, laughing shrilly and drinking everything from tequila shots to frozen drinks decorated with colorful little umbrellas.

"Oh. My." Brandi sounded amazed and impressed. "I didn't know about the contest." She handed her coat to the check girl.

"What contest?" Roberto smiled at the girl with special warmth, hoping that if he and Brandi had to make a hasty exit she'd remember which garments were theirs.

"The one where the woman dressed most like a slut wins. Yipes! Are any of these girls over twenty?"

Mossimo walked toward them, smiling, hand outstretched.

Brandi lowered her voice. "I assume the loser of the contest has to sleep with *him.*"

"It's whispered on the streets that his wife sends him into the arms of his mistress with a sigh of relief," Roberto said quietly.

"I'll bet." When Mossimo reached them, she dimpled and said, "Hello, Mr. Fossera, how good to meet you again."

"Hey! It's the lawyer," Mossimo said. "Whiskey, right?"

"What?" she asked in confusion.

"Your name's Whiskey, right?"

"My name is Southern Comfort," she corrected him smoothly.

She was smart-mouthing Mossimo Fossera, a man with no sense of humor and a damned touchy dignity. Roberto wanted to spank her.

Instead he chuckled indulgently. "Southern Comfort is also what she's been drinking." He patted her butt. "Run along and talk to the other girls, honey, and when I'm done here I promise to take you home and give you what you deserve."

"I'm so much more at ease with you, *darling*." Brandi gazed at him with wide-eyed and bogus adulation.

"As you wish." Roberto caught her fingers in his and kissed them. "She adores me and wants to be at my side always," he said—in Italian.

"I can see that." Mossimo watched her with a critical gaze and he, too, spoke in Italian. "But women need to seek their own kind, heh?"

"Well!" Brandi flounced with pretended indignation. "If you're going to be rude and speak Italian all night, I'm going to get a drink."

"Remember the special qualities of champagne," Roberto said.

Giving him a look that promised retribution, she headed off toward the knot of scantily clad women.

"She's quite the little firebrand," Mossimo said. "If you ever want someone to tame her—"

"I like wildcats."

"Your grandfather was the same way, but it's not good for a man to be under a woman's thumb."

"Ah, but you don't know what Brandi can do with her thumb." Roberto grinned. "Thank you for the invitation to visit you tonight, Mossimo. I especially appreciate the firm suggestion that I show up."

"Hey, I like to see my friends when I like to see my friends." Mossimo threw his arm over Roberto's shoulders and led him toward the men by the bar. "So . . . have you thought about the proposition I made you?"

"To steal the Romanov Blaze?"

"Sh!" Mossimo glanced at the caterers. "Don't be careless."

"Speak into the microphone, heh?" Roberto touched the flower in his lapel.

"Yeah. Speak into the microphone." Mossimo laughed weakly.

The Fossera men stood with drinks in their hands, watching Mossimo, watching Roberto, quiet, menacing . . . waiting.

"Ricky, man, good to see you again." Roberto shook hands with him. "Danny. Greg." His gaze swept the group. "But where's Fico?"

"He's around somewhere," Ricky said.

"Gone out for a smoke," Greg said.

"I hope I get to see him." How interesting that he had chosen to absent himself now. "But these guys I don't know." Roberto indicated the younger men, twenty to twenty-five, standing against the wall.

They were sullen; one even turned his back as they walked up.

"They're boys. They're not important." With a gesture, Mossimo ordered them to leave. "Go dance with your girlfriends."

Roberto watched as they drifted away, muttering at being dismissed so lightly. No wonder Mossimo was losing his grip on his family and the business. Trouble brewed among the testosterone-driven youths.

Brandi had stepped into the girlfriends' conversation and now chatted animatedly, but he saw the glazed amazement in her eyes as the young men slouched over and, without a word, took the girls by the hands and led them onto the dance floor.

The older women still stood with Brandi; they were Mossimo's mistress, Greg's mistress, Ricky's mistress, Fico's mistress. Brandi couldn't have anything in common with them, and he feared that if he left her alone for long she'd try to rally the women to a revolt— and that would make the shit hit the fan.

They needed to get out of here, so he got right to the heart of the matter. "Mossimo, you said it yourself. To steal the Romanov Blaze from the museum is a huge challenge."

The men moved into a circle around him, protecting him from eavesdroppers—for all the good it would do them.

Speak into the microphone.

"Are you frightened?" Greg taunted.

"Of course. Only a stupid man faces death without fear." But Roberto didn't show fear now. He showed nothing but a polite interest in the proposition.

"Maybe you can't do it," Mossimo said.

Roberto dismissed that with a flick of his fingers. "Can your guys get me in?"

"They can get you in."

"Then I can steal the diamond. I have a plan already. I just don't know why I should do it for *you*."

Before he could say another word, he found himself slammed up against the wall, Mossimo's forearm at his throat and Mossimo's gun pointed at his head.

So. Mossimo couldn't steal a jewel to save his ass, but he was still good with the strong-arm.

"Don't even think of betraying me." He shoved the cold pistol against Roberto's cheek. "I'll kill you. I'll kill your grandfather. I'll kill that pretty lawyer of yours, and damn it, I'll go to Italy to kill that whore of a mother of yours."

Roberto recoiled, ready to strike back.

But when he'd walked in here, he'd tacitly agreed to the deal and tacitly agreed that Mossimo was his boss. He couldn't balk now. Not because this worthless asshole called his mother names. Not because he'd threatened Brandi or Nonno. In this operation, timing was everything.

Mossimo held him against the wall for one more moment, cutting off his air, letting him feel the threat, before stepping away and holstering the gun.

Roberto sucked in air, trying to clear his spinning head. Across the room, he saw Brandi stalking toward them, and shook his head. *No.*

She stopped.

No. Don't try to help me. You'll make everything worse.

She inclined her head, but as she walked back to the crowd of wide-eyed women, she made it clear she left him with greatest reluctance.

When Roberto could speak, he said hoarsely, "You misunderstand me, Mossimo. While you're known for many things, you're not known for your generosity. What can you offer me that will make this worth my while? And don't tell me prestige—I can't take that to the bank."

Slowly Mossimo's scowl cleared. Greed . . . he understood greed. "You're a famous jewel thief. To work with you is an honor. Of course I know this. What do you want to do this job for me?"

"Tonight I dined at the home of Howard and Joni Patterson, and Joni was wearing a ruby on a chain around her neck. It was easily four point three carats and the color of fresh blood."

"I know of it." Mossimo bowed his head as if in shame. "But I can't get it. Their security is too good."

"Usually." Roberto examined his fingernails.

"What do you mean?" Mossimo asked alertly.

"Somehow, tonight their security in certain parts of their house was disabled," Roberto told him.

"Somehow, eh?" Mossimo began to smile. "Hey, you! Ricky! Get our friend Roberto some wine."

"Water." Roberto rubbed his bruised throat.

"Water." Mossimo pushed a chair under Roberto's ass, and they sat down for a low-voiced conversation.

When Roberto stood up again, the game was set. The bargain was made.

"It's a good deal," Mossimo said. "You bring the diamond to the Stuffed Dog, and I'll give you the Patterson ruby."

"Good." Roberto tapped Mossimo's belly. "Remember who has done you this favor, Mossimo, and give me and my *nonno* the respect and peace we deserve."

"Of course." Mossimo embraced Roberto, kissed both his cheeks. "This is a one-shot deal, profitable for both of us, and it's something to do with your time while you await trial, yes?"

Roberto nodded and noted how easily Mossimo gave him the kiss of betrayal. Judas would have been proud.

As Roberto strode across the floor, he crooked a finger at Brandi.

To his surprise, she obeyed him immediately and hurried to join him.

Taking his arm, she followed him to the hatcheck. "Congratulations, you discovered the one way guaranteed to make me respond to your every command. I'd do anything to get away from those women."

Roberto chuckled, took their coats when the girl handed them over, and gave her a hearty tip. "Awful, was it?"

"Awful hardly begins to cut it." Brandi let him wrap her scarf around her neck. "Did you know you can discuss a Brazilian wax for twenty whole minutes?"

"God, no. I don't even want to think about it for one minute." He shrugged into his coat and took her arm. Together they went out the door.

They hadn't taken two steps when the scent of tobacco hit him. He stopped.

She kept walking. "Yes, as a subject of interest waxing is right between acrylic nails and acid peels. . . ." She peered back at him. "What's wrong?"

Fico stepped out of the shadows, a cigarette tucked between two fingers. "Roberto, good to see you. And you." He nodded at Brandi. "It's cold out for a skinny thing like you."

"Brandi." Roberto jerked his thumb toward the limo.

"Sadly, I'm getting used to this." Brandi marched away.

The two men watched her go, and when Newby had opened the door and helped her inside, Fico said, "So, my man, did you listen to Mossimo's offer?"

"I did." What did Fico have on his mind?

"You know you don't have to do it."

Interesting. "But I do. I am very fond of my grandfather."

Fico stepped closer. "I can protect your grandfather."

"That's a spectacular promise, considering Mossimo's reputation."

"Mossimo has my greatest respect, always."

No answer, yet all the answer Roberto needed. "And for my fee, Mossimo has promised me a jewel."

"A dead man can't collect payment."

"So he plans to kill me after I get the diamond?" Roberto already knew it, but that Fico told him was confirmation of all he suspected. Fico wanted to take Mossimo's place. He'd do what he must to prevent the robbery.

"I'm telling you that you would be better off leaving this job alone."

This was tricky. Trickier than Roberto had imagined, because he *had* to do the job. "But Fico, knowing Mossimo plans to kill me adds excitement."

Fico threw his cigarette into the dirt and gravel. "Do what you like, then. But don't say I didn't warn you."

"No, I won't say you didn't warn me. In fact, I never saw you here tonight. It's a shame we missed each other." Roberto stripped off his glove and offered his hand.

Fico looked at Roberto's outstretched hand, then grasped Roberto's arm at the elbow. Roberto reciprocated, and the two men shook hard, once.

Against all evidence, Roberto liked Fico. The man wanted power, but not for the joy of inflicting pain. Fico was all about profit.

Taking a chance, Roberto leaned close. "Trust me. Fico, trust me."

Fico scrutinized Roberto's expression. "What would that gain me?"

"Exactly what you want, Fico. Trust me."

"Only a fool trusts anyone but himself."

"Then be a fool."

Fico considered Roberto for one more minute. "I will think."

"Do that."

They broke apart. Roberto headed for the car and hoped his instincts hadn't steered him wrong.

21

*T*he cold wind swept into the car with Roberto, chilling Brandi more than the last hour—and that was saying something. When Mossimo had slammed Roberto against the wall and pointed that pistol at his head, she'd tried to scream. But one of the bimbos, one who looked about sixteen, had slapped her hand across Brandi's mouth and said, "No. You'll get him killed for sure!"

Brandi itched to get out of that Knights of Columbus hall, and she couldn't leave. Of course, she could have run out the door—but for some inexplicable reason, it never occurred to her to abandon Roberto.

What had her life come to that she was responsible for a jewel thief who went looking for trouble?

So as Roberto slid close and the car smoothly drove off, she snapped, "You're some kind of superhero black belt. Couldn't you have knocked Mossimo ass over teakettle?"

Roberto stared at her as if he regretted knowing her name. Sighing hugely, he said, "It's at times like this when I realize why the Fosseras keep their silly bimbos. Smart women are a pain."

"I thought so. You could have kicked his butt! Why didn't you?" She wrapped her hands around his wrist, felt the girth, the muscles, the tendons in her grasp.

"Did you happen to notice the number of sports jackets in that place? And the number of holster bulges underneath those sports jackets?"

"I know." But for some reason, his words didn't ring right with her. This powerful man had allowed a fat old bully to shove him around. He'd gone in there knowing Mossimo would probably do it, and he had submitted without a qualm.

Somehow, it felt as if she didn't know all the facts.

Well. She didn't. Roberto didn't confide in her, and she should be glad. This way, when she got put on the stand and asked about the crime, she could truthfully say she knew nothing.

She subsided against the seat. "What happened after he took his gun out of your face?"

"I saw you coming across the floor to rescue me and almost had a heart attack. Are you crazy?" Roberto's usually smooth tone grew harsh. "Do you know what those men are capable of?"

His aggressive display startled her. Alarmed her. Sort of . . . thrilled her. "I can guess. So why were we there?"

"If you ever see me in trouble again, don't you dare try to rescue me."

"You think I'm going to stand by and let someone shoot you?" Her voice rose, too.

Newby glanced in the rearview mirror. He must have heard them through the glass.

"What good will it do if you get shot, too?"

"At least I won't have to live my whole life knowing I'm a coward!"

"Damn, woman." Roberto caught her in his arms as if he couldn't bear to be separated from her any longer. "You scare the hell out of me. Don't you know the world is full of sharks, swindlers, and sons of bitches?"

"Yes, I've had one remanded into my custody!"

He kissed her.

She'd been waiting for this ever since she'd left him on Sunday evening. Every minute she'd been with him, breathing his scent, hearing his voice, watching him watch her, she'd wanted to taste him again. Now she reveled in his heat, in her arousal, in the motion of the car that carried her toward someplace where satisfaction waited.

When finally he lifted his head, she was sprawled across his lap, her fingers clutching his lapels. "Don't stop," she muttered.

"Have to." He sounded as unintelligible as she felt. "We're here."

"Where?"

"At the ball."

She stared up at him, his face a contrast of shadow and light. "What?"

"The dance. At Mrs. Tobias's dance. We have to go . . . dance."

"Now?" She had been lost in the darkness with him, and she wanted to stay lost. "Now you want to dance?"

He laughed, a sort of helpless-sounding amusement. "Since your mother's in our suite—yes."

Her mother. Tiffany. She'd forgotten about Tiffany.

"We could . . ." Could what? Get into Roberto's bedroom without Tiffany noticing? Have wild sex while her mother slumbered in the next room? Fat chance. Even as a teenager, Brandi hadn't tried that. "Oh, fine." She gave up and sat up. "Let's go dance."

The gust of cold air helped freeze Brandi's desire.

Unfortunately, the inside of the California-style mansion was bathed in the warm colors of adobe and earth, with blooming plants climbing every wall and birds singing in tall cages, and her appreciation of her surroundings and her pleasure in her companion started a rapid thaw.

She could hear music. She hadn't danced for months, and then only in a crowded bar with other law students . . . and Alan. There the Rule of Highly Ranked Law Schools prevailed; students good enough to qualify had no social skills and no ability to keep the beat.

That night, it had become apparent that the rule applied to medical students, too, and that went double for Alan.

Now, as a waltz played by world-class professionals filled the air, the ballerina within Brandi stirred, and she flexed her legs.

"This is not so bad, heh?" Roberto smiled as if he correctly gauged her rise of anticipation.

"This is good, and the other would have been . . . " Not *bad*. She couldn't bring herself to say that sex between her and Roberto would be bad. "Unwise," she finished.

"Definitely unwise."

He didn't have to agree.

A thin, old lady of medium height with dyed brown hair and bright brown eyes hurried to meet them. "Roberto, how good of you to come. You're exactly the rogue I need to make this party a success." She extended her hand and allowed him to kiss it, then stood on tiptoe to kiss both his cheeks. Turning to Brandi, she said, "And this young lady must be Brandi Michaels."

Startled, Brandi said, "Yes, but I'm sorry—have we met?"

"No. But when a woman reaches my age she has to have a hobby, and mine is gossip."

Brandi's mind leaped to the kiss in the car, to the affair at the hotel, to this infatuation with Roberto that led her to commit reckless acts of passion. She had known someone was going to talk, and apparently she was right.

But Mrs. Tobias tucked her arm into Brandi's and led her toward the source of the music. "First your fiancé runs off and marries some floozy, and you show the world how little you care by getting Roberto remanded into your custody!"

What a lovely explanation. Brandi liked it very much.

"You lucky thing! Of course, if I looked like you, jewel thieves would fight to be remanded into my custody, so luck had nothing to do with it, right?" Throwing back her head, Mrs. Tobias chortled with old-lady glee.

"Is that all your gossip?" Brandi stumbled in her relief.

Roberto caught her arm. "Careful, Brandi; don't fall now."

"Do you have more?" Mrs. Tobias peered greedily at her.

"No, but I do have custody of the one jewel thief," Brandi said.

"So far." Mrs. Tobias led them through the sunny, open rooms toward the source of the music. "I'm sure they'll all be knocking down your door. Good-looking attorneys—did I say good-looking? I mean *decent*-looking—are hard to find. And one who can walk and chew gum at the same time is even rarer. There!" They reached the balcony above a grand ballroom. She waved an arm. "Isn't it glorious? I use it for my tennis courts the rest of the year, but this night is the night it was built for."

It *was* glorious. The huge room had a gleaming hardwood floor, gold plaster walls, and a raised dais for the twenty-man orchestra. A hundred people mingled in small groups, the men somber in black and white, the women glittering with diamonds and elegance. The dance floor covered half the room, and couples circled, swooping and dipping, as the orchestra finished its waltz.

"It's so grand." Brandi clung to the rail and watched, enthralled, quivering with the desire of a much-thwarted dancer. "I've never seen anything like it."

"It's not for you to look at; it's for you to join!" Mrs. Tobias placed Brandi's hand on Roberto's arm. "Roberto, take this girl dancing!"

"With pleasure."

Ballerina Brandi had always loved her recitals, loved moving to the tempo, loved the grace and the flow of movement set to music. As they descended the stairs, the music changed to a tango and she gave an excited laugh. "Roberto, can you tango?"

"But of course. My mother insisted I learn."

As soon as they reached the dance floor, he put his arms around her and she knew she'd hit the jackpot. He could dance. Really dance. He'd been well trained, but more than that, the music recalled the skill and grace of his lovemaking. And the frustration of being always together yet always apart made the anguish of the tango real to her.

The violent rhythm caught them up, taking them back and forth across the floor, one fleeing, one pursuing in exclusive, desperate passion.

The other guests gave way, clearing them a space until they danced inside a circle of enthralled observers.

Roberto's dark gaze never wavered from hers.

Brandi concentrated on him, saw only him, knew intimately what move he would make next.

The room faded to nothing more than a backdrop to their movements.

They were sex set to music.

Then Brandi caught sight of a familiar face on the edge of the crowd. It sneered with such contempt, she missed a step.

Roberto pulled her back into him, absorbing the motion, but he must have sensed something was wrong, for he guided her with more force, ruthlessly taking her through the motions, allowing her the time to get over her shock.

By the time the music stopped, she had disciplined herself enough to smile engagingly at Roberto and clap as if she had nothing on her mind except her admiration for him.

He acknowledged her, too, bowing and clapping, but he leaned down and spoke in her ear. "What is it? Who's upset you?"

"It's nothing." But that was stupid. Roberto was going to find out. "There. It's Alan."

Roberto searched the crowd with his gaze and unerringly settled on the handsome man with brown hair, blue eyes, pale, freckled skin, and muscled, lanky body. "Ah. I see him. The extremely foolish fiancé has returned."

Roberto made her smile with a little more sincerity.

"He's not at all as I pictured him." He sounded perplexed. "I thought he would be . . . well, not necessarily good-looking, but certainly I imagined he would have an imposing presence for I hear he has a brilliant future. Instead he's . . . just short."

"He's not short. He says he's five-ten."

"He's shorter than you."

"Only when I wear heels."

Roberto snorted. "And when don't you?"

She didn't answer.

"No. Don't tell me you catered to his fragile ego and wore flats. Brandi! No!" Roberto started toward Alan. "I must meet the man who so crushed my Brandi's individuality."

She caught his arm before he'd taken two steps. "He didn't crush my individuality."

Roberto looked down at her.

"Okay, he mushed it a little. Oh, come on!" Deliberately casual, she strolled toward the edge of the floor where Alan waited, a petite and curvaceous redhead clinging to his arm.

She was all too aware of the speculation running rampant through the watching crowd. Chicago society now knew who she was, that Alan had jilted her and that she had become Roberto's companion. They anticipated a scene, but Brandi was determined to keep it civilized. After all, Alan had made it more than clear that he didn't care about her, and she . . . Well, her sapphire earrings had gone far to mend her broken heart. Her earrings—and Roberto.

"Alan." She extended her hand. "How good to see you here. You're back from your honeymoon in Las Vegas, then?"

He didn't answer. Didn't take her hand. Instead he stood looking up at her—in her wedge heels, she was two inches taller—and shook his head in what looked like disbelief.

The chill of humiliation started, but Brandi would not allow it to control her. Alan had already controlled her through neglect and . . . oh, Kim was right. By an insidious kind of abuse. Lowering her hand, she smiled with quizzical amusement. "Come on, Alan, *you* walked out on *me*. You can be civil."

Alan looked as if she'd stung him like a wasp. "Don't be stupid, Brandi. We're not here to assign blame about who walked out on who."

She replied immediately, defensively, before she could stop herself. "I am not stupid, Alan."

Alan smirked.

"And I certainly hope you don't think I still care whether you walked out on me. I just think you should show some manners." But it was too late. Her fists and her stomach clenched.

Beside her, Roberto chuckled. Taking her hand, he smoothed her fingers and lifted them to his lips. "My darling Brandi, I deeply admire your ability to respond appropriately in any occasion."

Roberto had wrenched her attention from Alan's sour and offended face to him. To his warm appreciation, his generous support . . . his height.

"I would very much like to meet these people." He smiled broadly enough to show all his teeth. "I'm sure it will be a pleasure."

They shared a moment of intense communication. He didn't think it would be a pleasure, but no matter what happened, he was there to support her. "Of course, Roberto."

When she had done the honors, Alan accepted Roberto's outstretched hand and shook it, then quickly took his hand back.

Obviously he would have liked to ignore Roberto, except Roberto was too important to ignore. And too big. And from Alan's point of view, that rather odd sparkle in his dark eyes might look dangerous.

Fawn looked up at Brandi with the helpless amazement of a toddler viewing her first giraffe. "Alan? Alaannn? Does she have the diamond? Because I want the diamond."

"I don't have the diamond anymore," Brandi told her gently. "I pawned it."

"Oh, no!" Fawn turned to Alan. "She's a rich lawyer. Let's sue!"

Alan ignored his wife. "Brandi! I don't understand how you could have done something so stupid."

Beside her, Roberto lurched forward.

She stopped him with her hand on his arm.

Stupid. That was the second time Alan had called her stupid.

How had he come to assume he had the right to interrogate her and disapprove of her actions? Even now, when their engagement was over? Had she been so weak, so willing to go along with his dictates? Was she like her mother?

And if that was true, who did that make Alan?

Her father.

She stared at him. He looked nothing like her father, but he was the same. He was a manipulator. He was an abuser. And he'd done her a huge favor by dumping her.

Just as Roberto had done her a huge favor by showing her the way a man should treat a woman.

She glanced at him.

Roberto stood absolutely still, his laser gaze fixed on Alan. He might have been waiting for her cue.

But she could handle Alan. She turned back to him, to the short, petty, unhappy man she could now gladly walk away from. "You don't understand how I could do something so stupid? Like what? Pawn your ring? Spend the money on a day at the spa, a great dress, and some tall fuck-me shoes?" Her clear voice was carrying across the dance floor.

Wearing avid expressions, people pressed forward.

She continued: "Move into my apartment, start work, and get over you in less than a week? My God, Alan, when you got her pregnant"—she nodded at Fawn—"you didn't even have the guts to tell me not to come to Chicago. I uprooted my life for you, but you had to fly to Las Vegas and get drunk before you dared pick up the phone and admit what a weasel you are. I'm smarter than you, and unlike you, I'm not a coward, so don't you *dare* insinuate anything different."

In a clear, hard, carrying voice, Alan said, "No, Brandi. If you're over me so easily, it's obvious I did the right thing by marrying someone else. I don't understand how can you dance around the floor of an elegant ballroom draped across that man's arms like some kind of cheap whore."

22

$\mathcal{D}$ressed in her best black suit with her most dynamic red blouse, her most sensibly hemmed skirt and her highest stiletto heels, Brandi marched down the corridor toward Uncle Charles's thirty-ninth-story office.

Behind her, Roberto sauntered like a man out for a summer stroll.

Uncle Charles's secretary's workplace was twice as big as Brandi's cubicle, and the double doors leading into his private sanctuary were polished black walnut and without a word declared his importance.

Right now, Brandi didn't give a damn about his importance.

She tossed her mother's warm Gucci coat on a chair. Planting her fists on his secretary's desk, she leaned over and said, "Tell Mr. McGrath that Brandi Michaels is here to see him."

The secretary, a petite young woman with a face carved out of ice and a nameplate that said, MELISSA BECKIN, was not impressed. "Mr. McGrath is very busy right now, but I'll be glad to pass him a message when it's convenient for him."

Brandi recognized the heat as Roberto walked up behind her. She knew he smiled at Melissa, because that ice melted so quickly she feared a flood. And she hated it when he said, "Brandi and I both need to see Mr. McGrath. Is there any chance you could get us in right now?"

"Who should I say is asking?" Melissa fluttered like a bird wounded by the arrow of love.

"Roberto Bartolini." His Italian accent deepened. "Count Roberto Bartolini."

Brandi had never heard him use his title, and she'd liked that. It seemed to indicate some modicum of humility. But obviously he didn't know the meaning of humility. Or of constraint. Or of the basics of good manners. Last night had proved that beyond all doubt.

"Let me speak to him." Melissa shoved her chair back a little too hard and almost toppled backward. "Oops! Sorry. So silly of me." She stood and sidled toward the door. "I'll just check and see if . . . Hang on a minute . . . don't go anywhere. . . ."

"I'll be right here waiting . . . for you," Roberto assured her.

She fumbled for the doorknob, turned it, and slid inside without ever taking her eyes off Roberto.

As soon as the door closed behind her, Brandi swung on Roberto. "Why did you do that? You ruined her coordination!" Like Brandi really cared. "Were you trying to prove a point?"

"You wound me, Brandi." For a man who had danced half the night, he looked remarkably fresh. "You seemed hell-bent on speaking to Charles, so I got you in to see him."

"Thank you very much, but don't do me any more favors! I can't afford them."

"As you wish." With his hand on his chest, he made a little bow.

Continental. Suave. Mad, bad, and dangerous to know. He was all of those things, and if Brandi weren't careful, she'd be roadkill beneath his wheels, because she found him just as irresistible as did poor Melissa.

But she'd learned her lesson, and irresistible wasn't nearly enough for her. She wanted respect, damn it, and she was going to get it if she had to wring it out of Roberto's thick neck with her bare hands.

Melissa opened the door and smiled at Roberto. "Mr. McGrath will see you now."

"Thank you." He strode toward her, his long legs eating up the space between them.

Brandi watched, sure of his intentions, biding her time.

"*Signorina,* you have been so helpful." He took Melissa's hand and bowed over it.

Melissa fluttered like a bird enthralled by a snake.

By Roberto, the snake.

Brandi moved closer to the door.

He lifted Melissa's fingers to his lips. *"Grazie molto."*

While he was gazing into Melissa's eyes, Brandi slipped past him and into Uncle Charles's office.

Roberto whipped around.

Melissa whipped around.

The two of them stared, appalled, as she smiled and shut the door in their faces. She flipped the lock and turned to face Uncle Charles.

The old guy was dwarfed by his huge leather chair and broad wooden desk. "I'm so glad to see you. Come and give me a kiss on the cheek." He cocked his head, his eyes bright like some inquisitive, baldheaded bird. "How is your mother this morning? As beautiful as ever?"

"I don't know. She wasn't up when we left." In fact, Tiffany had been only a lump in the bed next to Brandi both last night when Brandi came in and this morning before she left, and she hadn't stirred to even offer her daughter a good-bye kiss. Brandi didn't really blame her—she could probably tell Brandi was furious by the way she moved, and Tiffany never looked for confrontation.

"Ah." Uncle Charles smiled. "Then what are you here about?"

"I am here about that man." She pointed through the door at Roberto. "Do you know what he did?"

Uncle Charles leaned back in his chair and steepled his fingers. "You've got ten minutes to tell me." He sounded brisk, no longer kindly Uncle Charles but the busy head of a large law firm.

"Last night he took me to three different parties and he treated me like arm candy." She stalked toward the desk. "He showed me off to the businessmen of Chicago as his 'lawyer.'" She created quotation marks with her fingers. "He took me to a party with his low-life Italian gangster friends and their mistresses, patted me on the fanny, and told me to go talk to the other ladies because he had business."

"What did you do about it?"

"Do about it? First I said no. Mossimo Fossera waited for him to . . . I don't know . . . discipline me, I guess, but he instead started talking in Italian. Fast."

Uncle Charles looked down. If he was trying to hide his smile, he wasn't doing a good job.

"So I went and conversed with the ladies! Who, by the way, were barely coherent in any language except hair spray and contraceptives." She leaned on the desk, hands flat, and silently demanded Uncle Charles look at her. When he did, she told him her greatest fear. "Listen, Uncle Charles, Mossimo Fossera wants him to steal something, and I'm pretty sure Mossimo is threatening Roberto's grandfather. What are we going to do?"

"Do? We're not going to do anything. If Roberto Bartolini decides to do a job for Mossimo Fossera, we can do nothing." When Brandi would have interrupted, Uncle Charles held up one hand. "Please remember who we are. We're not policemen, not FBI agents, not superheroes. We're lawyers, and our job starts and finishes in the courts."

"However, apparently I am a babysitter who's going to be held responsible by Judge Knight if Roberto does steal something."

Uncle Charles nodded. "Yes, if Judge Knight deems that any misconduct of Bartolini's could be laid at your door, he could create problems for us in the future. Make sure you stick with Bartolini so Knight has no reason to doubt your vigilance."

"But I'm losing my reputation as a reliable lawyer before I even start work!"

"Miss Michaels, if you believe that, you underestimate the prestige of this firm."

Miss Michaels. Okay, so she'd annoyed him. "I'm sorry, but do you know what it's like fighting your whole life to be taken seriously and having that undermined in an evening?"

"No." Uncle Charles stood up, came around the desk, and took her arm. "But I assure you, you'll find the gossip around the office among the other young ladies most envious." He led her toward the entrance. "Now, Brandi, you go ahead and dress up for Bartolini; I know he enjoys seeing a pretty girl as much as I do. Anyway, I always thought you worked too hard. When this is over and you're buried in dusty law books, you'll look back and wonder what you were complaining about." He unlocked the door. He opened it. "If you're worried about not having the right clothes—"

"That's not it!"

"—ask Melissa where we keep corporate accounts, and you can charge whatever you need on McGrath and Lindoberth." He patted her cheek. "That will be fun, won't it?" He ushered her out and shut the door while she stared at him in disbelief.

"Dress up for Bartolini?" she said to the solid oak. "Because he enjoys seeing a pretty girl?"

Dear God, Uncle Charles was a dinosaur. An insulting, patronizing, chauvinistic old dinosaur.

"Are you done?" Roberto asked.

Slowly she turned to face him.

He looked as charming as ever, but she detected smug satisfaction in his expression.

Jackass. "I sure am," she drawled sarcastically. "Make sure you stick close. I'd hate to lose you in the crowd."

She stalked past the glaring Melissa, out the door, and down the hall. She punched the button for the elevator.

Roberto walked up beside her, their coats thrown across his arm, elegant in the latest of his endless Armani suits. He wore a white shirt, a red tie, perfectly shined black shoes . . . yet his hair was tousled and untidy, as if he'd spent the night making love.

Not with her, though. Not with her.

Damned if she was going to give in to their attraction just to get the same kind of satisfaction she could get from any appliance that took D-sized batteries. Not after that talk with Uncle Charles. Especially not after last night.

"What did he say that made you so angry?" Roberto asked.

"I was angry when I got here."

"Yes, but you were angry at me. Now you're angry at both of us."

"He made it good and clear what my function is in this firm. He wants me to charge evening gowns on him so I can look good for—" She choked rather than finish the sentence.

"Me. Hm. Yes. I can see that would be irritating." The elevator opened, and Roberto held the door while she stepped in.

"Like you care."

"Of course I care."

"No, you don't, or you wouldn't make me go to these parties!" She punched the button for the ground floor.

"I'm not *making* you go to the parties. I'm going, and you're going with me." He took her hand as the elevator doors closed. "Last night I loved holding you in my arms for our first dance."

"Yeah, I loved it, too—right up until the time Alan and his bimbo bride saw us."

"What did you expect me to do?" Roberto's mouth tightened. "Allow him to show you such disrespect?"

"I didn't expect you to punch him in the face!"

"He called you a whore."

Yeah, he had. She hadn't enjoyed it, but she was the kind of woman who thought it was better to shrug off that kind of humiliating public display rather than compound it by making a scene. "You broke his nose."

"Perhaps next time he sees a lady he'll think twice before insulting her." No matter what she said, Roberto wasn't backing off. His brown eyes were flat and cold, his features rocky with disdain.

But retribution fostered retribution, and Alan had shot her a glare that promised trouble. "I saw flashes from the crowd. Someone took photos of us."

"It happens."

The elevator began its descent.

"Maybe to you, but I'm not a glamorous Italian count, and you've been remanded into my custody, and I'm supposed to keep you out of trouble, and if Alan presses charges—"

"*Sh.*" Roberto gestured her to silence.

"What do you mean, *sh*? I'm just saying . . ." Then she realized why he was listening. The elevator sounded . . . funny. Like something was slipping.

And they were going . . . too fast. "Roberto?" She clutched at him. Thirty-three, thirty-two, thirty-one . . . the floors went whooshing past. The elevator was almost . . . they were plunging to the ground.

"Roberto flung himself at the control panel, swearing, pulling emergency buttons.

And as abruptly as the drop started, it stopped.

Brandi fell hard.

When she opened her eyes, she found her cheek on the floor. She stared at the brown-and-teal industrial-grade carpet, at the expanse of polished wood wall, and at Roberto, sprawled beside her.

Stretching out his hand, he caressed her chin, but his fingers trembled. "Are you all right?"

"I don't know. How close are we to the ground?"

He lifted his head and looked. "We stopped on twenty-four."

"I'm awful." She was. She was sick with fear, her voice shaking.

"It could have started falling as soon as we stepped in."

That was so stupid she couldn't stand it. "Yeah, because if we hit the ground from twenty-four we'll be dead as hell, but if we fall from thirty-nine, they'll have to scoop us up with a snow shovel."

"Off the ceiling."

She didn't laugh.

In a reassuring tone he said, "Elevators have a lot of safety features."

"We just fell ten floors." Even terrified she could see the obvious.

"And stopped." He caressed her chin again. "That was no accident. There are governors that slow a plummeting elevator, and electromagnetic brakes—"

"And a really hard surface at the bottom if none of that works."

"The manufacturer guarantees the safety features will work. Plus there's a shock absorber at the bottom."

"If the manufacturer guarantees the safety features will work, why did he put a shock absorber at the bottom?"

"Ah, good. You're snapping at me. You are feeling better." He helped her to sit up. "Just a minute. Let me see if I can rouse anyone—"

A woman's voice blared through the speakers. "This is Officer Rabeck. Is there anyone in there?"

"Yes. Yes! There are two of us!" Roberto's Italian accent was deep and strong, as if the drop had shaken him back to his roots. "What happened?"

"We don't know, but don't worry. We'll get you out."

"What do you mean, you don't know? You've got some idea, I'm sure." Roberto slashed her with a CEO's authority.

Reluctantly the officer said, "It seems that the computer is malfunctioning."

"Malfunctioning? How is that possible?" He got to his feet and addressed the speaker as if Officer Rabeck were standing before him.

"We've got a hacker. The cameras in the elevators aren't working, the safety measures are barely holding—"

Brandi found herself on her feet. "So this is malicious?" she shouted.

"We believe so, but let me assure you, we have our best men on this. . . ." Officer Rabeck turned away from the microphone. Obviously she didn't mean for them to hear, but her tone carried. "What do you *mean,* they're trying to cut off the speakers right now?"

With a frying sound the speakers went dead.

Too stunned for words, Brandi looked at Roberto.

He leaned against the wall, his jaw outthrust, his eyes angry. "I'm sorry, *cara*. This is my fault."

"Your fault? I know you have a huge ego, but how do you figure it's your fault?"

"It's the Fosseras. They're having a power struggle."

"And you're involved . . . how?"

"Mossimo is a man barely hanging onto his authority. He's planned a job. He wants the Romanov Blaze."

Roberto's casual revelation took her breath away. "Aim high, I always say."

"I'm essential to completing that job."

"So you agreed to do it?"

"I did. But if Mossimo doesn't get the diamond stolen—"

"He'll fall and the next man will step in." She got the picture. Her knees gave out and she slid down the wall. "So they want to kill you."

"There's a lot of money in reselling stolen jewels, and head of the syndicate in Chicago is a prosperous position."

As if to reiterate his theory, the elevator dropped another few inches.

Brandi screamed.

"It's all right." He sat next to her and slid his arm behind her shoulders. "It's all right."

"My God." She sat straight and stiff. "We're going to die. We're really going to die."

He nuzzled the nape of her neck. "Have I told you how sexy you look in black and red?"

In astonishment, she turned to look at him. "How can you be so calm?"

He smiled, a tender curve of the lips. A lock of his hair flopped over his forehead. His eyes warmed her with heat and admiration. "*Cara,* there is no one with whom I would rather meet my end than you."

She *was* going to die, but in the arms of the handsomest, sexiest, most noble man she'd ever met. It didn't matter that he was a jewel thief or that he paraded her through Chicago like arm candy or that he planned to steal the Romanov Blaze and, if he lived, would no doubt succeed. He was a marvelous lover who'd led her to ecstasy. He'd taken her mother under his protection without complaint. And for all her protests, when she saw Alan sprawled on the floor, blood spurting from behind his hand, she had experienced a burst of joy. He'd given her that—a taste of savage retribution because he wouldn't allow a petty, foul-minded little jerk to abuse her.

The elevator dropped another few inches.

She didn't scream this time.

She attacked him.

With her hands on either side of his face, she held him still for a kiss that told him how desperately she wanted him.

He responded with an equal ferocity, thrusting his tongue into her mouth as if he needed the taste of her to survive. His fingers skimmed up her silky stocking to the lacy elastic around her thigh.

Her eyes closed when he touched the bare skin between her legs; she savored ecstasy while teetering on the sharp edge of disaster.

He pushed her back onto the floor and shoved her skirt up around her waist. From nowhere, a small knife appeared in his hand. His eyes narrowed; he looked cruel. He looked dangerous. He looked desperate. He looked like a pirate, and he sliced off her panties.

She almost came right then.

Instead she lunged for his zipper.

He unbuckled his belt.

Together they pulled his pants and underwear down to his knees.

She spread her legs and pulled him toward her.

He opened her with his fingers.

She whimpered. She was too sensitive. This was too intense. Too fast. Too driven.

Yet . . . she wanted more. She wanted him now.

He was so close she could smell the passion on his skin—an aphrodisiac that made her arch up to him. He placed his hips against hers. The head of his penis probed, then entered on a smooth, glorious glide.

And she came. And came. And came.

Roberto joined her, pounding into her, reaching deep.

One thought surfaced from among the chaos of sensation and glory.

If she had to die, this was how she wanted to do it. Entwined in Roberto's arms.

In love with Roberto.

23

"We've got it!" Officer Rabeck's voice blared across the elevator's speakers. "We've got control of the elevator! Are you two all right?"

All right? Brandi had never been so all right in her life.

But—*oh, God*—if the speakers were working, the security camera couldn't be far behind.

Roberto knew it, too. He touched his lips to hers and withdrew quickly. He dragged her skirt down, helped her to sit up. "We're fine," he called.

His voice was gravelly. Probably Officer Rabeck didn't know what that meant, but Brandi did. She recognized that sound. It meant he'd been well pleasured.

The elevator jerked.

Brandi gasped and clutched at him.

Then slowly the elevator rose, ascending as regally as a queen.

Officer Rabeck said, "We're bringing you up to floor twenty-five."

Roberto zipped up his pants, buckled his belt.

"There are emergency personnel here for you," Officer Rabeck continued.

Using the wall for support, Roberto worked his way onto his feet.

Brandi had drained him—and she was proud. And relieved to be alive. And . . . and she didn't know what she was.

He offered his hand.

She took it and let him help her stand. She pressed her trembling thighs together. He'd come inside her without protection. She had no panties. This was a disaster—and she didn't regret a minute of it.

She was alive.

She was in love.

She was such a fool.

"Don't hesitate to speak with the emergency personnel. They understand you've been through a trauma," Officer Rabeck said. "I'd recommend you go to the hospital, get checked out, and discuss your feelings with the doctors there."

As the doors slid open, Roberto leaned over, picked up a scrap of red, and stuffed it in his pocket.

Her panties. He'd gotten to them just in time.

A crowd of people stood staring at them—medical and emergency personnel, security, Uncle Charles and his secretary.

Roberto grasped Brandi's arm. He helped her out onto the solid floor.

She barely refrained from falling to her knees and kissing the carpet.

Uncle Charles grabbed and shook her like a parent who'd been frightened for his child. "Are you all right?"

"Fine. Really. Just stunned, that's all." She didn't want him touching her. She didn't want anyone touching her right now. She was still trembling with the aftershocks of violent orgasm. "I would like to go to the ladies' room."

He pressed a kiss on her forehead and let her go. "Of course. Melissa, would you go with her?"

"Yes, sir." Melissa moved to her side.

But before Brandi could walk away, Roberto slid his arm around her shoulders. In a low murmur meant only for her ears, he said, "*Cara,* we must talk."

She nodded. Melissa took one side of her, one of the medical personnel took the other, and they headed down the corridor toward the restrooms.

Roberto stood looking after her.

Damn! He'd fallen on her like a ravenous beast, taking her quickly, furiously, wanting satisfaction before he plummeted to his death. He'd demanded her satisfaction, too, and she'd given him that, but now she was avoiding his gaze. Avoiding him.

"Here." Charles handed him a clean white handkerchief. "Wipe the lipstick off your face."

Roberto stared at it, then into the knowing eyes of the older man.

"Don't worry. If I were in an elevator with a pretty girl and I thought we were going to die, I'd kiss her, too."

If you only knew . . . Roberto mopped his forehead as if wiping sweat off his brow, then cleaned his lips. He shoved the handkerchief in his pocket and buttoned his suit jacket to cover any other betrayals. Hell, as fast as he'd gotten dressed, his shirt might be sticking through his fly.

A policewoman with brown hair, gray streaks, and stern gray eyes stepped in front of him and offered her hand. "I'm Officer Rabeck."

"Officer Rabeck." Roberto smiled charmingly, but his gaze allowed for no prevarication. "Tell me what happened."

⌒

By the time security let them out of the building, it was three thirty, the temperature had dropped to twenty below, and the wind was picking up. Brandi and Roberto hurried to the limo parked at the curb and slid inside the dim warmth.

The emergency and medical teams had, with the best intentions, questioned them and suggested all manner of treatment for their trauma. They'd proposed the hospital, a psychiatrist, but Brandi just wanted *out* of that building. She didn't want to talk about her fear and her feelings, because sex had triumphed over fear and her feelings were none of anybody's business. Heck, she didn't even know what her feelings were.

She knew only that Roberto's grim expression made her worry that he regretted that moment of madness in the elevator.

She should regret it, too. She knew it, but telling herself so made no difference. Her mind might not approve, but her body was still singing. As Newby slipped the car into traffic, she turned to Roberto. "You said we had to talk." Abrupt, but she needed to hear what he was thinking.

"Yes. I spoke to Officer Rabeck."

"Officer Rabeck?" *Oh, no.* The cameras had come back on while they were still sprawled together.

"She said they had video of the two guys who hacked into the computer that controlled the elevator."

"Really." And Brandi cared because . . . ?

"They followed us into the lobby, sat down, and hacked into the wi-fi and through that into the building computers. Apparently they watched the security cameras until they saw us enter the elevator, then tried to take it down."

Oh. That was why she cared. She'd almost been killed.

But she'd also had the best, wildest, most demanding sex of her life. With the best, most amoral, most powerful man she'd ever met. "We need to *focus.*" And not on this. On the two of them.

She brushed her hand across her face. She had it bad. She had it so bad.

"I know." Roberto's rugged face was grim in the dim light, and the lips she'd kissed so passionately were a thin, determined line.

She wanted to kiss him again.

He continued. "We've got to get this figured out, because it's the same two guys who've been stalking us. Officer Rabeck showed me the video. The guys had scarves wrapped high around their faces, but I recognized the one running the computer by the violence of his cough."

Something about Roberto's description anchored Brandi's drifting attention. "His cough?"

"He's got some kind of cold or bronchitis or something. I actually caught him last night when I went to get your toothbrush."

Now Roberto had her full consideration.

"He followed me. I caught him, but like an idiot I let him go. They hadn't moved on us, so I thought their instructions were to keep track of us. I knew who they were, and I figured, better the devil you know than the devil you don't know." The lines around Roberto's mouth deepened. "My carelessness almost got us killed."

"Two guys. Two computer hackers. And one of them has a cough?" Memory stirred. She leaned back against the cool leather seat, trying to capture the picture stirring in her brain . . . last Friday. . . . "I wonder if they're the same guys as the ones in the pawnshop?"

"Pawnshop?"

"When I pawned my diamond ring, there were two guys in there, young guys. I didn't get a good look at them—they had their scarves pulled up and their hats on—but one of them had a cough. The shop owner said they were hackers. I was horrified, and he backed off and said they were just geeks." At the time, she'd been on the phone to Kim, so she hadn't been paying close attention, but she remembered that much. "He seemed scared, and I asked if everything was okay."

"Was it?"

"He said so."

"Think, Brandi." Roberto took her hand. "Why would guys you saw in a pawnshop stalk you?"

"I don't know. I pawned the diamond. I bought sapphire earrings. I got a check for the balance. They can't imagine I've still got the check, but . . . my apartment was vandalized when I got there Sunday evening, so . . ."

Roberto grasped her shoulders and turned her, fully facing him. "Your apartment was vandalized? Why didn't you tell me?"

"That note of incredulity doesn't cut it with me, buster!" She was starting to feel cornered. "I didn't tell you because we had agreed we wouldn't see each other again—although you *knew* better."

"All right." He rubbed her arms. "Why didn't you tell me later?"

"When, Roberto? At the courthouse, when you were mouthing off to Judge Knight? At the Stuffed Dog, where Mossimo's men were threatening you with a gun? At your grandfather's?" She was getting wound up. "I actually meant to tell you yesterday morning, but Tiffany appeared and I didn't want to explain why I hadn't told *her*, so I kept quiet. Then we moved to the hotel, then we went dancing, then you hit Alan, then we came to McGrath and Lindoberth so I could yell at Uncle Charles, for all the good it did me, then we got stuck in a murderous elevator, and now here we are—"

"Buono!" Roberto held up a hand. "You're right. We've been busy."

"Busy? It's been one damned thing after another!"

"You suspect the men who sabotaged the elevator and the men in the pawnshop could be the same men, and your apartment was vandalized."

"By two men. The security camera in the apartment building showed two men."

"Did they steal anything?"

"No, they just tore things up. Dumped out all the boxes—"

"So perhaps they were looking for something."

"Perhaps, but they were mean. They spray-painted graffiti on the wall, peed on the carpet, smashed my dragon . . ." To her horror, her voice broke.

Roberto noticed. Of course he would. The man, unlike most men, paid attention when she spoke. "Your dragon? It was special to you?"

"I bought it for myself before my parents broke up, and I've had it ever since. . . . Yes, it was special to me."

"My beautiful Brandi, you've been stalked. You've almost been killed." He ran his leather-gloved hand over her lower lip. "You don't need a dragon. You need a knight in shining armor."

"But I *want* a dragon." And she wanted Roberto.

"When this is over, I will find one for you. The best dragon in the world." He leaned forward as if to kiss her.

But the sexual flush was fading and logic was kicking in. They did need to discover who wanted to kill them, and the idea that she might be the target boggled her mind. She leaned away from him. "Don't be silly. The dragon's not important. What's important is finding out whether the same guys did it all."

Roberto straightened. "You're right, but *cara,* soon we do need to talk—about us." Reaching into the inside pocket of his jacket, he pulled out a smooth, flat, black metal box about the size of his hand. He slid his finger over the miniature keyboard and the three-by-four-inch screen came alive with color.

"Whoa." She leaned over his shoulder and watched as he used his thumbs to type in a code. "That's your computer? It's seriously wonderful."

"You like technology?"

"Love it. I used my father's old laptop during law school, and kept it running through a couple of viruses, one worm infection, and a hard drive failure. The vandals smashed it, which is probably what it deserved, but I lost everything I hadn't backed up. When I get my first paycheck I'm going to buy the newest, best—"

"What's the name of the pawnshop?" Roberto's thumbs hovered over the keyboard.

"Honest Abe's Pawnshop on Brooker Street."

Roberto typed rapidly.

She continued, "The owner's name is—"

"Nguyen?" Roberto asked.

She stared at the photo of Mr. Nguyen staring out of the screen and read the headline: *Pawnshop Owner Killed.*

"He was such a nice guy," she whispered. And she could scarcely comprehend that, once again, the situation had skidded out of her control and into a murky area called *danger.* She pushed her hair off her suddenly sweaty brow. "This isn't about you? Someone's really trying to kill me? Me, personally?"

"Call your mother," Roberto instructed.

Brandi was already dialing her mother's number.

"Have her pack," he said. "I want her out of the hotel and somewhere safe."

Come on, Mother. Come on. Come on and answer.

"Hello?" Tiffany sounded crackling-bright and cheerful.

"Are you all right?" Brandi asked.

"I'm fine! Just fine! Why?"

Brandi heaved a sigh of relief. She nodded reassuringly at Roberto. "Listen, Mother, we've got a situation here and no time to explain. I want you to go to Charles McGrath's house. Can you do that?"

"Um, honey? That's where I am right now. In fact—"

"Good." Brandi collapsed against the seat. "Stay there until we get this cleared up."

The cheer drained out of Tiffany's voice. "What's wrong? Brandi, I know that tone in your voice. What's wrong?"

Now Brandi polished her voice to a bright sheen. "I'm fine, but it seems that when I pawned Alan's diamond, I ran into trouble."

"Is Alan threatening you? Because I can talk to him." Beautiful, sweet Tiffany managed to make that sound like a threat.

"No, heavens no! Don't do that. It's not him, it's just . . ." Brandi tried to look back over the last week and pinpoint the beginning of the trouble. She couldn't. "Actually, Mother, when my pipes froze I would have been miles ahead if I'd licked them, gotten my tongue frozen to them, and stayed stuck until the spring thaw."

Beside her, Roberto chuckled. He brought up a blank e-mail. His thumbs flew as he typed a message.

Brandi tilted her head and tried to read it, but he hit SEND before she could.

"Is that Roberto with you?" Tiffany asked.

"Yes, Mother."

"As long as he's with you, I know you'll be safe."

When her mother said stuff like that, Brandi bristled. "He's just a man."

"Tomorrow I'll call and get you an eye appointment."

Brandi glanced at him in the fading light. Her mother had a point.

"Brandi Lynn, you let me know what's happening. Don't forget this time!" Tiffany ordered.

"No, ma'am. And you be careful, too!" Brandi hung up. "She's already at Uncle Charles's."

"His security is very good." Roberto held a memory chip in the palm of his hand. "If I show you the footage of the guys in the lobby, do you think you could recognize them?"

"I can probably tell you if they're the right age and size."

He slid the chip into a slot of the computer. "Officer Rabeck enhanced the picture for me. There we are, and there they are." He pointed at the door as first Roberto and then Brandi entered.

In a few minutes, the two young men followed.

The camera angle was high and to the right. The guys peeled off their coats. They wore black sports jackets and slacks. They kept their scarves high around their necks, but they looked respectable. One of them went up to the guard and spoke, gesturing at his friend and shivering graphically. The guard shrugged and gestured at a couch.

"While you were in the restroom, I talked to the guard." Roberto tapped the screen with his finger. "He said the boy—that's what he called him, a boy—told him they'd been waiting in their car for Jake Jasinski in International to come down so they could go to a family funeral. Jake had called them and said he was late and they were to come in and get warm."

"What does Jake Jasinski say?" She watched the two guys go and sit on the couch near a potted plant.

"That he's an orphan."

"I'll bet." She took a breath from a chest that felt tight and panicked. "Those could definitely be the men in the pawnshop. It's impossible to tell for sure, but—"

"The evidence is weighted in their favor."

"But . . . why did they kill Mr. Nguyen?" She took Roberto's wrist and looked into his eyes. "Why are they after me?"

"You said Mr. Nguyen was uneasy, so probably he knew they were going to hurt him, kill him." Roberto covered her hand with his.

"Why didn't he tell me something was wrong when I asked?"

"Maybe he was hoping to talk them out of it. Maybe he was a good guy who didn't want you to get hurt." Roberto's fingers clenched over hers. "But for some reason they're chasing you now, so I think there's a good chance he gave you something they want."

She touched her earrings. "I looked at them through the jeweler's glass. They're great stones, but those guys aren't coming after me for the sapphires. Not when they could have stolen them in the shop."

"So not the sapphires. How about the bag Mr. Nguyen wrapped them in?"

She spoke slowly, retracing that day in her mind. "I put them on in the shop. He gave me the case for them, but it's just one of those velvet jeweler's cases with the flip-top lid and the insert that sits in it holding the earrings, sort of, you know"—she gestured, trying to show Roberto the angle—"up for display."

"Where's the case?"

"In my coat pocket, which is why they didn't get it when they ransacked my apartment. Nothing's getting me out of my coat in this weather."

"Well . . ." His mouth quirked. "Something might."

At his reminder of their flagrant and reckless intercourse, heat washed through her.

She was being sensible. Yes, she was. But as always with Roberto, passion lurked close beneath the surface.

She'd changed since she met him. Had he changed, too, or was his life one long kamikaze escapade after another? Had she truly fallen in love with a modern-day pirate?

Of course she had. He planned to steal the Romanov Blaze.

This man—this criminal—had no place in her life.

At the realization, pain hovered very near. When she had time, she was going to sit down and cry.

But right now they had a crime to solve. "I thought we were having a rational and very necessary discussion."

"We are, although it's not the discussion I would prefer to have with you at this moment." He sighed soulfully, as if he regretted every moment he spent not in her arms. Then he gazed at her wrapped in the warm winter-white velvet Gucci and said briskly, "This coat is not the right one?"

"No, it's the London Fog, and it's in the closet at the hotel. Roberto, do you suppose those guys are at the hotel searching the suite right now?"

"No. I just e-mailed the FBI and told them what was going on."

"You told the FBI?" She was horrified. "But shouldn't you be trying to keep a low profile?"

"A man in my profession has contacts. After all, I spent a lot of time with the good agents while they questioned me about stealing Mrs. Vandermere's puny eight-carat diamond. If I can't use the FBI in this situation, what use are they?"

"But you did promise to do the job for Mossimo, and if the FBI starts watching us—"

"Little Brandi." Again Roberto put his gloved finger to her lips. "Listen to me. I swear to you, I will do the right thing. Trust me."

When he said that, she wanted to die from joy that he cared and anguish that she couldn't—didn't dare—believe him. "Roberto, I want to trust you. I really do. But—"

His computer beeped. He glanced at the message that popped up. "The FBI is at the hotel now. They're guarding our suite. And the stalkers must have discovered that their plan didn't work, because they're loitering in the lobby."

Newby brought the car to a halt outside the hotel.

Roberto nodded toward a man under the awning bundled up in a doorman's outfit. "That's our FBI protection."

"How can you tell?" He looked like a doorman to Brandi.

"I recognize him."

"Right." Brandi memorized his face. "Why doesn't he go in and arrest those guys?"

For a moment Roberto looked almost . . . guilty, and he sounded glib. "He can't do that until we know for sure who these guys are working for."

"What? Trying to kill us isn't a good enough reason to put them in jail?" Newby opened the door, and she got out of the car. "Do you remember when you were talking to Judge Knight, Roberto?"

Roberto followed her toward the hotel. "Yes," he said cautiously.

"I've decided you were right." As they passed the fake doorman, she spoke right to him. "The FBI really are a bunch of idiots."

24

$\mathscr{B}$randi knew Roberto had promised to steal the Romanov Blaze. She just didn't know when.

Roberto knew.

Tonight was the night.

In a few short hours Roberto would be in the Art Institute of Chicago, in the innermost sanctum, lifting the giant sparkling stone from its display case. Afterward, accompanied by the Fossera men, he would go to the Stuffed Dog and deliver it to Mossimo, and then . . . ah, then the stain on the Contini family honor would be expunged, and Roberto would have the answers to the questions that had plagued him this past year.

But before he could steal the stone, he needed to discover the identity of the stalkers who wanted Brandi dead. He needed to know that when he left her alone, she would be safe.

At this hour, the hotel lobby teemed with guests. The concierge gave him a salute. The desk clerk greeted him by name. One of the female guests asked him for his autograph.

Brandi observed the parade of sycophants. "Everybody adores you."

"But of course. I'm a celebrity. Don't you find it amusing that notoriety gives me the same respect as wealth and respectability?" When she frowned, he grinned. She was predictable, his Brandi, charmingly so. "Now excuse me; I have to speak to someone."

Going to the bell captain, he leaned close and murmured, "Do you see the two boys hanging around by the potted plants?"

"Yes, Mr. Bartolini."

"They don't belong in here. Throw them out."

"Yes, sir." The bell captain touched his forehead in an informal salute and signaled security.

Roberto rejoined Brandi, satisfied he'd done his part to make sure the stalkers were miserable and cold. It was the least Roberto could do for them.

Brandi waited for him by the elevator, and if Roberto hadn't been watching, he wouldn't have seen the small hesitation as she stepped on board.

"We could walk up," he suggested. "After a life-altering plunge, it's all right to be afraid."

"If you can take the elevator, I can take the elevator." Yet as it rose, she leaned against the back wall with her head pressed against the paneling and braced herself as if waiting for the fall. "Besides," she said as if he'd made a comment, "the suite's only on the fourth floor."

The elevator stopped.

She jumped.

The doors opened.

Roberto put his arm around her back. "Let's go find out what's in your coat."

His touch seemed to galvanize her, and she hurried out and down the hall—away from him.

She didn't trust him, and while he supposed she showed good sense, still he hated to see the misgivings in her eyes. His every action was that of an adventure-seeking opportunist, yet he wanted her to see beyond his exploits to the man he really was. He wanted her to depend on him, confide in him, believe in him, and he had only two tools on which to rely—his touch and his words.

If she chose to doubt those, he could do nothing to change her mind.

In the suite she went right to the coat closet. Pulling out her London Fog, she dug her hand into the pocket and unerringly pulled out the white velvet jewel case.

He remembered it. It had fallen out of her pocket at the courthouse. He'd picked it up, handed it over, and she'd thrust the case into her pocket once more. Thank God it had remained there until they could get to it now.

She flipped open the lid, lifted the insert that displayed the jewels—and a black-and-gold video chip tumbled out onto her foot.

"My God." Scooping up the chip, she gazed helplessly at Roberto. "It's really here."

Taking it from her, he walked to the desk. He ran his fingers across the lock on his laptop, pushing the right combination, and the lid slowly lifted.

"You have the best gadgets," she said.

She sounded so awed that when this was over, he resolved to get her a laptop with as many bells and whistles as money could buy.

"Let's see what we have." He inserted the chip.

At once the screen came to life and played a typical day in a small neighborhood pawnshop.

First they saw the counter and the cash register. They heard the door open and someone punch in the alarm code.

"There's probably another camera pointed at the door," Roberto said.

"Probably."

"When he first got the threats, he must have upgraded to a security system with sound."

"Probably," she said again.

They saw Mr. Nguyen come into the picture, go to the cash register with a bank bag, and fill the open till.

At the sight of him, Brandi took a pained breath.

Roberto understood. "It's a shock when you see someone who you know is gone."

"But I barely met him." She sounded bewildered.

"Death is always a surprise. About what time did you go in the shop?"

"Early. Probably ten thirty."

"Okay." Roberto fast-forwarded through Mr. Nguyen seating himself behind the counter and flipping through a magazine, and slowed when the door clanged. The shopowner looked up and flinched. Obviously he dreaded his visitors, but he called out, "Joseph and Tyler Fossera. What are you doing here? I told you to stay out."

Two young men swaggered up to the counter, and the oldest said, "Hey, you're nothing but an old gook. We don't have to listen to you."

"Yeah, man, he's a gook." The other boy laughed—and coughed.

"That's him; that's the kid I caught following me," Roberto said.

At the same time Brandi said, "That's them."

On the video, the oldest asked, "Are you going to take our offer?"

"I've checked around the neighborhood," Mr. Nguyen said. "You have no power here. It's your uncle who is the head of your family and if he knew that you were trying to set up your own protection racket in his territory—"

In a flash, the oldest punched Mr. Nguyen in the face.

Mr. Nguyen's head jerked sideways. He fell back, hitting the wall. Pictures clattered to the floor.

The younger guy said, "Joseph!" He sounded shocked.

"Shut up, Tyler." Joseph waited while Mr. Nguyen staggered up.

"Yeah, well, gook, we can protect you from *us*." Joseph thrust his head forward, a pugnacious little shit who needed to be taken out.

Mr. Nguyen put his hand to his jaw and gingerly moved it from side to side.

"I saw that bruise on his face," Brandi whispered. She couldn't take her gaze off the screen.

Roberto pushed the desk chair under her, and she sank down as if her knees could no longer support her.

"We're going to kill you if you don't pay us," Joseph said.

Mr. Nguyen shook his head as if clearing it, then rounded on Tyler. "And you! What are doing with this thug? You're smart. You program computers. You don't need crime!"

"He's with me!" Joseph grabbed Tyler around the neck. "Aren't you, man?"

"Yes, I'm with him." But Tyler didn't look happy. "You *have* to pay us. We're starting our own business. We're going to be rich, and everyone's going to pay!"

"Ask your uncle what he thinks of that, young Tyler!" Mr. Nguyen said.

Joseph pushed Tyler behind him and focused on Mr. Nguyen. "My uncle's old. He's lost his touch. Everyone says so. Someone new needs to step in. That's me."

"And me," Tyler said.

"No wonder they want the video," Brandi said. "This would convict them."

Roberto nodded. "If Mossimo didn't get to them first."

"Would he kill those boys?"

"The ones who challenged his power? You bet."

On the tape, Joseph said, "Yeah, Gook, Tyler is my second in command. So pay us"—he pulled a pistol and pointed it at Mr. Nguyen—"because I'm not kidding. We're going to kill you." His hand was absolutely steady, and he smiled as if anticipating the money or the kill.

Slowly Mr. Nguyen stepped back, his hands rising in the air.

Tyler was wiggling like a kid who needed to go to the restroom. "No, man, don't kill him; we'll get in trouble!"

"The weak link," Roberto said.

"Jesus, Tyler, you're such a chickenshit!" Joseph said in disgust.

"I'm not, either!" Without drawing breath, Tyler said, "Someone's coming. Shit, it's a girl."

All three heads swiveled toward the door.

"Didn't you lock it? You moron, what's wrong with you?" Joseph put his pistol in his coat pocket. He pulled his cap down and his scarf up. To Mr. Nguyen he said, "It's up to you. If you say one word, we'll kill her and you. Remember that before you say anything."

Mr. Nguyen nodded.

The boys moved down the counter.

The door opened, and Brandi heard her own voice saying, "It's cold outside. It's warm in here." She was talking to Kim, and in a second she appeared in camera range.

Roberto and Brandi watched as she pawned her ring and bought her earrings. They saw Mr. Nguyen take the white velvet case apart, then turn toward the camera. He looked into the lens and the expression on his face said it all. He faced death, but he took no one with him, and at the same time he hoped he brought the boys down.

He reached toward the camera. The chip went blank.

As the video ended, neither Roberto nor Brandi stirred.

She stood. "The little bastards!" she burst out.

He flinched at her vehemence. She called them bastards; if she knew the truth about Roberto, would she use that word so freely?

"They're not bastards," he told her. "They're Fosseras. Treachery is born and bred into their bones. Now let me copy this onto my computer and send it to the police." Pulling up the chair, he went to work, sending the video as an e-mail attachment to his contact at the FBI. Aiden would know what to do.

Walking to the window, she looked down. "I can see them from here. They look like a couple of innocent young boys shivering in the cold. But they killed Mr. Nguyen." She stared down at them, shaking her head as if she couldn't comprehend such violence. "I hope they get frostbite."

"They're going to get more than that." He finished the operation, then turned his attention to her. "But until they're in custody, they're dangerous men. Do you know how to shoot a gun?"

She faced him, exasperation clear on her face. "No, but I know how to do a flip on the balance beam."

"That's good, too." Going to the closet safe, he punched in the code and opened it. He pulled out his pistol, the small piece he kept handy for small jobs, and checked to make sure it was loaded.

Bringing it to her, he said, "Here's the safety. When you want to shoot someone, take the safety off. After that, point this end"—he showed her the end of the barrel—"at the largest part of the person you want to kill, and pull the trigger. It's not art. It's not science. It's security. Your own. Don't take any chances. Until the FBI has those guys under arrest, take this pistol with you every time you go out."

She didn't argue with him. Taking the gun in her hand, she got familiar with the weight, clicked the safety on and off, and nodded. "Okay. I might not do a good job shooting one of those guys, but it won't be for lack of trying. Where do you want me to keep it?"

"Someplace easy to get to." He opened the top drawer of the desk.

She placed the pistol there and smiled uncertainly at him. "What happens next?"

That Roberto couldn't tell her—even he didn't know for certain what would happen next. For all the work he and his grandfather had put into the plans to steal the Romanov Blaze, there was still an element of uncertainty. Any robbery could go sour; this one, with enemies around every corner, could prove lethal.

More than that, when Brandi discovered what he had done, she would be angry. It might take him several days to get back into her good graces, and he didn't want to wait. He wanted her as he'd had her today, as he'd had her last weekend, in his bed for the slow, heated loving, for the impetuous, graceless matings. He wanted her . . . always.

"Brandi, we need to talk."

At his expression she caught her breath. Color bloomed in her cheeks, and her eyes dropped as if she were shy. Then they rose, and she said, "Yes, we do. Do you know what I discovered today in that falling elevator?"

"What?"

"That I love you."

He gripped the back of the chair hard enough to make the metal crack.

"I shouldn't," she said. "You're the wrong man for me. You fit none of my requirements. You're flighty. You want adventure. You're immoral. You don't respect the law. But I can't help myself. I adore you."

"As I adore you. Brandi . . ." She stunned him with her fierce courage. He had been anguished that she believed the worst of him, yet was it not braver to open her heart to him when she credited him with a notorious character?

Lust, shimmering beneath the surface, roared into the full heat of an Italian summer. He found himself beside her, holding her head in his hands and kissing her. Kissing her with a rough need he could barely rein in.

She responded. . . . Their impetuous need in the elevator was nothing to this. Her mouth sought his again and again.

He slid his hands inside her jacket, relishing the narrow width of her waist, lifting his hands to her breasts and knowing that inside her bra, her nipples had peaked.

She shed her jacket and pushed his off his shoulders.

What was it about this woman? He'd had other beautiful women, yet she tasted fresh, new, and something about the way she reveled in his response hinted at the desperation that drove her to this moment, this night, and her own confession.

Twined in each other's arms, they stumbled toward the bedroom.

In between kisses, he said, "Brandi, I promise . . . I will be everything you want. Honest . . . I will be honest."

For one moment she buried her head in his chest as if she cherished his pledge. Then she lifted her head. "Don't make promises you can't keep. You've never lied to me. I know who you are. I couldn't bear it if I believed you were a knight in shining armor and discovered . . . you weren't."

But he had lied to her. He'd lied to her about almost everything, and unless he bound her to him now, she would lash out at him for making a fool of her. "I'm not a knight in shining armor. I'm what you want—I'm the dragon."

She laughed tremulously, pleased that he remembered.

Lifting her, he carried her to the bed. He laid her on the comforter. Leaning his forehead on hers, he said, "I promise to be the man you first imagined me to be. I *promise.*"

She struggled to turn her head away. She didn't want to fall into his enchantment.

"Brandi. Listen to me. I promise my heart—"

"Your heart?" Her gaze leaped to meet his.

"My heart is in your keeping. Surely you're not surprised?"

"Why would I think you . . . you . . ."

Her uncertainty amazed him. "Love you? Do you think I take every woman I meet to my room? Do everything I can to keep her at my side? Insult a judge? Get remanded into—"

Brandi shoved him away and sat up. "You did do that on purpose!"

"But of course. I would do anything for you. Only for you." He grinned at her indignation. "I wanted to be with you. I wanted to see if fate had at last given me what I most desired—a woman of intelligence, of beauty, and of kindness."

She gazed at him as if he were a strange beast. "You're not like any man I've ever met."

"I would hope not." He pressed her down on the bed again. "I don't want to remind you of anyone else. When you think of love, I want to be the only man you can imagine. But I promised you my heart. Can't you promise me your trust?"

She surrendered. At last she surrendered. "I trust you, Roberto. No matter what happens, I trust you."

25

A ringing noise woke Brandi out of a deep and satisfied sleep. "Roberto?" She groped, but he wasn't in the bed beside her.

The ringing noise continued.

Her cell phone. She fumbled, searching in the dark. Located it by the blinking red light that signaled a call. A glance at the clock told her it was midnight. Midnight. And—she stared at the caller ID—was that her father's phone number?

He never even called her in the daytime.

In a flash she imagined a heart attack. A car wreck. Some desperate need that made him want, at last, to talk to his middle child.

Flipping open the phone, she blurted, "Daddy. What's wrong?"

"What's wrong?" His wrathful voice blasted her ear. "What's wrong? I have a daughter who's a goddamn groupie, that's what wrong!"

"What?" She shoved the hair out of her eyes, trying to comprehend what he was yelling about. "Who?"

"You didn't think I'd see the pictures, did you? Your stepmother couldn't wait to show them to me. My wonderful daughter, the one I always compare that pathetic son of hers to, cavorting with a jewel thief!"

Daddy was talking about *her*.

"Kissing cheeks with a bunch of gangsters. Dressed like a two-bit hooker!"

She straightened up. "What pictures?" She might be half-asleep, but she didn't need to hear him call her a hooker again.

"In the paper on the front page of the society section. The *Chicago Tribune* has been slavering over that creepy Italian ever since he showed up in your town. I knew McGrath and Lindoberth was representing him, but damned if I knew you'd decided to sink your law career to screw him!"

She had that sick feeling in her stomach, the one she always got when she talked to her father. "I have not sunk my law career."

"You'd damned well better not have. You owe me for your education. You owe me big. Vanderbilt wasn't cheap."

She had hoped this was some sort of nightmare.

His nagging about money convinced her it was real.

"I got into one of the best law schools because I'm one of the smartest people in the country," she reminded him sharply.

"Don't take that tone with me. You're as stupid as your mother."

She'd heard that a few too many times. "I am not stupid, and neither is my mother!"

"Who are you trying to convince? Your mother still can't add two and two and get four, and *you're* sleeping with a client! Didn't Vanderbilt teach you anything about ethics?"

"Just about as much as you taught me, Daddy." She had the satisfaction of hearing him huff.

The satisfaction was short-lived.

He took a huge, angry breath. "Right, and if I don't have a check for your tuition—the whole thing—on my desk tomorrow, I'll repossess your ballet lessons."

His rage was contagious. She stood up on the mattress and bounced with temper. "You'll get your money. I've got a good job. Tomorrow I'll go to the bank and take out a loan to pay you so I won't ever have to talk to you again. You're a controlling, abusive bastard, and I am done trying to please you."

She had to give him credit: He recognized what she'd done; she'd washed her hands of him. And he replied with all the spite and malice of which he was capable. "You're no better than your mother. A goddamned, stupid, spineless ballerina worth nothing. When I'm dead, you won't even have the guts to come to the funeral and spit on my coffin."

"You're absolutely right, Daddy. I'm not coming to your funeral to spit on your coffin. I don't like standing in long lines." She waited until he stopped sputtering. "Now, Daddy—you're the last person to criticize anybody for messing up their lives, so next time you want to shout at someone, don't call me." She almost shut the phone.

Then she brought it back to her ear. "And don't call my mother, either."

Then she hung up.

She hung up on *him*.

She rubbed her stomach and waited for the ache to start, that sick sort of roiling that told her she'd had another run-in with her father.

But it wasn't there.

She was angry, yes. Furiously angry at him for thinking that providing money for her college gave him the right to shout at her, and mad at herself for being foolish enough to fall into his trap instead of taking out a student loan.

But mostly she felt free, as if telling him off had released her from that spell of fear he'd cast the day he'd walked away from her and her mother. It didn't matter whether he called her stupid. It didn't matter whether he admired or despised her. She was done with him. She was an adult. He and his cruel words and his endless spite didn't have the power to hurt her anymore.

She took a long breath and released it slowly.

But in this world there was someone who did have the power to hurt her.

Roberto.

Where was he? Why hadn't he come back to bed to see what was going on? She needed to be held and praised, to be assured there was more between them than good sex.

Yet the suite was very, very quiet.

Slipping out of bed, she pulled on his robe and walked into the living room.

It was empty.

She checked the bathroom. Both bathrooms.

They were empty.

She looked in the extra bedroom. She looked under the bed.

She stood in the middle of the floor and took a long breath. This couldn't be happening. There had to be another explanation than the obvious . . . that Roberto had sneaked away from her and right now he was stealing the Romanov Blaze.

Picking up the hotel phone, she called down to the concierge. In her most charming, carefree voice, she said, "This is Brandi Michaels in room . . . oh, dear, I can't remember what room I'm in!"

"You're in room four-oh-three, Miss Michaels." The concierge sounded warm, entertained—and male.

Male. At least she had some luck tonight. "Oh, thank you. I never can remember numbers! Is this the helpful and handsome Mr. Birch?"

"You've guessed right, Miss Michaels."

"It's not a guess, Mr. Birch. I know *you*." An older man, dapper and smart, good at his job and happy to be of service. The concierge should never give out information on a guest, but Mr. Birch liked women, and he liked her. If she struck the right notes, she could pull this off. "I am such a silly woman. I forgot to ask Mr. Bartolini if he would get me a bottle of my favorite nail polish while he was out. It's L'Oréal's Lollipop Pink; it's such a beautiful color, and it smells like candy! I just love it! Can you catch him before he leaves?"

"Just a minute." Mr. Birch put her on hold.

As she waited, she tapped her fingers on the table. The foolishness of her actions infuriated her. Looking under the bed. Calling the concierge and pretending to be a blithe, untroubled lady of leisure. But she couldn't stand not knowing the truth.

She had to know if Roberto was gone. She had to know if he had lied to her.

The concierge popped back on, and he sounded a little wary. "We're not sure if he left. There was a man, but he had his scarf over his face and his hat down, and he went out through the kitchen."

"He wanted a snack. I *told* him to order room service. He probably charmed some hapless cook out of a cookie." She lowered her voice and confided, "I swear, Mr. Birch, it's not fair that Mr. Bartolini can eat all the time and still be so thin!"

"So true." Mr. Birch sounded relaxed again.

"He's not here. He has to be somewhere. . . . I wish I could find his cell phone number!"

"He met three men behind the hotel."

"Yes, he went out to have a drink." If life were fair, she'd receive an Academy Award for Most Indulgent and Amused, when actually she was Most Infuriated and Deceived. "With the Italian guys, right?"

"I couldn't venture a guess about that." Mr. Birch responded in the same spirit of amusement.

"Dark hair, dark eyes, all speaking Italian?"

"I believe that's right."

"Great! I do have Greg's cell phone number. I'll call him and catch Roberto that way. Thanks so much, Mr. Birch!" She hung up briskly—then flung the phone across the room. It thumped against the wall. It skittered across the table and bounced across the carpet. The antenna broke off with a snap. And that small act of violence wasn't enough—she wanted to stomp it to smithereens.

Roberto had sworn he wouldn't steal the Romanov Blaze. He'd promised her he would never steal anything again, that he would live on the right side of the law. For her. He'd said he would do it for her.

And instead the bastard had screwed her senseless, left her sleeping, and gone to do just what he'd promised he wouldn't.

Her father had called her a groupie and a hooker.

She was worse than that; she was a fool. She was as stupid as

Daddy had insisted she was—because with her father and Alan as examples of what men could be, she had still chosen to trust Roberto.

She put her hands to her forehead.

Could she be any dumber? She had known Roberto was an international jewel thief with an eye for women and a way with words spoken in an irresistible Italian accent. Why was she surprised to discover he'd slipped it to her, then slipped away?

Her stomach didn't hurt, but her heart did.

She hated Roberto. She *hated* him.

Yet according to the courts and her boss, she was responsible for Roberto Bartolini. Her job depended on her keeping track of him, and if she was going to pay her father back—and by God, she was—she needed her job at McGrath and Lindoberth.

But how to find Roberto?

She eyed Roberto's laptop. She stalked toward the desk. She would do it like one of the big boys.

A touch on the keyboard woke the computer from hibernation. But the screen that appeared didn't hold a conveniently labeled PLANS FOR ROBBERY icon.

Yet not for nothing had she made it through law school with a decrepit computer prone to viruses. She knew a few things about searching for secrets hidden in the program code.

Settling down in the chair, she worked through the levels of passwords and encryptions until she had a file on screen that showed the briefest, barest of agendas for the robbery.

She had no time. No time to prepare. No time to plan.

Because if all was going as scheduled, Roberto was at this moment at the Art Institute of Chicago confounding the myriad traps and alarms around the great diamond and removing the Romanov Blaze from its case.

If all was not going well . . . he was dead.

She sat, her fingers still on the keyboard, frozen by the thought.

At this moment Roberto could be lying in a pool of his own blood, surrounded by the guards, by the police, by professionals pleased to have caught him before he laid hands on the diamond. He would be alone, with no one who knew his voice, his smile, his body, his mind. They'd call the coroner to put the body into a bag—

Brandi found herself on her feet.

She couldn't bear it. She couldn't bear the idea that she'd never see him again, that he'd be nothing but a noted criminal gunned down by the police.

Because she might hate Roberto, but she loved him, too.

"Damn it!" she whispered. She glanced at the rest of the schedule.

He was due to deliver the diamond to Mossimo at the Stuffed Dog in one hour and forty-five minutes. If she could intercept him, she could make him take the diamond to the police. He'd have to confess, but the courts would be lenient because he'd repented his crime.

Yes, she'd make him surrender the diamond if she had to shoot him to do it.

She opened the desk drawer and pulled out the pistol.

Aim at the largest part of the person you want to kill.

She'd aim at his fat head.

But she didn't have much time. Going to the window, she looked out. The Fossera boys were still there, waiting for her to come out. Worse than that, that FBI agent was watching the Fossera boys. Brandi knew she could ditch Joseph and Tyler, but she wasn't so sure about the professional skulker.

Picking up the phone, she called the one person she could always depend on. "Tiffany?" She could hear music and laughter in the background.

"Hi, sweetheart, how are you?" Tiffany sounded distracted.

"Not so good." Tears prickled Brandi's eyes.

"What's wrong?" Brandi had Tiffany's full attention.

"Mama, I need help."

26

"*D*arling." Tiffany swept through the door of the suite dressed in a long dark coat with her blond hair hidden by a fuzzy hat and her face concealed by sunglasses. "I can't believe Roberto did this to you. This is an outrage!" She swept Brandi into a still-chilly embrace.

"I'll make him sorry," Brandi promised. She had the television on the local all-news channel, watching for a report of a break-in at the museum.

So far there had been nothing.

Roberto was still alive.

She'd make him sorry about that, too.

She gestured at the rolling suitcase Tiffany dragged behind her. "Did you bring the stuff?"

Tiffany inspected Brandi's face. "Yes, and you've done a wonderful job with the makeup and the hair. This is such a clever plan, Brandi. I'm so glad you included me!"

"No one else could possibly understand." Brandi rolled her eyes at her mother, but she couldn't tell whether Tiffany saw her.

Tiffany was still wearing her sunglasses.

Odd, because her mother had very strong opinions about a person who failed in the essential courtesies of removing her hat or her sunglasses, and while sunglasses helped with her disguise, it *was* nighttime. She didn't need them in here.

Peeling off her coat, Tiffany flung it at a chair. Kneeling beside the suitcase, she popped the latches. "I know you wanted one of my action outfits, but darling, I was packing for elegance."

"It's okay, Mama. Whatever you brought is fine with me." Brandi knelt beside her.

Tiffany took clothes out of the suitcase—a pair of Calvin Klein chocolate-brown wool slacks, a matching cashmere sweater, and Jimmy Choo stiletto heels in chocolate with an an orange flower on the toe. Tiffany's tone was worried as she said, "This was the best I could do. The heels are last season's, but they're my favorites, and I think so kick-ass. Don't you?"

"It's all right, Mama. I know one thing—I might not be able to run in those heels, but running isn't what I do well. What I do well is walk and smile and make men forget good sense, and I'm going to need every weapon in my arsenal to pull off this diamond rescue without landing in jail." Brandi grinned, expecting her mother to appreciate her sentiment.

"You can do it," Tiffany said, but her mouth trembled.

"Did you break a nail on the suitcase latch, Mama?"

"No. Why would you think that?" Tiffany's breath caught, and her fingers trembled as she brushed her hair back from her face.

"Mama." Brandi carefully removed Tiffany's sunglasses. "What's wrong?"

"With me? Nothing! Right now, I'm concerned with *you*." But her eyes looked as if she'd been crying.

With her own bad experiences to guide her, Brandi leaped to the logical conclusion. "Was Uncle Charles mean to you?"

"Charles? Heavens, no, he's the best man in the world. . . ." Tiffany choked a little. "It's just that you . . . you . . ."

"Me?" Brandi was taken aback. "What have I done?"

"You haven't done anything! It's just that . . . since the divorce . . . you've always called me *Tiffany* or *Mother*."

"You *are* my mother," Brandi said, bewildered.

"Yes, but tonight you asked for my help. Oh, honey, you haven't asked me for help since the day Daddy announced he wanted a divorce." Tiffany sniffed. "You always treat me like some sort of imbecile."

"I don't think you're an imbecile." But Brandi stirred uncomfortably. She hadn't thought her mother was an imbecile, but she'd never seemed bright about anything but men and decorating.

"Tonight you called me *Mama*."

Brandi sat back on her heels. *Mother* or *Mama*? Shades of gray, unimportant in her eyes, or so she had told herself. But not really, because in her own mind she recognized the difference. *Mama* was the cry of an innocent, loving child. *Mother* was a teenage girl's criticism. "I hadn't realized you cared."

"I know you didn't," Tiffany hastened to assure her. "I know I wasn't any good as the head of the family. But sometimes I dreamed of the old days when you were ten and ran to me with your problems as if I could fix everything. You were such a sweet little girl!"

"Not so sweet as a teenager, huh?" Brandi remembered her disappointment as her mother went from one job to another and their income sank lower and lower, and she remembered, too, what a snot she'd been about it. What a snot she'd been ever since.

"I wasn't cut out to hold down a job. I knew it, but I wanted to make you proud of me, so I kept trying, thinking someday you'd remember you loved me and call me *Mama* again."

"My God." As Brandi viewed her mother's distress, revelation slapped her hard. "I'm turning into my father." And she'd been engaged to her father. The man she'd most despised in her life, and she'd been imitating him. Why?

Because he didn't feel. He didn't hurt.

"No, you're not! I didn't mean that. Oh, dear, I shouldn't have started this. I knew I'd mess it up."

"You haven't messed anything up." Brandi started to place her hand comfortingly on her mother's back, then chickened out. For a long time she'd barely touched her. The wall of their differences had seemed too high to breach.

But Daddy was like that. Touching no one. Connecting with no one.

Brandi couldn't afford to be like him.

Taking a breath, she put her arm around Tiffany's shoulders. "I have."

"No, you haven't!" Tiffany touched Brandi's cheek. "You're just a beautiful girl struggling to find her place in a world that thinks beautiful girls are stupid, like me. I'm so proud of you. You're so smart, like your father, but you're a good person, too, and I've wanted your approval for a long time."

"You're not stupid, and you don't need my approval," Brandi said fiercely. "You're wonderful just the way you are. Everybody thinks so. I've been a shit."

Tiffany laughed a little. "Maybe. Sometimes. But no matter how you act, I love you so much."

"I love you, too, Mama. I always have."

They hugged each other hard, in accord for the first time since the day they'd been left to face the world alone.

"You'll tell me when I say the wrong thing now, you hear?" Tiffany said.

"You mean stuff like, 'As long as Roberto's with you, I know you'll be okay'?"

Honestly bewildered, Tiffany asked, "What's wrong with that?"

"It sounds like you don't believe I can take care of myself."

"Oh, darling." Tiffany put her hands on Brandi's cheeks and looked into her eyes. "You are the most competent person I know. Of course you can take care of yourself. But two heads are better than one, and . . ."

"What?"

"I don't want you to have to spend your whole life alone. It's nice to have a man—or in Kim's case, a woman—to come home to. A bad relationship is just awful, but no relationship is very lonely." Tiffany sounded wistful and looked . . . well, lonely.

"You need someone."

"I have someone."

Brandi blinked. She knew her mother had refused one man after another all the time Brandi was in high school and college—men who wanted another trophy wife or, more likely, a trophy mistress. She'd been proud when, time and again, her mother refused.

Now, at last, Tiffany had taken a lover. "Who is it?"

"Charles McGrath."

"Uncle Charles?" Brandi shouted.

Tiffany tentatively smiled.

Brandi got a grip on her incredulity and said a little more quietly, "But he's . . . old."

"And he's rich. And kind. And he doesn't cheat on his wife," Tiffany pointed out. "He wants to marry me and shower me with clothes and jewels, and I want him to."

"But"—Brandi shuddered—"you have to sleep with him."

"Love makes all things better."

"You *love* him?"

"Possibly. Maybe." Tiffany waved an airy hand. "But that wasn't what I mean. I mean, I know he loves me. He worships me. And when Roberto's old and gray, won't you still want to sleep with him?"

"Roberto? You mean . . . you know?"

"What? That you love him? Whew. Honey. If I weren't here, you could never sneak out of the hotel. You *glow*."

"But Mama." Brandi took a breath. "What if he gets himself killed tonight?"

"Roberto? Get himself killed?" Tiffany laughed aloud. "I know men, and you could drop that man twenty stories and he'd still land on his feet."

"Actually, twenty-four stories," Brandi said reflectively, remembering the elevator.

"Honey, Roberto Bartolini is not going to get caught, and he's not going to get killed. Don't you worry about that. You just get yourself in and out of this mess tonight without getting hurt. That's all I ask."

"I'll be careful," Brandi promised. Tiffany's assurances made her feel better. Tiffany was right: Roberto did always land on his feet.

"Come on, then!" Tiffany said. "We've got to get you ready to go. We don't have much time." Taking her makeup bag, she went into the bathroom.

"The dress is hanging on the hook," Brandi called. "Everybody saw me in it, and apparently the pictures were in all the papers."

"Yes, you're famous!"

"Infamous," Brandi corrected. Tossing the bathrobe aside, she donned her briefest thong and the beige slacks. She poured her boobs into her pointiest bra. She pulled on the beige turtleneck sweater. She looked down and grinned, then headed into the bathroom. "Look, Mama. Look at what I've got!"

"Oh." Tiffany put down the mascara wand and stared. "Oh, my."

Brandi surveyed herself in the mirror. "This'll knock their eyes out."

Tiffany giggled. "Or poke them out."

"Whatever's necessary." Brandi sat on the lid of the toilet and pulled on her trouser socks and her stiletto heels, then stood and stretched her arms over her head. "I'm ready for action."

"Not quite." Tiffany took off her large white-gold brooch sparkling with rhinestones, and pinned it on Brandi's right shoulder. "There."

"Thank you, Mama. It's perfect. It's so bright it's almost blinding." And not at all her mother's style. "Where'd you get it?"

Then together they said, "Uncle Charles."

"I'm working on his taste in jewelry." Tiffany put the finishing touches on her hair. "What do you think?"

Brandi turned Tiffany to face the mirror. She stood beside her.

Tiffany looked like her daughter, and Brandi looked like . . . well, she looked liked Brandi, but if all went according to plan, the Fossera boys would be miles away by the time she left the hotel.

Brandi handed her mother the velvet winter-white coat she'd worn last night and the video chip Mr. Nguyen had hidden in her earring case. "Now remember: Have the cabbie go to the police station, but tell him to take the long way around. Once you're inside you'll be safe, and if the Fossera boys actually try to follow you in, you can give the chip to the officers and tell them those were the guys who killed the pawnshop owner. That should fix them."

"I won't forget," Tiffany promised. "This will be fun!"

Picking up the long, dark coat Tiffany had worn into the hotel, Brandi pulled it on. She pulled on Tiffany's fuzzy hat and her sunglasses. She checked the safety on the pistol and put it in her pocket. With a brisk nod to Tiffany, she said, "Let's go."

Holding hands, they descended in the elevator. Tiffany tried to smile. "You're the smartest, prettiest girl in the whole world, and I have absolute confidence you'll make all the right moves."

And that was the difference between Tiffany and everybody else's mother. She didn't say, *I'll worry about you, so be careful.* Instead she said, *You're going to succeed.* In fact, now that Brandi thought about it, Brandi had been so successful not because she'd inherited her father's intelligence, but because her mother had always shown absolute confidence in her daughter's superiority.

And no matter how big a fool Roberto Bartolini had made of her, she still knew her father was wrong. She wasn't stupid. She was smart, she was ruthless, and she was coming out of this alive.

And she would make sure Roberto did, too.

"Thank you, Mama. I will succeed." Taking a leaf from her mother's book, Brandi hugged her hard and said, "You will, too, because you're the smartest, prettiest mother in the whole world. Joseph and Tyler Fossera don't stand a chance."

As the doors opened into the lobby, Tiffany stepped out, shoulders back, dress clinging to every curve. She was the picture of insouciance with the white Gucci coat draped over her shoulder and caught on one hooked finger. She smiled at the bellman, the desk clerk, and every late-night reveler that she met, searing them with the heat of her beauty. As she approached the doors, the doorman leaped to open it for her, and she strolled out into the freezing cold wearing nothing but a blue velvet dress and a steely determination.

The doorman summoned her a taxi and helped her in.

The cab drove off.

The Fossera boys grabbed the next taxi.

The FBI man leaped for his car and followed them both.

Brandi grinned. The diversion had worked.

Her mirth faded. And she'd sent her mother into danger.

"Be careful, Mama," she whispered, her hands folded in prayer. "Please be careful."

27

*H*ead down, Brandi strode toward the door.

Nobody in the lobby glanced twice at her.

She walked out and down Michigan Avenue and to the next hotel, where she caught a cab. "Take me to the Stuffed Dog," she said. "And hurry. There's a good tip in it for you."

"Sure, lady." Before they pulled up to the small diner, they'd been airborne three times.

She paid the cabbie, giving him enough to make him say, "Thank *you*!" She stepped into the street.

It was almost two in the morning, a clear night with stars so cold they looked brittle. Steam covered the windows of the Stuffed Dog. Inside Brandi could see a dispirited waitress sitting on a stool at the counter and two bedraggled customers hunched over cups of coffee.

Mossimo Fossera sat with his back against the far wall. The table before him held an empty plate and dirty silverware shoved off to the side and a silver laptop. He was tensely watching a movie on the monitor.

But she knew it wasn't a movie. It was the real thing. Inside the museum the Fosseras were filming Roberto as he worked and sending the feed to Mossimo.

Mossimo faced the door so she couldn't see the screen, but she was able to read his body language. It was like observing a man watching a football game. He flinched. He dodged. Once he stood up, then sat back down. She knew everything was going well or he wouldn't still be there. Yet frequently his eyes narrowed and his lips moved in a disgruntled manner.

She could read that, too. No matter how ruthless or clever he was, he had none of Roberto's skills. Jealousy ate at him, greed kept him in his seat, and she was freezing to death waiting on the streets for Roberto to arrive.

She shivered as the wind swirled under her coat.

Unfortunately, she *was* literally freezing to death. She glanced at her watch. If everything went according to schedule, Roberto would be here in twenty minutes. Until then, she had to walk or she'd turn into a Popsicle before she could even start to save him from prison for eternity.

She hurried down the empty street, then walked back to the Stuffed Dog and glanced in the window again.

Mossimo was on his feet, grinning, holding his arms over his head and shaking his fists.

Roberto had stolen the diamond.

Well. He had landed on his feet. He was still alive.

She paced away again. Her stiletto heels *tink*ed hollowly on the frozen sidewalk.

When she was at the end of the block, she heard a car coming. She turned.

The brown Infiniti F45 stopped at the curb, and two guys draped in coats and scarves jumped out and went into the restaurant.

She hurried toward the restaurant and arrived in time to see them peeling off their hats. She recognized them: two of the guys from Mossimo's party. They handed Mossimo a small case; he opened it, nodded, and put it in his pocket. The two men took chairs behind Mossimo, and they listened as Mossimo waved at the screen and told them what had happened. Then they faced the door in an attitude of waiting.

A woman's slurred voice spoke near her shoulder. "I didn't know they played football this late at night."

Brandi swung around.

What looked like a short bundle of rags stood there weaving in the wind, but when Brandi looked closer she discerned two bright eyes and a smiling mouth.

"It's probably a rerun," Brandi said. "It's awfully cold and late." And Roberto and Mossimo's men were coming with the diamond. Then the trouble would start. This woman needed to be well away. "Don't you have someplace to be?"

"Don't you?" The little thing was a foot shorter than Brandi. She smelled of whiskey and garbage, and she shoved at Brandi as if urging her to leave.

"I'm going to stay here until my boyfriend comes to pick me up." Which was not really a lie. When he saw her, he was going to pick her up and run with her out the door.

She hoped.

"You see, that's not a good idea." The woman's voice wasn't as slurred now. "This is a bad neighborhood at night, and a pretty girl like you shouldn't be out here. Why don't I call you a cab and send you back to the hotel?"

"What?" How did she know Brandi came from a hotel?

"I can get you a cab," the rag woman said clearly. Then she jumped as if stung. She pressed her hand to her ear. "Shit. All right. I'll get in position."

Brandi stared as the woman shambled up to the door of the Stuffed Dog.

Had the voices in her head told her to go in?

A lone car drove down the street toward the restaurant.

Brandi stepped into the shadows to see if it would stop.

It did, and Roberto stepped out and headed for the door. Ricky, Dante, and Greg Fossera piled out and followed him.

Brandi slipped in on their heels.

Nobody paid any attention to her. The two Fosseras with Mossimo stood up and met the guys with Roberto, and the younger Fosseras laughed, slapped one another on the back, and generally acted like new fathers who had delivered their own baby.

Roberto stood in the middle, smiling and accepting their congratulations as if they were his due.

Stupid, lying, heartbreaking son of a bitch.

The old rag lady and two customers seemed oblivious to the celebration—probably drunk or hungover or just too smart to get involved.

Brandi wished she could be like them.

Mossimo sat at his table, watching and sneering, looking like a fat toad.

Brandi slid over close to the bar and the light switch, watching the scene, waiting for her chance, wondering if she really had the nerve to shoot someone and hoping that, if she did, it would be Roberto.

Putting his fingers in his mouth, Mossimo gave a shrill whistle.

The revelry died down at once, although the young Fosseras still grinned.

"Where's Fico?" Mossimo asked.

"He didn't show," Ricky said.

The men exchanged significant glances.

"The next time anyone sees Fico, kill him," Mossimo said.

The restaurant grew chilly and quiet. The customers slid low into their seats. The rag lady slipped behind the counter and crouched down.

Brandi slowly, quietly slid the safety off the pistol in her pocket.

"But we didn't need him," Dante said. "There was an alarm we didn't know about, but Greg here figured it out—"

Greg wagged his head.

"—and I disarmed it," Dante continued with a return of exuber-ance. "Then Roberto went to work. He's an artist. An artist, I tell you! No one even knows the Romanov Blaze is gone, and unless they look hard they'll never know, because the fake we replaced it with looks good!"

"Yeah, man," Greg said. "We were slick! We were clean! We got the diamond!"

"We did get it," Ricky pointed out.

"So where is it?" Mossimo snapped his fingers and pointed to his empty palm.

Ricky indicated Roberto while Greg and Dante pretended to prostrate themselves before him.

He drew out of his pocket a package about the size of his fist and wrapped in a black velvet drawstring bag.

Stupid, lying, heartbreaking son of a bitch. When Brandi finished this, she hoped the feds would give her a cell next to Roberto's so she could shriek her opinion of him for the next twenty-five years.

He started to hand it to Mossimo.

Heart pounding, Brandi drew her pistol.

Roberto stepped back. "But first, Mossimo, what about my ruby? You promised me the Patterson ruby in exchange for my work."

Brandi slid the gun out of sight.

Mossimo pulled the case out of his pocket and offered it to Roberto.

"Let me see it," Roberto instructed.

"So distrusting," Mossimo said in a chiding tone, but he opened the case and showed the gem to Roberto.

The setting glittered, and shafts of fire glinted off its glowing red facets.

Roberto nodded and smiled. *"Bella."* He accepted the case, snapped it closed, and stowed it in his pocket.

Then with the air of a showman, he cradled the diamond. He gave it a warm kiss.

Brandi wanted to shoot him so badly the hand holding the pistol started shaking.

He started to give it to Mossimo.

Again Brandi pulled her pistol. She pointed it at him. "Roberto!" she shouted.

Roberto wheeled around. At the sight of her, his incredulous expression gave way to terror.

"Give me the diamond," she said.

28

Guns appeared in every Fossera hand, pointing at Brandi, at Roberto, at one another.

Mossimo snatched the diamond away from Roberto. "Kill her!"

"Don't shoot," Roberto shouted. "For the love of God, don't shoot!" He ran toward her, knocking chairs aside.

One chair took Greg out at the knees.

Greg's pistol blasted. Ceiling tile and insulation rained down.

Another chair sent Ricky backward over a table.

In Roberto's hands, the chairs were weapons.

He raced halfway across the restaurant. One of the customers tackled him. They crashed to the floor and slid along the linoleum, hitting chairs like dominoes.

"Kill them all," Mossimo shouted.

He left Brandi no choice. She leveled the pistol at Mossimo.

From behind, someone grabbed her by the hair.

She went down on one knee, the pain bringing tears to her eyes.

"I got her," the guy yelled, and twisted.

Her hat slid over her eyes. She shoved it off.

Joseph. It was Joseph, Mr. Nguyen's murderer, the little prick who'd tried to kill Roberto and Brandi.

How had he gotten here? Where was Tyler? What had he done to her mother?

Getting her foot under her, she stomped on his instep, sinking her stiletto heel deep into his shoe.

Yelping with pain, he let her go.

"Brandi, get down!" Roberto shouted. "Drop to the floor!"

So Joseph could kick her to death? No way.

"Bitch. I'm going to kill you!" Joseph grabbed for her again.

Ballerina Brandi performed a grand jeté that would have made George Balanchine proud. In stilettos. She hit Joseph right in the chest.

He went down, arms flailing.

She landed off balance, fell against the counter. She righted herself, but when she tried to put her weight on her foot, her ankle twisted.

She glanced down. Her mother's shoe. When she kicked Joseph, she'd broken the heel on her mother's favorite Jimmy Choo shoe. Furious, she turned back to Joseph.

Pandemonium reigned in the Stuffed Dog. Another chair smacked the wall. Fists hit flesh, and something cracked. Men and women were shouting, "Drop it! Drop it!"

Joseph's livid gaze had settled on Roberto. He lifted his knife, aimed it with the skill of a professional—

So she shot him.

The recoil slammed her elbow into the counter. The retort blasted her ears.

The knife whistled past so closely it sliced off a piece of her newly highlighted and beautifully cut hair.

Joseph screamed. Screamed like a little girl. He writhed on the floor clutching his thigh. Blood seeped through his jeans.

Incensed, gun raised, she turned back to the room.

The whole scene had changed.

The rag lady was pointing a pistol—not one like Brandi's, but a big long one—at Mossimo Fossera. The waitress held a shotgun. The two customers were pointing guns at the younger Fosseras, who were carefully putting their pistols down on the floor. People—agents— were pouring into the restaurant from the back and from the front, and they were all carrying guns. Shotguns and . . . well . . . some kind of really long guns.

Roberto leaned against a table, shaking his hand as if it hurt and glaring at Dante, who was flat on the floor and holding his bloody nose.

Brandi was a smart girl, but it didn't take brains to figure out that Roberto had never faced a threat here. He couldn't be any safer in a monastery.

The agent who had been guarding the hotel, the one Tiffany had lured away, walked in. He looked at her in disgust. "You and your mother. Couple of smart-asses."

By that she assumed Tiffany was fine. *Thank God.*

Roberto looked up at her. He sagged with relief.

Then his expression changed. He frowned, and a fire lit his eyes.

Yeah, she would bet he was mad. She'd interfered and screwed up his whole heroic operation.

Too damned bad. Maybe he should have trusted her, like he kept saying she should trust him. "Bastard," she said.

With the noise in the restaurant, he couldn't have heard her, but he read her lips. He walked toward her.

"You double-crossed me!" Mossimo shouted, clutching the diamond to his chest. "You bastard son of an Italian whore! You double-crossed me!"

Roberto stopped. He turned back to Mossimo. In a move so clean Brandi never saw it happen, he knocked Mossimo's feet out from underneath him. The whole restaurant shook as Mossimo landed flat on his back.

Roberto leaned over the wheezing bully. "The nice FBI agents are going to take you away now, Mossimo, and while you may not be happy to go to prison for two hundred years, I know one Fossera who will be glad to see you go."

"Fico. That turncoat Fico," Mossimo said.

"No," Roberto said, "I was talking about your wife."

The FBI agents laughed.

Brandi didn't.

"That jewel you're clutching? It's cubic zirconium," Roberto said. "The real Romanov Blaze left the country three days ago."

Mossimo unwrapped the stone. He held it up to the lights. The facets glittered with glory, mocking him.

Mocking Brandi.

As hard as he could, Mossimo threw the fake diamond at Roberto.

Roberto caught it, and in a gesture that celebrated his triumph, tossed it in the air. It landed in his open palm, and with a grin he closed his fingers over it.

Celebration. Sure. If Brandi had pulled off a sting this complex, with the faked theft of a phony famous Russian diamond, the real theft of an authentic ruby, and the fall of an entire family of his grandfather's enemies, she'd celebrate, too.

For the whole time she knew him, Roberto had been working for the FBI. Had been working to trap Mossimo Fossera and his men in the process of stealing and receiving the Romanov Blaze and put them away forever.

And like a cat in a fan belt, she got caught up in the plot.

All of this—the worry about her job, the unwanted socializing, Roberto's swaggering, her angst about having unethical and totally great sex with a client, her fear he would die and this wild chase across Chicago at night armed with a pistol and the resolve to rescue Roberto from his own folly, her mother's broken shoe—had been for nothing. For a sham.

The damned diamond she'd put her life in jeopardy to protect wasn't even the real thing.

Tonight, when she had woken up and thought Roberto had broken his promise to her not to steal the Romanov Blaze, she had felt like a fool.

Now she knew the promise he'd made, the one that had made her heart trill—never to steal anything again, to live on the right side of the law *for her*—was as big a fake as the cubic zirconium he held.

Because, hell, how could he steal the diamond out of the Art Institute when it had been out of the country for three days?

Carefully, before she could give in to her desire to shoot Roberto right in the chest where his nonexistent heart should reside, she placed his pistol on a table. She turned toward the door.

From the floor, she heard Joseph shout, "For you, Mossimo!"

Off balance, she spun and saw him aim a pistol at her head.

Roberto hurled the cubic zirconium.

With a thump it hit Joseph right between the eyes. He fell backward, unconscious, a huge, bloody welt on his face.

One of the FBI agents scooped up the pistol.

She stared at Joseph's prone body.

She was *so glad* she'd shot him.

Of course, he was only a substitute for the man she really wanted to shoot—Roberto.

Roberto, who again started toward her. He looked wary. He looked furious. He looked like a man who'd been hiding the truth from her almost since the moment she'd met him.

She held up her hand. In a clear, carrying voice, she said, "I'm going home now. I won't be seeing you again. I'd wish you a good life, but actually I hope you step outside and get hit by a flaming meteorite. That would be fitting retribution for what you've done to me."

Roberto continued to stride toward her.

She limped out the door.

A gust of wind hit Roberto in the face. It smelled of rain and felt almost warm.

The cold snap had broken.

Aiden grabbed Roberto by the arm.

Roberto turned on him, furious to be stopped.

"Let her go. She's pissed off and you can't blame her." Aiden was a stocky man with short, sandy hair and hazel eyes, and Roberto's collaborator for the whole operation.

They'd known each other for years, and when Roberto had heard the rumor that Mossimo Fossera intended to steal the Romanov Blaze, he took it to Aiden. Aiden had had the authority to make the deal Roberto wanted, and Roberto had the expertise Aiden needed. They had been a good team—until now.

"She can't walk around Chicago at two thirty in the morning looking for a cab," Roberto said impatiently.

"One of my guys is taking her back to the hotel. No, wait." Aiden put his hand to his earpiece. "She wants to go to Charles McGrath's. She'll be safe there. More than safe."

"Safe from me." Roberto knew Aiden was right. He was right, but Roberto hated it. She'd seen the whole operation go down, and right now she despised him. No explanation he made could change that. He had to rely on her own good sense to soften her feelings toward him.

Brandi was a rare, very rare woman—one who used logic on a daily basis. When she thought about it, she'd know he had had no choice but to lead her on. And she'd probably understand that he'd wanted her close as he went to those parties to be feted as an infamous jewel thief.

Hm. Perhaps it would be best if he took her flowers when he went to explain.

Mossimo Fossera was on his feet, his hands cuffed behind him, the rag lady holding a gun to his back. "This is entrapment! I didn't steal anything!"

"You accepted stolen goods," the rag lady said. "The Patterson ruby and the Romanov diamond."

"It wasn't the Romanov diamond," Mossimo screamed.

"Could have fooled me." The rag lady smiled.

"I want my lawyer," he brayed. "I want my lawyer!"

"Shut up!" Roberto told him.

So Mossimo changed to, "You're dead to us. You betrayed us. None of the thieves will speak to you again. Traitor!"

"Yeah, Count Bartolini here is really worried about that," the rag lady said.

"Count?" Mossimo laughed hoarsely. "He's no count. Everyone thinks he's so smart, so rich, so continental, but he's a bastard. Everybody knows it! The bastard son of Sergio's whore of a daughter."

"Get him out of here," Aiden said.

The rag lady and one of the customers shoved Mossimo out the back door.

"I hate that guy," Aiden said.

"Yeah, but I got what I wanted from him," Roberto said.

"Revenge for what he did to your grandfather?"

"That, too." Roberto touched his pocket.

New agents entered with cameras and tape measures to document the crime scene.

Aiden kept a close eye on the proceedings. "Let me tell you, Roberto, when my man at the hotel realized he'd been suckered into following Miss Michaels's mother to the police station, and my agents here realized the woman watching Mossimo was Brandi, no one knew what to do. They were screaming in my earpiece like I could do something when I was following you."

"Couldn't they have gotten her out of here?" At least then she wouldn't have actually seen the sting.

"If we'd had another five minutes, but we didn't. We planned for everything except *her.*"

"That makes two of us." She'd worn the strangest expression when she looked at him. Angry, yes, he expected that. But pained, too, as if she'd been hit below the belt too many times and was bleeding internally. "I've got to go after her."

"Not right now. There's someone here you want to meet." Aiden nodded toward a tall, gangly young man who'd come in with the agents.

He sat in the booth, observing Roberto with keen curiosity.

"Who is it?" Roberto asked.

"He's the guy with the information you did all this for."

The news shook Roberto to the core. "He knows who I am?"

"He knows it all." Aiden shook his head. "The poor son of a bitch."

"He's here to tell me now?" Roberto glanced around. The fluorescent lights glared onto the upturned tables and shattered chairs. The agents worked, talked, and took pictures. Blood stained the floor. When he'd begun his quest, he'd never imagined it would end in Chicago in the Stuffed Dog at two thirty in the morning.

Aiden obviously saw nothing odd about the scene. "We made a deal, didn't we? You did your part, and I thought you wanted to know as soon as possible."

"I do." Yet Roberto wasn't ready. He didn't know if he'd ever be ready to know the truth about the man who had really fathered him.

A Chicago patrolman stepped in the door. "What the hell is going on?"

Aiden shouted, "Hey, the restaurant is closed. This is an FBI crime scene!"

"The hell it is!" the patrolman bellowed.

Aiden walked over to fight with the indignant, pugnacious policeman.

He left Roberto to introduce himself.

The young man was about twenty-three, tall and broad-shouldered. His hair was as dark as Roberto's; his eyes were dark and intelligent. He watched as Roberto walked toward the booth, scrutinizing Roberto as Roberto scrutinized him.

"I'm Roberto Bartolini." Roberto extended his hand.

The young man shook it. He looked into Roberto's face as if seeking something. In a voice tinged with the accent of an East Coast aristocrat, he said, "My name's Carrick Manly. I'm your half brother."

29

The next day, neither Tiffany nor Brandi would answer when Roberto called. It took a trip to McGrath's mansion for him to discover the two women had moved back to Brandi's apartment.

Charles McGrath was none too complimentary about the way Roberto had handled the whole situation. "Damn it, boy, when I told you and the FBI I'd help with this operation, I didn't mean I wanted to lose my fiancée to a crisis with her daughter! I had Tiffany living here with me. I was buying her things, she was helping me decorate the house, we were going to parties. We were happy! Then Brandi comes to the door sobbing, Tiffany finds out I was in on the sting, and now neither one of them is speaking to me. Thank you very much!"

So Roberto loaded his flowers and his presents back in the BMW— Newby was an FBI agent, and now that the sting was over Roberto was driving himself—and went to Brandi's apartment.

When he rang the doorbell, Tiffany answered. "What lovely flowers!" She relieved him of the cheerful mixed bouquet of golden sunflowers and purple asters. "Are the gifts for Brandi?" She took them, too. "Not that any of this is going to work," she said cheerfully. "You'll have to do better!" She shut the door in his face.

He stood there, sure she would now open the door and announce she was merely joking.

She didn't.

After two days of leaving first reasonable, then abject, then angry messages on Brandi's answering machine, he finally had no choice. He called in an expert—Count Giorgio Bartolini, who had been married to Roberto's temperamental mother for over thirty-two years.

When the count heard the whole story, he sighed deeply. "All these years, and you still know nothing? This young woman, Brandi—you admire her intelligence, you love her independence, yet you used her."

Roberto was outraged. He had expected his father to take his side. "It wasn't like that, Papa."

"Most certainly it was. She has her pride, and you made a fool of her." Roberto could almost see his father shaking his dark head in disgust. "Love that survives trial and strife withers at the sound of laughter."

"I did not laugh at her." Roberto was beginning to think this call was a mistake. "I phoned so we could talk sensibly about strategies to win her back. Instead you make it sound as if this rift is all my fault!"

Papa said nothing for a long minute. "If you were here with me in Italy, I would slap your face. Of course it's your fault! With a woman, you don't worry about *sensible*. With a woman, even if it's not your fault, you take the fault! That is what being a man is!"

"I have been a man for a long time, Papa, and no woman has ever required me to take the fault."

"No woman has ever saved your insignificant life before."

Roberto began to feel backed against the wall. "I saved hers in return!"

"That *is* what a man does. Do you love this Brandi?"

"Yes, but—"

"Then find a way to make her listen to you, admit you were wrong, and if you're lucky, perhaps she'll forgive you!"

"Roberto Bartolini crawls for no woman!"

⁓

"Good-bye, honey. You're going to make them all love you!" Tiffany kissed her daughter as if she were a girl going off to her first day of school.

In fact, Brandi was a woman going off to face the gauntlet of disgruntled McGrath and Lindoberth employees who now were sure her work ethics were lousy. "I'd settle for a little tolerance."

"I know it's going to be rough, but you have to go. You've got to pay off that loan from the bank!"

Ah, yes. The loan from the bank. The loan she'd taken out to pay back her father. The loan for which Uncle Charles had cosigned. "I've got three years to pay it back. Three years of working at McGrath and Lindoberth with people who will make my life hell." Brandi took a breath. "Three years isn't so long."

"That's the spirit!" Tiffany's cheerleader training was showing through. "Don't forget, you look great!"

Brandi did look great in a blue Dolce & Gabbana suit, a white cowl-necked sweater, and Donald J. Pliner pumps. Yesterday Tiffany had pulled out the credit cards Uncle Charles had given her and assured Brandi he had *begged* them to indulge in retail therapy. Brandi would have refused—knowing Uncle Charles had been in collusion with Roberto made her none too happy—but she had to do something about her hair. Joseph Fossera's knife had whacked off a one-inch-by-two-inch piece of her hair close to her scalp, and she desperately needed a professional to create a new style.

So Tiffany and Brandi had gone to the spa. Brandi's hairdresser had been horrified, then driven to a frenzy of creativity that resulted in an asymmetrical cut that made Brandi look almost French. A manicure and shopping had made both Brandi and Tiffany feel better about their lousy love lives.

Talking to Kim did *not* make either of them feel better about anything—Kim was madly in love, and while she tried to sympathize with their plight, it was clear nothing could penetrate her happiness.

But Brandi and Tiffany had had fun, and if Brandi was given to sudden bouts of tears disguised as temper, she never directed it at Tiffany.

Now, as Brandi entered the McGrath and Lindoberth building, the guard waved her in without checking her badge. "Don't bother, Miss Michaels; I know who *you* are."

She nodded and smiled, figuring that after the elevator incident every security guard in the place knew her name.

She closed her eyes as the elevator took her to the twenty-seventh floor and tried not to think about falling. The trouble was, when she emptied her mind, that opened it to the memories of lying on the floor with Roberto between her legs, coming with a desperation that shook her still. And to the memory of that moment when she'd realized she loved him.

But what good was love when the man was a lying creep?

When she'd posed that question to her mother, Tiffany had waved a hand at the presents and flowers and said, "He may be a lying creep, but he's a lying creep with excellent taste."

Brandi looked around at the open boxes filled with jewelry, glass objets d'art, and books selected especially for her. "We're not keeping that stuff."

Tiffany's answer left Brandi breathless. "But darling, we shouldn't let our dislike of him spoil our pleasure in the gifts. We want to hurt him, not ourselves!"

Even with their newfound accord, Brandi didn't know how to reply to that.

When the elevator doors opened, someone yelled, "She's here!"

Brandi opened her eyes to see the hallway lined with people—attorneys, law clerks, the secretarial staff—staring at her. She braced herself for a ration of trouble and instead heard a sound she had never expected to hear from them—applause.

Were they making fun of her? Was this some kind of office joke?

Brandi stepped cautiously out of the elevator and walked down the hall past the gauntlet of smiling people.

Diana Klim was bouncing while she clapped.

Tip Joel punched the air as Brandi walked by.

Even Sanjin smiled and clapped—coolly, but he clapped.

When Glenn called, "Good work, Brandi!" she knew the elevator had dropped all the way to the ground and she was dead and in some kind of purgatory.

The sight of Shawna Miller standing outside her cubicle clutching a legal pad gave Brandi a measure of sanity. Shawna hated her. She would tell her what was going on without prettying it up.

"What's with everyone?" Brandi asked.

"We saw the pictures," Shawna said. "We read the story! Oh, my God, you must have been so scared, but you looked cool as a cucumber."

Brandi stared at the bubbling Shawna. "The pictures? The story?"

"We got the memo yesterday afternoon, and the story broke on the *Chicago Tribune* Web site this morning." She dragged Brandi inside her cubicle and indicated her computer. "You're in the *paper.*"

Front and center on the *Tribune* Web site were two photos of Brandi—one looking elegant and graceful in Roberto's arms as they danced the tango, and one in the Stuffed Dog looking intent and calm as she pointed her pistol at Joseph.

Brandi sank into Shawna's chair. "Where . . . ? How . . . ?" She started reading as fast as she could.

> Brandi Michaels . . . new attorney for McGrath and Lindoberth . . . volunteered to assist international businessman Count Roberto Bartolini in a sting operation to thwart the nefarious plan to steal the Romanov Blaze . . . infamous kingpin Mossimo Fossera is under arrest . . . FBI agent Aiden Tuchman said, "At great risk to her own life, Miss Michaels

entered the fray and removed a threat to the operation with a kick to his chest, and when he again attempted to thwart us, she was forced to shoot him . . . cool under danger . . ."

"I don't believe it." Somehow Brandi had gone from dupe to heroine.

"That picture of you shooting that guy was so cool. You're my new hero!"

"Yeah. Thanks." The pictures must have been culled off the security cameras, or maybe the FBI agents had been wired. Brandi didn't know how this worked, because she hadn't been in the know. No matter what the *Tribune* said, Roberto had made a fool of her. But if the *Tribune*'s story smoothed her way at McGrath and Lindoberth, she would be ungrateful to complain.

"You'd have volunteered to help with the sting, too, if Roberto Bartolini was in on it," Brandi said as she stood. "It was no sacrifice on my part."

"You did get to go to parties with him, but no way. He's a hunk, but when the FBI told me there was going to be shooting, I'd have been out of there. He isn't worth getting killed over!"

"No, I suppose not." Brandi certainly shouldn't think so.

As she walked past Mrs. Pelikan's office, Mrs. Pelikan called out, "Miss Michaels, if I could see you for a moment?"

Mrs. Pelikan didn't sound nearly as infatuated with Brandi as the rest of the office, and she was shuffling papers when Brandi stepped in. "It would seem we need to assign you to a different case." She peered over her glasses at Brandi, and her brown eyes were cold. "Since this one was a front for you and Mr. Bartolini, and all the work we did on it useless."

From far off down the corridor, Brandi heard a rumble. Conversation? Laughter?

"Yes, Mrs. Pelikan. I'm sorry, Mrs. Pelikan." Brandi warmed to the woman who so greatly resented being lied to and used. Brandi could relate to that.

The rumble got louder. Definitely laughter.

Mrs. Pelikan relented. "I know you couldn't tell me, but what an immense amount of work for nothing!"

The sound of many voices carried more and more clearly into the office.

What was going on out there? "I promise, I won't be doing anything exciting ever again."

Mrs. Pelikan looked over Brandi's shoulder. She subdued a smile. "I don't know that I'd agree with *that*."

From the doorway, Roberto said, "Brandi, I'd like to speak to you."

Brandi stiffened. Slowly she turned.

And found herself facing a six-and-a-half-foot dragon.

30

The dragon was mostly green. Small green scales on his pointed snout, large green scales on his ridged back, green scales on his fat, three-foot-long tail, iridescent green scales on the ridiculously small wings that sprouted from his shoulders. Pointed white teeth grew from his long mouth. His black eyes, set deep into the sides of his head, shone softly. But it was the gem in the middle of his forehead that really caught her attention.

It was the fake of the Romanov Blaze, and it glittered with the same violet fire as the real thing.

Roberto looked . . . ridiculous.

"Brandi? Can we talk?" It was definitely Roberto's voice coming from inside the dragon.

"I don't talk to mythical fire-breathing reptiles." But she had to cover her mouth to hide her grin.

The whole floor, maybe the whole building, was watching. The men dug their elbows into one another's sides. The women giggled softly.

"You have to talk to me. I'm your dragon."

Her amusement died. "My dragon is broken."

"I know, and I'm sorry. I can't fix him, but if you'll let me, I can fix the things *I* broke."

"I don't want to talk to you." Brandi had been stomped by enough men lately. She didn't need to give this one a second run at her. Especially since this one was the only one who mattered.

"What did you break?" Shawna asked him.

"Her trust."

Brandi snorted. *And my heart.*

Roberto continued, "But if she'd listen to me for just a few minutes . . ."

"Brandi, you ought to be nice to the dragon," Diana said. "We don't want him to start breathing fire. There are a lot of papers in this place."

Their onlookers chuckled.

It wasn't fair. How had he gotten her whole office on his side? "Give me one reason why I should listen to you."

With his hands, Roberto opened the dragon's mouth and looked directly at her. "Because I love you."

Their onlookers *aah*ed.

The impact of his dark, intent eyes and firm declaration made her back up two steps. "Tell me why I should care."

He came toward her, claw outstretched. "Give me a chance and I will." Then his large backside caught in the door.

"As touching as this is, I've got work to do." Mrs. Pelikan looked over her glasses at the people crowded into the corridor. "As does everyone in this department. Sanjin, they're going to borrow your office. Show them where it is."

Sanjin stood immobile, his face blank with astonishment. "But I have work to do, too!" A jab in the side brought him to his senses and he said, "Follow me."

Roberto shuffled backward and gestured to Brandi to precede him. She walked down the hall, clutching her briefcase, acutely aware of the dragon shambling on her heels.

Damn Roberto. He made her want to laugh. He charmed her. And no matter how mad he made her, no matter how he hurt her, she still loved him.

Damn him. Damn him.

Sanjin opened the door to his office and gestured them in. He had a desk, a chair, a file cabinet, a view of the next building, and so little floor space the dragon made it a tight fit. He had to squish his tail sideways so Sanjin could shut the door behind him.

Even though most of Roberto was just a costume, she backed to the far side of the desk. "What made you think of doing *this?*"

"I wanted your attention." He opened the dragon's mouth again and looked at her. "My father told me I'd better crawl, and I said absolutely not, no woman was worth that, and he said . . . he said rather rude things." He winced as if they still stung. "He's a man whose opinion I respect very much, so I followed his advice."

"Because you respect him."

"No." He waggled that enormous, outrageous head. "Because every minute you're apart from me, my heart bleeds."

"Nice. Poetic. I'm not impressed." Although she sort of was, but he didn't need to think he could spout some romantic nonsense in that deep Italian voice of his and she would roll over like some kind of dragon groupie.

"In your absence, I wanted to know everything about you, so I begged Charles for photos and stories about you. I saw your baby picture. I saw ballerina Brandi in her first recital." He reached out a claw. "I heard all about your father."

She opened her briefcase and fussed with the contents, arranging the already neatly arranged notebook, pen and pencil, PDA, and shining-new laptop. "How nice of Uncle Charles to tell you *that.*"

"But I am not like your father."

"No, you're a whole different bag of beans."

"Nor am I the son of Count Bartolini."

She looked up. She shut her briefcase. She placed it on one side of the desk and seated herself on the other. "Okay. You win. You have my complete attention."

"Two years ago, my mother was diagnosed with breast cancer."

"I'm sorry." And why was he telling her *this*?

"She got very ill, and she believed—we all believed—she was going to die. So she called me to her bedside and told me the secret of my birth." Roberto clasped his clawed hands across his scaly chest. "My father is a man she got involved with while at college, a man who got her pregnant and left her. She came home to Nonno, who sent her to his family in Italy. Before she gave birth to me, she met the count. She married him, I was born, and I grew up believing he was my father."

"No one told you differently?" That was hard to believe.

"Except for my mother and the count, no one knew the truth. Everyone thought they'd had an affair during his visit to the States. Gossip said that they fought and my mother, in her pride, refused to tell him of her pregnancy, but when she went to Italy, they found each other again and married."

"Look, I hate to dispute you, but Mossimo knows. He called your mother a . . . he called your mother names."

"Mossimo suspected the truth, and probably there are rumors. But really—does anybody believe Mossimo when he spouts venom?"

"No. No, it never occurred to me to pay attention to him." She swung her foot and watched the motion. "What has this to do with you and me?"

"My mother would not tell me who my father is."

"Ah." That would grate on Roberto. He would need to *know*.

"She says she sinned. She says she's ashamed. She says that he isn't a good man, and she would not tell me his name. I would make a scene, but thank God she's in remission, doing very well, and I don't want to upset her."

"What about your father? The count, I mean."

"He's in every way a good parent to me. I can't tell him that I need to know"—he shook his dragon head as if his own emotions bewildered him—"to *see* this man who begat me. What was it about him that made my mother reject him and flee in such horror?"

Brandi began to understand the events of the last week. "But you had to know, so you searched for a way."

"And I found it. I'm not an international jewel thief—not usually—but I know the family business and I keep up the Contini contacts. Nonno called and said that Mossimo Fossera intended to steal the Romanov Blaze. I used my contacts. I went to the FBI and told Aiden Tuchman that if he would find out who my father was, I would help him bring down the Fosseras." The dragon shrugged his massive shoulders. "It's as simple as that."

"As simple as that—for you. For me, I made a mistake. I saw you at Charles's party and I thought it was fate."

"That was no mistake. It was fate, for once I saw you, made love to you, I wanted you with me. When I discovered you were one of my lawyers, I thought fate had given me the woman of my dreams." He touched his claw to his chest. "I was wrong."

"Not the woman of your dreams, huh?" For a man who was good with words, he was lousy with words.

"Definitely the woman of my dreams, but not *given* to me."

"Oh." Better.

"Not given to me. I had to earn her. Still have to . . ." He shut the mouth. He looked down.

He bonked her in the head with his snout. "Ouch!"

"*Cara!* I'm sorry!" He tried to get close and got stuck between the wall and the desk. "Are you all right?"

She rubbed the bruise. Green glitter drifted onto her shoulders. "I'm fine, but I think you mashed his nose."

Roberto felt around and found a misshapen nostril. In a mournful tone, he said, "Now when I breathe fire, I'll singe myself."

"You're ridiculous." He made her want to laugh again, and that would never do. Laughter would indicate softening, and if there was one thing Tiffany had taught her, it was that a man should work if he wanted a woman, and then work some more. Besides, Brandi might still love Roberto. She might still want him. But he had lied by omission . . . although now she understood why . . .

Hastily, before she could think of more reasons to become sympathetic, she said, "So you trapped Mossimo. Did Aiden come through?"

"Yes. The night of the sting, after you went storming out the door, I met my half brother."

She leaned forward, her interest well and truly caught. "Your father's child by another woman?"

"Carrick Manly. He's the only legitimate son of billionaire industrialist Nathan Manly."

Memory stirred. "Nathan Manly. Didn't he steal all the capital from his collapsing industry about ten or fifteen years ago and flee to South America?"

"That's the rumor. I thought that on my mother's side I was the descendant of an ancient clan of jewel thieves. It turns out I'm also the son of the corrupt man who stole the livelihood of thousands of his employees and stockholders." Roberto laughed bitterly. "He also, before he left, spread his sperm throughout the land, impregnating young women indiscriminately and without conscience. I'm one of those who knows how many of his children. Of his *sons*—apparently he fathered only sons."

"So you have a whole family spread out across the country and you don't know who they are?" She could almost hear her mother's voice in her head. *Don't feel sorry for him, Brandi! Don't you dare! He hasn't given you a single gift today!*

But he sounded so grim and sad. He was a man who had known his place in the world. Then his identity had been whisked away and replaced by uncertainty. Being Roberto, he hadn't moaned or complained; he'd taken action, and now the mystery he had sought to solve had deepened.

"Carrick is tracking down my brothers. He wants whatever information they have about his father."

Brandi noted that Roberto didn't call Nathan his own father. His father was the count.

"Carrick's mother has been accused by the federal government of being in collusion with Nathan to steal the money. Carrick says she's innocent. Certainly she has no money. I don't know, but I told him I would help him find my brothers. For him. And for me." Roberto tried to squeeze closer to her. "No one else knows the whole truth, Brandi. Only me . . . and you."

She stared at him, trying to resist the appeal of a man who *did* trust her enough to confide in her.

"Tell me, did I forever ruin my chances to love you as you deserve to be loved?"

Don't let him seduce you with green scales and big white teeth! "Take off that stupid dragon suit."

"I have sworn to wear this until you agree to marry me." He put his claw over his heart.

"That is the dumbest thing I've ever heard." Which it was. Also the most romantic.

"So tell me you'll be my bride."

"Tell me one reason I should marry you, Roberto." *Oops.* Impatience had driven her to indicate how very much he charmed her.

He knew it, too. "I have two. I love you. How can I not? And when you thought I was in trouble, you came to rescue me. No woman has ever done that before."

"I was an idiot." That was the real problem. She'd gone off to rescue a man who didn't need rescuing.

"No. You were a woman in love." His voice took on that warm, intimate tone he used during sex.

"Like I said—an idiot." When she thought about how humiliated she'd felt when those FBI agents poured into the restaurant, she could . . . she could shoot Joseph again. The little weasel. "But I'm not going to be an idiot anymore. You made a fool of me, and I don't trust you."

"How can you not? I've told you what no one knows. I trust you with everything I am." As he took a step toward her, his large, scaly foot kicked over the trash can. It clattered against the desk. Wadded-up papers rolled across the floor. "Can you learn to trust me again?

I'll spend my life making you happy." He scooped up her hand with his claw and raised it to his teeth. "I beg you, Brandi, please marry me."

She looked at her fingers. They were covered with green glitter. She looked at him. He was an insensitive jerk who never stopped to think that he might be hurting her by dragging her along on his adventure. Yet he flattered her because he had been unable to leave her behind.

And he was sensitive enough to recognize the importance of a dragon in her life. . . .

"Just a minute." Opening her briefcase, she located her PDA in its pocket. With her stylus, she flipped through her lists until she found:

Qualities Required in a Man.
1. Honest
2. Dependable
3. Goal-oriented
4. Sober . . .

She pushed ERASE ALL.

The list disappeared forever.

Carefully she placed the PDA back into her briefcase, shut it, and turned back to Roberto. "Take off the dragon costume and we'll *talk* about the *possibility* of marriage."

He crowed like he'd already won.

Man, he was irritating. "I said *talk.*"

"I have a gift for you."

Irritating, but he knew just the right words to say. "What gift?"

"Can you see the zipper under the dragon's arm?" He twisted sideways.

"Yes. What do you have for me?" She pulled it down.

"A ring."

"I threw the last diamond ring at the toilet." She hoped he realized what that meant, coming from Tiffany's daughter.

"It's not a diamond. Open the zipper wide. Can you see my pocket?"

"Yes." He was wearing a T-shirt and jeans that fit like a glove.

"Get the ring out."

So she had to grope him. He was a very clever strategist. Slowly she slid her hand into his pocket. His hip was firm against her hand, tempting and warm, and she just stood there a minute, her eyes closed, as she relished the chance to touch him once more.

She was so easy.

"Are you having trouble finding it?" He sounded amused and pleased.

"Yeah! I mean, no, it's right here." She delved all the way to the bottom and felt the small, smooth circle. She drew it out, then stared at the old, worn yellow gold and the polished stone in puzzlement. She'd seen this before. On Mossimo's hand. "It's Mossimo's ring."

"No." He touched her cheek with his claw. "It's the Contini ring, stolen by one of my ancestors so many years ago its origins are lost in myth. The head of the Continis wears that ring. My *nonno* wore it until he married; then he gave it to Nonna with love and honor. She wore it until she died; then my *nonno* put it back on his finger. It should never have left him until the moment he passed on the mantle as head of the Continis."

"How did he lose it?" As if she couldn't guess.

"When Mossimo smashed Nonno's hand, he stole the ring."

When she thought how she and Roberto had faced off against that beast, she wanted to faint from fear and beam with pride. "And how did you get it back?"

Roberto opened the dragon's mouth and grinned at her. "At the Stuffed Dog, I lifted it off Mossimo when I threw him."

He looked so pleased, so mischievous, she couldn't hold it back anymore. She laughed. "You are so bad!"

"Nonno told me to give the ring to you." Roberto put his scaly arm around her shoulders. "I would be honored if you'd wear it and add my name to yours."

She carefully placed the ring on the desk. She laid her head on his scaly chest. "I do like dragons, but I like Roberto better."

In a flash the two of them started tugging, trying to free him from the costume that encased him.

They thumped around Sanjin's office.

"There's got to be another zipper."

"Don't you know how you got in here?"

"The person at the shop dressed me, and I didn't know if you were ever going to let me out." As they struggled to free his head, his tail repeatedly hit the door.

"You liar. You knew all you had to do was bat those beautiful dark eyes at me and I'd melt." She found another zipper. "Here. Right here. That's it!"

"That's not true." He almost tumbled over.

She caught him. They teetered on the verge of falling. "You just don't want to admit it until we've got you out of the costume."

"Shouldn't you be glad to marry a wise man?"

She jerked on the ridge on his back, and suddenly his head was free, his shoulders were free, and she could see his face without gazing through white pointed teeth.

The tussle suddenly stopped. They stared at each other, and Brandi could think of nothing but how much she loved him.

"Give me the ring," he whispered.

Without looking down, she groped until she found it. She handed it to him.

Taking her left hand, he slid it on her third finger.

She looked at the smooth green stone and knew she held the weight of Roberto's history in her hand. Slowly she said, "It doesn't matter who your father is, or your grandfather, or your mother. I treasure them all, but only because they brought you into this world. For me. Just for me."

"Yes, I am just for you. And you are just for me." Still half in the dragon costume, he caught her in his arms and kissed her. "The ring . . . do you know what they call the Contini ring?"

She kissed him back. "What?"

"The dragon's scale."

She laughed. And laughed.

Fate had an interesting sense of humor.

They fell over in Sanjin's office.

In the corridor outside, Sanjin heard the sound of Brandi's mirth and again heard the rhythmic thump of the tail against the door. With an exasperated sigh, he walked away.

Tongue in Chic

✑

For my wonderful editor, Kara Cesare,
who suggests and titles and revises with tact and genius.
Here's to a long and fruitful relationship!

Acknowledgments

Thank you to Kara Welsh for a fabulous promotion and publishing schedule, and to Anthony Ramondo and the NAL art department for gorgeous covers that fly off the shelves.

And as always, thanks to the Squawkers, friends, booksellers, and fans who make writing and life in general such a pleasure. All my love.

Prologue

*I*n the fourth-floor studio in the majestic Waldemar House, Isabelle Benjamin finished the last painting she would ever do there. Over the past week, the light had been good, the humidity oppressive but manageable, and the temperature had never topped eighty degrees. Now, when she stood back and studied the canvas, she nodded in satisfaction.

This was, without a doubt, her best work to date.

Taking a thin brush, she dipped it in black paint and, with a flourish, she signed her name.

She covered the pots of paint and cleaned her palette. She wiped her brushes on a rag, washed them in the sink, and carefully arranged them on the table. Untying her apron, she hung it on the hook.

She didn't know why she bothered. When she was gone, Bradley would throw everything that reminded him of her into the garbage. But she was betting—betting her daughter's future, in fact—on the probability that he couldn't stand to throw away her painting. If she was wrong . . . well, it would be a loss to the art world.

But then, no one would ever know.

She picked up the canvas. It was large and awkward and still too wet; nevertheless, she carefully maneuvered it into the heavy gilt frame. She tapped at the nails that would keep it in place, then turned the whole thing around and studied it. Her fingers had smeared a little of the detail along the edges, but she'd figured on that and created an unfocused background that hid the damage. The paint would seal the canvas into the frame; no one would try to separate the two. Certainly not Bradley . . . A bitter smile twisted her lips, and a single tear escaped and trickled down her cheek.

But she dashed it away. Enough of that. She'd cried too much over the last two years.

Her marriage was over now, and past time, too.

Picking up the painting in both hands, she carried it down to the third-floor nursery.

The room was absolutely perfect. Pink ruffled curtains hung in starched splendor at the long, old-fashioned windows. A colorful alphabet danced across the wall, and each teddy bear occupied its proper niche. The gleaming antique crib was fitted with white sheets over an appropriately firm mattress, and the sleeping three-month-old inside was swaddled in a pink blanket, and rested on her stomach to discourage colic. Her sweet pink lips moved occasionally as she dreamed of milk, and Isabelle's heart broke again when she remembered how her husband and her mother-in-law had bullied her out of nursing her child.

But no more bullying for Isabelle. No more cold, hard, proper nursery for Sharon. They were escaping. Going free.

The sour-faced nanny sat in the rocker reading a *Reader's Digest* condensed version of *Les Misérables*.

Isabelle appreciated the irony.

At Isabelle's entrance, Mrs. Graham stood as a gesture of courteous—and false—respect. "May I help you, madam?"

"I've come for Sharon. Would you carry her downstairs for me?"

"If madam would allow an experienced nurse to advise her, after a baby has been put down for the night it's not a good idea to disturb her. Such an action sets a bad precedent and leads to reprehensible habits later in life."

"According to you, so does holding her when she cries and feeding her when she's hungry."

Mrs. Graham stiffened in offended horror.

Isabelle had never spoken to her that way before. Before, she'd tried to make the best of a bad situation. Tried to compromise and create change from within.

But now she had a child to consider. She couldn't allow her baby to grow up loveless, stifled, fit into a box furnished with white lace gloves and hats held under the chin with an elastic band, friends picked by their income and family background, and a debutante ball at seventeen that led to another tearstained marriage, another loveless childhood.

"Please put the knit hat on Sharon, wrap her in her down blanket, and bring her to me. I'll be in the library," Isabelle instructed.

"As you wish, madam." Mrs. Graham bobbed a curtsy that mocked Isabelle and promised that another phone call would be made to Mrs. Benjamin.

Isabelle didn't care. Not even the threat of her mother-in-law's displeasure could dissuade her from her course.

She walked down the two flights to the library. The painting, held carefully away from her body, got heavy. Her arms grew tired. And this part . . . this part she dreaded more than any other. But when it was over . . . it was over forever. And she'd be relieved. So relieved.

She walked into the lofty room with its shelves packed with leather-bound books, its massive desk and old-fashioned chair, and the alcove where two snarling lions guarded a marble fireplace.

As she expected, she found Bradley in his easy chair, his bourbon on the table beside him, his smoking cigar between his fingers.

He was a handsome man with a shock of dark brown hair. When

she first met him, his appearance had been what turned Isabelle's head. That, and the flattering experience of having a wealthy older man paying court to her. He'd said all the right things. He'd enjoyed her conversation. He'd been indifferent to her poverty.

Most important, he'd admired her art. For the first time in her whole life, someone who'd visited the Louvre and Florence and the Taj Mahal had seen in her paintings enough promise to call in the foremost art expert in the world.

Bjorn Kelly had been half Scandinavian, half Irish, with an eye patch, a limp, and an incredible charisma that mesmerized and enticed. He also had no patience with being dragged halfway across the world by the infatuated Bradley to look at a stupid woman's paintings—until he'd seen them. Then he'd yelled at her for bad technique and no vision, told her to stop drawing like a girl, and given Bradley the names of two American art teachers worthy of her genius.

That was the term Bjorn used—*genius*.

When Isabelle remembered that moment and how her love for Bradley had swept through her heart, she wanted to break the painting she held over his stubborn, handsome head.

Instead she walked with firm footsteps across the library—no more tiptoeing around—and leaned the painting against the fireplace facing him.

As if stung, he half rose from his chair. "What the hell is that? Some kind of cruel going-away present?"

"It's a gesture of my appreciation, Bradley. Without you, I would never have been able to create a painting like this." She dragged the wooden chair away from the desk and over to the fireplace.

"Without me—and that damned Kelly." Bradley's lips were so stiff they hardly moved as he spoke.

"Yes. Damned Kelly helped me, too."

"Don't be smart with me," Bradley snapped.

Isabelle looked him right in the eyes. "Or what?"

The silence between them grew and seethed until Mrs. Graham bustled in, breaking the spell.

"Sharon is still asleep," she said, her tone making it clear that she didn't expect the condition to continue, and that it was all Isabelle's fault. Mrs. Graham was an officious, judgmental woman who for thirty years had served the best Southern familes and fancied herself above Bradley Benjamin's upstart wife. Mrs. Graham would be delighted to see the back of Isabelle.

She wouldn't be quite so delighted to see her employment disappear at the same time.

"Wait there," Isabelle told her. "I'll take the baby when I'm done." She stood on the seat and lifted the old painting off the hook. She stepped down, walked over to the bookshelves, and placed it there. Picking up her painting, she stepped on the chair again. It rocked under the weight of her and the heavy canvas.

Bradley surged to his feet, caught her waist, and balanced her.

The two of them stood motionless, joined by the sensation of touch and all the old feelings: lust, fury, pain . . . so much pain.

Then Bradley stepped away and wiped his palms on his pants.

The insult broke what was left of her heart, and she almost doubled over.

But she couldn't lie to herself. She had known what would happen when he accused and she acceded.

Her hands trembled as she placed the wire over the hooks. She straightened the painting as well as she could, then asked, "Is it level?"

"Yes." His voice was gruff.

"I'm leaving you my best work."

"You're a damned whore." He rejected her with his voice, with his words, with his stance and his accusing gaze.

Mrs. Graham inhaled with shock.

"I know." Isabelle looked down at him. "But I won't contest a divorce or ask for support. I won't take anything of yours. You're free to find the woman of your dreams." She stepped off the chair and dragged it back to the desk. Going to Mrs. Graham, she took Sharon and hugged her close to her heart.

The baby stretched and wiggled, opened her eyes and closed them again. "Do you want to say good-bye to her?" Isabelle asked Bradley.

"Why?" He seated himself in his easy chair and picked up his bourbon. "She's nothing to me."

Any man who could say that about the infant he had cradled had ice in his veins.

Isabelle was doing the best thing for herself and her child. "You're right." She nodded and walked to the door.

When she turned back to look at him one more time, he was sitting in his easy chair, staring at the painting over the top of the fireplace.

1

Lightning flashed. Shadows of bare limbs clawed the tangled path, and the lithe, black-clad trespasser stumbled. Paused. Shuddered. Then continued toward the Victorian house set high above the ocean. The roar of thunder shook the ground, and the next flash of lightning followed hard on its heels, blistering the massive structure with harsh white light. The spires on the fourth-story cupola stabbed at the roiling clouds, the wind gauge spun wildly, and on the beach the waves growled and pounded. The posts on the second-story balcony stretched and twisted, and a hard gust of wind drove the first burst of rain up on the porch.

The figure ran lightly up the steps and toward the imposing double doors. The large silver key slid neatly into the lock. It turned easily and was quickly pocketed. One black-glove-encased hand rested on the beveled glass, then pressed, and without a sound the door swung open.

No lamp lit the interior, but the intruder confidently strode into the foyer.

Then the lightning struck again, blasting away the shadows. Thunder boomed. The figure halted and spun in a circle.

The wide hall soared two stories above the floor. Gold blazed off every picture frame, every finial, off the coved ceiling. Stern eyes watched from nineteenth-century portraits, and wide stairs stretched up and out of sight. The blast of thunder made the crystal chandelier shimmer, and the prisms sent colored light shivering across the walls.

Then the lightning was gone. Silence settled like dust in the house.

Shoulders hunched, the intruder crept toward the second entrance on the left. The beam of a tiny flashlight slid around the room, touching briefly on shelves crowded with leather-bound books, the massive carved desk, the incongruously modern office chair. In an alcove in one corner of the room, two overstuffed chairs faced a tall fireplace finished with marble and flanked by two snarling stone lions.

The flashlight blinked out, but stayed in the intruder's hand. Each step fell soft and sure on the wide, custom-woven rug, headed in a straight line for the cozy sitting area.

The figure halted behind one of the chairs and stared up at the painting over the fireplace. The flashlight flicked on again and scanned the wall, once, twice. The picture there, that of a stodgy twentieth-century businessman and his dog, drove the intruder to cast the light around the room in an increasing frenzy. "Oh, Grandmother. You promised. You *promised*. Where . . . ?"

The overhead light flared.

A man's deep Southern voice demanded, "What are you doing here?"

The intruder half turned. One gloved hand flew up to protect against the brightness.

A tall, dark-haired man stood in the doorway, his hand on the light switch, his face craggy, tanned, and harsh.

He was the most striking, arrogant, handsome man Natalie Meadow Szarvas had ever seen.

The lightning flashed so fiercely static electricity skittered across the floor. In the yard something broke with a loud crack. The thunder roared and the windows shook.

She'd descended into hell.

She tried to run.

Her feet tangled in the fringe of the rug.

She tripped.

She grabbed for support. Missed. Hit the floor—hard.

Her head and the lion's head collided.

The lion won.

When the stars had ceased sparking behind her closed eyelids, she took a long, trembling breath. Her bones ached from hitting the floor. The fringed rug smelled good, like citrus and sandalwood. Her head . . . her head really hurt. She lifted her hand to touch the pain at her temple.

Someone caught her wrist. "Don't. It's bleeding."

The man. The one with the contemptuous brown eyes. How had he managed to get from the door to her side?

The explanation was easy. She'd been unconscious. But she didn't remember being unconscious. She remembered only . . . she remembered seeing *him*.

"Sir, should I call the police?" Another man. Eager. Quiet. Efficient.

"Call the doctor," Mr. Arrogant said.

"Then the police?"

"Just the doctor."

"Yes, sir." The other sounded disapproving—and obedient. His footsteps retreated.

Mr. Arrogant pressed something soft to her forehead.

She winced and tried to flinch away.

"Leave it," he instructed. "You're bleeding on the rug."

"Okay," she muttered. *Wouldn't want to bleed on the freaking expensive rug.*

"Open your eyes," he said.

She must be mistaken. This couldn't be the handsome one. A guy who used a tone that rude to a girl sprawled bleeding on his floor couldn't be attractive.

She opened her eyes. She looked up at him.

He looked back at her, a cool, assessing stare.

Her heart stopped. Her breath stopped. She was immobile.

Because she was right about one thing: He wasn't handsome—he was harsh, breathtaking, his glance striking like lightning and leaving her dead.

And what a way to go. If this was her punishment for trying to steal a priceless painting, then burglary had just become her way of life. "Wow," she said again.

Mr. Arrogant sat on his heels beside her. He wore a crumpled, starched white shirt with the cuffs rolled up.

Nice arms.

And a pair of blue jeans that caressed his thighs.

He held Meadow's wrist in one hand, and pressed a swathe of white to her forehead with the other, framing her in his arms, sheltering her with his shoulders.

Her heart jumped into a frenzy of action.

"Who are you?" he asked.

"Um . . ."

Apparently she wasn't fast enough with a reply, because he shot a second question at her. "What are you doing here?"

"Here?" She lifted her head and tried to look around. The instantaneous headache and nausea made her relax back against the floor, close her eyes, and mutter, "I'm going to barf."

Gently he placed her hand on the cloth on her head. She heard sounds—him standing, moving away, coming back. "If you must, here's a basin."

She opened her eyes the smallest chink and looked.

He held an etched-glass vase with gold decoration, absolutely exquisite, done in the Regeletto design.

Aghast, she asked, "Are you insane? That's a Honesdale vase, an original. I can't barf in that!"

For a second, the merest twitch of an eye, she thought she saw amusement.

But no. Mr. Arrogant was as forbidding as ever when he said, "Of course. Pardon me. I lost my head." He glanced around him. "Can you barf in a Limoges punch bowl?"

"No problem. But"—she took long breaths—"I think I'm okay now. I just have to be careful and not sit up."

"You have a concussion."

His certainty made her faintly belligerent. "You're no doctor."

"No, of course not. I wouldn't have sent for one if I were."

"Ha." She'd met way too many doctors lately, and while he acted superior enough to be a physician, he was too intense to fit the medical profile.

He continued, "But it doesn't take a surgeon to see that you hit the lion hard enough to break his tooth."

Cautiously she checked out the lion. He still snarled, but lopsidedly. "I hope that's not an omen."

"If it is, I don't know how to read it."

The other guy, tall, bulky, with Asian eyes and a dark brown complexion, returned and hovered. "The doctor's on her way."

"Sam, make sure I'm not bothered."

Without a glance or any acknowledgment of her, Sam left, shutting the door behind him.

"So who are you?" Mr. Arrogant slid the clip off her head—and smiled as her hair tumbled free.

People, especially men, tended to smile when they saw the fall of shining copper curls. In fact, people, especially men, tended to smile at her all the time, no matter what.

Not this stern-faced, hawk-nosed interrogator. His smile vanished at once, like a mistake he wished to call back.

She had more composure now, no desire to explain her mission, and a few questions of her own. "Who are *you*?"

"I'm Devlin Fitzwilliam."

Which told her absolutely nothing. "And you're here because . . . ?"

"I live here."

She stared.

"I own this house," he said helpfully. "The one you broke into. The one with the Honesdale vase and the now snaggletoothed lion."

"You own Waldemar?" She struggled to comprehend the incomprehensible. "What about the other guy . . . ? The one who used to own it?"

"Bradley Benjamin? Is that who you're asking about?" Devlin picked up her wrist again. He stripped off her black leather glove. He kissed . . . *Oh, my.* He kissed her fingertips. "Which Bradley Benjamin? The third or the fourth?"

"I, um, don't know." She hadn't prepared for this conversation. She had planned to break in, grab the painting, and depart, not talk to a guy whose ruthless eyes demanded the truth and whose lips carried on a dialogue all their own.

"Bradley Benjamin the third sold me the house," Devlin said. "Bradley Benjamin the fourth—I call him *Four,* which irks him no end—likes to visit and whine."

"Oh." Grandmother was wrong. So wrong. Bradley Benjamin *had* sold the house. This stranger *did* live here. The painting was *not* in its place.

And Meadow was in deep, deep trouble.

"Who do you think you are, breaking in here?"

"I'm . . . Meadow." Not Natalie Szarvas. That was her professional name, and if he knew that, she didn't stand a chance of getting out of this mess. "I don't . . . I can't . . ." How stupid was this? She should have considered that she might get caught. Prepared some kind of story.

But Grandmother had been so sure . . . and now some guy with cold eyes and warm lips kissed her fingers and cross-examined her, and soon she'd find herself on the way to jail. And how was she going to explain that to her parents living just outside the small town of Blythe in Washington State, when they thought she was teaching a glassblowing seminar in Atlanta?

"You don't remember?" Devlin kissed her wrist.

Nice. Very nice.

His lips, not his questions.

"That's right. I don't remember. Because I . . . I . . . I have amnesia!" *Good one, Meadow! That's thinking on your feet!*

Lightning struck nearby. Thunder boomed.

Meadow jumped. It was as if God Himself called her a liar.

And Devlin's mouth twisted. He didn't believe her.

Hastily she added, "I don't remember what I'm doing here. I've probably had some kind of mental breakdown." A pretty clever lie, because what was the worst that could happen? The police would send her to an asylum for a few days' evaluation; then she'd be out on her own and she could try again.

Or perhaps the Almighty would send a bolt of lightning to strike her dead.

"When you didn't recognize me at once, I was afraid of this." Devlin gazed into her eyes so soulfully she didn't dare blink. "My darling, somehow you managed to find your way back."

"Huh?" She had a bad feeling about this.

Tenderly he gathered her into his arms. "I know you don't remember—but you're my wife."

2

"Are you crazy? We're not married!" Someone was shouting, and the noise made Meadow's head throb. Because, she realized, the shouting came from her own mouth.

"You poor thing. You don't remember, but we married eight months ago."

Lightning struck. Lights flickered.

"Right! That's why you welcomed me with open arms!"

"You left me. On one of the worst days of my life you disappeared, and I didn't know what happened to you. I've been worried to death, and when you showed up, hale and hearty and pretending not to know me, I . . . I just . . ." He did a good imitation of a man choking on his emotions.

Except he wasn't choking on his emotions; he was trying to think of a new lie to tell. She knew it—because she'd never met him before. Ever. She would remember him.

Any woman would remember him. He had the face of a dark angel and the eloquence of Satan's right-hand man. The flashes from outside danced across his craggy features like stage lighting in hell.

"You just what?" she insisted.

"All the months of uncertainty, of not knowing whether you were alive or dead. I wanted to shake you. But your poor bruised head saved you, and now I've got my senses back and I can hold you. Hold you as I've longed to."

Which was tightly and with an intimacy that took the edge off her pain and made her heart beat too fast. Of course, she'd had a scare. Probably that was why her heart thumped. It couldn't be the pleasure of discovering that the scent of citrus and sandalwood came from his skin, or that she could see the shadow of his beard darkening the cleft in his chin. Beneath his shirt, his chest had that taut warmth that made her want to run her hand over his pecs and down his belly. . . . Without a doubt he worked out, and while she liked a guy who was, as her grandmother would have said, built like a brick shithouse, Meadow was perfectly happy to view the bricks from a distance. In her experience, men who kept themselves buff were self-absorbed, and a brick shithouse–worthy man who wasn't self-absorbed would be deadly to her peace of mind.

Especially if he smelled good.

Good heavens. Was her nose buried in his chest?

She pulled away.

He gathered her closer again. "What caused the amnesia, darling?" he asked solicitously. "Did you hit your head then, too?"

"I don't know. I don't remember ever being with you." *Pin him down.* "Where did you say we were married?"

"In Majorca."

"Majorca." *Majorca?*

"A beautiful island off the southeast coast of Spain."

"Right." She didn't feel sick anymore. More like . . . giddy.

"I have a home there."

"Well, of course you do."

"You don't believe me?"

"I believe you've got a home on Majorca."

"And you can take my word, my darling amnesiac, that we met and married there. After all, you don't remember anything different, do you?"

She looked at him . . . at his tanned, rugged face, his dark, rumpled hair, his brown eyes . . .

A man like this—a man whose perpetual expression was harsh intensity—made it difficult to imagine he could be amused. But he had to be . . . didn't he? Was he punishing her for breaking into his house by playing a practical joke? Did the absurdity of the situation make him want to laugh?

Did he ever laugh?

She got the feeling she would wait a long time before he grinned and admitted he was teasing.

Which left her where?

"My head hurts." From trying to figure a way out of this maze.

At the sound of voices in the foyer, he glanced around. "The doctor's here."

"Wow. You got a doctor to make a house call? I thought they only did that on old reruns." In her experience, doctors never did anything to make matters easy on the patient.

"I hired Dr. Apps to be on call for the hotel. You've given us the opportunity for a dry run. Keep your hand on my handkerchief." He pressed Meadow closer to his chest, slid his arm under her knees, and very slowly stood with her.

"A hotel? What hotel?" She grabbed the soft linen as it slipped.

"Good girl." He spoke to her as if she were an obedient dog. "This hotel. The Secret Garden."

"This is a hotel?" Maybe her brain *was* affected by her fall. Or hell had frozen over.

Devlin had a sure way of moving that minimized the dizziness and, yes, he probably did it so she didn't throw up on his rug, but he made her feel secure, the way a Honesdale bowl must feel when she cradled it.

"The grand opening is in three weeks," he told Meadow; then his attention left her, and he spoke to someone else. "Dr. Apps, thank you for coming." Placing Meadow on the couch, he went to intercept the doctor at the door. "Meadow fell. . . ."

As he gave Dr. Apps the details, Meadow carefully lifted her head and looked.

Dr. Apps looked back and smiled with that mechanical interest medical people showed when faced with an unspeakably boring case. She had nice teeth. Nice face with a minimum of makeup, and lipstick that was a nice shade of pink. Nice, well exercised, extremely tall body. Nice brown hair done up with a nice clip.

Talk about unspeakably boring.

With Devlin's attention and his scent and his body elsewhere, Meadow relaxed against the cushions and tried to organize her thoughts.

Bradley Benjamin had sold Waldemar.

Devlin Fitzwilliam had bought it and was turning it into a hotel.

Her beautiful plan was in tatters.

The paintings had probably all been moved according to some decorator's idea of where they would be most attractively placed. Or they'd been appraised and sold. . . . No, she would have heard about that.

So what to do?

Stay here and poke around, of course.

But Fitzwilliam claimed she was his wife, and she didn't know why. Or what he wanted.

Of course, there was the usual thing a man wanted from a woman, but he wasn't a rapist. She snorted. More likely he had to defend himself against hordes of pursuing women. And why bother with a concussed female when he could have someone like the doctor? The doctor whose voice she heard crooning at Devlin. The doctor who couldn't have made her interest more obvious if she'd wrapped herself in pearls and presented herself on a clamshell.

Meadow moaned softly.

No response. Her *husband* kept talking to her *doctor,* and neither one of them paid her a bit of attention.

She moaned louder.

"Darling!" Devlin returned to her side.

That's better.

"Let's have a look at her." The doctor nudged him aside.

He went easily.

"Hello . . . I'm sorry, I don't know your name."

Meadow had heard Devlin tell Dr. Apps her name, but she was willing to play along. "Meadow. I'm Meadow."

"Tell me what happened, Meadow," Dr. Apps invited. She wore a blue smock with big pockets loaded with all kinds of doctor stuff, and she listened to Meadow's heart, shone a light in Meadow's eyes, examined Meadow's bump on the head, and listened with seeming inattention while Meadow confessed to breaking in, falling down, and blacking out.

"How long were you out?" Dr. Apps asked.

"I don't know. Long enough for him to get to me." Devlin stood off to the side, and Meadow indicated him.

"How long?" Dr. Apps asked him.

"Less than a minute," he answered.

Dr. Apps nodded. "Pupils look good. Nice and even. Eyes are tracking well. Any loss of memory?"

Here it was. Meadow's chance to escape. "You bet. I have amnesia. I don't remember what I'm doing here."

"I thought you said you broke in?" Ruthlessly Dr. Apps cleaned the wound on Meadow's head.

"Sure! He said I did"—she indicated Devlin—"and I'm sure he's got the security cameras to prove it."

Devlin nodded.

Great. When he dragged her into court, they'd show the video and throw her in prison for the rest of her life. "But I don't remember that at all. I don't remember anything."

"But you told me your name." Dr. Apps didn't appear to believe her any more than Devlin did.

"That's the only thing I remember. I don't know my last name." Meadow was starting to feel like Klinger in *M*A*S*H*—trying desperately to convince the doctor that she was crazy. "I only know I woke up with my head bleeding."

"Hmm. How unusual." But Dr. Apps wasn't looking at her. She was staring at Devlin as if he'd said something. Which he hadn't. He was still standing there, impassive and waiting.

"Really." Desperate to get her attention, Meadow got up on her elbows. But that made her head throb, so she slid back down. "You ought to take me to the hospital for a mental evaluation."

Dr. Apps returned her attention to Meadow. "Any nausea?"

"Not anymore," Meadow said.

"She threatened to throw up in a Limoges punch bowl." Devlin perched on the arm of the couch.

"Oh, dear. Oh, no." Dr. Apps pursed those lovely, lipsticked lips in real distress. "Those bowls are exceedingly valuable, Meadow." Obviously the woman fancied herself a connoisseur and Meadow a Philistine.

Devlin made no move to correct her.

Meadow glared at them both. "So's the rug, and at least you can run a bowl through the dishwasher." She savored the sight of Dr. Apps's sputtering horror.

"Darling, stop teasing. You know what happened the last time you ran a Limoges bowl through the dishwasher. All the gilding washed off." Devlin dusted Meadow's forehead with his fingertips. "But I'm afraid she's telling the truth, Dr. Apps. She doesn't remember a thing. She doesn't even remember that she's my wife."

Dr. Apps looked at the two of them. Looked again. And laughed so heartily Meadow would have liked her if she weren't a doctor. "Devlin, you jerk. You set me up, didn't you? You wanted to see how well your emergency medical plan works, and you called me in on a fake case."

He shrugged as if admitting guilt, but answered, "I would hardly bash Meadow over the head to check out your response time."

"So one of your cleaning staff fell and you took advantage of the opportunity." Dr. Apps stuck her stethoscope and her eyeball light into her capacious pocket. She pulled gauze and tape out of her other pocket, and in swift motions and with no care for Meadow's discomfort, bandaged her with tape and gauze. "You would have suckered me completely if not for the story including breaking in *and* having amnesia *and* her being your wife. That last is a little too much to swallow." She patted Meadow on the arm. "Did you make all that up yourself?"

Devlin smirked. "Meadow, next time, stick to the script I give you so we can get through a practice run."

"I did! You're the one who said . . . I told the truth!" *Mostly.*

It would serve them both right if Meadow did barf in a Limoges punch bowl. Unfortunately her nausea had subsided under her indignation at being accused of lying.

Sure, she was committing perjury, but not for such a paltry reason as Dr. Apps imagined.

"She really did hit her head," Devlin pointed out.

"She's going to have a headache, maybe dizziness, maybe irritability. She might need bed rest for a day. Let her make the decision, but no heavy lifting or hard work tomorrow. I'll leave a prescription for pain relief. And tonight someone needs to wake her every hour to make sure she's conscious. Don't worry; she's going to be fine." Dr. Apps talked about Meadow as if she weren't even there, and as Devlin rose, she tucked her hand into his arm. "Now—how did I do on my dry run?"

"Very well. It took you less than ten minutes to arrive." He escorted her toward the door. "I was sorry to wake you, but it was too good an opportunity to miss."

"I understand. Don't hesitate to call whenever you need me."

The thunder cracked again, shaking the sofa and the floor. "Those storms won't stop coming," he said. "I'll send you home in one of my cars."

"It's less than a mile," the doctor protested, but she sounded pleased.

"And you'll get drenched." He sounded firm.

Their voices faded.

Outside, lightning struck and thunder cracked.

Inside, Meadow fumed. Not only did they both patronize her, but the doctor didn't believe she had amnesia. Of course, neither did Devlin, but if she denounced him for saying they were married, she'd have to confess that she didn't have amnesia—and he'd have her thrown in jail. She couldn't fool herself; he looked like the kind of man who would prosecute her to the full extent of the law. He'd probably set his snaggletoothed lion on her.

But if she didn't confess, she was stuck here.

Stuck. Here. At Waldemar. At her grandparents' home, looking for a painting she desperately needed, and which was nowhere in sight.

Her plan had been simple.

Break into Waldemar.

Steal the painting.

Get out of Waldemar.

Sell the painting for an absurd amount of money.

Use the money to pay for her mother's very expensive treatments.

She turned over to stare at the fireplace. That pompous old gentleman mocked her.

No matter how many times she stared at it in disbelief, it never changed. It was the wrong damned picture.

3

*H*ow was that possible?

In Meadow's pocket, the key poked her in the hip. Pulling it out, she looked at the length of silver, the huge teeth, the ornate handle. This she should hide. She might need it again.

Hearing Devlin's footsteps, she hastily poked the key between the couch cushions and the back, down far enough that it wouldn't be easily discovered by the cleaners.

Lightning danced across the portrait, making the haughty gentleman's eyes glint with disapproval. She didn't care. Disapproval of any sort was of no importance to her. Finding the right painting was.

She reclined just as Devlin Fitzwilliam walked back into the room. She looked up at him.

He looked so . . . tall. And . . . austere. And . . . intent. On her.

If he gave a damn about Dr. Apps, he hid his interest well.

"Ready for bed?" Without waiting for an answer, he scooped her into his arms and headed toward the door. "Tell me if you feel sick."

"I'm fine." Except for the fact that he held her against him as comfortingly as a man might hold his beloved wife—and she liked it. She almost felt he wanted her here.

He climbed the long, elegant sweep of stairs. The place smelled of fresh paint and wallpaper glue, and everywhere she looked she saw antique lamps, gilt-framed mirrors, and designer touches that echoed an elegant age. Waldemar had been refurbished into a showcase of comfort and ease.

"It looks great," she mumbled.

"The house? Yes, it came out well." His gaze roamed the corridor, and he looked grimly pleased. "We have a saying in Charleston. 'Too poor to paint, too proud to whitewash.' Bradley Benjamin didn't have the money to maintain the old girl like she deserved. I did the house a favor when I bought it from him."

"And him? Did you do him a favor, too?" So that was why Bradley had sold the house? He was broke?

"No. Old Benjamin and I have a deal—I don't do him favors, and he doesn't call me a bastard. At least, not to my face. Not very often." He turned sideways as he went through a doorway. He carried her through a sitting room decorated with masculine furniture in claret tones. "Here we go."

She caught a glimpse of a huge, lush bedroom painted a warm gold and touched with claret highlights. They entered a huge en suite bathroom with swathes of black marble, a black tub, a sleek and gigantic glass shower done in claret tile, and fresh gold chrysanthemums in blue Chinese vases.

He placed her on the counter, her head against the wall, her feet in the sink. The cold from the marble leaked through her slacks, chilled her flesh, and brought her halfway to perkiness.

"I imagine you want to use the bathroom before you go to bed." He looked down, his eyes hooded and enigmatic, and he didn't take his arms away.

"Yeah." He was warm. Toasty.

"Can you manage on your own, or shall I . . . ?" He tugged at the hem of her black turtleneck T-shirt.

"Hey!" She caught at his hand. "I can do it!"

A lovely sort of half smile cocked his mouth. "Are you sure?"

She wouldn't have thought it, but this austere man looked almost . . . charming. "I can do it. You go out. If I need help, I'll call."

"Promise? I don't want you to hit your head again."

"None of us want that. I'll call you if I need to." She turned, dangled her feet off the counter, and watched as he strolled away.

"There are new toothbrushes and whatever else you need in the top drawer. There's a robe on the hook by the shower." He walked with a long-legged grace that made her fingertips tingle.

She would really enjoy touching his ass.

He turned at the door and lifted his eyebrows. "Are you sure you don't need me?"

Maybe. But not for the reason he was thinking.

She slid to her feet. "I'm not dizzy. I'm not sick."

"You just don't remember who you are."

"I certainly don't remember being your wife."

"I promise I'll do everything in my power to remind you." He studied her openmouthed consternation, then firmly shut the door behind him.

"Oh, no, you won't!" she said to the closed door.

It didn't answer.

She looked into the mirror at her pale, strained face, at the white bandage partially taped to her hair, at the faint smear of blood on her forehead.

She'd lived through the last two grueling years with her faith in good thoughts and good living intact. She'd faced the challenges with a smile, knowing she kept everyone's spirits up.

Now she looked like hell. She felt like hell. And she blamed Devlin Fitzwilliam.

Her mother would make the case that Meadow was responsible for the events of the day.

In an excess of guilt, love, and determination, Meadow dropped her head into her hands. Her mother. If her mother knew where Meadow was and what she was doing . . . Meadow moaned at the thought.

"You need to go to bed and get a good night's sleep," she said to herself. "Tomorrow you'll know what to do." Because tonight she was so confused.

She had lied to Devlin about having amnesia. Did he believe her?

Of course not. He didn't, did he?

He'd lied about their being married. If he didn't believe she had amnesia, then he knew she knew they weren't married.

Possibly he was trying to wring a confession out of her. But it didn't feel that way. The way he acted, he wanted her here. And why? What was he up to?

Worried, she pulled off her sweater. On a good day, her boobs were an A cup, and this athletic bra mashed her flat. She didn't have much of a rear end, either, and her black leggings, the ones she wore to yoga, hugged her body. Devlin had seen the package, so clearly he wasn't after her voluptuous body.

She leaned on the counter and stared into the mirror.

Or her face, which at this moment looked singularly cheerless and unappealing. And unattractively pale and sweaty. And worried. Really worried.

So what was he after? What did he want? What was his plan—and *why*? Why was he doing this?

She opened the drawer and found every soap and lotion a woman could want, all in sample-size bottles. She brushed her hair back and washed her face, avoiding the bandage. She slipped out of her shoes, her pants, her socks, and dropped them in a heap on the floor. She put on the plush white bathrobe. Like all hotel robes, it was huge. The hem brushed her at midcalf, and she had to roll up the sleeves to see her hands. She tied the belt into a knot, then opened the door.

The bedroom was empty.

He hadn't gone far. He'd promised to come if she called, and she recognized a man who kept his word.

She climbed into the tall four-poster bed and sighed as the mattress, the pad, the cool, soft sheets enveloped her. She pulled the comforter up; it was light yet lavish. Nine feet above her, the ceiling glowed the same warm gold color as the wall, and the intricate cove molding was painted to look like cherrywood.

The artist in her admired the craftsmanship. The exhausted woman wanted nothing more than to close her eyes and go to sleep.

Except . . .

Did this guy want her here? A weird idea—but why else would he tell such a whopper of a lie? Why would he say she was his wife, and go through such incredible gyrations to keep her at . . . what did he call it? The Secret Garden?

She knew only one thing for sure—his reasons for trapping her here could not be good.

~

Meadow's beautiful blue eyes, the eyes that had betrayed her, were closed in slumber. Her copper-tinted hair glowed like a nimbus on the pillow around her face, and the flickering lightning caught each shining strand. Her skin was tinted like a peach and was—Devlin ran his fingertips over her cheek—just as soft. Her lower lip was rosy and slightly swollen—every time she told her silly lie, she bit into the tender skin.

The doctor's bandage was a large white blot on her forehead, and that, combined with the dark circles under her eyes, gave her a fragile appearance.

He suspected that was a mirage.

He knew so much about her already—and so little.

She had a name, Meadow. But he didn't know exactly who she was.

She was a thief, and here for a reason. But he didn't know what it was.

When it came to art, she had a discerning eye. But he didn't know what she did.

Yet he knew more than she could ever imagine. People in the

South had embarrassingly long memories, especially when a scandal was involved, and Meadow's grandmother had been the biggest scandal in a generation. No one in Amelia Shores had ever stopped talking about Isabelle, or her affairs, or how thoroughly she had humbled the proud Bradley Benjamin.

Devlin had never met Isabelle, but he liked her.

For years, when he was young, Bradley Benjamin had made Devlin's life hell. The reasons were myriad and diverse—two hundred and fifty years of rivalry between the Fitzwilliams and the Benjamins, Bradley Benjamin's old-fashioned dislike for successful women like Devlin's mother, and most of all, Bradley Benjamin's pure, unmitigated hatred for a child born out of wedlock. A bastard.

Like Devlin.

Bradley despised him. And why?

Because Devlin reminded Bradley of his own well-publicized failure, and the humiliation that had followed him ever since.

So when the opportunity for revenge presented itself, Devlin had seized Waldemar, storming the ancient bastion of Benjamin superiority. Even better—the sheer stupidity and incredible incompetence of Benjamin's own son had been the reason he'd been able to obtain their ancestral home as his own. And what a lovely, delicious dollop of warm pleasure on the cold dish of revenge—rather than living in the home, which Bradley would have hated and mocked, Devlin had turned the grand old mansion into a posh hotel.

That was what bastards did.

He smiled down at Meadow, an unpleasant curve of the lips.

Now, sleeping in his bed was the possibility of more and even better revenge.

Would Bradley Benjamin recognize Isabelle's granddaughter?

Probably.

Would he wait and cringe, fearing that moment when everyone in Amelia Shores identified her, and all the gossip started up again?

Definitely.

Would he give a damn that Devlin had married her?

Yes. Just . . . yes.

Bradley Benjamin hated Isabelle, but she had once been his, and if there was one trait Devlin shared with Bradley, it was their possessiveness about their property. He would hate to think of his former wife's granddaughter in the filthy clutches of the Fitzwilliam bastard.

Devlin touched Meadow's throat and noted the contrast between his tanned hand against her fair, freckled skin.

Bradley would hate to think of Devlin and Meadow thrashing together on a bed.

Best of all, the whole maneuver would cost Devlin nothing.

Well . . . except the investigation into Meadow's background.

He didn't know exactly who she was—according to gossip, she didn't exist—but by the time his detective had finished with her, Devlin would know her age, her birth weight, and the names of every man she'd ever dated.

Taking Meadow's cell phone, he flipped it open.

It was searching for service.

Of course.

He searched for her call list.

Nothing.

He looked for the numbers she'd last dialed.

Nothing.

The smart girl had wiped the memory on her cell phone clean before she'd broken in.

Only she *hadn't* broken in. Somehow she'd unlocked the door and walked in. The cameras hadn't caught her sleight of hand, but something she'd done had overridden the security chip in the huge old-fashioned lock. Of course, the motion sensors had caught her as she walked through the foyer, setting off the silent alarms, but still, he wanted to know—his security man wanted to know—how she'd done it.

With a touch of uncharacteristic whimsy, he wondered if it could be something as simple as the house knowing she belonged here.

But he didn't care whether she belonged here and he didn't. He would solve all of her mysteries and in the process take a pound of flesh from Bradley Benjamin.

Devlin had always had the luck of the Irish.

Meadow proved he hadn't lost his touch.

4

*M*eadow woke to sunshine pressing against her eyelids, a rebound of her optimism—and someone in bed with her. Behind her. Spoon fashion.

A man. Most definitely a man. Most definitely the man who'd been there to wake her up every hour all night long.

No wonder she was feeling optimistic.

She flipped over and found herself facing Devlin's rugged, handsome, unsmiling face. "Good morning, darling." His fingers caressed her cheek. His chocolate brown, dangerously intense eyes plumbed the depths of her soul.

Her soul, ridiculous thing, stretched and purred under the flattering attention.

"All right." She managed to sound stern. "What are you doing here?" Like she didn't know. He'd seen an opportunity and moved to take advantage.

"Where else would I be except in bed with my beloved wife?" He slid closer, his legs tangling with hers.

"I'm not your beloved wife!" *Oops*. Panic reaction. Because of his words. Because the robe she'd wisely slept in last night was open from the waist down and the waist up, and her bra and panties left her very bare. And because he wore only a soft cotton T-shirt and . . . well, she didn't know what he wore below the waist, because the blankets covered him, and she wasn't about to grope him to find out.

"Darling, of course you are. You just don't remember." His fingers wandered down the slope of her throat. "I'll help you."

"Stop that." She slapped at him and inched back.

"Does your head still hurt?"

"A little." A nagging headache behind her eyes. Certainly not enough to stop her from doing what she must.

"The doctor said you could stay in bed today."

"The doctor is an idiot. I'm fine." And thoroughly irritated that he should quote Dr. Apps to her while he was horizontal with *Meadow.*

"You're grouchy." He shook his head sadly, as if he actually knew what her moods were like, when he didn't have the foggiest idea. "You *should* stay in bed today."

"I am not grouchy. See?" She smiled, grinding her teeth all the while.

He smiled back, all allure, ease . . . and seduction. "I'll let you get up on one condition: You promise that if you feel faint or ill, you'll let me know."

"As if you really cared." Maybe she was a little grouchy.

He touched his lips to her forehead.

"What do you want?"

"I want you back. I want to be together like we were in Majorca. I want the romance, the talk, the passion. . . ."

She ought to say, *That never happened.* And *Tell me why you want me here.*

Maybe she would. Later. When her thigh wasn't trapped between two of his. "I don't remember."

"Then I'll make it happen again. We could go down to the beach and meet by accident—"

"We met by accident?"

"With Fate as our matchmaker. I was worn out from making the deal on this house, and bitter about the acridness of business. I'd lost my way, my pleasure in living, and I was leaning against a boulder, staring out at the sea. . . ."

The sun warmed his upturned face. The waves lapped at his feet, and the Mediterranean smelled briny, while a hint of lavender wafted through the air. This moment was perfect, a gem set in the restless flow of time . . . yet an unusual yearning tinged his soul with melancholy. All his life, he'd enjoyed his own company, cherished his solitude, his moments snatched away from the swift and cutthroat business of making deals, renovating warehouses into trendy apartments, constructing luxury boutique hotels on dilapidated properties.

But today didn't feel like solitude. Today he was alone. Very alone.

Out of the corner of his eye, he caught a swift slash of color. He turned to see a woman, a tall woman with hair shining like a new copper penny—

Meadow interrupted. "I'm not tall. I'm only five-five."

Devlin placed his finger on her lips and reproved her with a shake of his head. "The flow of your sundress made you look tall, and your long, leisurely strides made me think of only one thing. . . ."

"Yeah, and I'll bet I know what it was."

He knew this was the woman for whom Fate had intended him.

"I would have lost that bet," she said.

She held her sandals in one hand. She kicked the sand while she walked, her gaze fixed to the horizon, where the blue sky blended with the blue sea. Her expression was far-off and wistful. He thought she looked as lonely as he felt, and when he stepped forward, her eyes were first startled, then wary, then . . . warm. Without a word, she took him in her arms and kissed him, and since that moment, nothing had been the same.

"Wow," Meadow whispered. He was good. She knew it was all garbage, but when he wove his story, he pulled her in and she almost believed it. Almost lived it with him.

"Maybe you don't recall me, but your body knows mine. Your

body yearns for the pleasure I can show it." His voice sounded the way black velvet felt—soft, rich, seductive. His hand cupped her wrist and slid beneath the wide sleeve to the inner bend of her elbow. His thumb stroked back and forth on the tender skin. "We don't need warm white sand and Mediterranean breezes. We don't need palm trees and glass-bottomed boats. All we need is each other . . . and the world drifts away."

He wasn't so much encroaching on her body as he was seducing her with his words. Each phrase sank into her mind and sent a thrill down her spine to places that had nothing to do with marriage and everything to do with mating. His thigh rubbed hers over and over, and distractedly she tried to recall the last time she'd shaved her legs.

Then she decided she didn't care, because she wanted to rub herself against him. In fact, her hips were headed in his direction when some remnant of sense stopped her.

She wore almost nothing. He wore . . . who knew? Dangerous ground for a woman whose one fledgling affair had faded under the pressures of family illness.

She turned her head away from his fingers and her gaze away from his. "Don't."

He rose onto his elbow. "Look at me."

She did. She had to. She needed to observe his moves, try to keep ahead of him. If that meant she obeyed him, there was no help for it. If her gaze intertwined with his again, and those heated brown eyes stripped away her pretensions and left her bare to his scrutiny, there was no help for that, either. He had a way of making her feel helpless—and making her like it.

"We're lucky." He slipped his hand around her waist and splayed it in the small of her back. "Most couples have only one first kiss. We'll have two."

Her thoughts might be muddled, but her instincts were crystal clear. She should run. She should run *now*.

Instead she let him pull her closer, into the heat and the scent of him.

But it was okay. Because he was wearing boxers.

Specious reasoning, Meadow.

His head dropped toward hers. His breath whispered across her skin near her ear. "Sometimes when two people meet, they know that a touch would be enough to set off a wildfire, but they never have the chance to set the spark. We have the chance . . . and it would be a crime against nature not to find out. . . ."

She turned to look at him, to tell him to back off.

Somehow her lips met his—and the spark leaped into instant, glorious conflagration. Her eyes fluttered closed. The lightning from last night shivered between them, setting off flashes beneath her closed lids. Her hands rose and grasped him, one behind his neck, one against his shoulder, and the lightning crackled from her fingertips into his skin and back again, like magic performed by a cartoon magician.

What he did with his lips was wicked, an overload of temptation. His hands didn't wander; rather, they held her closely, and the heat that built seemed to ignite their scraps of clothing, leaving nothing but bare skin and the flare of desire.

Her breath came more and more quickly. She was blind and deaf to anything but him: his breath in her mouth, his scent filling her nostrils, the fire he created as he rubbed his hips against hers.

She liked his tongue. She liked that he used it against her teeth and lips to taunt and touch. She liked that he gave up control when she wanted to explore his mouth. She savored the vibration of his moan as he rolled onto his back and pulled her with him.

He was solid beneath her, a great, strong beast of a man who radiated heat and moved her without effort. As she pressed him into the mattress, kissing him with growing intensity, he ceased holding her against him. Instead his hands wandered, pushing her robe aside so that only the tie remained between their bodies. His palms caressed her buttocks, cupping them, pressing her against his erection, and moving her in a pulsing rhythm.

Vaguely she knew things were moving too fast. She couldn't get intimate with a man who had lied to her. Not when she was lying to him, too. But on this sensual, physical, earthy level, they were far too attuned.

At least, she was attuned to him.

Maybe he was simply good at this stuff. She'd heard that some men worked miracles with a woman's anatomy, although she'd had little experience with that. But here and now, each shift of their bodies wrung another sensation from her taut nerves.

She searched out the hem of his T-shirt and slid her hands beneath it, climbing the ladder of his sculpted belly up to his ribs and then to his nipples. He stretched his arms above his head, inviting her—challenging her—to strip him.

As a girl, she'd once taken a dare to jump off the roof of the studio onto their trampoline. She'd broken her leg. While the doctor set it, he'd sternly warned her of the dangers of accepting dares.

Too bad Meadow's besetting sin was impetuousness.

Don't do this, Meadow.

Sitting up, she straddled Devlin.

You're going to be sorry, Meadow.

Peeling him out of his T-shirt, she tossed it aside.

Her conscience was wrong. She was *not* sorry.

Smooth muscles rippled beneath tanned skin. On his arms. On his chest. On his belly. She couldn't resist; she touched him with her fingertips, sliding up hills and down valleys, following his love arrow down his breastbone, over his navel, to the waistband of his underwear. The contrast between her pink nails and his dark hair fascinated her, and she gloated over the strength and glory of his chest. "You're in great shape."

"After you left me, I had nothing worthwhile to do except practice making love." He flexed his biceps. "By myself."

Damn the man! How did he know she was sucker for guys who made her laugh? "Practice makes perfect."

"Let's see." He slid his fingers under the waistband of her panties.

She had only one thought—*Take them off.*

She leaned forward.

He pushed them down her legs.

Stupid Meadow. Don't do this, Meadow.

She kicked them away.

His palms stroked the bare globes of her rear, raising the fine hairs all over her body. His fingertips skimmed the crack that led to the space deep into her body.

She tensed with anticipation.

He slid his thumbs over her clitoris.

She sank her nails into his skin.

He slipped—just barely—his finger into her body.

She gave a moan that revealed far too much.

"It was exactly like this in Majorca," he whispered in her ear. "You kissed me and we went up in flames."

A warning pealed loud and shrill in her head.

"Majorca?" He'd mentioned Majorca before, and it behooved her to remember—she'd never been to Majorca.

She wasn't starting out a relationship based on lies.

Devlin's lies.

Her lies.

"I'm out of here." She vaulted off the bed, one hand sinking into the mattress, the other mashing his stomach.

He *oofed* as she drove the air out of him.

It was farther to the floor than she expected. She stumbled when she landed, then stood with her back to him and took a long breath— a long breath that did nothing to restore her good sense.

Her brain clamored for her to get far away. Her body urged her to climb back on the mattress and make it rock.

And her common sense insisted on asking the logical question— had he mentioned Majorca on purpose? Had he wanted to stop them before they went too far? That suggested that a cool mind still operated beneath the heat of passion, and that one thought brought her temperature down to a reasonable simmer.

She pulled the robe closer around her, covering herself. She faced him.

He reclined on the bed, sheet to his waist, arms tucked under his head. Muscles bulged on his chest and pecs; hair dusted his armpits and breastbone. His hair glowed like a dark halo against the white pillowcase. His eyes smoldered with intensity.

He didn't look like a man in possession of a cool mind. Maybe he'd mentioned Majorca by mistake. "Are you always so reckless?"

"Never." He sat up on one elbow. "That's why I fell in love with you—you transform me from a dull businessman into a dashing beachcomber who knows what's important in life."

"What's that?"

"You."

She swayed toward the bed, pulled by the gravitational force of his desire.

Think, Meadow. Think!

She pulled back. "You're good." She'd always appreciated flattery as much as the next girl. Apparently she appreciated it a little too much.

"Let me put on my clothes. They're harder to get out of." She headed into the bathroom, sure she had seized control of her destiny again, and determined to ward off any more of his lightning-fast, underhanded, seductive maneuvers.

"I threw away your clothes."

5

Meadow caught her breath in outrage. She stopped. She turned.

Devlin smiled a panty-dropper smile.

Too bad she wasn't wearing panties.

"Excuse me?" She stepped toward the bed, a half smile on her lips, fire in her eyes. "You threw away my *clothes?*"

"The shop downtown is sending out outfits appropriate for my wife." He sounded so . . . innocent. So reasonable.

"Outfits *appropriate* for your wife?" Her voice rose. "What does that mean?"

"It means I like the way you dressed in Majorca."

"And that would be?"

"In sundresses. With flowers in bright colors." He wiggled his fingers over his chest to indicate something. Bright-colored flowers, she guessed.

"Sundresses? With . . ." Normally she wore jeans and T-shirts. And Birkenstocks. With socks. "If I'm your wife, why don't you have my clothes from Majorca?"

Promptly, he said, "I left them there, hoping you would return."

The fresh-washed morning sunshine lit one half of his body and face, and left the other half in shadow. Who did he think he was?

Some supervillain capable of lightning-fast changes designed to amaze and confuse her?

Because someone needed to bring him down to earth.

Like targets, his nipples drew her gaze. Grabbing one, she twisted. *Hard.*

"Ouch!" He grabbed himself. He looked down at the bruised nub. "What was that?"

"A purple-nirple." She watched in grim satisfaction as he rubbed the ache. "And no normal woman wears a flowered sundress for everyday. I wear jeans."

"You can't know that. You don't remember." Sarcasm. Definitely sarcasm.

"Are you trying to make me into a Stepford wife?" A spooky thought. Was that his intention? "I know what kind of woman I am. And I certainly know what I wear. What all women wear. You need to look around."

"I don't look at other women. I'm married."

She snorted. "I'll call and get you an eye appointment."

"That's a very wifely duty."

Conversation between them wasn't an exchange of ideas; it was a fencing match.

Worse, she was enjoying herself when she was actually angry at him. Very angry about . . . something . . . *Oh, yeah.* "Don't ever get high-handed and toss my clothes again."

"Of course not. I won't have to." He swung his legs out from under the sheets. "Not now. You're here with me, and I intend to keep you close."

Devlin was too tall. The way he loomed distracted Meadow, made her aware of his erection tenting his dark blue boxers, her bare feet on the cool hardwood floor, their recent and all too steamy intimacy. The things he said sounded less like banter and more like a threat, and when a woman had gone as far as she had—and that was far too far—she would be a fool to ignore her alarm. "Keep me close? What does that mean?"

"You're not well. You have a concussion—"

"Minor!"

"And you have amnesia about the most important moment of our lives."

She hated that he held that trump.

"More important, I'm opening a hotel here on the private, exclusive shores of South Carolina. It's the wave of the future; all of these old homes are falling to reduced incomes and increasing costs. But the wealthy here are still wealthy—and hostile to me, and there've already been incidents of sabotage."

"Oh," she said blankly. Such a scenario was so out of her league, she didn't know what to say. "Like what?"

"A few of the more important families made it clear that the merchants in town would find their mortgages inexplicably foreclosed on if they sold us anything. I'm trucking in groceries from Charleston."

"That's medieval!"

A smile quirked his mouth. "That's South Carolina. It's one of the original thirteen colonies and still run by the same families."

"You're kidding." She was from the West. From the mountains of Washington and a family of bohemians, artists. Of course, her grandmother had told her about the old South Carolina family traditions that choked the life out of a person. But Isabelle had run away, and the stories she told sounded like fairy tales from long ago.

Now Devlin was saying nothing had changed? One look at his stern face convinced her he was serious. "What else have they done to the hotel?" Meadow asked.

"I built a cell tower behind the hotel. Someone knocked it down."

"Cell tower?" With a jolt she remembered. "My cell phone." She slapped her rear as if expecting to find a pocket. "Before you tossed my pants, did you retrieve my cell phone?"

"It's here on the nightstand." Sitting down on the bed, he extended his hand. "I have guards patrolling this place—"

"So how did I get in?" She didn't think he was lying about this.

"A guard who found shelter from the storm when he should have been making his rounds, combined with untested generators that allowed power outages. The problem will be fixed today."

"Fixed? You mean, the generators will be up and running?"

"And the guard replaced." His gaze grew cold.

She didn't like that expression. It reminded her of last night. It reminded her only too clearly that he had some ulterior motive for this farce he was playing, and if she didn't get that painting and get out of here fast, he was going to squash her like a bug. "Ah, come on. That was a heck of a storm!"

"I pay top dollar, and I expect the best."

"Yes, but . . . the poor guard! He's got no job."

She saw no visible softening on Devlin's face. "He should have thought of that before he signed the contract."

"I guess." Meadow honored her own contracts, but at the same time, her heart ached for the unknown man.

"Look. These people who want to stop me from opening are determined, and they've got the money to back that determination. I can't take the chance that someone will seize the opportunity to hurt my wife, and a sloppy guard would expose you to danger. You do understand, don't you?" Charm thawed his expression. With his dark hair disheveled from the night and that quirk of his lips, he looked almost . . . sincere. Intent. Interested in her. Only her.

Reluctantly she placed her hand in his. "Sure. Except . . . are you really going to tell people I'm your wife?"

"Of course." He rubbed his thumb back and forth across her palm.

It was on the tip of her tongue to ask what excuse he would make when she disappeared. But then he'd ask why his wife would disappear, and she'd be stammering around, trying to come up with a good lie. Her mother always said there was no such thing as a good lie, that the universe rewarded the truth and punished a falsehood.

Meadow's gaze fell on their joined hands, then on the bed. With last night's debacle and this morning's precipitate passion as cases in point, Meadow had to admit that her mother was right.

She could reveal the truth—she cast a glance at his harsh face—and be arrested for breaking and entering with intent to commit grand theft. *Good idea, Meadow.*

Devlin watched her flounder with the dilemmas of truth versus lie, him versus prison; and the way he smiled made her suspect he found her struggles all too amusing.

Jerking her hand from his grasp, she picked up her phone.

As she flipped it open, he said, "I looked for numbers, but the phone is blank." He strode across the room to the dresser and pulled a pair of jeans out of the drawer.

"You snooped in my phone?" He'd had the nerve!

"I thought it might reveal some names that would tell us where you've been." He pulled on the jeans.

"Oh. Yeah." Thank God Judith had thought to have Meadow wipe the memory or he'd be talking to her mother right now. Meadow could imagine how her mother would sound—as disappointed and upset as the time she'd caught the thirteen-year-old Meadow eating a hamburger—meat!—at her friend's.

What a horrible memory that was!

"So there's no cell service out here?" To avoid his gaze, she watched the little signal searcher do its gyrations.

"Until last year, the residents of Amelia Shores hadn't allowed anything so crass as a cell tower to pollute the ambience of their elite village, and even now the signal doesn't reach out to the mansions."

"Medieval," she muttered again.

"I'm building another tower for the hotel's guests, but it isn't scheduled for assembly until the day before the grand opening. Then the frenzy of disapproval from the other mansions' residents will be at its height, and they won't even notice the tower going up behind the house."

"Yeah. Probably not." She snapped her phone closed. "I want a shower."

He opened his mouth.

"Alone."

He closed it.

"So where are these flowered sundresses?" She needed to search the house for the painting, and she needed to search fast.

"They're not here yet. I'll see what I can find you in the gift shop." He started for the door.

"Jeans. A T-shirt," she called after him.

"It's going to be eighty-five today."

"Shorts and a T-shirt, then."

He stopped and ran his unsmiling gaze over her.

"What?" She spread her hands.

"Five-five, one hundred and twenty-eight pounds, A cup, pants size six, shoes a size eight." Then he continued out, shutting the door behind him. He didn't ask if he was right.

"One hundred and twenty-*six* pounds. What's wrong with that?" A man with such acute powers of observation could probably read every thought before it crossed her mind—and she prided herself on keeping an open mind.

She was in such trouble.

She had to find that painting and get out of here. She wanted—desperately wanted—to go home to her parents with enough money to pay for her mother's medical treatment . . . and now Meadow had a second reason for haste.

She needed to get away from Devlin—before he lay further siege to her wary self, and ruined all of her well-made larcenous plans.

6

Meadow dove for the corded hotel wall phone.

She dialed frantically, then slammed down the receiver. Would Mr. I've Got Security Everywhere know she was using the phone?

Probably.

But she felt pretty sure it was illegal to bug the phone lines in a hotel room, so her conversation should be private.

Besides . . . did she have a choice?

No.

Really, he probably hadn't had time to bug this phone.

And she had fallen over the edge into the pit of paranoia.

She dialed again, calling the one person who had listened to her rage and disappointment, encouraged her to look for a solution, helped her make her plans, and promised to be the contact in Blythe while Meadow was away.

Judith Smith had arrived on their doorstep when Meadow was fourteen, hungry to learn everything she could about art and painting. Before she was done with her apprenticeship, Judith had settled in as part of their family. She'd stayed for months, creating mediocre paintings, but the first time her art was rejected she had quit.

Privately, Sharon told her daughter that the only person who could declare an artist a failure was the artist herself, that Judith's demand for immediate success had put a stranglehold on her talent, a talent Judith refused to allow to mature.

So she'd quit and gone on to other careers—she didn't say what they were, but apparently she had money, for she came and went as she pleased. She'd helped Meadow get into the art program at Stanford and suggested she study abroad. Her mother, her father, and her grandmother had built Meadow's spirit and mentored her art, but when Meadow had left their mountain home and gone out into the world, Judith had been her real-life mentor.

Now Meadow held her breath, waiting for the first ring.

Judith answered before it was completed, her nasal voice tipped over the edge into panic. "Who is it?"

"It's me." Meadow hunched over the phone, keeping her voice low.

"Thank God. I've been so worried." Judith took a long breath. "Why aren't you answering your cell phone? What happened? Where are you?"

Meadow answered the questions in order. "Cell phone doesn't work out here. Got caught breaking in. At Waldemar."

"Oh, my God. Are you all right? Did you find the painting? Did you get hurt?"

"I got hurt a little. Nothing important. But the painting wasn't on the wall."

"I did try to tell you that was possible. People do rearrange their houses."

Judith sounded so calm, Meadow wanted to shriek at her. "Grandmother promised me it would be here."

Judith's voice sharpened. "Do you think she lied to you?"

"She didn't!"

"I'm so sorry. I didn't mean that. There's simply so much riding on this." Judith sounded contrite and embarrassed. "But you did say that sometimes there toward the end, she was a little confused."

"Yes. But the painting probably was there—once. The trouble is, people sell their houses." Meadow listened as Judith breathed hard.

"Waldemar is sold?" Sometimes, in moments of stress, Judith's voice sounded like pure New York. This was one of those moments.

"To a man named Devlin Fitzwilliam."

"Devlin Fitzwilliam," Judith said slowly. "Devlin . . . Oh, my God. *Devlin Fitzwilliam* caught you breaking in?"

"Yes, and he— Wait a minute." Judith's panic caught Meadow's attention. "Do you know him?"

"Everybody knows Fitzwilliam. He was the quarterback for Florida State."

"Quarterback. That's football, right?" The way he was built, that made sense.

"Yes, dear. That's football. The man's been profiled in the *Harvard Business Review. Forbes. Entrepreneur.* He's one of the Fitzwilliams of Charleston, the son of Grace Fitzwilliam." Meadow could almost see Judith wringing her hands. "Do you recognize *that* name?"

"No. Not really." Meadow put her back against the wall and slid down, sitting on the floor, knees up, eyes fixed on the door.

"You ought to watch TV every once in a while. Grace Fitzwilliam is a home decorator with a nationally syndicated show. She demonstrates how to turn your house into a traditional Southern paradise."

"Oh." Meadow liked television. So did her father. But her mother wouldn't allow a set in her house, and Meadow had been living with her parents for the last—difficult—year and a half. She was out of touch and knew it—and, much to her surprise, she was happier than when she had been at college and very much in touch.

Sharon was a smart cookie.

"Is it a reality show?"

"More like Martha Stewart. You do know who Martha Stewart is, don't you?" Judith was half laughing, half sarcastic.

"Yes. Judith, I can't talk for long." Meadow needed to get off this phone before she was caught, but she couldn't resist hearing about Devlin. "Tell me what I need to know to manage *him*."

"Fitzwilliam is a genius at developing profitable properties."

"He's turning this into a hotel."

"I'll bet. He's got a reputation as a ruthless son of a bitch out to make his fortune bigger."

"Ruthless."

"He's nobody's fool, and everybody knows it—or finds out to their peril. He runs over anyone who stands in his way. He's the son of that billionaire, Nathan Manly, the one who bankrupted his company, stole all the money, and fled to South America about ten or fifteen years ago. Bet you never heard that story, either?"

"No." Nor did she care, except as it related to Devlin's personality—and remembering his comment last night about Bradley Benjamin calling him a bastard, it obviously did. "So Fitzwilliam wants to prove he's not like his father?"

"That, and Grace's family didn't take it well when she popped up pregnant. She wasn't married to Manly—in fact, he was married to someone else."

"Every child born is a new thought of God."

"The Fitzwilliams are against new thought."

Realization dawned. "They're one of the families he was talking about. The ones who still control everything."

"That's right. So he carries chips on his shoulder as big as epaulets, and rumor says he's a real asshole when someone tries to screw him over."

"Oh." And Meadow had sort of liked him. Found him enticing. But maybe that was the hormones talking.

"So you have to be careful. Very careful." Meadow could hear the worry in Judith's voice. "Now, what's your next move?"

Meadow couldn't bring herself to confess her ridiculous amnesia lie or his absurd marriage lie. The whole thing sounded like a Shakespearean farce, and it played like one, too, except for those kisses . . . which played like porn. "I talked him into letting me stay."

Judith hesitated, and Meadow could almost hear her brain whirling. Judith was probably more intelligent than any person Meadow had ever known. Not more talented, but more intelligent, and although she tried to hide it, hungrier for fame. Mom had once quietly confessed to Meadow that she felt there were teeth in that hunger, but Judith had never shown them to Meadow. "Do you think it's wise to stay? Maybe there's another way."

"I think there's no choice. He's got guards and security all over the place. I won't get in again. And I have to have that painting." Unbidden, the picture of her mother with a handkerchief tied over her bald head rose in Meadow's mind. She swallowed sudden tears. "We haven't heard it's been discovered, and we would be the first to know. Gossip in the art community spreads like wildfire. So it's got to be here in the house somewhere. I only have to find it."

"Yes. You're right. But if he's got all that security . . . how?"

"I'm a smart girl. I can turn off the security for a while, then turn it back on again."

"Oh, my dear, I'm so worried about you!" Judith burst out.

"I know." Meadow took a breath. "How's it going at home? Do they really believe I'm in Atlanta at a retreat?" She felt awful lying to her parents, but if her mom knew Meadow was here and what she planned to do, she'd be disappointed, and her mother's disappointment was a crushing weight to bear.

So it was better for them both if Meadow lied. Any guilt her mom would have made Meadow feel about stealing a lousy picture was nothing compared to the guilt Meadow would feel if she could take action and didn't.

Not to mention the fact that Grandmother would come back and haunt her.

River was a gifted artist and a great father, but he was a disaster at making sure they had food in the fridge, talking to their agent, and paying the bills, so Meadow had made Judith promise to stay with her parents and handle the day-to-day stuff that her mother usually handled. Now Meadow tried hard to feel relief and instead suffered a clawing anxiety.

"Yes, don't worry! Just concentrate on your job. And don't call them—I told them your retreat won't allow cell phones."

"Oh, but . . . " She talked to her mother almost every day, touching base, needing to hear that familiar, warm voice and know her mom was still in the world.

"You're a lousy liar," Judith said with brutal frankness, "and if you call your mother, she's going to know you're up to something. You don't want to worry her."

"No. You're right."

But that brought Meadow right back to the problem of Devlin Fitzwilliam.

If she was such a lousy liar, why was he keeping her here?

⌒

Judith hung up the phone and looked around the piece-of-shit room she'd rented at the Amelia Shores Bide-a-Wee Motel.

She'd worked years to get to this moment—she shouldn't pull back now just because the big cockroaches kept pet cockroaches. Besides, she'd been here once before, eighteen years ago this September, and yes, it was seedier than it had been then, but she was so close to her goal, she could almost taste it.

In some ways she felt bad lying to that kid. She'd known her for years, and Meadow was as genuine and open as her parents.

On the other hand, Meadow was as talented as her parents, too, and that made Judith's gut burn. It wasn't fair—why some people were geniuses and others . . . others were just good. In the art world, *genius* won you international appreciation. *Good* won you a place in the traveling Starving Artists' Shows and a painting on a restaurant wall with a two-hundred-dollar price tag stapled on the frame.

That wasn't what Judith had wanted. All her life she had needed to *be* someone. She wanted people—critics—to notice her, praise her, recognize her. And twenty years ago, five years after getting out of college, she'd had to face harsh reality. She didn't have genius—so she went about getting her fame a different way.

She was going to find a lost masterpiece.

It wasn't hard. It could be done. It merely took a little research and the willingness to track down rumors to their source. Not all the rumors had panned out, of course, and she'd spent a lot of time viewing really lousy art masquerading as masterpieces.

After about a year she heard a rumor about famed artist Isabelle and the masterpiece she'd left behind. She'd heard another rumor, and another, and finally she'd bought enough drinks for the bitter old nursemaid, Mrs. Graham, to get confirmation. The masterpiece was real, and it was in the grand old mansion of Waldemar.

But Mrs. Graham was so deaf she shouted every word, and such a lush she'd give up her information to anybody with enough cash for a mimosa and some pretzels. Judith hadn't had a choice, and really, it wasn't hard to spike her twelfth glass of the evening with a little rat poison. When the police found her the next day in the alley outside the bar, they'd carted her away and listed her death as "natural causes."

Southerners had a real way with covering up the ugly side of life.

Judith's break-in at Waldemar had yielded no painting that fit the description. It had, however, yielded some dog-teeth marks on her ass and a perfect description of the thief by one furious Bradley Benjamin. For those reasons, she hadn't dared try again.

So she had gone about matters a different way. She'd gone looking for the papers of the famous—and infamous—artist Isabelle . . . and instead found Isabelle's *supposedly* dead daughter.

The whole setup was too perfect. The grand old artist Isabelle had announced her daughter had been killed in a car wreck in Ireland at the age of four. She'd "adopted" Sharon, then kept her out of the limelight, and ever since, Sharon had been hiding in plain sight, not avoiding the press, but not courting them, either.

After Sharon married River Szarvas, they'd used the money Isabelle had made from her art to establish an artists' colony, one dedicated to fostering talent and training the next generation of geniuses. They funded scholarships. They trained their successors, for shit's sake. They always had ragtag kids who imagined themselves artists hanging around, sleeping on their floors, eating their food, talking about their art with burning eyes. . . . It hadn't been hard to show up at the household in Blythe and move in as Judith, a woman seeking her muse.

And for a while, she'd thought she'd found it. She created the best paintings of her life while living there and breathing that rarified air. For a while, she'd forgotten the stupid lost masterpiece and painted at a fever pitch, sure she'd at last tapped her inner genius.

Then, when she had shown them to an art critic, he gave her the name of a restaurant willing to hang and sell paintings for a commission.

She wanted to put poison in *his* coffee.

Instead, she'd crawled back to the Szarvases', listened without interest to Sharon's pep talk, and volunteered to transcribe Isabelle's diaries into the computer. Sharon felt sorry enough for her to let Judith do it, and while Judith discovered eye-popping gossip and fascinating insights into the female artist's life, she'd found nothing about the masterpiece.

She had tactfully probed Sharon's memory, trying desperately to become the kind of confidante Sharon would trust in all things.

But Sharon had held back; her acute eyes had made Judith think that . . . well, they had made Judith think Sharon saw through her.

At last Judith took an interest in Isabelle's granddaughter, and hit gold.

Isabelle had told the child everything. *Everything.*

A quick trip to Amelia Shores had revealed that the painting was no longer hanging above the fireplace.

Of course not.

That would be too easy.

And she couldn't figure out how to stay there and search. Old man Benjamin was still alive. The police still had the description of her. She got in and out of town in a hurry.

Right about then, her money had run out. She put her father, the meanest son of a bitch who had ever lived, in an asylum, sold his home, and cashed in his assets. That gave her another two years.

Then she needed funding.

Mr. Hopkins made his offer so promptly, it was as if he had been observing her. Of course, knowing what she knew now, he had been.

She could have the fame.

He wanted the painting.

She'd never seen him. He'd been a voice on the phone, counseling her to be patient. She'd thought *she'd* been patient all the long years, but he defined staying power, and in the end . . . he was right. With his help, her moment had come.

The painting—and the glory—was within her grip. She would allow nothing to stand in her way.

Nothing—and nobody.

7

Gabriel Prescott stepped into Devlin's office.

"Hey, Gabe." Devlin didn't glance up. He didn't have to. He sat before the banks of video screens set into the handsome, old-fashioned bookshelves. He'd been watching, so he'd seen Gabriel come through the front door. He'd seen every step Gabriel made all the way to the office.

But he was still viewing the screens, a slight smile on his face.

"What are we doing?" Gabriel shut the door behind him.

"We're watching her."

Always interested in a *her* that put that tone in Devlin's voice, Gabriel came to stand behind his shoulder. The monitor showed a woman wandering down one of the corridors—and she was gorgeous. Her red hair glowed like a candle flame about her pale skin. She had long legs and curvy hips and small, high breasts, all lovingly arranged by a master hand. She wore a pair of white shorts, a yellow tube top, some silly-ass flip-flops decorated with rhinestones, and over it all, a man's large white starched shirt with a knot tied in each front corner. She wore a yellow Band-Aid on her forehead—from here it looked as if it was decorated with happy faces—and she moseyed down the corridor, stopping at every other painting and staring.

Gabriel pulled up a chair and seated himself so he could see the screen, too. "Anytime you need help looking at her, I'm your man. Who is she?"

Devlin shot him an enigmatic look. "My wife."

"Your wife?" *Misstep!*

"Meadow."

It took Gabriel a moment to realize Devlin meant that was her name. "Really." He'd known Fitzwilliam for a long time, ever since his firm had first started installing the security on Devlin's projects, and never had Devlin mentioned a wife.

But then, they weren't friends. Devlin was a grim, secretive son of a bitch with no sense of humor and an adversarial way of making conversation. He was also damned possessive about his properties, and watching him watch Meadow made Gabriel feel sorry for the girl. She was in for a bumpy ride.

"What's she doing?" Gabriel asked.

"She's searching for something."

"A painting?"

"She could very well be." Devlin sounded satisfied.

Okay, fine. Devlin was feeling enigmatic today. Might as well get to business. "I hear there was a break-in last night."

"There was."

"And you caught him."

"Her." Devlin nodded at the screen as Meadow turned a corner and moved to a different monitor.

"Her?" Gabriel was getting confused. "Your wife broke into your hotel."

"Right."

"Why don't you tell me about it?" Because Gabriel sure as hell couldn't think of any reasonable explanation.

"No, *you* tell *me*. How'd she get in without setting off the alarm on the front door?"

Gabriel's people had done their work before he got here, so he knew the answer. "She opened the door with a key."

Devlin swiveled to face Gabriel. "A key? Why wouldn't a key set off the alarm?"

"People still use keys, so as standard operating procedure we make sure a key will open a lock without setting off the alarm. That's been changed." And the guy who didn't ask what the owner preferred was kicking shit down the road right now. Gabriel operated the biggest security firm on the East Coast. He'd built it from the ground up. He didn't accept mistakes like that.

"So any key would have opened the door?" Devlin asked.

"Any key that fits that lock, and there aren't many that will. It's a Sargent and Greenleaf lock. They've been a solid, innovative firm for a hundred and fifty years. That lock was fitted on the door when it was put in place, the work of master craftsmen." Sargent and Greenleaf constructed the kind of lock that made work like Gabriel's easier. "It's never easy to pick, and it wasn't picked this time. There weren't scratches inside or outside the lock. It wasn't forced. We found fresh metal residue inside a very old lock that had not been used for months, probably not since the former owner moved out." He sat forward, his arms on his knees. "More interesting, the metal was silver. That's an antique key, and even then it's rare—and it fit the lock."

Devlin stared at Gabriel long enough and with enough concentration to make the hairs stand up on the back of Gabriel's neck. Getting up, Devlin walked to the large desk and opened the belly drawer. He pulled out a key, a large, ornate silver key, and held it up. "Like this?"

"I would guess just like that." Gabriel examined it. "Fascinating. Does it open the front door?"

"No. Old Bradley Benjamin didn't give me the key to the front door. Claimed it was lost. But this was stuck in the back of this desk, so we went looking for the lock. Had a dickens of a time finding it—it opens a gate in the yard."

"What's on the other side of that gate that's worth a silver key?"

"A garden." Devlin's tone was flat and uninterested.

"A garden." Gabriel turned the key over in his hand. The silver glinted in the light. "Somebody must have loved that garden."

"Probably. The Benjamins are notorious for wasting their time with foolishness." Devlin dismissed both the Benjamins and their foolishness with a wave. "Where do you suppose Meadow got a rare silver key that fit the front door?"

"She's your wife. Why don't you ask her?" That seemed only logical, but the whole situation—a wife breaking into her own husband's house with a mysterious key—wasn't logical.

"I will." Devlin stood and clapped his hand on Gabriel's shoulder. "Thanks for coming in."

"I had to. It's not often someone breaches our security."

"I'd swear she didn't realize it when she did it." Devlin started for the door, then returned and shut off the monitor for the corridor where Meadow still wandered.

Yep. Possessive of his property.

"Have a cup of coffee," Devlin said. "Stay for dinner. The chef is trying out his new dishes in preparation for the grand opening. I've been eating like a king for two weeks."

"I'd love to, but I've got to catch a plane. There's a family gathering in Texas I want to attend. My youngest sister just had a baby, and we're getting together for the christening."

Devlin didn't understand how happy it made Gabriel to say that. "Sure. Next time."

Gabriel sobered and got back to business. "I'll be here for the grand opening. I intend to see that nothing goes wrong with security. I hired someone new, a female with great references."

"Where'd she work before?"

"A guy in Atlanta by the name of Hopkins. Do you know him?"

"I've heard of him. Runs an import/export business." Devlin recalled another tidbit. "And lives on the shady side of the law?"

"A polite way of putting it." Gabe's mouth curled with distaste. "*Mr.* Hopkins, as he is always referred to, is never seen. No one knows where he lives. No police reports are ever made about him.

Yet there are a lot of rumors circulating—that he rewards betrayal with a single gunshot to the back of the head. That he enforces his will with threats and torture. That he always keeps a few of Atlanta's politicians and judges in his pocket."

"Good God. Do we *want* his security?"

"Absolutely. Who has better security than a man who is never seen?"

"Right."

"Besides, female personnel are necessary for surveillance—guys can't watch the ladies' rooms in the public areas—yet damned hard to find. The weekend of the grand opening, there'll be no trouble at all." Gabe was a handsome guy, one of those blends of Hispanic and Anglo who had taken the best from both. He was tall, muscular, with black hair and green eyes that made women take a step back, then a step forward.

Devlin knew; he'd seen it happen. He liked Gabe. More important, he trusted him. "I know." His computer chimed. He had e-mail.

"I'm off to talk to my people." Gabe gave a wave and went out the door.

With anticipation, Devlin opened the e-mail—and frowned.

The report was short and decisive. *At the age of four, while in the company of her stepfather, Bjorn Kelly, Sharon Benjamin was killed in a car accident in Ireland. Isabelle Benjamin had no other children.*

Bullshit, Devlin typed back. *Dig deeper.*

8

*M*eadow needed a floor plan. She'd left her room thinking she would look the hotel over, retrieve the house key from the couch, check out the paintings and find the one she came for.

Hey, she believed in positive thinking.

Besides, this time she had a lie ready—if caught, she'd claim she was lost.

But she became fascinated by the renovations that had turned a house called Waldemar into a hotel called the Secret Garden. The grand old house her grandmother had so carefully described had been changed.

Walls had been rearranged to create rooms where none had existed before. The long corridors were rabbit warrens bounded by closed and locked doors, and without windows of any kind. On the third floor, Meadow met a crew of a dozen maids pushing linen carts, running vacuum cleaners, and making beds. One guy was installing a Coca-Cola machine next to an ice maker.

She said hello to them.

They said hello to her.

She briefly considered asking if they'd seen the painting, but as soon as they spoke, they returned to work with a frenetic energy that told her more clearly than words how tight their schedule must be.

And asking about the painting wasn't clever; if Devlin was keeping an eye on her, as he'd practically threatened he would, he'd know who she talked to and perhaps question them later.

So she strolled along, looking at the art on the walls, but it was unremarkable—impressionistic landscape prints mixed with typical late-nineteenth- and early-twentieth-century family portraits done by artists long forgotten. She glanced at the prints and dismissed them, but scrutinized the portraits, longing to catch a glimpse of a feature, a smile, a familiar posture. She'd gone up grand stairways and down elevators, but so far she'd had no luck.

Now her lie was the truth. She really was lost, and the corridors were eerily empty.

Maybe she didn't need a floor plan. Maybe she needed a compass.

She decided to head downstairs—as soon as she found more stairs or another elevator—in the hopes of finding the kitchen, where surely someone was cooking or getting ready to cook or something. At least, she hoped so. She was hungry.

Hearing voices somewhere—around the corner—she hurried forward.

"Why did the tree blow over?" It was Devlin's voice.

"Rotten to the core, sir." She recognized the voice of the guy who replied. It was Sam from last night, the man who had wanted to call the police on her.

"Must have been old Bradley's favorite tree. All right, I want it and the other one, the one struck by lightning, taken out today."

"I don't know if I can get the local guy out today."

"Then get someone in who'll do it."

She paused. Devlin sounded different than he had earlier. Harsh, driven, uninterested in excuses.

"I want the damned tree gone, the stump removed, and the landscaping done and growing before the grand opening." In fact, his tone and his words recalled last night before he'd declared she was his wife, and her first impression that he was cold, ruthless, and unfeeling.

"Yes, sir." Sam's submissive attitude only bolstered her feeling.

"What about the mattresses?" Devlin's attention whipped from one subject to another.

"They'll be here today. The company apologized for the mistake and offered to pay overtime to get them installed."

"Very sweet, but that's hardly enough to make up for the inconvenience."

"I know, so I told them to throw in mattress pads for each mattress. They did." Sam sounded pleased with himself.

"Excellent." Devlin gave brisk approval. "How are we doing at hiring more help before the opening?"

"I've got six new people starting today, and some woman who says she has experience in laundry called and is coming in for an interview. The trouble is, we've tapped out the number of people in town who are willing to take on the old guard."

"I hope those farts burn in hell." Devlin sounded vicious. Vindictive. Every emotion that was bad for his soul.

Before he could call down more bad karma, Meadow headed around the corner, talking as she went. "Whew! I'm so glad I found you guys. I've been lost for an hour!"

Devlin made the switch from hard-nosed businessman to smooth operator without a hitch. "We were about to send out a search party."

Sam started to move away, but she headed right for him, hand outstretched. "We didn't meet formally last night. I'm Meadow."

"Sam." He put his clipboard under his arm and briefly shook her hand.

"You must be part of the security team," she said. He was built like a linebacker, and Devlin's abrasiveness seemed to have scratched away any sense of humor.

"Actually, I'm Mr. Fitzwilliam's personal secretary," he said.

She laughed, then realized he was serious. "That's wonderful. What made you take a job usually considered the province of women?"

"Mr. Fitzwilliam pays well." He walked away.

She waited until he was out of earshot before turning to Devlin. "Did I hit a tender spot? I simply meant he's confident in his masculinity."

"Don't worry. You can't offend Sam. He's not much of a talker." He looked her over in a way that made it clear he'd dismissed Sam from his mind. "Is that my shirt?"

Recalled to a sense of grievance, she advanced on him while holding out the shirttails. "It sure is. I had to cover myself somehow. What made you think I would wander around this hotel in an outfit better suited to some prepubescent teenager than a—"

"Married woman?"

"Yes. No!" She narrowed her eyes at him. "Don't try to confuse me. I told you I don't remember getting married."

"You still don't remember anything?" Catching her hand, he tugged her closer.

"No." Inspiration struck. "But what do *you* know about me?"

"What do you mean?" He twirled a curl from her hair around his finger.

"We got married, and I must have told you about my life. Tell me about myself."

"I could." He drew out the pause while he leaned into her and took a long breath above her hair. "But I won't."

"Because . . . ?" She took a long breath, too, and his familiar scent started a chain reaction of longing, lust, and wariness. Because she did recognize his scent, and she'd slept in his arms, and come alive at his bidding.

He was a man to guard against.

"You have amnesia. It would be best if you discovered the truth on your own."

Damn, he was good! She couldn't catch him out no matter how

hard she tried. "My amnesia seems to be spreading. I don't remember eating breakfast this morning."

"Hungry?" He spoke close to her ear, so close his next move would be to kiss her.

"Starving." She shoved his head aside.

"You could have called for room service." He placed his hand at the base of her spine and guided her down the corridor. "After all, you know where the phone is."

She braced herself, waiting to see if he recited parts of her conversation with Judith.

He didn't. He left the comment hanging, and said, "Come on; I'll show you where the kitchen is. We can beg something for you."

"I didn't know room service was working." As they walked, she leaned into him. She didn't know why. He simply felt as if he could support her—in every way.

If this farce continued for long, she was afraid she'd start to believe in him and his silly marriage story.

"The people working on the hotel need to eat," he said, "and the kitchen staff and service people need to practice. The Secret Garden's grand opening is in three weeks. So, yes. We have room service." He led her around a corner and there they were, face-to-face with an elevator. He pushed the down button.

"I came up on an elevator, but when I turned around it had disappeared." She glanced around. "And this doesn't look at all familiar. Do you think it wanders when no one's looking?"

"There are two elevators. You came up the other one."

"Oh." *Yep.* He'd been watching her.

"I have to get to a map," she said.

He showed her a speaker set into the wall. "Did you see any of these?"

"Yes. They're for music, right?"

He didn't laugh at her. She had to give him that. "They're intercoms. See this button? Anytime you're lost, push it. Someone will direct you or, if you're really confused, come and get you."

She blushed. She couldn't help it. She'd seen intercoms at the university, but it hadn't occurred to her how useful they would be in a house as big as this. "I guess you think I'm a hick."

He ushered her inside the elevator. "I think you're delightful."

"I'd still like a map." Because she didn't want everyone to know where she was searching.

Well . . . apart from Devlin. And the security people. And anyone else watching the monitors.

"You can have whatever you want." He smiled whimsically, and that was an expression she would bet he didn't often wear. "Except . . ."

"Except what?"

"Except for your own bed at night."

As the doors closed he kissed her, a warm salute of appreciation, one so genuine she could almost taste the salt from the Mediterranean on his lips.

9

As the elevator slowed to a stop, Devlin lifted his head and examined Meadow's upturned face. Her flushed cheeks and supple lips showed a woman who had been thoroughly kissed, and when her eyes gradually blinked open, they were a soft, blurry blue.

Those eyes. Those beautiful, expressive, betraying eyes. "Let's get you that breakfast now," he said.

"Hmm?" She smiled at him, a smile of pure pleasure.

Then he saw her snap back into consciousness. He stepped out of the elevator and held the door.

"Hey. Wait a minute." She followed him out. "You never answered me about this outfit."

"I've never answered you about a lot of things." He viewed the kitchen with satisfaction.

Jordan Tapley ran a taut ship. The black granite countertops and black gas ranges shone brightly. The range hoods held nary a speck of dust or grease. The two cook's assistants chopped and rolled, their shoulders hunched, their faces unsmiling, and neither looked up, not even at Devlin's entrance.

Jordan himself had his head buried in the commercial-size refrigerator, flinging produce into the garbage with vicious abandon while demanding in a thick New Orleans accent, "Who is the idiot that okayed this asparagus? This celery? These tomatoes? None of this is fit for pigs. Do you hear me? Pigs!"

"Jordan. Come and meet my wife." Jordan had already tried to ban him from the kitchen, so when handling the temperamental cook, Devlin made it his practice to keep his voice low and his gaze level.

Jordan spun around, a graceful movement for a man with an immense girth and three chins. "Your wife? I didn't know you had a wife."

Nonsense, of course. Devlin knew that since last night word of his unexpected marriage had swept the hotel.

Slamming the refrigerator closed, Jordan minced over, his feet tiny compared to the immense bulk above. "Miz Fitzwilliam, it's good to meet you."

"I know you. You're the famous Jordan Tapley." Meadow went to meet him, arms outstretched wide. "I've got your cookbook!"

Before Devlin's astonished eyes, Meadow and Jordan hugged and kissed, both talking at the same time. His voice was loud and sounded like New Orleans. Hers was low and warm and without any hint of an accent. Yet the two of them were instant friends. Devlin heard indecipherable terms like *andouille sausage* and *garde-manger* flung about with abandon. For the first time ever, Devlin saw Jordan's teeth flashing, not in annoyance, but in an exultant smile.

As if waiting for an explosion, the two assistants watched the display warily and muttered to each other.

When Meadow and Jordan managed to untangle themselves, she bounded toward the assistants. "These must be your sous chefs!"

Jordan followed, beaming.

Devlin trailed behind, wondering how the quiet, chilly, professional kitchen had disintegrated to this boisterous cheer so quickly.

"They aren't all of my local staff, of course. I have three people coming for training this afternoon." Jordan waved a big hand at the thin, middle-aged, nervous-looking woman chopping onions. "This is Mia—she's very talented. In the fall, when we open the restaurant, I'm going to promote her to saucier."

Mia's mouth dropped open. "You *like* my sauces? Really?" At Jordan's outraged glare, she hastily turned her attention to Meadow. "I mean . . . good to meet you, Mrs. Fitzwilliam!" Wiping her hand on her apron, she offered it to Meadow.

Meadow hugged her around the shoulders. "Is that for dinner tonight? Then don't stop!"

"Thank you, ma'am." Mia had the softest, most timid voice, with an accent that sounded almost like Devlin's. Almost, but a little less educated and little more country.

"This is Christian. He's new. He has all his fingertips." Jordan dismissed Christian's inexperience with a snort.

"I hope he keeps all his fingertips and becomes your head sous chef!" Meadow hugged the pudgy young man, too.

"Thank you, Mrs. Fitzwilliam." Christian's accent sounded sort of Southern, sort of twangy.

"My head sous chef is coming from New Orleans a week before the grand opening," Jordan told her. "I'm training this boy as pastry chef."

"You are?" In astonishment, Christian looked at the piecrust he was rolling on the marble slab.

"Yes—if you remember to *keep a light hand*!" Jordan thwapped him on the back of the head.

At once Christian lifted the rolling pin. "Yes, sir! Good to meet you, Mrs. Fitzwilliam."

"Now." Jordan rubbed his hands together. "Miz Fitzwilliam, you look hungry. What can I get you for breakfast?" He glanced at the huge clock on the wall. "Or lunch?"

It was time for Devlin to remind them he was here. "We're going into town for lunch."

At the news, Jordan settled for an outraged glare at Devlin, then switched his attention to Meadow. "So . . . do you like blueberries?" Jordan rummaged in the bread box and filled a plate, then placed it on the counter beside her. He broke off a piece of scone and popped it in her mouth.

"That's wonderful!" she mumbled.

"Biscuits and homemade blackberry preserves?" A chunk of biscuit followed.

"Ummm." She closed her eyes and shivered with pleasure.

Devlin was getting hungry. For food. And for Meadow.

He wanted her to look at him with the same lust she showed for homemade blackberry preserves.

Why hadn't he turned her over to the police last night? If all he was interested in was humiliating Bradley Benjamin, he could have easily announced that he'd caught Isabelle's granddaughter breaking and entering, and the resultant scandal would have been a lovely taste of revenge.

But when Meadow had looked up at him with those big blue eyes and proclaimed she had amnesia, she'd been so sure she'd plucked a get-out-of-jail-free card. He saw her congratulating herself, and something in him—some previously unknown quirk in his character— rose to the challenge, and he'd declared she was his wife.

His wife. Of all the tales he could have invented, why had he made up that one?

"The cold quiche is delicious." Jordan's fork flashed. "Traditional. Bacon, eggs, cream, Swiss cheese, and Christian's pastry."

She held up a hand. "I'm a vegetarian."

Devlin could pretend he wouldn't be bested when it came to telling outrageous falsehoods.

But Devlin Fitzwilliam did not deceive himself.

When he held Meadow in his arms, when he breathed her scent and saw the shining tumble of her copper-colored hair, he felt as if a strong, fresh wind had blown into a life grown stale and grim.

And when she threatened to puke . . . he'd wanted to laugh.

He hadn't really laughed a real belly laugh in years. Maybe never.

"Of course you are a vegetarian. You are skinny." Jordan polished off the piece of quiche.

"I wish," she said.

"She's perfect," Devlin said.

Jordan and Meadow both flashed him a startled glance. Had they forgotten he stood here? Or did he so seldom give compliments?

"Of course she is perfect. Just too skinny." Jordan turned back to Meadow. "Vegan?"

"No." She shook her head. "No meat."

"Good! So much easier. So much tastier. So much better for you!" Jordan pinched her cheek. "Some iced tea? Today it is ginger-peach. Very good!"

"That would be great!"

Devlin had never imagined such a mutual admiration society would flourish between his cook and his . . . between his cook and Meadow. He didn't understand it, either. Jordan had been like Devlin's other employees—dour, hardworking, determined to take this opportunity to head a world-class hotel and restaurant. Now he was smiling, handing out compliments, and flirting with Devlin's wife.

And the other two cooks . . . they were smiling!

What the hell had happened? What kind of effect did Meadow have on people? Why didn't she ever beam that smile at him?

Sure, he was lying to her, and she was lying to him, and they both knew they were deeply involved in one hell of a game. But they'd slept in the same bed. They'd exchanged the kind of kisses that branded a man's soul.

And she couldn't spare him one of those open, generous smiles?

Jordan bustled over to the bread box. His knife darted, and before Meadow could respond she held a plate mounded with golden pastries, a small bowl of unsalted butter and one of jam, and a napkin in a silver ring. In the other hand she held a frosty glass filled with sweet tea.

"Thank you!" She kissed Jordan on the cheek. "I'll make sure we're here for dinner!"

"We were always going to be here for dinner." Devlin knew Sam had already informed Jordan of that, because Sam always did his duty.

Jordan ignored him. "Good! I'll fix something especially nice for your first night in your new hotel."

"She was here last night." Concocting a foolish story about having amnesia. Being surprised when he concocted a story right back.

If their perjuries were getting in the way of her smiling at him, he'd do the right thing. He'd give her a chance to tell him the truth.

She wouldn't do it, of course. Like every other person in the world, she'd tell herself a story to justify her larcenies and her lies. Nevertheless, he'd give her the chance.

"She came late, not in time for dinner." Jordan sounded impatient with Devlin.

Impatient. With Devlin!

Jordan shooed her toward the stairs. "It's a beautiful day. Go into the garden and eat."

"Come on," she said to Devlin. "We need to get out of Jordan's way. The man's an artist—he needs room to work."

"Could I have a glass of iced tea, too?" Devlin injected a note of polite sarcasm into his voice.

"Sure 'nuff, boss. Here you go!" Jordan answered with exactly the same note of polite sarcasm coupled with some mocking old-fashioned subservience.

Meadow laughed, a laugh so bright the air in the usually dour kitchen sparkled like champagne.

With unaccustomed surprise, Devlin realized he wasn't going to win this round.

What surprised him more was . . . he didn't mind.

No. He couldn't turn her over to the police. He would not let her go.

Not yet. Not until she smiled at him without wariness and with joy. Not until he had uncovered her mysteries. Not until he'd discovered why she made him feel . . . alive. Different. Newborn.

And not until he'd slept with her.

Especially not until he'd slept with her.

10

*D*evlin followed Meadow up the stairs and held the heavy utility door for her.

They stepped out into the sunshine. In the distance he could hear the chain saw as someone removed the fallen tree. Nail guns whooshed as the carpenters erected the gazebo, and the trucks came and went, dumping loads of bark mulch for the gardeners. The estate sounded busy.

Good thing. They needed to clean up the havoc wrought by the storms and keep the schedule for the grand opening, or heads would roll.

"Isn't it a beautiful day?" she asked.

The humidity hovered at about eighty percent, the temperature at seventy degrees. He informed her, "This is average for this time of year."

"Average? There is nothing average about this day." She took a deep, long breath. "I love the way the salty scent of the sea and the spicy scent of the pines mingle. Don't you?"

He sniffed. To him it smelled of the sea, of the earth the gardeners had turned. It smelled of immense wealth and cruel snobbery brought down by inbreeding and stupidity—and his own ruthless intelligence.

It was a good smell.

"Look at the basil!"

He tried, but the tiny plants all looked the same to him, and he'd bet at least half of them were weeds. "This is the kitchen garden. The gardeners have been working getting the rest of the estate ready for the grand opening. They haven't touched it in here."

"So it's even better out there?" She walked toward the spring-hinged gate, hit it with her hip, and headed out into the estate.

Waldemar had been ramshackle when Devlin had gotten his hands on it. For all his pride, Bradley Benjamin hadn't been able to afford to maintain the gigantic house and immense grounds.

But Devlin had thrown his seasoned legion of interior decorators, cleaners, painters, and gardeners at the place, and now it boasted eight acres of seashore, forest, and lush gardens, with the freshly painted, newly cleaned, and redesigned house set high on the bluff overlooking the waves. An impressive iron gate announced the entrance to the estate, and from there the road wound past a carriage house—well maintained and serving as the eight-car garage—across the expanse of lawn and blooming wild roses.

This was what the estate was meant to be—and a slap in the face of Bradley Benjamin's overweening pride.

"This place is beautiful. Alluring." The tone of Meadow's voice changed from wonder to . . . thoughtfulness. "A woman could be seduced at the idea of owning this."

"Yes." He watched her and understood exactly what she was thinking. "Are you seduced?"

"What?" She blinked at him. "Oh. No. I've been taught better than that."

He knew why. He wondered if she did.

A crew of gardeners trudged into view, shovels over their shoulders, pushing wheelbarrows full of soil and flowers. At the sight of Devlin and Meadow, they stopped and backed up.

"They don't have to leave. I don't want to get in the way of their work." Meadow started toward them.

Devlin caught her arm. "They've been instructed to stay out of sight of the guests. That's the rule. Let's not confuse them."

"I'm hardly a guest."

"You're much more important. You're the wife of the owner." He enjoyed saying that; enjoyed, too, her wide-eyed, blinking dismay. She didn't know how to handle him—and he suspected that was a unique situation for the nimble Meadow.

"Let's sit over there." He indicated the picnic table beneath a huge ancient live oak with moss in its crown, and branches so huge and outstretched they touched the ground.

"What a great old tree." As Meadow walked ahead of him, the sun shone through his white linen shirt, outlining her body, reminding him of the morning when he'd woken with her ass pressed against his crotch. He'd been lucky the night before when she had appeared at Waldemar; his luck had moved to a new level this morning when her eyes had widened at the sight of him and she'd caught fire in his arms.

Something about her chemical makeup responded to him.

If revenge was a coin, he held a rare gold antique.

She ate with a gusto that surprised him. No dainty picking at her food for Meadow—she consumed a scone and two biscuits with jam before wiping her lips with the napkin, sighing with satisfaction, and surveying the area. "Look at those rhodies!" she said. "Aren't they glorious?"

He glanced at the rhododendrons. They were blooming. They were pink. Wasn't that what they were supposed to do? "Glorious."

"Why do you call the hotel the Secret Garden?"

He loved it when she gave him an opening like that. "Don't you remember, love?"

She blinked uncertainly at him. "You love the Frances Hodgson Burnett book?"

"I'm not familiar with it."

"You're not familiar with *The Secret Garden?*" In an excess of horror, Meadow pressed her hand over her heart. "It's a wonderful book about a girl who's closed off from love, and a boy who thinks he's a cripple, and his father who's so bitter about his wife's death he won't love his own son, and this secret garden that heals them all."

"Sounds . . . mushy." A polite way of saying he didn't believe in such emotional revelations.

"No! It's inspiring."

She couldn't be so naive—could she?

No. Of course not. She'd broken into Waldemar in search of that painting. She'd been willing to steal from Bradley Benjamin—Devlin had no problem with that—but now she planned to steal from him. No one took anything that belonged to Devlin and got away with it. She'd find that out soon enough. No one, no matter how attractive, stole from him.

With ruthless intent, he smiled into her eyes and said, "I remember. . . ."

Hand in hand, they explored the island of Majorca and found a sun-drenched island of tourists, beaches, cliffs, scrub, and gardens. Wonderful, glorious gardens. Each day brought a new adventure, a sense of the world made new, for he saw it through her eyes. Then, high atop a hill overlooking the sea, they discovered a small, forgotten patch of earth overgrown with weeds and brambles . . . and climbing roses and tiny crocuses thrusting out of the soil.

"You know what a crocus is?" she asked incredulously.

"I do now. You showed me."

She narrowed her eyes. "*I* know what a crocus is?"

He gestured around, "You know what a rhododendron is."

She nodded once, grudgingly. "Go on."

The garden had the remains of a house beside it, a place so old it had no roof and half the walls had tumbled down. She had screamed at the sight of a tiny mouse—

"I've really changed, then, because I'm not afraid of mice."

"Then maybe I screamed," he said impatiently. "Do you want to know about the Secret Garden or not?"

"Of course." She leaned her chin on her hand, and a smile lit her eyes.

The garden was enchanted. That was the only possible explanation he could imagine for the breeze that made the blossoms dance and the grass ripple. The food in their hamper tasted of honey and love, and when they kissed, the world disappeared. Only the two of them remained, entwined on the blanket, while around them the garden sang around its siren song.

On that blanket, in that garden, was the first time they made love.

"So in honor of you, I bought an estate with a secret garden on its grounds." In honor of her, Devlin Fitzwilliam, a man whose life had been ruled by logic and profit, had woven fantasies guaranteed to charm her.

What spell had she cast on him, that he should be so adroit, so romantic?

"Here? At Waldemar? Has it got walls and a door?" Her blue eyes were bright and mesmerized.

"Walls of stone, and a door with a lock." He loved to look at her like this, her lips softly open as if he'd just seduced her.

"With winding paths and flowers of every fragrance and color?"

"And at its heart, an expanse of velvety blue grass where you can dance." He sat solidly on a bench in the middle of his yard, watching the breeze off the Atlantic made the blossoms bobble and the grass ripple . . . and tousled the bright strands of Meadow's hair.

And she watched him as if he were the embodiment of her every dream.

He had used his voice to enchant her. Now he found himself enchanted as well.

"Well." She tore her gaze away from his and patted her cheeks. "It's very warm here."

She was blushing. Blushing at the thought of making love to him in a garden.

"I thought the temperature was quite . . . comfortable." And she was quite adorable.

"Yes. I'm not used to the humidity."

He watched her face as they spoke, weighed which of her words were lies and which were truths, and wondered which truths he could use to discover everything about her. "It's not humid . . . where you came from?"

"I guess not." She didn't take the bait.

He was almost glad. He was doing what he should, of course. He'd given the house detective the number she'd called this morning and sent him to search Atlanta—the area code placed it in Atlanta—to see if he could find any information on whom she called. But Devlin didn't want this farce to end so soon. He was enjoying himself as he hadn't for years.

No. That wasn't true.

He was enjoying himself as he never had.

"Why did you come here now?" he was asking. He was coaxing. He, ruthless bastard Devlin Fitzwilliam, wanted to end the farce between them and start anew.

And he waited on tenterhooks, watching her eyes widen with uncertainty, inwardly urging her to trust him.

Instead, she bit her lower lip, then cleared her throat. "I'll get you a copy when we go into town."

"A copy?" He leaned back, all his cynicism confirmed. "A copy of what?"

"Of *The Secret Garden.*"

He laughed, a brief bark of amusement. "I'm in the last stages of opening a hotel. I don't have time to read." Certainly not a sentimental bunch of drivel like *The Secret Garden.*

"I'll read it to you."

Long afternoons curled up on a hammock in the garden, just the two of them rocking as she read him a girlie story . . . why did that sound appealing?

But it did.

His little liar offered him a world he had previously scorned, and made him want it almost as much as he wanted her.

For the first time he realized she was more than a challenge and a distraction—she was dangerous.

A third voice intruded, a man's laughing, charming, aristocratic voice. "How touching. The sweet girl's going to read a children's book to the big, mean developer."

With a thump Devlin stepped ankle-deep into a pile of reality. He turned to find a blond, well-dressed, and far too familiar figure standing behind him, glass in hand. *Shit. Not him. Not now.* "Four. I told you to go away and stay away."

"So you did." Four swung his leg over the bench and sat next to Meadow.

"Then what are you doing here?"

"I live here."

11

"Or I used to." Taking Meadow's hand, Four raised it to his lips. "I'm Bradley Benjamin the fourth. I'm handsome, kind, generous, trustworthy, and irresistible."

Meadow grinned at his insouciance. "I can see that."

"In other words, the exact opposite of stodgy old Devlin over there."

"Oh, I don't know." She was still half-aroused with the pleasure of Devlin's description of the Secret Garden. "I think Devlin's incredibly charming." Although he didn't look charming right now. He sat with his arms crossed over his chest. His mouth was grim, his teeth clenched.

"Devlin? Devlin Fitzwilliam?" Four stared at Devlin with bug-eyed disbelief. "Not this Devlin Fitzwilliam, the meanest son of a bitch—begging your pardon, ma'am—ever to walk the streets of Charleston?"

"The very one."

"You have a smiley-face bandage on your forehead." Four touched it lightly. "Tell me the truth. You fell and knocked all the sense out of yourself."

His guess was close enough to the actual events to frighten Meadow into flashing Devlin a questioning glance.

"Where did you hear that story?" Devlin asked.

"I didn't *hear* anything. But that's the only explanation I can imagine for her bad judgment." Four took a biscuit. "Never allow Devlin's temporary attempts at civilized behavior to fool you. The milk of human kindness has curdled in his veins."

She studied Four as he slathered the biscuit with butter and jam and ate it in two bites. He seemed sincere enough, but . . . "Devlin seems indestructible."

Four snorted. "He hides everything. His feelings, his thoughts . . . then, wham! He hits you with a broadside and knocks you catawampus." He lifted the half-eaten biscuit. "But his cook is far superior to Father's."

"Yes." Devlin didn't waste time with graciousness.

"And your liquor cabinet is stocked with the best." Four saluted Devlin with his sweating glass.

"Help yourself." Like a stubborn case of athlete's foot, Four irritated Devlin.

Meadow could see why. Devlin appeared rugged, like a mountain man who had gotten lost and stumbled into this soft, warm, humid environment where the birds chirped and the sun trickled through the thick leaves.

Four was very different. He had a look about him, one she'd seen in her grandmother's black-and-white Fred Astaire movies— whipcord thin, world-weary, well dressed, and wealthy. Very, very wealthy. He wasn't tall, only about five-nine, but his blue polo shirt stretched across muscular shoulders, and his gray slacks were belted tightly around a trim waist. His hair was expertly cut—and thinning. She'd swear someone armed with an airbrush had sprayed on his tan. He smelled of stale cigarettes and expensive cologne, and he sounded eloquent and nobly Southern. But most important, he oozed charisma from every pore, a kind of jaded, old-world dissipation.

She didn't imagine he was anything like his father.

He took a drink from the glass he'd placed on the table. It was the same kind of glass from which she sipped iced tea. The liquid was brown like tea. But a few green leaves floated among the ice cubes, and the sweet odor of bourbon wafted through the air.

It was barely eleven in the morning. "I'm Meadow."

"Meadow. That's beautiful, and so appropriate. You're as fresh as a mountain meadow. But I didn't catch your last name." Four's hazel eyes danced with amusement as he observed Devlin's impatience.

"I didn't give it," she said.

At the same time, Devlin said, "Fitzwilliam."

"You're romancing your cousin?" Four guessed. "Isn't that a little traditionally Southern for you, Devlin?"

"She's not my cousin," Devlin said.

She studied her hands in her lap and wished she could stuff her napkin down Devlin's throat.

Four studied them, then reached the inevitable conclusion. "She's not your . . . *wife?*" He choked on the liquor. He coughed until tears sprang to his eyes. Until she hit him on the back to clear his air passage. He waved her away and croaked at Devlin, "You're married? To her? You're pulling my leg. Since when? Don't tell me—you married in *Majorca!*"

So he'd heard at least some of the tale Devlin had spun for her. His eavesdropping made her uncomfortable and a little disgruntled. The fantasy was her story, a present from Devlin, and she didn't like sharing it with anyone. Most certainly she didn't want Four asking questions about a ceremony that had never occurred.

"Actually, Four, this is such bad timing." Devlin's sympathetic tone was at odds with his glee. "My wife and I are on our way into town. So go away."

"We are?" It was the first Meadow had heard of it.

"We need to pick up your prescription," Devlin said.

Her head ached, but not much, yet when she started to say so she encountered a warning glance from Devlin.

All right. They were going to town. "We can pick up a copy of *The Secret Garden* while we're there."

"Another good reason to go into Amelia Shores," he said with almost indiscernible exasperation.

"Great!" Four said. "I'll go with you."

"No, you won't." Devlin was firm. "We're taking the Jeep. There's no room for you. There's no backseat."

"Devlin, that tone will never work! You can't tantalize with the news of your marriage, then get rid of me! I have a reputation as a gossipmonger to maintain. I drove out here. I'll drive back into town." Four laughed lightly and took another drink, more carefully this time. "While we're there, you can give me all the juicy details of the romance of the century."

"You don't take a hint, do you?" Meadow admired the man's impervious nature.

"My dear, if a person listened to all of Devlin's rejections he'd think he wasn't liked. In fact, I'm his best friend."

Devlin snorted.

"If I'm not, who is?" Four challenged him.

"My wife," Devlin said.

"That is so romantic," Four began.

But Meadow wasn't prepared to make up any stories about meeting on the beach and exchanging a kiss before they exchanged a word, and she certainly couldn't imagine expanding on the preposterous imagery of lying among the shrubs in a secret garden behind a crumbling house and making love . . . not until she was alone, anyway. "So your family used to own Waldemar."

"For over a hundred years." Four's pride unfurled like a flag. "It's the foremost estate near Amelia Shores, and Amelia Shores is the last and most important refuge for the hidebound and stinking rich of Charleston. My family—the most hidebound and stinking—held this place for a hundred years, through the Great Depression and every kind of tax. And we had to sell it to the most famous blue-blood bastard—pardon me, ma'am—illegitimate son who ever lived."

"It wasn't so much a sale"—Devlin locked gazes with Four—"as a surrender."

"Wow." Meadow looked between them, saw Four's clenched jaw and Devlin's insolent smile. Their malice acted like acid to corrode her pleasure in the morning.

But she was a fighter. If they were going to piss on each other's shoes, she was at least going to know why. "You guys get nasty fast. What happened? Did you have a fight in prep school?"

Four turned to her in surprise, then laughed and relaxed. "I'm older than he is, and too smart to pick a fight with little Devlin and his bony fists. He had a reputation for making the other guy bleed, no matter what the odds."

"Really?" That was the Devlin she saw in his unguarded moments— mean as a junkyard dog, overwhelming as an earthquake.

"But then, the whole Fitzwilliam family has been trying to destroy my family and its pride for two centuries." Four's grin turned malicious. "With no success."

"The problem is not your pride, but the lack of reason for it." While Four was growing angry, Devlin was growing cold.

Fascinated, she looked between the two of them. "Is this a real live family feud?"

"Rooted in tradition," Four said.

"For generations," Devlin added.

"What started it?" she asked.

Both men shrugged and looked away. They knew, but they weren't talking. Whatever rivalry prompted the sharp exchange was old and acrimonious.

"Slander? Robbery? Murder?" She searched her mind for something that would really upset these guys so much. "Lynching?"

Four took a drink of his bourbon. "Broken betrothal," he muttered.

Meadow sat there, waiting for the rest of the story. When nothing more was forthcoming, she asked, "That's it? Your families have been fighting for . . . for—"

"Two hundred and fifty years," Devlin told her.

"Two hundred and fifty years over a *broken betrothal*?"

The two men nodded.

She burst into laughter. "How *girlie* of you!"

They were not amused.

"In early America, a broken betrothal was a huge point of honor," Four said stiffly. "When John Benjamin, who was a wealthy planter, did the honor of offering for the hand of Anne Fitzwilliam, who was his housemaid, she accepted, then decided she couldn't stand to marry him and left him at the altar."

"Thus showing that the Fitzwilliams have a long history of good sense," Devlin said.

"She was probably in love with someone else." Still smiling, Meadow watched the two men snipe over an old romance gone bad. A *really* old romance.

"She died a spinster," Four said.

"The ultimate insult." An offensive smile played around Devlin's mouth. "If she'd married someone else, the Benjamins could claim she'd lost her mind for love. Instead, she preferred to work as her brother's housekeeper—by all accounts, a thankless job—while he made his fortune shipping cotton to Britain."

"He made his fortune in trade," Four sneered.

"Yes, and the only difference between him and you is that he did it well."

Four stood up, knocking over his glass.

Ice clattered across the table. Brown liquid rushed toward Devlin.

Devlin scrambled to his feet, but not fast enough to avoid a lap full of bourbon.

Meadow would have sworn he was ready to leap across the table and beat Four.

Then Four laughed.

The sound of that insolent amusement acted on Devlin as the ice cubes had not. His flush faded and his expression cooled. "How clumsy of you, Four."

He wasn't talking about the spilled drink.

"Okay!" Meadow stood up, too.

Four ran his gaze up her legs. "Nice."

"Thank you." Exasperated at the way he used her to get at Devlin, she used Four's pride to get back at him. "And what a gentlemanly way of saying I look attractive."

He flushed. "Point taken."

"Make sure that it is."

Devlin slid his hand around Meadow's waist. "Let's go change now, darling, and we'll be on our way."

"Of course, darling." She fluttered her eyelashes at him. He didn't seem nearly as smug about her outrageous outfit now. Apparently it was one thing for him to appreciate her figure, and quite another for Four, with his lascivious smile and his handsome face, to enjoy it. "After we clean up this mess."

"I'll call for a crew." Devlin took the walkie-talkie off his belt.

"We can do it." Meadow stacked the glasses onto the plate.

Devlin ignored her, giving orders to the housekeeper on the other end. When he finished, he gestured at the wet spot on his pants and said to her, "Let's go."

"You don't need me to help you." She did not want to go into that bedroom with him again. Not while he removed his pants. As Sharon always said, it was easier to shun temptation than to fight it.

"He's not going to let you stay here alone with me. I might decide to avenge the insult to my ancestor by seducing Devlin's wife." Four thrust his hands in his pockets and grinned.

"What a jackass you are," she said cordially.

"What did I say?" Four glanced at Devlin in honest bewilderment.

Devlin's satisfaction couldn't be denied. "I believe my wife just said she wouldn't be seduced by a pretty face and a big ego."

"You almost got it right." Meadow pinched Devlin's chin and smiled deliberately into his face. "*I* won't be seduced *at all*."

Devlin understood. He understood very well, but he didn't accede. He stared back, answering her challenge.

Neither of them backed down. Nothing broke the silence.

Until the cleanup crew clattered out of the door and started toward them.

At the sign of discord between them, Four beamed. He opened his mouth to speak.

Meadow looked at him. Just looked at him.

He shut his mouth.

She approved Four's common sense with a simple, "Good man." To Devlin, she asked sarcastically, "Which of my flowered sundresses do you want me to wear?"

"Put on jeans," Devlin directed.

"Jeans. What a good idea." She'd won! She'd won! "I wish I'd thought of getting some jeans."

Or had she won? If jeans were already in her room, he'd ordered them when he'd thrown away her burglar outfit, and all that talk about only flowered sundresses was simply nonsense.

She didn't understand what drove Devlin—what he wanted with her, why he lied to Four, what he intended with his elaborate charade. She knew while she donned her outfit only that whatever it was she decided to wear, she would lock the door.

It was simply safer.

12

Amelia Shores was a town of four thousand in the off-season and twelve thousand during the tourist season. Right now, in the spring, the bed-and-breakfasts had been freshly painted, Wendy's and McDonald's were hiring smiling faces, and the restaurants along Waterfront Row rolled out their striped canopies to cover their outdoor tables.

A few tourists were already there.

The hordes were coming.

As they wandered along the sidewalk, the Atlantic on one side and the street on the other, Four told Meadow, "The shops are gearing up for the high season, so before the tourists get here the regulars come down to D'Anna's for lunch and stay for a leisurely dessert, coffee, and gossip."

"Who are the regulars?" Her head swiveled between the beach and the shore. She'd never visited the East Coast, but no matter their location, coastal towns shared common sights and smells. Waves curled, and sunbathers wiped sand off their lotion-damp skin. Shops advertised with bright bikinis and intricate kites hung in the windows. Tourists traipsed along Waterfront Row in cover-ups donned too late to protect against the sunburn that seared their shoulders.

She didn't fit in; in a fit of rebellion against Devlin she had donned a silk flowered sundress and strappy yellow sandals, and now the breeze played with the edge of her skirt, and she had to use her hand to keep her wide-brimmed straw hat on her head.

"The regulars are people who live here." Four waved at a shopkeeper. "The people who work here."

"The regulars are the old farts who used to own the whole town and still control the city council." Devlin walked behind them, and his words were so at odds with his unemotional tone that Meadow turned and walked backward to stare at him.

He wore faded jeans and a white shirt with the sleeves rolled up to his elbows. He looked like a construction worker—except for his darkly sardonic eyes, which watched her with such intensity.

Could he see through her sundress? But no; the halter and skirt were lined, the hem reached midcalf, and he might not have been happy that she defied his instructions about the jeans, but he openly appreciated the smooth line of her shoulders and throat.

"You don't like the old farts," she said.

"They want to halt the march of time," he answered.

"And you *are* the march of time," she guessed.

"He's like an army battalion tromping through a flower garden. He leaves nothing in his path." She heard a sour note in Four's voice. "You're going to trip." Four caught her arm and turned her forward.

"If you didn't want to sell Waldemar to Devlin, why did you do it?" she asked.

Four did trip on a crack on the sidewalk, and when he righted himself she saw that some of his charm had eroded like gold vermeil off well-worn silver.

"Four didn't sell the house to me," Devlin said. "His father did."

"Over my objections." Four looked toward the restaurant perched on the highest spot on the street. There uniformed waiters moved among the outdoor tables carrying bottles of sparkling water, and the fringe on the large round umbrellas fluttered in the breeze.

"He had no choice." Devlin continued his barrage on Four's dignity. "I made him an offer he couldn't refuse."

"Are you the Godfather?" Meadow laughed, then realized that Four's cheeks were ruddy with fury and Devlin was smiling that hateful smile. They were ready to come to blows again.

"He has aspirations," Four said grimly.

"Yet my ambitions are thoroughly crushed. The original Godfather of Amelia Shores isn't ready to step aside yet." Devlin indicated the group of gentlemen who sat along the metal railing, watching the street. "That's his father up there."

Meadow stopped still in the street and looked up. From across and down the street, they looked too similar to tell apart—five older men dressed in tasteful, expensive leisure clothing and sipping aperitifs from tall glasses. "Which one is he?"

She tried not to sound too intense, too interested.

She doubted that she had succeeded.

Four stopped with her. "Left to right—Wilfred Kistard, toupee, and a crusty old gentleman with a kind heart. Penn Sample, bald, portly, ear hair, twinkling blue eyes that hide a shrewd brain. He's the one who thought of cutting Devlin's local supplies to the hotel."

"Did he?" Devlin didn't appear particularly worried.

But Meadow was learning a lot about Devlin, and she knew that as of this moment, if Penn Sample were drowning and going under for the last time, Devlin would throw him an anchor.

"H. Edwin Osgood. Never married, lives alone in his mansion—not a bit of trouble making his payments, I can tell you—and fancies himself quite the ladies' man. Hair color for men. Bow tie and thick glasses. He's my father's sycophant." Four grimaced. "'Nuff said. Scrubby Gallagher, thinning white hair. He's my godfather, the oldest, and the only one of the bunch who's ever lived anywhere besides Charleston and here."

Meadow had been raised in her parents' art studio outside the small town of Blythe in the Cascade Mountains in Washington. She'd attended college at Stanford in California. She'd spent a semester in Rome taking classes and living with an Italian family. She was only twenty-two—and these old guys had never lived anywhere else? She couldn't imagine being so confined in her mind and heart. "Where did he live?"

"Atlanta."

She laughed briefly.

Four laughed with her. "Yes, quite a change of pace. His experience broadened his world scope—a profound character defect—and that's why the others pay him so little heed." He looked sideways at Devlin. "And it's the reason he's forward-thinking enough to invest in Devlin's hotel."

Devlin studied Four. "How did you know that?"

"I only suspected until this minute." Four smirked so obnoxiously, Meadow wondered that Devlin didn't hit him.

Four was smart; he'd figured out something Meadow knew must be so secret only Devlin and Scrubby Gallagher knew. Yet so stupid; he had to taunt Devlin with his sly intelligence.

One of the gentlemen, the one with the whitest hair, waved.

She waved back.

Four didn't. "That's him. That's my father. He's only made two mistakes in his life—all the women he married, and all the children he fathered."

"Really?" Meadow considered Four. "How many wives and children has he had?"

"Four wives. One child. Me." Four pulled a cigarette from his shirt pocket and lit it with a match, protecting the flame from the ocean breeze with his body and his hand.

"Four wives." She had had no idea. "Did all the marriages end in divorce?"

"All," Four confirmed. "Three of them—number two, number three, and number four—cited mental cruelty. He's an indifferent old prick."

"And the first wife?" she asked.

"He divorced her, citing irreconcilable differences." Four chuckled, amused and ashamed by his amusement. "Actually, it was infidelity."

"Really?" She watched Four.

Devlin watched her.

"Mind you, this was before my time, but from what I've managed to gather, Isabelle was a beauty. Not appropriate, of course. Not one of our class."

"Shocking!" Meadow said.

"For my father it was. He must have been mad for her. She was fooling around with her art teacher, and when the old man confronted her, she admitted it without a bit of shame. He threw her out, of course, and the baby with her." Four shook his head. "Cold as ice. Apparently the kid was only a couple of months old, and Isabelle had no funds and nowhere to go."

"She had a baby?" Meadow's skin should have been warm in the sun. Instead a chill worked its way along her nerves.

"My closest shot at a sibling—except she was fathered by the lover." He flicked his ashes into the wind. "I wish she hadn't been. She might have taken some of the expectations off me."

"Not likely," Devlin said. "He doesn't expect much of a woman."

"He expects them to be decorative." Four's gaze swept Meadow, not insultingly as before, but appraisingly. "He'll approve of you."

"You can imagine my relief," she said coolly.

"He'll like that air, too. He detests a woman who's demonstrative about her feelings. In fact, he's not fond of feelings at all."

"Because the one time he gave in to his own, his wife betrayed him." Meadow looked between the two men's surprised faces. "Honestly, don't you guys ever think of this stuff?"

"Don't you gals ever think of anything else?" Devlin countered.

In a flash of irritation, she said, "On occasion, but we *gals* have our priorities right. Family and feelings first."

"Except Isabelle." Devlin lifted Meadow's hand to his mouth and kissed her fingers. "Isabelle didn't think of her family and their feelings when she had that affair."

Meadow snatched her hand from his. "I suppose that's right."

Four watched the interaction between them curiously, as if he saw something askew.

He was correct, of course. She and Devlin were two actors in a nightmare play, performing onstage without knowing their next line, their next scene. And beneath the trappings of civilized manners and banter, dread and anticipation bubbled through her veins, caused not only by the fear that she would falter and betray her mission.

She also sensed that she was being stalked. Devlin was stalking her, maybe for sex, maybe for . . . she didn't know why.

She knew only that she, who was so good at reading people's motives, did not understand a single thing about Devlin. She knew only that when he watched her as he was watching her now, the blood flowed warm and thick in her veins and she wanted to go somewhere with him and be alone to kiss and touch . . . and mate.

"No photos of Isabelle exist in the family album," Four said thoughtfully. "Father tore them up. Is that why? Because he gave in to his feelings and she betrayed them?"

Meadow looked away from Devlin's mocking eyes, down at the ground, then out at the ocean. "Probably."

"How do you know he tore them up?" Devlin asked.

"One day I was digging through the boxes of his pictures and realized she was missing. I got curious, so I asked." Four took a long drag on his cigarette. "He about snapped my head off."

"He sounds delightful," Meadow said.

"He'd get worse when Isabelle's picture was in the paper. You see, his wife Isabelle, the one who made my father forever a cuckold in the eyes of his compatriots, went on to become a famous artist." Four clearly relished imparting the news.

"Really?" Meadow opened her eyes wide in astonishment.

"She was *the* Isabelle, acclaimed darling of the wilderness art world. Are you familiar with her?"

"Who isn't familiar with Isabelle?" It should have been a rhetorical question, but Devlin was looking at Meadow. Mocking Meadow.

And Meadow could scarcely keep from squirming in guilt.

"Her canvases command upward of a hundred thousand, and they're appreciating in value all the time," Four said.

"He must hate that." She hoped so.

"He really hated that whenever she took a lover, it was reported in the gossip columns. He got particularly nasty then." Devlin actually put his hand on Four's shoulder. "Do you recall when he reamed you out in front of the whole school?"

"You told him to stop, so, asshole that he is, he asked what last name you were going to give your children—and the other kids laughed."

"That was the first time he used that line," Devlin said.

"That was the first time she slept with a Kennedy." Four smirked.

Meadow looked between the two men and realized how much in common they shared. No wonder they were friends—or as much friends as Devlin would allow them to be. "Why would he say such a stupid, unreasoning thing?"

"He recites a chant over and over to remind him and the Amelia Shores Society of Old Farts of a world order that faded many years ago," Devlin said.

"It faded in most of America. But not here. Not in this tiny town, where the elders will kill to maintain their goddamn—pardon, ma'am—world order and their goddamn—pardon, ma'am—place of importance in it." Four took a long drag, then ground out the cigarette with his foot.

Meadow looked him right in the eye. "You pick that up."

He did.

"Good boy. Now, shall we go meet Bradley Benjamin?" While she was fortified by renewed indignation.

She started up the stairs to the restaurant.

As they approached, the old guys stood up. They were exactly as Four had described—and Bradley Benjamin was exactly as Meadow had imagined.

Of the old guys, he was the tallest. His posture was military, shoulders back, spine straight. His large, noble, aging nose drooped at the end. His shock of white hair was wavy and thick, his brows white and wild. His eyes were gray, cool and considering. He looked like an old-world aristocrat—and a surge of hatred caught Meadow by surprise.

This man had thrown her grandmother and mother into the street with no money, no support, and no remorse. He'd let Isabelle take her baby to Ireland to live with her art teacher, and when she sent word that Bjorn Kelly wished to adopt Sharon, Bradley had signed the papers without hesitation. And when Bjorn had been killed and Isabelle had announced her daughter's death with him, Bradley had not sent a word of condolence.

Isabelle had insisted that he had emotions. That they were stunted and warped by his upbringing and his background, but that he had them.

If that was the truth, Meadow wondered what he would do when he discovered . . . what had really happened.

13

"*F*ather." Four shook the old man's gnarled hand. "Good to see you."

Bradley Benjamin grunted and ignored his only son, as he'd been doing from the day he was born. His gaze went beyond Four to Devlin. "Fitzwilliam."

"Sir." Devlin offered his hand, too.

Bradley took it, shook it, and dropped it as if the contact would contaminate his skin. He scrutinized the pretty girl dressed in silk flowers, and his gaze warmed. "Who is this young lady?"

"This is Meadow Fitzwilliam," Devlin said.

She smiled at Bradley, that open, happy smile that Devlin had come to realize characterized her personality. The one she so seldom wasted on him.

She might have secrets, but she didn't allow them to prey on her mind.

"Good to meet you, Bradley." She shook his hand heartily.

Bradley Benjamin stiffened.

She'd slipped in his assessment. This was the South, the Old South, and young ladies did not call their elders by their first name. In Benjamin's day, they didn't shake hands, either.

Then she smiled at Bradley again, and her sheer charm melted his reserve.

One at a time, Devlin introduced her to the old farts.

They twinkled. They beamed. Penn Simple even blushed and sucked in his stomach, and H. Edwin Osgood studied her with narrowed eyes, like man scoping out his next conquest. They all proved the truth of the adage, *No fool like an old fool.*

Damn the old fools.

She was like a weapon in Devlin's hands, to be used to get what he wanted, when he wanted, and all he had to do was sight down the barrel and squeeze the trigger.

Old Benjamin held her chair. "Won't you honor us with your presence?"

"Thank you." She seated herself and removed her hat, and the glow of her copper hair caught the gaze of every man in the place.

Devlin pulled up a chair without being asked and placed himself just behind and off to the side of her right shoulder. From here he could watch the door, watch the street, and, most important, watch the old farts, especially Bradley Benjamin.

"Meadow is my wife."

The collective gasp was satisfying.

Benjamin's narrow-eyed outrage made Devlin want to laugh out loud. Devlin could almost hear him accusing Devlin of ruining a young woman's life, then of bringing a fortune hunter into their midst, and finally of deceiving the old farts by presenting them with a woman of charm and not immediately identifying her so they could snub her properly.

At last, predictably, Benjamin's attention turned to his son. "Devlin is married."

"I would be married, too, Father, if Devlin hadn't discovered the lovely Meadow first." Four performed a sitting bow in Meadow's direction.

"Congratulations, Devlin. I can already tell you don't deserve her," Penn Sample said.

"That's very true," Devlin answered easily. "No man alive deserves someone as delightful as Meadow—but I have her, and I will keep her."

She glanced over her shoulder at him, her eyes wide, and he realized how that must have sounded—and that, at this moment, he meant it.

"When and how did this marriage occur?" Benjamin asked.

"I went to my house in Majorca to vacation, and Meadow found me there," Devlin said.

"I wasn't asking you, young man," Benjamin snapped, "but your lovely wife."

Devlin didn't want her to say the wrong thing, but he shouldn't have worried.

"Let's just say—Devlin and I have had a tumultuous relationship, and leave it at that, shall we?" Meadow laughed. "Now all his lovely wife wants is a drink, and a chance to sit back and talk."

She handled the old farts so well. She only fumbled with Devlin, and that pleased him more than he could say.

He signaled for service.

The waiter appeared at Meadow's elbow. "Ma'am, what may I get you?"

She smiled at him, a zit-laden college kid, with exactly the same amount of pleasure she showed Benjamin and the other old farts. "Don't call me 'ma'am'! My name is Meadow. I would love a bottled water, and can I get a menu? I'm starving!"

"Yes, ma'am. Yes . . . Meadow." Dazzled, the waiter started to leave.

"Excuse me, Dave!" Four was half laughing and all annoyed. "I'd like something."

Dave came back, flustered. "Of course, sir. What will it be?"

"A mint julep for me, and for Devlin—"

"I'll take a bottled water, too," Devlin said.

"Have a julep," Four urged. "Daddy runs a tab."

"Water will be fine," Devlin told the waiter. "For all of us."

Four started to protest the edict, but Devlin subdued him with a glance.

Damn Four. He'd tricked Devlin into admitting Scrubby's investment in the Secret Garden. And not that Devlin thought Four would deliberately tell the other old farts, but when he got drunk, he said too much and acted like an ass.

Scrubby had risked his standing in his community to show faith in Devlin, and he deserved better than betrayal.

"Of course. Water is my favorite beverage." Four seated himself and lit a cigarette, as debonair, as privileged, and as annoying as ever.

"Mrs. Fitzwilliam, I know you're not from South Carolina, but I can't place your accent."

Trust old Benjamin to ask the questions Devlin needed answered.

"Now, how do you know I'm not from South Carolina?" With startling speed, she developed an accent.

"You have a good ear." Osgood spoke with a slight lisp, and his thick glasses distorted his watery brown eyes to an unnatural size. That, and the unskillful application of dark brown hair dye created a man better suited to a farce than to this elite group of privileged old men. "Usually when a Yankee tries to imitate us, the sound grinds like a chain saw."

"I do have a good ear." She sounded cockney, then smoothly switched to a Hispanic accent. "I tried drama in college, but I couldn't cut it as an actress."

Did she have an accent or didn't she? Devlin was suddenly unsure. Could she have fooled him from the moment she'd fallen on his stone lion?

He wanted to know her name. He had to discover her true identity. He needed to know everything there was to know about the mysterious Meadow . . . and before their affair was over, he would. He swore it.

"A lovely young woman like you? I would think you'd be a Hollywood star by now!" While Penn Sample pried, charm oozed from his pores like 3-IN-ONE oil.

"I cried when I played the sad parts and laughed at the funny ones." She laughed now. "As my coach said, that's not acting; that's audience participation."

Wilfred Kistard blotted his damp forehead with a snowy handkerchief, looked uncomfortable, and said, "Hot out here already."

Dave arrived with the waters. He twisted the top off one bottle and handed it to her, then delivered the menu with a flourish.

She glanced at the menu. "The house salad sounds marvelous! I'll have that with blue cheese dressing on the side, and the pasta primavera." She turned to Devlin. "Do you want anything?"

"Ham on rye, hold the mayo, deli mustard," Dave recited. "I remember."

"He is such a nice boy!" Meadow said as Dave left. Tilting up the bottle, she drank the whole thing, and each of the men around her watched her throat as she swallowed. She lowered the bottle and sighed with contentment. "That was wonderful! I was dehydrated."

"Another reason I know you're not from the area. You're more brash than a Southern lady, more forthcoming." Old Benjamin was not paying her a compliment.

"Thank you, Bradley. That is so sweet of you!" Devlin recognized the overly vehement note of pleasure in her voice, but no one else here knew her well enough to identify her annoyance.

Benjamin wasn't used to being misunderstood, and he visibly struggled against telling her what he had meant.

That gave Devlin the opportunity to say smoothly, "Yes, that was one of the many reasons Meadow succeeded where so many have failed. She's less stifled by tradition and the weight of expectations than the typical Southern lady."

Benjamin gladly turned his reeking frustration on Devlin. "We're all surprised, Devlin, that you've married at last."

"Thirty-two is hardly a great age, sir. After all, I believe you were as old when you took your first wife." Devlin was pointed in his comment.

The other old men moved uneasily. The story of Isabelle and her infidelity always made them uncomfortable, recalling their own marital misadventures and the possibility—slight, in their minds, but always there—that not every female knew her place.

"Now, see, there's the difference between Devlin and me. He married me because I'm a child of freethinkers." Meadow grinned cockily. "I married him for his money."

The old farts sputtered with shocked laughter.

"And his good looks." Turning around, she looked mischievously into Devlin's eyes as she pinched his cheek.

All he had to do was sight down the barrel and squeeze the trigger. Too bad the damned weapon had a mind of her own.

And why in the hell did he enjoy having her make fun of him in front of the assemblage of old farts? If he wasn't careful, she would make him liked in this town.

"What did you say, young lady, when you discovered your husband was a bastard?" Benjamin baldly asked the question, clearly hoping to catch Meadow by surprise, maybe tell her something Devlin hadn't had the nerve to tell her.

"Oh, Father." Four covered his eyes with his slender, uncallused hand.

"Good shot," Osgood said.

It wasn't lack of nerve that had kept Devlin from informing her, but lack of time—they'd met only last night, and he seldom spoke of his fatherless state, certainly not within twenty-four hours of meeting a woman.

"What? Oh, I suppose he wants me to call him illegitimate." Benjamin challenged Devlin with his curling lip. "But I believe in calling a spade a spade."

Devlin waited, as curious about Meadow's reaction as the rest of the group.

"There's no excuse to call it a bloody damned shovel, at least not in polite society." Meadow's tone could have frozen pipes in August. "Perhaps when you wish to be rude, Mr. Benjamin, you should stick with calling me brash and hope I don't catch the slight."

Benjamin's gaze flew to hers, then dropped beneath the lash of her contempt.

"Brava!" Four clapped his hands softly. His eyes lit up, and he visibly admired Meadow.

Devlin schooled his face to impassivity, but marveled at Meadow's defense of him. He marveled, too, at how well Meadow read these men and used their weaknesses to manipulate them. She held her own formidable weapon—and Devlin needed to remember she held it.

"To answer your question, Mr. Benjamin, I have no interest in Devlin's parents except in the way they influenced his upbringing. It's the man himself who fascinates me." She turned her head toward Devlin and smiled. "I can hardly fault his charisma, his charm, or his kindness."

Either she was a better actress than she claimed, or she believed what she said—and Devlin didn't know which idea disturbed him more.

Benjamin recognized defeat when it stared him in the face, so he quit that battle and took up another. "So, young Devlin, what have you done with my house?"

"In three weeks, the Secret Garden will be an accredited five-star small hotel and receive its guests," Devlin said.

"Yet I hear you're having trouble getting goods from the local merchants." Wilfred Kistard leaned back in his chair and folded his hands across his round, sagging belly.

"The local merchants do what they must." Devlin had been pulled aside more than once while some storekeeper feverishly explained that his defection was temporary and if Mr. Fitzwilliam would simply have patience . . .

"You've had some accidents on the property." Scrubby tapped the table. "Any more problems?"

"Security has been tightened." Devlin met his anxious gaze and nodded.

"How bad is it if you don't get that five-star rating?" Penn Sample smacked his lips. "I'd say that would cause a significant loss of revenue."

"True. So true." Osgood's shoulders slumped as he looked toward Bradley for guidance.

"My hotels do not lose revenue." Devlin looked around the table. "The invitations to the grand opening will be going out in another week. Look for it in the mail. It will be the event of the season."

"Do you really imagine anyone will show up to see you desecrate the sacred traditions of Amelia Shores?" Benjamin asked.

"You will. Your curiosity won't let you stay away." Devlin's certainty ran headlong into Benjamin's outrage.

Benjamin's wrath faltered. He would, indeed, be there.

Four ground out one cigarette, then lit another immediately and took a long draw like a man in need of a much stronger drug.

Bradley watched him with ill-concealed contempt. "You're too old to be smoking those things. Those are for adolescents. Try to be a man about one thing, at least."

"You want him to be a man about smoking?" Meadow asked. "How would he do that?"

"There's nothing like a cigar." Bradley held up his hand to forestall any comment from her. "I know some ladies don't like the smell, but there's nothing like the smooth, warm smoke of a good cigar."

Four must have really been irritated by his father's reprimand, especially in front of Meadow, for his voice ground with exasperation. "I don't like cigars, sir."

"I don't see why you value mouth cancer from a cigar more than lung cancer from a cigarette. They both end in mutilating surgeries, awful bouts of chemotherapy, and death." Meadow smiled, a slight upward tilt of the lips and the least genuine smile Devlin had ever had the privilege to view.

The contrast between that and her regular smile was so great, every old fart there looked taken aback, and Bradley harrumphed in perturbation. "Young lady, that's a harsh view of a pleasant pastime. We raise tobacco in this state, and we don't believe all the propaganda about cancer-causing agents and such."

"Mr. Benjamin, if you had ever once visited a cancer ward, you would believe." Taking the burning cigarette from between Four's fingers, she stubbed it out in the ashtray. "Never mind the cigars," she said to him. "Just give it up."

Bradley started to speak.

She looked at him straight-on, and did the one thing Devlin thought was impossible: She stared him down.

Bradley looked away. "Cheeky."

In the background, Devlin saw Scrubby grin, and Kistard and Osgood leaned back in their chairs, crossed their arms, and waited for further entertainment. Bradley was well respected, but by no means popular.

A young mother came out onto the deck. She wore the tourist's usual uniform—flip-flops, a bathing suit, a cover-up, and drifts of sand. But she carried an extra decoration—a car seat hung over her arm. She looked hot and tired, and the baby wailed for attention.

"Oh, for God's sake!" Benjamin exploded with disgust. "Can't these people see this is a nice restaurant?"

The woman heard him. Of course she did. Her sunburned cheeks got redder, and her shocked, hurt eyes filled with tears.

Meadow was on her feet at once, arms extended. "Let me help you get settled so you can take care of the baby. Where would you like to sit? In the shade, I'll bet."

The mother shook her head and glanced anxiously at the table of old farts.

"Don't worry about him." Meadow's voice carried as clearly as had Benjamin's. "His arthritis is acting up." She found the woman a comfortable spot, sent Dave for water, and all the while chatted about vacations and seashells and eating carrots sticks with sand on them.

Slowly the mother relaxed and responded.

And all the while the old guys and Four and Devlin watched, because they couldn't take their eyes away from Meadow's gleaming copper hair.

Meadow lifted the three-month-old out of the car seat.

Out of the corner of his eye Devlin saw Bradley Benjamin start. Devlin looked over.

Benjamin stared at Meadow, frowning, puzzled.

She bounced it against her hip, smiling and talking in the low croon of an experienced caretaker.

Benjamin took a sharp breath. The color drained from his face. He grimaced and put his hand to his chest.

Devlin leaned back with a sigh of contentment. His plans were proceeding as he wished.

Bradley Benjamin had recognized Isabelle's granddaughter.

14

"*Do* you have a copy of *The Secret Garden?*" Meadow leaned across the counter toward the owner of the Amelia Shores Bookstore.

Mrs. Cognomi, middle-aged, stout, with a mustache and suspiciously black hair, glared as if she were offended. "Of course I have a copy. It's popular vacation reading for children. Hardcover or paperback?"

"Hardcover." As Mrs. Cognomi bustled off to fetch it, Meadow called, "I want it for Devlin." Without visible qualm, she indicated him.

Two other customers browsing the shelves turned to look at him, standing beside Meadow. One woman smirked at him. The other turned her back and silently laughed.

With one simple sentence, Meadow had ruined his reputation as the meanest son of a bitch in Amelia Shores.

Mrs. Cognomi fetched an oversize hardcover with an impressionistic painting of a young Victorian girl. She handed it to Meadow, who received it with soft, cooing noises.

Mrs. Cognomi straightened her black glasses and looked him over so critically she reminded him of his first-grade teacher. "You know, Mr. Fitzwilliam, you should consider putting a copy in each room in your hotel."

"Yes! That's brilliant, Mrs. Cognomi." Meadow turned to Devlin. "That would be a nice touch."

"Who would care?" Devlin stood there stoically, his arms crossed across his chest.

"All the women who read *The Secret Garden* when they were young." Meadow confided to Mrs. Cognomi, "My husband has never read it."

Mrs. Cognomi *tsk*ed. "Yet it's a lovely story with lessons for us all. Would you like me to order the hardcover edition for the hotel?"

"I don't think—" Devlin said.

"No. People steal towels. Can you imagine how fast they'd snatch up a book like this?" Meadow slid it across the counter to Mrs. Cognomi. "Do you have it in trade paperback?"

"Yes, and a good choice indeed, Mrs. Fitzwilliam." Mrs. Cognomi approved of Meadow. Of course she approved of Meadow. Who didn't? "How many copies do you need?"

"Let's start with sixty," Meadow decided.

"There are only forty-five rooms," Devlin said.

"Yes, but we have to figure on loss during the grand opening," Meadow said sensibly. "So, Mrs. Cognomi, sixty copies to begin with, and we'll let you know when we need more."

"Lovely." Mrs. Cognomi pulled out her order pad and began filling it out. "How would you like to pay?"

"Devlin, give her your credit card," Meadow instructed.

Devlin couldn't believe he had suddenly accrued such an absurd expense. An expense that should be coming out of the corporation. But he knew his CFO. She questioned every receipt. And damned if he was going to try to explain why he had ordered sixty copies of a girlie children's book. As he flipped through his wallet, he asked Mrs. Cognomi, "If you do business with me, aren't you afraid Bradley Benjamin will foreclose on your store?"

"He doesn't own the mortgage on my store. Nor does he own the building my store is in." Mrs. Cognomi folded her arms across her belly and smirked with satisfaction. "I do."

Devlin developed a sudden liking for Mrs. Cognomi. "Better make it ninety copies."

"With the bulk discount, that'll be four hundred eighty dollars, plus tax. They'll be delivered here next Tuesday. I'll bring them out to you—I'd love to see the restoration work you've done." Taking Devlin's card, Mrs. Cognomi swiped it through the cash register. "Bradley Benjamin is the type of man who scorns fiction and reads newspapers and business journals."

"I don't understand that kind of joyless approach to life," Meadow said. "But let's not say anything disparaging about Mr. Benjamin. They just took him away in an ambulance suffering from angina."

Mrs. Cognomi looked unimpressed. "He's gone to the hospital before. He always survives. Only the good die young."

"It sometimes seems that way, doesn't it?" For a telling moment, Meadow's lower lip trembled.

Devlin noted . . . and wondered.

Then she lifted her chin and smiled. "Don't forget to charge us for the hardcover copy! I'm going to read it to Devlin."

"Good for you." Mrs. Cognomi looked right at Devlin, her protuberant brown eyes enlarged by her lenses. "It would be too bad if Mr. Fitzwilliam became as joyless as Bradley Benjamin, wouldn't it?"

Devlin scowled with so much annoyance, Meadow knew she could get away with murder right now. Good thing she wanted so much less. "Mrs. Cognomi, can I use your restroom?"

"Of course, dear. They're through the swinging doors to your right."

"I'll be in the Jeep," Devlin called.

Poor guy. He couldn't wait to get out of here.

Meadow slid into the tiny ladies' room, flipped open her cell phone, called Judith—and groaned when her call went right to voice mail. In a low voice, she said, "I'm in Amelia Shores, I'm going back out to Waldemar, and so far—except for a confrontation with Isabelle's husband, who almost had a heart attack afterward—everything's okay. But how's Mom, and where are you?" She hung up and leaned against the cool door.

Half an hour ago she'd been livid with Bradley Benjamin. She didn't care if he offended her, but to be cruel to Devlin about his illegitimacy had not been acceptable behavior, and his rudeness to that poor single mother had made Meadow want to smack him. She'd gone to help the mother just to keep her own hands off Bradley—and then he'd suffered that attack.

Four had had to give him the nitro he kept in his pocket. Dave had rushed over with water. The old guys flapped around like a bunch of excited peahens, except for H. Edwin Osgood, who kept his head and dialed 911. And when Devlin had offered his assistance, Bradley had shouted at him to go away. The ambulance had drawn up to the restaurant, and when she'd tried to wish Bradley well, he'd pretended to be unconscious. Pretended to be—she'd seen his eyelids fluttering.

Now she felt guilty for being so irked with Bradley, and even guiltier for wanting him to live so she could use him. Nothing was turning out as she'd planned, and now she had to go back to Waldemar with Devlin. Devlin, who watched her like a cat at a mouse hole.

Unfortunately, the cheese he used to bait his trap was truly tempting.

She splashed water on her cheeks and wished she'd brought those pills the doctor had given her, because she had a whopper of a headache.

She wasn't going to admit it to Devlin, but maybe she'd overdone it on her first day with a concussion. She needed to go back to the hotel, crawl in bed, and take a nap.

She headed out through the restaurant and onto the street, where Devlin had parked the Jeep.

The top was off, and she could see Devlin seated behind the wheel.

Four stood facing him, his hand on the roll bar. "I make a pleasant dinner guest, and your chef needs practice. I'll ride out with you."

"You will do no such thing." Devlin's impatience couldn't be hidden.

"That's right. No backseat. So I'll drive myself," Four insisted.

"No." Devlin revved the motor and glanced toward the bookstore. He caught sight of Meadow, and for an instant she thought his gaze warmed.

But she must be imagining what she wanted to see, for in the next moment he summoned her with a jerk of his head.

He *had* to be kidding.

She stopped walking. She jerked her head in imitation. She lifted her brows.

Four turned, watched the pantomime, and grinned.

Devlin looked as if he were about to choke with frustration, but his voice was warm and adoring when he called, "Darling, come on! Sam has already called from the hotel. The tree movers dropped the blasted trunk on the brand-new gazebo before the paint was even dry."

She resumed walking.

Four helped her into the Jeep, murmuring in a voice just loud enough for Devlin to hear, "He's a beast who's far too used to getting his own way, but you're training him, and he does take instruction well."

"Which is more than I can say for you." Devlin drove off so quickly Four leaped backward to avoid being run over.

Meadow scrambled for her seat belt. "Devlin! That wasn't nice."

"Don't worry about Four and his hurt feelings. They've been subdued by a large infusion of bourbon over ice. *My* bourbon over *my* ice." Devlin shook his head, but Meadow thought she discerned a faint fondness for the only Benjamin son. "He's almost certainly skipping toward his stupid little car right now, ready to drive out to the hotel."

"You're probably right. Four seems remarkably resilient, especially for a man with a father like Bradley Benjamin." She removed her hat and gathered a handful of her hair into a band at the base of her neck.

"When I was a boy, I used to long for a father like the other kids had. Then I'd meet old Benjamin and watch him abuse Four and count my blessings."

She hesitated, torn between so many questions that needed asking. Finally she settled on, "Bradley doesn't seem too fond of you, either."

"You heard him. I'm a bastard, and he reserves his most vitriolic abuse for me."

"Because you remind him of his wife's infidelity and the child he lost to it." She pulled on her hat and tied her scarf around it to keep it on her head.

"That's a new theory."

How could he be so obtuse? "There has to be a reason for him to care so much, and by all accounts he loved Isabelle; he just didn't know how to open his soul to her."

"You got that from what Four said?" The wind whipped past as Devlin cruised toward the edge of town and onto the southbound road toward the line of mansions.

She had to be more careful about revealing what she knew. "While you were talking to Sam on the phone, I talked to Scrubby." That was true. She had talked to Scrubby—just not about Bradley Benjamin's marriage.

"Did you two incredibly intuitive souls talk about me and my inner feelings, too?"

"No," she snapped. "We only talked about people we were interested in."

"Good."

He didn't say anything else, slowing where the pavement gave way to well-groomed gravel. He took the dip smoothly, then sped up again, not quite as fast this time.

She wished she hadn't succumbed to irritation. Because she wanted to know about his inner feelings. She always thought people were like pieces of art glass—strong enough to handle and use, delicate enough to shatter under a strong blow, and filled with swirls of color that fascinated the eye. But while most people—and most glass—

allowed light through, she could discern nothing of Devlin's heart and soul through the smoke and mirrors he held before him.

And she was a curious girl. She loved people. She loved to ask them about themselves. Loved to listen to their stories. Flattered herself that she understood them . . . and she was lying to herself if she thought her curiosity about Devlin was anything similar to her curiosity about other people. With Devlin, she wanted to know everything about him. She urgently wanted to know what made him tick.

"Are you nervous?" He looked at her sideways. "I'm actually a very safe driver."

"What?" He drove so confidently she relaxed into the seat and watched the ocean. "No, I'm fine."

"You're tapping your foot."

"Oh. It's a nervous habit. When I'm thinking. So tell me about your childhood." *Smooth. Very smooth.*

He laughed. "I wondered how long you'd be able to keep your questions to yourself."

"How long did I?"

"Maybe a minute."

"It was longer than that."

"You're right." He waited two beats. "At least sixty-five seconds."

"That's better. So . . . your childhood."

"Comfortable. My grandparents were disappointed with my mother, but they didn't throw us out in the snow. We lived with them until I was five. At that point I got big enough to beat the tar out of my older cousins when they made fun of me and my mother. Mother had to move out to avoid blood on the antique rug in Grandmother's dining room, but by then she had her interior decorating shop established and her toe in the media. I went to an exclusive school—that's where I met Four—and before long I was beating the tar out of a variety of boys, some of whom were still my cousins."

"What is wrong with the people here?" Meadow burst out. "It's not the fifties! Women are allowed to have a baby with or without the option of marriage, and that child is valuable, a piece of God put on this earth."

"You're an innocent. People always love to gossip, and children always love to be cruel to kids who are different. It's an eternal law, never to be changed." He sounded so sure.

How had he come from being that boy so free with his fists to a man closed to honest emotion?

"In addition to the onerous weight of human nature, I was born in Charleston. Charleston is old-fashioned. Then there was my mother's conviction that my father, Nathan Manly, was going to divorce his wife and marry her. So she lorded her conquest of him over her fellow debutantes—my mother is the slightest bit competitive."

Meadow heard a heavy dose of irony in his voice.

"Put all of those ingredients into the situation and you have a recipe for social . . ." He hesitated.

"Disaster?" She marveled that he was at last opening to her.

"Difficulties. Fortunately for my mother, her talent and ambition have allowed her to triumph over her former rivals, although not in the traditional way, with a rich husband and two socially correct children. And if challenges form character, then I have enough character to make up for Four's lack of it."

"I don't think it works that way. I think he'll have to develop his own. And what you need to develop is—" She stopped herself. She was thinking out loud again, and every time she did that, she got into trouble.

"What do I need to develop?"

Patience. Kindness. A belief, however unproven, that men are good at heart. Automatically, she said, "You're perfect as you are."

"A lovely thought. But you don't believe it."

"You're exactly who you should be at this point in your life." She knew the correct things to say.

He cast her a sardonic glance. "Where did you learn to babble such nonsense?"

"It's not nonsense!" She did believe it was true. The trouble was, she wanted to fix people. As her mother pointed out time and again, Meadow could only fix herself, and until the moment when she'd achieved nirvana, that should be her lifelong project.

But it was so easy to see what was wrong with other people and give them good advice.

"Right." The road wound away from the ocean, following a curving path into the woods filled with cedar and moss-draped live oaks. He pulled off to the side. Turning to face her, he put his arm across the back of her seat. His gaze captured hers. "I've confided in you. Now you tell me—when, my dear amnesiac, were you in a cancer ward?"

"A cancer ward?" she repeated. "What makes you think I was in a cancer ward?"

"When Bradley Benjamin instructed Four on smoking cigars, you ripped into him with a passion and a sarcasm reserved for serial killers." Shade dappled the Jeep and offered a false mellowness to his face.

She stared at Devlin, caught in the horror between a lie and the truth. Should she tell him?

My mother has cancer, she needs treatment, and if I don't get her a quarter of a million dollars fast, she might—probably will—slip out of remission and die.

Would he understand?

Maybe he would. But even if she found the painting, he wouldn't let her take it. He owned the house and all its contents. The painting, if it was still there, was his.

What was it Four had said? *The milk of human kindness has curdled in Devlin's veins.*

She believed it. She'd heard his hard-nosed handling of Sam, seen his impatience with Four, witnessed his satisfaction when Bradley Benjamin had suffered his attack. She couldn't take the chance and trust Devlin. Not with her mother's life at stake.

Devlin still sat there, waiting for his answer.

She looked away. "I know things. I know my first name. I know I don't like it when you summon me like I'm one of your maids, and you shouldn't treat any human being like that. I know what I think about life. I know what I think about smoking."

He leaned back. He looked her over, his eyes black with disappointment. "But you don't know anything about how your thinking got the way it is."

"No."

"Right." His arm slid away from her seat. "I give only so many chances, Meadow."

Her heart gave a hard, frightened thump. "What do you mean?"

"You know what I mean." He faced forward, put the car in gear, and got the Jeep up to speed. As he drove the narrow curves the tires spit gravel, and the silence felt like a weight on Meadow's guilt-ridden soul.

Maybe she should trust him. Her heart said she should. It was her fears that held her back. "Devlin, listen—"

She didn't know exactly what she was going to say.

Then it didn't matter.

He tried to make the bend. The steering wheel balked. He swore. He hit the brakes. His arms strained as he fought the turn.

They weren't going to make it.

15

Fear and adrenaline surged through Devlin's veins. The steering was stiff—he'd lost it at the crucial moment in the curve. He worked the brakes, fought to control the skid on a damp gravel road.

The ditch was about a foot deep and full of last night's rain. The front tires smacked hard and deep. Water flew. Branches snapped as the Jeep ripped through them. The stand of cedars rushed toward them.

They hit a good-size tree head-on.

The air bags ripped the wheel out of his hand.

They skidded sideways. The side panel smacked another tree.

And they stopped.

The air bags deflated. The warm and comforting scent of cedar—no longer warm and comforting—filled the air.

In the sudden lack of motion, lack of sound, he could hear his heart thundering in his ears. Or was it Meadow's heart he heard?

She clutched her head.

Damn it. That concussion! "Meadow. Are you all right?"

She didn't answer. She was conscious, but she wasn't talking. And if Meadow wasn't talking, there was definitely something wrong.

He unhooked her seat belt. "Is anything broken? Can you move everything?" Two minutes ago he'd been furious with her. Twice today he'd given her the chance to tell him everything, and she'd refused. More than twice today she'd laughed with other men, charmed other men.

Then she'd had the nerve to look at him warily, as if he could be as dangerous and unforgiving as Bradley Benjamin and his cohorts.

A thought niggled at him—maybe he was more like them than he wished.

But he dismissed it when she said, "I'm fine." She wiggled various body parts to show him, but she kept her hand on her head.

He lifted her chin to look into her eyes. They were tear-filled. Pain-filled. "Meadow. Are you all right?" He enunciated each word slowly.

"I'm fine," she said again.

Yeah. Sure she was. She looked like hell. Her red freckles stuck out in stark relief to her white complexion. She closed her eyes, as if keeping them open were too great an effort, and leaned her head against the headrest.

He sure wasn't mad at her anymore.

"Damn it!" They were halfway between the Secret Garden and Amelia Shores. He pulled out his cell phone and looked. They had no service. They were alone out here with no protection. . . . His head whipped around.

A car was coming.

He leaned into the Jeep toward the pistol he kept locked in a box close at hand—and relaxed when Four's stupid damned MINI honked from the road.

"What happened?" Four climbed out, a long-legged clown out of an absurdly tiny car, and rushed toward them. "Did you miss the corner?"

"Yeah. I missed the corner." Devlin leaped out and hurried to Meadow. "Honey, I'm going to send you with Four." He slid his arms around her.

"I can walk," she said.

"But you don't have to." He headed for the MINI.

Four took one look at Meadow, then backed away as if he were afraid she'd hurl—and hurl on him. "Is she okay?"

"Take her to the hospital."

Four tiptoed after them and opened the passenger-side door.

"I'm fine. I'm just tired," she said, but she didn't open her eyes.

Last night she'd been lively even after hitting her head. Today she looked drawn, exhausted; and with a pang, Devlin realized he shouldn't have taken her to town, shouldn't have relied on her to tell him whether she was tired. Meadow didn't complain. Not while there was life to be lived.

Devlin slid her into the seat. "I want Dr. Apps to check her out. Don't take no for an answer." Taking Four's shoulder, Devlin looked him in the eyes. "Don't leave her alone, and don't let anything happen to her. Or I'll kill you."

"Right. I know. Don't blame you a bit. She's great." Four's breathless agreement could be anxiety for Meadow—or it could be guilt.

Had Four had a hand in this accident?

No. No, Four might be mad at Devlin, but he wasn't vicious. He never had been.

"What are you going to do?" Four asked.

"Call Frank Peterson," Devlin said tersely.

Four knew Frank, the mechanic and handyman. "I don't think he can fix *that* car."

"No. Probably not." But he could answer the question Devlin wanted answered.

Because this accident wasn't an accident.

⟜

Miss Louise "Weezy" Woodward, teenage volunteer at the Amelia Shores Regional Hospital, hustled out of the waiting room like her tail feathers had been scorched. She stopped by the nurses' station. "Mrs. Peterson, did you see that Devlin Fitzwilliam while his girlfriend was in having a CT scan? I offered him a cup of coffee and a smile, and he about ripped my throat out."

"Of course he did. He's madly in love with her. Haven't you heard?" Jazmin Peterson, nurse in command on this floor, grinned at the chance to impart the news and take pretty Weezy down a few notches. "That's his wife."

"His wife?" Weezy's cheeks turned as bright pink as her hospital jacket. "He's not married! He can't be. Who told you? When did he marry?"

Jazmin leaned on the counter and drawled every single syllable. "It is the most romantic thing. I heard all about it from my Frank, who's working out at the hotel doing odd jobs—and there are a lot of odd jobs to do, too, with stuff going wrong all the time, and half of it fishy stuff, if you know what I mean."

"I heard old Mr. Bradley Benjamin was so mad he swore to kill Mr. Fitzwilliam."

"I heard that, too. But Mr. Benjamin came through here not too long ago, and he's in no shape to kill anyone." Jazmin nodded wisely. "If he don't have a angiogram pretty soon, he'd better start preparing for the long journey home."

"Never mind him!" Weezy grabbed Jazmin's arm and shook it. "Tell me about Mr. Fitzwilliam and how he got married without any of us knowing it."

"A long time ago, Mr. and Mrs. Fitzwilliam met and got married in Hawaii, then they had a big fight and she left him. That's why Mr. Devlin's been so ugly to everyone for so long."

"He was dying of frustrated desire," Weezy said.

"Yes, until she showed up on his doorstep last evening. They shared one night of passionate reunion; then he almost killed her by driving into a tree. That poor man. He's swimming in guilt."

"That is the most romantic thing I've ever heard." Weezy pressed her hand over her heart.

"And all true." Frank had said there'd been gossip that Mrs. Fitzwilliam broke into the house, but Jazmin figured that was just crazy talk, and she wasn't the kind of woman to spread crazy talk.

Weezy, who was Amelia Shores to the bone, asked, "Who is her family?"

"No one knows. She's some Yankee girl, but I'll tell you one thing for sure—she's not rich. I saw the calluses on her fingers myself." That had made Jazmin like her a lot.

"What's young Mr. Benjamin doing hanging around here?"

"I don't think but he's in love with her, too," Jazmin said wisely. "He's the one who brought her in, and you should have seen him. He was white-faced and shaking like a leaf."

"That is not fair. She can't have the two of them!" Young Weezy stomped her foot.

"I guess she can." Jazmin gestured down the corridor. "There they go now."

They watched the wheelchair roll toward the exit. Mr. Fitzwilliam walked beside the wheelchair, holding Mrs. Fitzwilliam's hand.

Four walked behind them, weaving slightly.

"Do you suppose he's been hitting the bottle again?" Weezy asked. "You know he always keeps that flask in his pocket."

"And fills it up at Waldemar, according to my Frank. He just hangs around out there like some sorrowful ghost. Rumor has it he's the reason Mr. Bradley Benjamin had to sell the house to Mr. Fitzwilliam."

"No! Why?"

"Young Mr. Benjamin's not got a head for business."

Dr. Apps stepped into the doorway of the examining room and watched her patient leave.

Jazmin lowered her voice. "Dr. Apps must have agreed to send Mrs. Fitzwilliam home. She didn't want to—Mrs. Fitzwilliam was arguing like crazy—but Mr. Fitzwilliam said he would make sure his wife stayed in bed if he had to stay there with her. Dr. Apps looked as if he'd slapped her, and got real quiet."

"Dr. Apps had aspirations toward him."

"She wasn't the only one." Jazmin looked meaningfully at Weezy.

"Well, why not?" Weezy plumped her ample boobs with her hands. "I'm a good-looking girl, and there aren't that many handsome millionaires in this town."

They didn't call her Sleazy Weezy for nothing.

"Devlin Fitzwilliam is not a handsome millionaire." Jazmin chuckled. "He's a handsome billionaire—and honey, you are so out of luck."

16

Jordan hustled into the kitchen, and Mia flinched. She always flinched when he was around. He was so critical. He bellowed so loudly. And now that he'd said she was going to be his saucier, the stakes were higher. If she messed up he would throw her out, and she needed this job. The divorce had left her with nothing except bills and two teenagers who hated her because their no-good daddy had skipped town.

"Come on!" Jordan clapped his hands. "We're going up to stand on the porch and wait for Miz Fitzwilliam."

"They're not keeping her at the hospital?" Christian asked.

"Yes, but they're releasing her in the morning, so we'll stand there all night." Jordan rolled his eyes. "Of course they've released her. Now, *vite*! They've turned in the gate."

The two assistants took off their aprons and headed after their boss.

The sunshine made Mia blink, and so did the size of the crowd. She worked in the kitchen. She had no idea there were so many employees at the Secret Garden.

"There must be fifty people here," she whispered to Christian.

"Sixty-five, last I heard, and Mr. Fitzwilliam's secretary was hiring again today."

"I've lived here my whole life, and I don't know half these people." She hung back and let Jordan push his way toward the front. She hated crowds. She hated meeting new people. But she'd liked the new Mrs. Fitzwilliam, and she was glad Jordan had let them come up to offer their support on her return.

"Plenty of them heard there was work to be had and came in from other towns. Mr. Fitzwilliam brought some in from Atlanta and such. And you know there's always some people who drift in for the summer because they want to live on the beach." Christian wasn't originally from Amelia Shores—in fact, he talked twangy, like a Texan—but he'd lived here long enough to think he was an expert. "It was probably one of them who nicked the steering fluid line with something sharp."

"No! On purpose?" She wrapped her hands around her waist.

Christian nodded. "Frank told Mr. Williams, who told Miz Burke, who told me that it happened while Mr. and Mrs. Fitzwilliam were in town with Mr. Four."

"Mr. Four didn't do it!" Mia liked Four.

Christian laughed. "Yeah, he is sort of a doof, isn't he? I heard it was his fault old Mr. Benjamin had to sell this place. I heard Four got into debt to Mr. Fitzwilliam, and this place was the only payment Mr. Fitzwilliam would take."

"How do you hear this?"

"I take my breaks in the break room instead of the kitchen. You should try it sometime."

Mia ignored that. "There they are," she said as the long limo pulled up to the steps.

Like a colorful aluminum can tied to the bumper of the real car, Mr. Benjamin's MINI followed.

"Mrs. Fitzwilliam is such a nice lady—and she's married to *him*." Christian shuddered. "I guess that proves any guy can get a wife if he's got enough money. Mr. Fitzwilliam scares me to death."

Mr. Fitzwilliam scared her, too. He was that kind of man. But he'd been kind to her, more than anyone else in Amelia Shores, giving her a job based on nothing except a stint as a cook at a long-vanished restaurant in town and presenting her to Jordan as a permanent employee. Her knees might quake when Mr. Fitzwilliam was around, but she was grateful to him. "I don't think he's that bad."

"Oh, yeah? Cecily said she got behind cleaning her rooms and he almost threw her out."

Mia gloated a little. She did have some gossip Christian didn't know. "Cecily didn't tell you everything. She got caught taking a nap on the bed she was supposed to be making, and the only reason she got a second chance was that she pleaded a dependent child. That, and the fact that Mr. Fitzwilliam's having a hell of a time getting enough help, between the tourist season starting and old Mr. Benjamin dissing him all over town."

They watched as Devlin lifted Meadow from the backseat of the limo.

"Whew. Look at that. He's picking her up so carefully, like she's a diamond." Mia's heart trilled as it hadn't since the day she'd fallen in love with her louse of a husband. "And we didn't even know they were married."

"That's because it was a runaway marriage. Her folks are rich—"

"I thought they were poor!" Because Mrs. Fitzwilliam didn't seem like a rich girl. She was too nice.

"I heard they were rich."

"Does anybody really know?" Mia felt as if she were talking to one of her kids.

"C'mon, that makes sense, because her parents didn't want their little darling marrying that carpetbagger."

Sometimes Mia didn't much like Christian. "Mr. Fitzwilliam is not a carpetbagger. He's from Charleston!"

"He's buying up every piece of property he can get his hands on and make a profit with. What else does a carpetbagger do?" She tried to object, but Christian talked over her. "Plus, he's a bastard, and the man who got his mother pregnant was a bigger scoundrel than Mr. Fitzwilliam any day."

"I heard that, too." Folks were stretching to touch Mrs. Fitzwilliam as Mr. Fitzwilliam carried her past.

Four followed them. He darted a look around and hunched his shoulders. He wiped his palms on his trousers.

Mia hated to admit it, but he looked guilty of *something*. She hoped not; he wasn't a good man, but he was a nice man.

"You can't blame her folks for not wanting that pretty girl to marry that mean son of a bitch." Like a boy caught tattling, Christian ducked when Mr. Fitzwilliam glanced his way.

As Mia said a silent prayer for Mrs. Fitzwilliam's recovery, she watched the way Mr. Fitzwilliam cradled his wife. The way he looked at her, and her all covered with white powder from the air bag, with dirty hair, and sporting a bruise on her cheek.

He was in thrall to her.

"Who knows what she has to put up with," Christian said.

"All . . . night . . . long."

"What?" Christian shook his head in confusion.

"That man has a look about him. He can go all night long," Mia drawled. "Trust me on this."

Christian looked as horrified as if his neutered spaniel had humped his leg.

Stupid boy. He thought that because she was twenty years older than him and didn't say much, she was a sexless nothing. She might be plain, and she might be divorced, and she might have been abused, but she recognized a man who knew his way around a bedroom. She added, "Besides, this morning it looked as if Mrs. Fitzwilliam had him wound around her little finger."

"Yeah, he isn't the only one." Christian nudged her and indicated their boss.

"My poor skinny little *poulet.*" As Mr. Fitzwilliam walked by with Mrs. Fitzwilliam, Jordan clasped his huge hands together under his chin, and his big brown eyes swam with tears. "I will make you a vegetable broth that will cure all your ills and bring roses to your cheeks again."

"Thank you, Jordan." Meadow would have said more, but Mr. Fitzwilliam didn't stop. He headed right for the open front door.

"She has to go to bed now," he said. "And she's not getting up for forty-eight hours."

"But I want to thank everyone for coming out to greet me," Mrs. Fitzwilliam wailed.

"In two days you can thank everyone. For now, you're going to bed." They disappeared into the house.

"See?" Christian whispered. "I told you he's scary."

Mia smiled at his naïveté. And sighed with gladness for Mrs. Fitzwilliam.

Maybe not tonight. Maybe not tomorrow night. But someday soon, Mrs. Fitzwilliam was going to be one very happy woman.

All . . . night . . . long.

Sam rushed ahead of Devlin into the bedroom and turned down the bed.

Tenderly Devlin laid Meadow down and covered her with the sheets. "How do you feel?"

"I'm fine." A line was etched between her brows.

"Lying will only get you into trouble." He watched her closely. "More trouble."

She jerked as if she'd been electrocuted. "I'm not lying!"

"You don't have to try to fool me." He smoothed the hair back from her forehead. "You can trust me. I'll take care of you."

"Will you give me forty million dollars?" she asked truculently.

His hand stopped in midair. "Why do you need forty million dollars?"

"If you trusted me, you wouldn't care."

"Right." She was as cranky as a child. Dr. Apps had said she might be—Meadow had no serious injuries from the wreck, but she was exhausted and stressed. "You've got the worst damned headache you've ever had."

"I suppose," she said sulkily.

"And a sore wrist and a bruise on your cheek"—his thumb skimmed the black mark on her fair skin—"caused by the air bag slamming your hand into your face."

"I guess."

"So you can admit that you feel lousy."

"I don't feel lousy." She hesitated on the edge of major perjury, then gave in with a flounce and a wince. "I want a shower."

"Not right now. Sam, get some water." Devlin took the bottle of pills out of his pocket and shook one out.

Sam headed for the bathroom.

"I'm dirty. I've got that air bag powder on me." She rubbed her arms and the powder came off in little pills.

"Tomorrow you can have a bath."

"I don't want a bath. I want a shower. And I want one now."

"As soon as the drug takes effect, you can get up and take a shower."

"Do you think I'm stupid? Do you think I don't know what that pill is supposed to do?"

"No. What?"

"Put me to sleep!"

"That is a problem, isn't it?" Devlin took the glass from Sam and offered her the pill. "But at least while you're asleep you won't think about being dusty."

She turned her head away. "I don't like drugs."

"You need to sleep."

"Then I'll drink some chamomile tea."

He handed Sam the pill and the glass. He seated himself on the bed beside her, taking care to put his hip against her hip. He put his hands on either side of her, leaned forward until their noses were almost touching, and said, "Darling, forty-eight hours from now you can go back to charming the staff, scolding old farts, and just generally being Meadow. For now, you are going to do exactly as you are told."

"And how are you going to enforce that?" Her weary blue eyes shot lively sparks.

"To start with, you'll take this pill or I'll climb into bed and make love to you until you're so tired you'll fall asleep in my arms."

"Devlin!" Her horrified gaze flew past him. "Not in front of Sam!"

"Then you'd better take the pill." Devlin accepted the pill and the glass from his stoic secretary. He helped her sit up, watched her swallow the pill and drink the water, then slowly let her back down onto the pillow. "Now go to sleep. I'll be here if you need me."

She turned her back on him. "I won't need you."

"I'll be here anyway." He tucked her in and turned to Sam. "We'll work in the sitting room."

"Yes, sir." Sam headed toward the door.

"So much for being here," she muttered.

Devlin went into the bathroom, wet a washcloth, and returned to her. "Turn over," he instructed.

She did, and he wanted to laugh at the rebellious, sulky, wary expression on her powdery face. "Here." He smoothed the wet, cool cloth across her cheeks, her chin, her forehead.

Her eyes closed in pure bliss.

"Does that feel good?" he asked.

"Yes. Thank you." She rubbed the back of her hand against her nose. "I'm sorry I've been a snot."

"I wouldn't say a snot. More of a brat." He stroked the cloth across her mouth, then kissed her. Her lips were velvety and relaxed, but when he opened his mouth slightly, she responded. Reluctantly and just a little, but it seemed to him she couldn't help but answer him. "Go to sleep now."

She nodded, her eyelids drooping.

He stroked her hair one more time, tossed the washcloth in the bathroom, then walked out to the sitting room.

Sam sat at the desk, laptop open.

Devlin had found Sam eight months ago during a search for a temporary secretary. Sam had presented himself as a man who excelled at being an administrative assistant. He'd proved himself invaluable time and again—and never had he betrayed one bit of personal information about himself.

Devlin liked it that way.

Now Sam looked up, unsmiling. "The line was definitely cut. However, a sabotaged steering fluid line is not an attempt at murder."

"Yes, but there's always a chance of incompetence." Devlin seated himself in front of the desk. "Perhaps whoever it was, was trying to cut the brake line—and murder me."

Sam inclined his head. "True."

"Who would have the motive to kill me?"

"It would be a shorter list if we asked who doesn't have the motive to kill you." Sam wasn't being funny. In fact, as far as Devlin could ascertain, Sam didn't have a sense of humor.

"Don't sugarcoat it, Sam."

"How about Mr. Bradley Benjamin the fourth? Or more probably, Mr. Bradley Benjamin the third. Or someone in Amelia Shores who doesn't like the hotel. Or one of the people you've angered for one reason or another, and those are legion. Or a rival hotel owner. Or—"

"Okay, I get you. But I don't believe in coincidence, and the fact that Four showed up within five minutes of the accident doesn't play well with me." Neither did the fact that someone tried to hurt Devlin and had hurt Meadow instead.

In fact, that put him in a rage.

"I have been in contact with Gabriel Prescott. He's sending ten of his top men to patrol the Secret Garden inside and out."

"Good." He trusted Sam to handle the situation and give him reports as needed. "Tell me about the gazebo."

He listened to Sam describe the damage to the gazebo and how long it would take to fix, but all the while he was thinking that he'd pulled Meadow into this farce. He had figured he would use her and set her aside and hurt nothing more valuable than her feelings.

Instead, he'd almost gotten her killed.

She wasn't his wife, but she *was* his responsibility, and he was a man who took his responsibilities seriously.

So when he found the son of a bitch who had hurt her . . . he would kill him.

It was as simple as that.

17

The shrilling of the phone beside Four's bed made him groan and, without opening his eyes, grope for the receiver. "What do you mean, calling me at the outrageous hour of"—he cracked a lid and checked the clock—"nine o'clock in the morning?"

"Mr. Benjamin, how delightful to talk to you once more."

The smooth, warm, deep Southern tone shot Four into the sitting position. "Mr. Hopkins! How did you—"

"Get through to you? I have my ways. You ought to know that by now."

"Yes, sir. I do." The sunlight blinded Four. His head throbbed. But he couldn't loll in bed while he talked to this son of a bitch.

He'd never actually seen Mr. Hopkins's face. Right before he'd been knocked unconscious, he'd caught a glimpse of silver hair and the shine of pale blue eyes. And vaguely, through the haze of pain, he recalled an impression of a sagging chin and bent shoulders.

But he recognized the voice. It was the voice of pure evil.

"How's the hunt going?" Mr. Hopkins asked.

"I . . . I haven't had much chance to look yet, but—"

"I'm not interested in excuses. I want what you promised me."

"I know. I know, but I just . . . are you sure it's here? Or even that it exists?"

"Are you trying to void our deal?" The voice didn't change. Mr. Hopkins sounded just as genial, just as kindly interested.

But Four had once made the mistake of underestimating Mr. Hopkins. He wouldn't do it again. "No. No! It's just that . . . I lived here for a lot of years. There are a lot of paintings, but I don't think I remember anything like you described."

"You're not there to think. You're there to search. Please remember, Mr. Benjamin, what happened last time you tried to weasel out of this deal."

Four ran his finger over the notch in his ear, and shuddered. "I remember," he said faintly.

"I could hold the rest of your ear in the palm of my hand. Or a finger. Or . . . I could hurt someone you care about."

Four found himself standing beside the bed, phone clutched to his ear. "What do you mean?"

"When a man's as amiable—and useless—as you are, it's hard not to care for people. Isn't it? A man like you makes friends, and that gives a man like me . . . leverage."

Four could almost hear the smile in Mr. Hopkins's voice, and his mind made the logical connection. "Did you cut that steering fluid line? *Did you?*"

"Just keep searching, Mr. Benjamin. Keep searching, and no one else will get hurt."

Four heard a soft click as the connection was cut. He stared at his hand holding the phone. If something happened to Devlin . . . Devlin despised him, but like a brother despised his weak-willed sibling. Yesterday in Amelia Shores, Devlin had put his hand on Four's shoulder. For the first time since Four had screwed up so badly, Devlin had reminisced about the events that bound them in remembered hardship.

And Meadow . . . she was the most wonderful woman Four had ever met. Of course, she wouldn't bother to give him a toss—women never did when Devlin took an interest in them—but he liked her. He liked her.

And somehow Mr. Hopkins knew.

Someone here was watching him and reporting back to Mr. Hopkins.

He had to find that painting—before Devlin or Meadow or Four got killed.

⌒

"I like Josh and Reva the best." Meadow shoved another pillow behind her so she didn't have to crane her head to watch the fifty-inch television on the wall.

"They're *old*." Katie was sixteen, the youngest of the seven maids gathered in various poses around Meadow's bedroom to eat Jordan's hors d'oeuvres and to watch *Guiding Light*.

"Hush up. They're not old. They're classic." Rashida, forty, tall, black, opened her lunch bag, pulled out her sandwich, and used the bag as protection for her lap.

"Here, use the bed table." Meadow took it off the mattress where she'd shoved it and handed it over. "It's easier."

"Thank you, Mrs. Fitzwilliam." Rashida nudged Buzzy, next to her on the couch. "I told you she likes me best."

Buzzy shoved her and laughed. "You silly old woman. She doesn't know me yet."

The two women were different ages and different colors, but best friends of long standing.

Meadow watched their camaraderie with envy. Her best friend was miles away in Washington, the daughter of Russian immigrants, and Meadow had far too little time lately to spend with Firebird. When the doctors said Sharon was completely well . . .

When Sharon was completely well, Meadow would visit the Hunters' tiny home. She would be respectful of Konstantine, because he was a typical Russian patriarch—big, strong, and a little scary. She would tease Firebird's brothers. Zorana would pack a basket full of wonderful food, and she and Firebird would run off into the forest and have a picnic, and Meadow would tell her friend all about Devlin. . . .

"I like Gus and Harley, and they're classic, too." Katie sat on the Persian rug, a bowl of popcorn in her lap, an apple in her hand. "I love that she was wrongfully convicted of murder and suffered—"

"Is that Harley?" Meadow used a fistful of popcorn to point at the TV.

"That's Tammy," Buzzy said. "Mrs. Fitzwilliam, do you mind if I use your phone to call my mother? She's home alone, and I like to check on her during my lunch hour." She added hastily, "I already asked Mr. Fitzwilliam if I could use the hotel line, and he said it was okay."

"Of course I don't mind." Meadow handed over the receiver, then watched as Buzzy dialed.

As it rang, Buzzy told Meadow, "Mama watches *Guiding Light*, too, so we do the rundown during the commercials." Her attention switched to the phone. "Hi, Mama! Did you see what happened?"

"Her mama has MS," Rashida told Meadow in a low voice. "It's tough for Buzzy, but they're awfully close."

Meadow nodded. She understood. Sharon's illness had been a trial for everyone in the family, but the anguish and the worry had changed them—the family that had lived to celebrate life seized each moment more intently, showed their emotions more freely, and treasured the time given them.

She liked watching Buzzy talk to her mother, seeing the affection, hearing the warmth.

"Oops. The show's back on, Mama. I'll call you at break, okay? Love you, too!" Buzzy hung up and handed the phone back. "Thank you, Mrs. Fitzwilliam."

"Is she okay?" Meadow asked.

"Some days are better than others." Buzzy used the kind of language that let Meadow know her mother was suffering.

Meadow swallowed. She hadn't been away from her mother since

Sharon had been diagnosed. It was stupid to feel so anxious, as if a week away would make a difference to Sharon's health . . . but the anxiety was there, growing with each hour.

She wanted to call her, but she feared Devlin was watching the calls that went out of her room. Of course, Sharon always said, *Where there's a will, there's a way . . .*

If Meadow could just figure out the way . . .

The idea came in a lovely burst of genius. If all the maids made one phone call a day off her phone, that would be probably fifty phone calls, and that would surely confuse the issue. She sat up straight and announced, "You should all feel free to use my phone. Anytime! Long-distance!"

"You'd let us call long-distance?" Katie brightened. "Because my boyfriend's in Wisconsin and my folks get mad when I call him, and make me pay the bill."

"Mrs. Fitzwilliam doesn't mean long-distance," Rashida said.

"Really. Please." Meadow flashed a big, we're-all-one-happy-family smile. "It would make me happy to know you're in touch with your boyfriend. And everybody, don't forget your families!"

Katie stretched out her hand. "Please give me the phone."

"I'm next," Shelby said.

Meadow relaxed against the pillows and hoped her plan would work.

By the time the next round of commercials was over, Shelby had handed the phone to Rashida, who had called her brother in California.

When the show came back on, Teresa, their resident *Guiding Light* expert, pointed to the screen and told Meadow, "When Tammy was little she lived in foster homes; then her mama got married and she lived with her and her new daddy; then that daddy died; then her mama married a prince, but her real father kidnapped her—"

Meadow had already discovered that the wrap-up on these characters could take an hour, and ruthlessly interrupted. "So she's a good person."

Teresa's perky golden curls bobbed as she nodded. "But so put upon, poor lamb."

"I think she's stupid," Katie said. "Everybody could see that Jonathan was a creep, and she slept with him and set fires with him and—"

The outcry that followed caught Meadow by surprise.

"But he was cute—"

"He was just bad—"

"She's better off now—"

Passions were running high when Devlin stepped through the door.

His arrival cut conversation as if with a knife.

His cool gaze surveyed the scene. "What's happening here?"

Meadow lifted her chin at him. "The second cleanup crew is taking their lunch hour with me."

He'd been enforcing her prescribed bed rest: standing by while she showered, taking her clothes and leaving her pajamas and a robe, having her meals delivered on a tray, shutting the curtains when he decided she needed sleep. Worse, he was always right. Somehow he knew when a headache threatened. Somehow he knew when she was tired.

He had been *observing* her.

Now she was ready to shriek with the need to rise, to search the hotel, to escape this place before . . . before he . . . well, before he made good on the promise to spend the night with her. Because she knew one thing for sure—this time she wouldn't escape his bed unscathed. No woman ever had a *casual* affair with Devlin. It would be intense, desperate, passionate—and Meadow didn't have time. She needed to find that painting. She needed to get back home. Her mother needed her. Her father needed her.

So why did this whole episode feel less like a mission and more like escape?

"You're supposed to be resting." He glanced toward the television and frowned.

He had better not try to chase out the cleaning crew. He had better not. Belligerently, she said, "I am resting. I have been resting for the last forty hours. See? I'm in bed, I have pillows, I have pain reliever, which makes me feel *just* fine." She wiggled her eyebrows at him. "*Just* fine."

"How does your head feel?"

"*Just* fine."

"Vicodin," Rashida told Buzzy.

"I can tell." Buzzy's jowls trembled as she laughed.

"When the second cleaning crew finishes their lunch, you'll rest," Devlin said.

"Of course I'll rest. Just like I'm doing right now. Because the third cleaning crew is coming by for their lunch hour to watch Oprah. Oprah has Hugh Jackman talking about his new movie, and he's going to sing . . ." Meadow allowed her attention to stray from Devlin, and as she did an image on the screen caught her attention: a gorgeous guy crouched in the bushes and holding a crowbar. "Wait! Who's that spying on Tammy?"

"Oh, my God!" Teresa came to her feet and pointed. "Would you look at that? He's back!"

"I don't believe it!" Katie said.

"I told you so! Didn't I tell you so?" Buzzy exchanged high fives with Rashida.

Devlin stood in the midst of the screaming women, a lone male awash in a sea of estrogen.

"Who?" Meadow sat on her heels, bouncing on the bed. "Who? Who is he?"

Devlin swam toward her, caught her shoulders, picked her up, and laid her flat on her back. He held her there until she stopped struggling. He locked gazes with her. And he said, "This is not what the doctor ordered, and I won't allow you to hurt yourself out of pure obduracy. Now you can watch this soap, and you can Oprah, but only if you promise me you'll rest afterward."

He was so domineering. So macho. So . . . hot.

He made her want to lock her legs around his waist, bring him down on the bed with her, and show him exactly how rambunctious she felt.

How humiliating to discover that caveman behavior made her want to come right here, right now.

But she was very aware of the complete, riveted attention of the women of the second cleaning crew. Plus she had to face the fact that she couldn't handle the power of coitus with Devlin. Not because she was fragile. Oh, no. Because everything about him—the way he loomed over her, the grip of his hands on her shoulders, his scent of citrus and sandalwood, and that overwhelming air of sexual competency—convinced her she would expire from joy.

And she was too young to die.

"Okay," she said in a tiny voice, "I'll rest afterward."

He nodded once—the jerk never had a doubt she would do as she was told—and stood and faced the room.

Pink-cheeked, Meadow sat up.

"Ladies." He nodded pleasantly and walked out.

Each head followed his every step.

When he had disappeared, Katie whispered, "Whoa."

"I couldn't have said it better myself." Rashida's brown eyes were wide and awed.

Everyone looked at Meadow with a kind of ripe envy. Nobody paid a bit of attention as the credits rolled on *Guiding Light*.

Yep, Meadow needed to get away from the Secret Garden. Fast.

She had to take the chance she had sworn she wouldn't take.

She cleared her throat. "I was wondering . . . I would like to, ah, change that painting." She pointed at a print of *Water Lilies* by Monet.

Really, what a boring painting. It *did* need to be changed.

"During my wandering around the hotel, I saw a painting, but I can't remember where. . . . It looked like an oil of a Dutch domestic scene from the seventeenth century, a lady cooking while her husband taught the children their lessons. Have any of you seen it?"

Everyone shook their heads.

"Strong lighting effects, warm colors, a sense of tranquillity and contemplation . . ." She tried to express the elements that created a masterpiece.

Again the heads shook.

She had hoped that if she asked, someone would remember seeing the painting and she could be on her way. Instead, she now risked one of these ladies mentioning it to Devlin. Then he would be on his guard, and he had the resources to find the painting and the capacity to discover why she sought it. Disappointment tasted bitter in her mouth, and she lay back against the pillows. "If anyone sees that painting, would you let me know?"

"Of course, Mrs. Fitzwilliam." Rashida stood up. "Come on, girls. Time to go back to work."

Buzzy stood up, too. "Mrs. Fitzwilliam, would you like us to tell the third cleaning crew you're tired so you can rest up? For, you know . . . later?" She weighed the last word with significance, and glanced eloquently at the door where Devlin had left.

The others giggled.

"No! Really! I'm fine. Mr. Fitzwilliam simply overreacts; that's all." Meadow blushed again.

"Is *that* what you call it?" Teresa picked up her lunch. "How many more days are you supposed to rest, Mrs. Fitzwilliam?"

"I can get up tonight."

"If I were you, I'd angle to stay flat on my back," Buzzy said.

As the women left, laughing, Meadow heard someone say, "Amen, sister. Amen!"

18

When Meadow stepped into the office, Sam was already staring at the door with a resigned expression, as if he expected her. "Mrs. Fitzwilliam. How can I assist you?"

"I came to see my husband. I want to show him I've completely regained my health." Actually, she'd come to view the paintings Devlin hung on his walls, because she really needed to get out of Waldemar, hopefully before she spent another night sleeping with a very warm, very active, very horny Devlin.

"Your recovery is a relief to us all." Sam's flat tone belied his voiced concern.

But she knew that with the right incentive—and someday she would figure out what that was—he could be cajoled into a smile.

"Mr. Fitzwilliam is busy right now. Would you like to wait?" he asked.

"Sure." She wandered around, examining the office. "You've got a great place here." He did. The room was spacious and nicely furnished, with large windows looking out toward the ocean, oak file cabinets, a printer/fax/copier, and absolutely no interesting paintings on his walls.

Rats.

She wandered toward the file cabinet. "What did you do before you worked for Mr. Fitzwilliam?"

Sam looked up from his work and glowered.

Hastily she added, "Not that I have gender-biased thoughts about a guy being a secretary—"

"Executive assistant."

"Yes, executive assistant. That's what I meant to say. But you"— *with your constant scowl and impatient efficiency and your eyes, which are way too observant*—"seem to be more of a general." *Or a serial killer.* "Someone in command."

"I *am* in command. Of Mr. Fitzwilliam's time and a good deal of his organization." Sam went back to shuffling papers.

"I'm sure Mr. Fitzwilliam is glad to have you." And now she knew better than to ask Sam personal questions. Maybe he *was* a serial killer. "Is there a map for the hotel? I keep getting lost."

"There's a stack of maps on the corner of the credenza by the door."

She nabbed one, folded it up, and stuck it in her pocket.

"And if you remained in your room, you would not get lost."

It was obvious the guy didn't like her, and since he knew that she'd broken into the house, and suspected she wasn't really Devlin's wife, she supposed she could see why. But that didn't stop her from trying. "I get bored. You understand, Sam. You're very fit. You must play sports. Keep active. You must play football, like Devlin?"

"I lift weights and I run. Those are the two most efficient methods of staying fit."

"What do you do for fun?"

"Fun?" His brow knit in puzzlement.

Okay. That line of questioning wasn't going to pan out. She glanced at the open door to Devlin's office, and sidled toward it.

"Won't you have a seat while you wait?" Which was Sam's less-than-subtle way of telling her to sit down and shut up.

"Sure." She sat down in the chair opposite him, and smiled.

He didn't smile back.

"I guess Mr. Fitzwilliam keeps you really busy? Do you always work this late?" She glanced at the clock on the wall. "It's after five."

"Yes, he does. Yes, I do. So it is."

Not much of a conversationalist, our Sam. "How late do you usually work?"

"Very late. In fact, right now I need to finish typing up the requisition list for the groceries for the next week." He turned to his computer. His fingers hovered over the keys.

"That's a great telephone." She turned it toward her and examined it. "It's got four lines. Do you answer them all?"

"Yes."

"Is that all the lines for the hotel?"

"No. But I do monitor the use of all lines on that switchboard." He indicated the electronic panel hung on the wall. "For instance, I've noticed that your line has been almost constantly in use since about eleven." He bent a dark frown on her.

"How about that?" she asked cheerfully. "Is someone using it now?"

"Yes. One of the maids, I suppose."

"I suppose. Can we listen in?"

"It is against the law to listen to private calls in a hotel."

"Oh." She barely managed to keep from rubbing her palms together.

"Do you have any more questions?" Before she could speak, he added, "Because these last few days I've had very little sleep, and until this is done, and all the jobs after it, I won't be able to sleep tonight."

Testy. "I don't want to keep you from your work." She stared at him while he typed.

She didn't know if he was dedicated to his work, or immune to her charm, but he didn't pay her any attention.

Standing, she wandered over to the fax machine and frowned at it. "I'll bet this gets a lot of use."

"Yes."

If only she could get a glimpse into Devlin's office without having to actually confront Devlin . . . She wandered closer to the open door.

She could hear voices. Devlin's deep, distinctive Southern accent, and a woman's thin, frightened tones.

"I'm sorry, Mr. Fitzwilliam. I won't let it happen again. At least . . . I'll try to make sure it doesn't happen again."

"Mia, I don't understand. Until three days ago you were a model employee. What's happened?"

"It's . . . it's my son." The cook sounded miserable and embarrassed. "He dropped out of school. He's getting in trouble. I try to keep control of him, but he's seventeen. Mr. Fitzwilliam, I told him we're going to starve if I don't keep this job, but he said he had a way to provide . . . provide for us . . ." Mia's voice was wobbling. "And I'm afraid . . . afraid . . ."

"Sit down. Take some Kleenex. For God's sake, stop sniveling." Devlin's voice was a slap in the face after Mia's miserable recital.

What a jerk. Didn't he see Mia needed special care right now?

"Yes . . . yes, sir," Mia said.

With a glance at Sam, typing furiously, Meadow moved close enough to peek into the office.

Mia sat in the chair opposite the desk, dabbing at her nose.

"Mia, are we romantically involved?" Devlin snapped.

She lifted her outraged face out of the tissue. "No, sir!"

"Then blow your damned nose. I don't care what it sounds like." Devlin scowled ferociously. "I just want you to stop sniveling."

She blew.

What a jerk! He really was as awful as everyone said. Meadow ought to go in there right now and tell him—

"All right. Look at me." Devlin leaned forward and stared right into Mia's eyes. "Your seventeen-year-old son has dropped out of school, your husband has abandoned you, you've got a thirteen-year-old daughter, and you're afraid your son's involved in drugs. Have I included everything?"

"My son cashed my last paycheck, and I don't know what he did with the money." Mia started to cry in earnest and stood. "I'm sorry, Mr. Fitzwilliam. I know it's not your job to worry about my family. Do you want me to leave now?"

"Not until we've figured this thing out. Sit *down*."

She sat.

"Now. Look at me."

She did.

"I have a project working on the island of Elmite."

"Where's Elmite?"

"In the Caribbean. I bought it."

"The whole island?"

"It was uninhabited. No water. I drilled. There's a huge reservoir under the island. I'm building a resort."

"Okay." Mia nodded.

"Since your son has already dropped out, what do you say I give him the incentive to get back in school?"

Mia stared, the beginning of hope flickering on her face. "Okay."

Perhaps Meadow had misjudged Devlin.

"If he were kidnapped"—Devlin paused to see if Mia would object—"and sent to work construction, hard construction labor, on an uninhabited island for the summer—"

"How soon can he go?" Mia's voice changed, became cool, poised, eager.

"Mrs. Fitzwilliam!" Behind her, Sam whispered, "Are you eavesdropping?" He tried to move her.

"Shh." Meadow shoved back at him. "I want to hear this."

Devlin glanced at the door, saw them, then returned his attention to Mia. "He'll go tonight."

She didn't waver. "Take him."

"On your way out, give my secretary the information he needs to find him. Then go back to work, and good luck. Jordan's in one hell of a mood today."

"I know, sir. Thank you, sir." Mia stood. As she marched past

Meadow, she nodded—and for the first time since Meadow had met her, she looked happy.

Sam tried to move Meadow aside. "I'll announce you."

"Don't bother." She bounded into Devlin's office and shut the door in Sam's face.

Devlin did *not* look pleased to see her.

Yeah, because the big, bad, ruthless developer had been caught in a generous act.

She rounded the desk.

He stood up. "You should be in bed."

"Forty-eight hours are up." She shoved him back down on his chair, followed him down, and straddled his lap. "You are so nice."

"Mia's a good cook."

"The nicest man in the whole world." She put her lips to his and kissed him.

When she released his lips, he said, "If I fired her, Jordon would be furious."

"The nicest man in the whole world," she repeated, kissed him again, and pushed her hips further into his lap.

By the time she took her tongue out of his mouth, he would have agreed with anything she said. "I'm the nicest guy in the world." He looked into her eyes, a half smile on his damp lips, his hands holding her hips. "Did you lock that door?"

"No. Why would I have to? The nicest guy in the world doesn't screw women in his office chair."

"No, but he would screw his wife."

"You silver-tongued devil, you." She was as close in his lap as she could be, her arms wrapped around his shoulders, her breasts almost touching his chest, her scent warm and womanly. . . .

My God, she was smiling at him. Not at Four. Not at the old farts. Not at the maids or Sam or Mrs. Cognomi, but at him.

Yet he felt compelled to speak. "Really, I didn't want to lose one of the few people from Amelia Shores willing to dare the displeasure of the old farts and work for me." What was wrong with him? Why was he talking her out of thinking well of him? He *wanted* her to smile at him.

But not to reward him for being a Boy Scout. Which he was not. He wanted her to smile at him because she felt at ease with him, because she wanted him.

Hell. She was smiling at him for the wrong reasons, and before this moment, he hadn't even known there were wrong reasons.

It took a discipline he didn't know he possessed to move her hips away from his crotch. "Look, I'll get my money's worth out of the kid, too. He's going to work like he's never worked before."

"Tough love. I get it. But without your help, Mia wouldn't stand a chance." Meadow kissed him again, then slid off his lap.

He wanted to stand up, but he couldn't move without groaning.

"Wow, look at all the monitors." She faced the wall where they all hung. "Man. What a bunch of monitors." She sounded uneasy, and she glanced around.

Her gaze lingered on the wall behind him—or rather, at the paintings on the wall behind him.

Damn it. She hadn't come here to smile at *him.* She'd come to check out his art.

As she walked down the corridor toward her room, Meadow took the map from her pocket, spread it out, and examined it. Every corridor was marked. Every room was clearly shown. This was exactly what she was looking for.

She glanced around her. But how spooky to know that every second someone—Devlin—was observing her. She'd known it before, but seeing those monitors had made the sensation of being watched so vivid that the hair stood up on the back of her neck. She was glad to get into the refuge of the sitting room, glad to be able to spread the map out on the table and with a pen, plot her explorations.

She didn't understand Devlin. One minute he was holding her on his lap and looking at her as if she were God's gift to South Carolina;

the next minute he dumped her off, figuratively speaking. Then, as she was looking around, he grabbed her arm, hustled her out of his office, and, before he shut the door on her, he told her to order room service.

And Sam didn't let her open that door and charge back in, either. He must have been in football, because he blocked her attempts just by standing in front of the doorknob.

She had just wanted to tell Devlin he shouldn't be embarrassed because he'd been nice to Mia. Meadow wasn't going to tell anyone and ruin his image as a big, bad, ruthless developer.

She glanced at the phone. She wanted to tell her mother all about him, but Judith had said not to call.

Was Sharon okay?

Picking up the phone, Meadow ordered a room service dinner. When it arrived, it was succulent, glorious, and vegetarian. The hotel's reputation for fine food would be secure. She ate, she chatted with the room service server who picked up the tray, she took a shower, put on her nightgown, settled down to watch *Training Your Spouse*, a really lousy reality-TV show . . . and all the time she worried about Sharon.

She missed checking in with her mother. Missed hearing Sharon's assurances. Missed her earthy wisdom. And she worried, worried so much, about Sharon's health. If she could at least give her mom a hint, not about what she was really doing, but about *him*, Sharon would be interested. Distracted from her illness.

And why not call her?

Meadow stared at the phone.

Why not?

She could tell Sharon some story about how she was sneaking a phone call during the seminar. A simple tale, because Mom had a way of hearing when Meadow lied.

And if Sam was still in the office, he might see that she was making a call, but he couldn't listen in.

Meadow looked out the window at the rapidly falling spring darkness, and made the decision she needed to make for her own peace of mind. Quickly she dialed her parents, and as it rang, she gripped the phone as hard as she could.

When she heard that beloved voice on the other end, she relaxed. "Mom. I have to go back to the seminar, so I can't talk long, but . . . how's it going with you and Dad?"

⌒

Sharon hung up the phone and lay back on the bed. Sweat beaded her upper lip and her forehead, and her face had that pallor that made River want to cry.

But her smile was genuine. "That was Meadow. She's having a wonderful time."

"How's the seminar?"

"She didn't want to talk about that. She wanted to talk about this guy she met."

"She met a guy?"

"She said he's different—grim and driven and intense. But he fascinates her."

"He doesn't sound like our kind of guy."

"He doesn't have to be. He has to be *her* kind of guy."

"I guess." River wasn't quite as altruistic as Sharon when it came to men dating his little girl, but they'd taught Meadow to trust her instincts, and now he had to trust them, too. He handed Sharon a glass of water and held out a handful of pills. "When is she coming home?"

"She asked if we minded if she stayed for a couple of weeks."

"A couple of weeks?" Dismay mixed with River's interest. "She really likes him?"

"I'm glad. She's only twenty-two, and it's been a rough couple of years for her. This is a break she needs."

"Yes, but . . ." He watched while Sharon struggled to sit up, and fought the impulse to help her. She hated that; hated being treated like an invalid.

"Don't you want to spend some time alone with me?" One at a time, Sharon took the pills and, with great effort, swallowed them. Smiling, she stroked his cheek, then slid back on the pillow.

"Yes. Of course I do." He watched helplessly as she closed her eyes and put her hand on her stomach, a clear sign that nausea, always so close, threatened again. "You told her you were fine." He didn't mean to, but the words came out as an accusation.

"I'll tell her the facts when we know them. When the final results come through. I promise I will. Let's let her be happy for a few days."

He surrendered to Sharon. He always did. She had a strong will and a clear sense of wrong and right, but this time . . . he didn't know if she'd made the correct decision. He wasn't sure at all.

19

Seated in his office, Devlin watched the video screens.

It was close to midnight. The moon was full. And Four staggered up the stairs, drunk as a skunk. He didn't even drink that much; he just couldn't hold his liquor.

Was Devlin ever going to get rid of this guy? While Devlin was distracted by Meadow's injury, Four had taken up residence, and the trouble was, during his daily visits to the sickroom, he'd charmed Meadow. She liked him—far more than she liked Devlin.

To Devlin's surprise, that irked him.

How the hell did a guy like Four, who couldn't manage himself, much less a successful company, win over every woman he met? Did Four conceal hidden depths?

No. Devlin had known the guy for twenty-five years. If Four had hidden depths, they were buried too far beneath layers of vanity, cowardice, and alcohol to be accessed.

Now, as Devlin watched, Four reeled from wall to wall. He was lost, of course. The son of a bitch had lived here, on and off, since he was a kid—and he still couldn't find his damned bedroom. He claimed it was because of the changes Devlin had made; Devlin believed it was because Four was a dissolute idiot. Four was weak, without morals, and a lousy businessman. So much for Bradley Benjamin's proud breed.

Devlin wasn't wrong about Four. He wasn't wrong about Meadow. He sure as hell wasn't wrong about himself.

Devlin lifted the walkie-talkie from his belt and, without looking at the small screen, said, "Mr. Benjamin is on level two, corridor T-three. Send somebody to escort him to his bedroom."

A deep female voice came back. "Yes, Mr. Fitzwilliam."

Startled, he glanced down.

Gabriel had told him he'd hired a woman, but Devlin hadn't yet caught a glimpse of her. Even now he couldn't see her well—she stood somewhere outside. He caught a quick impression of middle age and competence, and an Eastern European stockiness. Gabriel had assured him she was experienced, so Devlin clicked off the walkie-talkie. "Sam!"

Sam appeared in the doorway. He looked tired—both of them had been working flat-out since five this morning trying to trace the sudden loss of water pressure to the hotel.

Of course, they both knew who was behind the sabotage, but that didn't make it easier to fix.

"No luck so far, sir. The manager of the water treatment plant still says he can't get anyone on the problem until next week." In frustration, Sam ran his hand through his hair.

"You know where he lives. Send someone over to knock on his door."

"Right now?" A measured smile grew on Sam's lips.

"Absolutely, right now. Then go to bed." With familiar bitterness, Devlin said, "Until we figure out a way to get a monkey wrench locked around Bradley Benjamin's nuts, there's going to be more trouble, and we'll never figure out a solution without sleep."

Devlin glanced toward the video screens. He rubbed his eyes. He should go to bed, because he was hallucinating. He had to be.

He thought that was Meadow running down the dim corridor outside their bedroom—in her bathrobe.

"What the hell?" He sat forward.

Sam joined him. "It's good to see that Mrs. Fitzwilliam is feeling so much better," he said in a neutral tone.

Meadow was flitting along without any care to a stairway or obstruction or a sudden veer, when one more smack on her head might actually give her what she claimed to already have—a memory loss.

At least she wasn't looking for paintings.

"By the way, the detective e-mailed. He's following up on all the phone calls from Mrs. Fitzwilliam's room, but so far he has eliminated only two numbers. Most people aren't home. One won't speak to him, and another threatened him with a lawsuit if he called again. Three go right to voice mail every time. He says caller ID is the bane of the detective. If a person doesn't know the number, they won't pick up. If they don't know the person who leaves a voice mail, they won't return the call. And the kind of questions he asks trip off all kinds of concern." Then Sam looked at Devlin, just looked at him, and the questions were clear in his eyes.

Sam hadn't been along on Devlin's trip to Majorca. He couldn't say for sure that Meadow wasn't his wife. But he knew better than anyone how Devlin had reacted when he'd first seen her, and of Devlin's search for her origins. Sam didn't believe they were married.

But Devlin's motivations were none of Sam's business, any more than Sam's lack of a personal life was Devlin's.

Sam had no relatives to plague him, no home that called him, no dog to pee on his rug. The guy showed a flair for business, but apparently had no desire to start his own, and occasionally Devlin wondered if he should keep an eye on Sam, because really—how could a guy so talented not have a single fault?

Yet based on Sam's impeccable references, Devlin had hired him, and until the day Sam announced he was seeking his fortune elsewhere, Devlin would utilize his skills, pay him really damned well, and trust him—or trust him as much as he trusted anyone.

"Where are the calls going?" Devlin asked.

"Most are local, but several calls went to Atlanta. California. Wisconsin. Texas. Washington. Florida. And New York."

Devlin never took his gaze off her. "She's a clever girl."

"Yes, sir," Sam said without an ounce of inflection.

Devlin took the ornate silver key out of the desk drawer and pocketed it.

Meadow headed toward the back door. She was going outside.

"I'm going for a walk to clear my head." He set off at a run.

He thought he would catch her before she left the house; instead, he arrived at the back door as it clicked shut behind her. He caught it and stepped out on the porch.

After his trek through the dim corridors, the moonlight almost blinded him. It turned the estate into stark etchings in black and white. The shadows beneath the trees sprinkled the lawn with dark coins, and when he looked up, he could see the full disk of the moon floating through a black sea decorated with stars.

Across the lawn, Meadow was running, her copper hair the single color in a black-and-white world. Only she wasn't really running. She was . . . skipping like a schoolgirl, her arms in the air as if to embrace the night.

Damn. The drugs had made her crazy.

But he knew that was bullshit. The drugs had nothing to do with it. She was just . . . crazy.

He spoke into his walkie-talkie. "Mrs. Fitzwilliam and I are going to be in the walled garden. We'd like our privacy. Tell the other security personnel to stay away."

"Yes, sir." It was the woman again, speaking to him from somewhere out in the yard. It didn't matter where she was—where any of them were—as long as he herded Meadow toward the walled garden. There they would have privacy.

He turned off the walkie-talkie.

Meadow disappeared over the rise toward the beach.

He sprinted after her. When he topped the rise, he saw her bathrobed figure on the winding path headed over the dunes toward the beach. "Meadow," he called. The breeze carried his voice away, so he bellowed, "Meadow!"

She turned. He thought she would frown at him, as she had when he broke up her soap opera party, or clutch her robe together in that maidenly skittishness she displayed whenever he showed the tiniest hint of his sexuality.

But no. She grinned and ran back to him. "Did you come out to play, too?"

"Come out to play?" He hadn't heard that term since third grade.

"Isn't it beautiful?" She waved an all-encompassing arm at the lawn, the dunes, the sky. "Don't you love living here? Don't you love the sound of the waves and the smell of the ocean and the scent of the pines?" She seemed giddy.

"Did you hit your head again?" he asked warily.

She laughed without a worry as to who might hear. "It's the full moon. Come on!" She grabbed his hand. "Let dance!"

She pulled him along, holding his arm in the air, stomping her feet in some weird version of Greek dancing.

"Isn't this fun?" she called.

He felt stupid, like an onlooker at a drunken party. Plus, security was watching for saboteurs coming up the beach, and he'd be damned if they were going to see him prancing around like a sailor on leave. He stopped and, like an anchor, hung on to her.

She stopped, too—she had no choice—and glared at him in exasperation.

"I have a surprise for you," he said.

"You do not." But she lavished that stunning smile on him. "What?"

"Come on." He led her along the winding path back into the depths of the estate.

"What's that?" She pointed at the ivied walls rising ahead.

"That's where we're going." He led her toward the tall, heavy, timbered gate. Pulling the key out of his pocket, he showed it to her.

He felt her flinch. He heard her draw a breath.

So she recognized it. It probably matched the one she'd used to get into the house.

Fitting the key in the lock, he turned it. He experienced an odd sensation, a sort of breathlessness, although he didn't know why. Then he realized—he actually anticipated the look on her face when he showed her. . . . He pushed the door open and stepped aside.

Her expression of delight was everything he could have wished. "Look. It *is* the Secret Garden!" She bounded in, her robe fluttering behind her.

Her enthusiasm bubbled up like champagne, intoxicating him, and he hurried after her, calling, "Would you slow down?"

"Don't be silly!" She disappeared around the corner, and her voice called back, "How could I slow down when the moon is full and I'm in the Secret Garden?" She laughed, one of those full-bodied laughs that made his testosterone levels surge. Then, "Oh!"

He came around the corner and almost ran into her.

She stood stock-still before the wide expanse of lawn that was the heart of the garden. A tangle of pine and rhododendrons occupied one corner. An immense live oak spread its branches over a marble bench. An artificial waterfall sparkled over real boulders and into a pool, and frogs called their love songs.

And at the center of the broad sweep of the glade was a pergola where an ancient wisteria vine twisted up and over, thick with blooms.

It was just the way he'd planned it. He'd seen in the garden a marvelous asset. He'd approved its cleanup, the plantings, and the installation of the waterfall. Transforming the garden from a tangled jungle into a romantic hideaway made financial sense—after all, the value of the Secret Garden increased once lovers started hiring the hotel to plan their weddings.

But he wasn't thinking of finance while he basked in the awe on her face.

"This is . . . so beautiful." Her voice choked with tears.

In the moonlight, the garden glowed with light and shadow, glory and mystery.

So did Meadow. The moon's glow lit her face, and at the same time she radiated pure joy. "Thank you for bringing me here. Thank you for showing me this. I don't care what everyone says about you. You're wonderful!"

Leaving him speechless, she danced away.

She twirled in a circle, around and around, laughing lightly. Then she did something that stopped his breath.

She shed her robe.

The moon shone through the thin white material of her nightgown. As she whirled, he could see her legs, her hips, her waist, her breasts in silhouette.

She was glorious, a white candle topped by flame.

Then . . . she pulled her nightgown up and off over her head.

He'd seen his share of naked women. He'd visited Mediterranean beaches where toplessness was a way of life. But he had never seen anything as bold and innocently sexy as Meadow worshipping the moon. She paid him no heed, but swayed to an inner rhythm, her feet bare, her thighs strong and muscled, her small breasts high and pale.

If he believed in witches, he would believe in her. She made him want to dance in the moonlight. She made him want to shout, to sing, to fuck.

She made him want to live. And that was goddamn stupid, because he was already living.

Except . . . as he watched her, he knew he was lying to himself. He hadn't been alive for years. Maybe he'd never been alive.

Her expression was fiercely exultant, as if the night were her lover and she the only woman who could satisfy him.

But no. Devlin wanted to be her lover.

He discarded his shoes.

Stupid move, but not fatally stupid, because he kept his pants on. As long as those pants were on, the two of them were safe from something so impetuous, it would be madness.

He walked toward her, seeing nothing but her.

As she twirled toward him, her smile blossomed.

"Let me show you what moonlight is made for." Sliding his arm around her back, he placed his hand on her bare back.

And for the first time, he got real benefit out of his Southern-gentleman training. Unhurriedly he guided her through the basic steps of the waltz, teaching her; then, as she gained confidence, he took her in wider and wider circles, speeding up, carrying her along with him.

She felt small in his arms, and with each turn her body brushed against him, teasing him. Her scent rose in his nostrils and fired synapses in his brain until he knew that if he were blindfolded and shoved into a crowd of women, he would identify her. The breeze sang in his ears, the trees and flowers and pond and pergola whirled past, and she smiled up at him as if *he* had enchanted *her*.

And she was naked in his arms.

Later he didn't remember planning to do what he did. He was a man who plotted and schemed every moment of his life, his business, and his revenge, yet a silent melody and a merry face swept him away to someplace where only the two of them existed.

The circles got wider and slower.

Her smile dissolved. Her wide eyes focused on him—just him. The two of them loitered through the last steps, their bodies pressed together.

They stopped and stared at each other.

She broke away.

She took his hand.

And she led him toward the pergola.

20

*I*nside the pergola the fragrance of wisteria hung heavy in the air, and the moonlight lay shattered in bright bits on the marble bench, the flagstones, and Meadow's face.

She struggled to get Devlin's jeans unbuttoned and unzipped.

He didn't help her. Hell, why would he, and miss the accidental touches to his groin and occasionally—okay, more than occasionally—the touches to his dick?

For how could she not touch it? It was *gigantic.*

He wanted to chuckle at himself for his testosterone-fed flight of imagination. Trouble was—his dick felt gigantic. It felt powerful. *He* felt powerful.

She pushed his jeans off. His boxers. She ran her fingertips from his balls to his tip.

No other touch had ever felt so good, and he groaned like a callow boy.

"Do you want to dance now?" she whispered, and her husky voice trembled with suppressed laughter.

"You little tease." Picking the robe off the bench, he spread it over the marble. In one efficient motion he twirled her around and flat onto her back.

For the first time she saw him with a face stripped of guile. The moonlight showed her his soul before the circumstances of his life had stripped away his pleasure in life. Tonight he wasn't a control freak or a tycoon or a mystery. Tonight he was just a man.

No, he was a *guy*, controlled by his testicles and happy to obey their dictates.

And who was she? A woman who had disregarded her mother's warnings about the fatal combination of moonlight and men.

Now she was as helpless as he was.

She held up her arms to embrace him.

His dark eyes gleamed in the shards of moonlight, and his teeth flashed as he smiled. With his hands on her shoulders, he pressed her back.

Then those hands wandered . . . down across her breasts, brushing them, learning their shape, their sensitivity.

Her eyes closed as he caressed the curve of the underside, the small circle of her nipples. He knew exactly what he was doing, touching her in such a way that she thought only of the slow, warm slide into arousal.

She didn't know what to do with her legs. Put her feet on the ground? The bench would be between them. She would be revealed, and it seemed too early for that. Yet when she bent her knee and put one heel against the seat, he murmured, "Darling," and kissed her inner thigh.

They were going to make love, in this secret garden on this perfect night . . . and maybe this was what she'd planned all along. Her untried emotions felt new and raw, different from any she'd experienced. She felt like an adventurer visiting a place she'd only imagined.

When he slid his hand up her thigh and buried it in the carefully trimmed thatch of copper curls, she arched off the bench in a tumultuous excess of anticipation. "Devlin," she whispered.

"What? Do you like that?" His finger slid inside her, a deep, leisurely violation. "And this?"

Her eyes opened wide, and when she looked up at him, she saw a handsome face made wondrous by the desire he could fire in her. He was all strong muscle over heavy bones, a man made tough by the fight for success, for honor, for his identity.

He thrust his finger inside her again, and she was swollen, damp—her body betrayed her need with excruciating detail.

She wanted that shirt off him. She wanted it off now. "Take it off." It was *not* a request.

He smiled. He withdrew his finger from within her and straightened. His hands went to his buttons. One by one he unfastened them, and as unhurriedly as he moved, she might have thought him indifferent to passion.

But as his shirt fell open, she saw his sculpted chest and belly . . . and the proud erection that reached up from his groin.

He stood between her legs, one knee on the seat, masculine, dominant—yet he needed her desperately. She didn't even know if he realized how much he needed to be civilized . . . no, not even civilized.

Humanized.

The shirt still hung from his shoulders as he leaned down to kiss her breast, taste her nipple. Goose bumps rose in a wave, rushing away from the sensation like a wave, cresting in the sensation that lifted her hips toward him.

He laughed again, very much the man in command, the conquering hero.

She couldn't allow that.

She sat up on one elbow. She licked one finger and, with its damp tip, she swirled it around the head of his penis.

He groaned—a spontaneous, vibrant sound that made her laugh for joy.

She licked her finger again, but before she could touch him, he caught her wrist and squeezed. Not painfully, but somehow she knew . . . the moonlight, the scents, the passion had broken his fierce will.

They stared at each other, eyes locked.

Then he picked up her knees and spread them wide. He sat on the seat and dragged her toward him until they were groin-to-groin.

The pressure of his erection against her wrenched a moan from her. She wanted . . . needed . . . She tried to position herself to thrust herself on him.

He didn't allow her that. Didn't allow her any control. He rubbed himself against her, a long stroke that massaged her clit and made her whole body clench in anticipation. He found the entrance to her body and gradually thrust inside.

He lifted her hips toward him, and each inch filled her past the point of comfort, but she didn't care. It wasn't comfort she sought; it was satisfaction, and the craving made her supersensitive.

The scent of him mixed with the fragrance of the night-blooming flowers, the grass, the air. Above him she could see the wisteria hanging off the arbor like ripe clumps of grapes, and beyond that the night sky and moonlight . . . so much moonlight. She could hear the rough rasp of his breath as he thrust all the way in, then reluctantly drew out, and she wanted to clutch at him, make him stay tightly inside her.

But like some Greek god, he sat above her, looking down at her, his gaze never leaving her. He held her hips and directed their movements until she wanted to scream with frustration.

Yet she did nothing but writhe and moan . . . because everything he did to her felt so good. Too good.

She clutched the robe-draped sides of the bench, bunching the material in her fists in building frustration. Each time he lifted her, he leaned in so his groin connected with her clit, and the pressure . . . the pressure built.

Her skin grew so sensitive that even the cool breeze felt like a caress. It hurt to breathe, hurt to have Devlin thrust inside, hurt to have him slide out. "Please. Please, please, please, please . . ."

She didn't care what he thought, whether her begging constituted some triumphant mark on his supremacy scoreboard. She knew only that he had better do something about this intense compulsion that drove her to madness or . . . or she really would lose her mind and her memories, and be lost in some glorious place with Devlin.

"Please." She kissed her fingertips and placed them on his lips.

His lips returned the kiss. Then his stark features tightened; his lips parted as he pulled air into his lungs. He lifted himself—and her—and rode her in a driving rhythm.

Her back went taut as a bow. She wrapped her legs around his hips, accepting him, welcoming him, taking him as he took her— and finally, finally climax seized her.

Thank God.

Devlin had held her off too long, and her orgasm was almost painful in its intensity. She screamed. Her hands went over her head and gripped the bench behind her. She heard him say one word: "Meadow!"

To hear his deep, warm, Southern voice call her name sharpened her response, and the climax, already so powerful, blotted out the rest of the world . . . except for Devlin. Always she was aware of Devlin.

And he was aware of her. Even as his balls drew up tight against his body and that shudder ran up his spine, he couldn't stop observing her—the way her small breasts lifted as she clutched the bench over her head, her taut belly, her expression of mingled agony and exaltation. She was the most beautiful thing he'd ever seen. He wanted to spend every moment of his life inside her, kiss her mouth, her breasts, her belly. He wanted to pleasure her until she believed the tale he wove of their love, until she remembered no life except with him.

He wanted this moment to go on forever . . . and he couldn't stop the rush of semen that spurted from him. He laid claim to her in the ancient, primal way dictated by the moon for generations past . . .

And it wasn't until he finished, until he rested on her, panting, and felt the rise and fall of her chest as she gasped beneath him, that he realized—he hadn't used protection.

For the first time in his life, he hadn't used a condom.

21

Clad in the innocuous black-and-white uniform of a security guard, Judith stood under the huge live oak and watched as Meadow and Devlin pranced toward the house.

They'd had sex. Great sex.

So freaking lovely for them. The only time Judith had had great sex was when she was alone and had an unending supply of D batteries. Men didn't seem to be interested in a woman with a broad chin, thin lips, legs like tree stumps, and a waist as broad as her beam. It wasn't fair, but she was used to "not fair."

What *was* fair was acquiring a sponsor like Mr. Hopkins, who helped her get a job in the right place at the right time doing the right thing—being a security guard at the house where Isabelle's painting was hidden. Here she could keep tabs on Four and Meadow as they searched Waldemar, and when they found it . . . she would be the first to know.

But never for a second did she imagine she would end up with custody of the painting. She had made a deal with the devil, and better than anyone in the world, she understood the nature of evil—her father had taught her that—and respected its strength.

Besides, in the end, she would get what she wanted. Mr. Hopkins had promised she would have the credit for discovering that painting.

⁓

"Why are we sneaking back into the house?" Meadow stage-whispered.

"Because every security person in the place is watching and—" Devlin broke off. Why *were* they sneaking into the house?

He couldn't herd Meadow across the lawn and through the corridors to their bedroom without every security person on duty—and probably a few who weren't—seeing them. And he knew damned good and well the conclusion they would draw from their disappearance—the right conclusion. Especially since he claimed Meadow was his wife. And because she was still dancing, although now she wore her nightgown and robe—but only because he made her.

And she was smiling. She was so happy.

Damn it. Damn it. Damn it.

He couldn't believe he'd been so criminally careless.

He couldn't believe he let her take his hand and swing it as they walked. He should have explained the danger they'd courted. Instead, he let her blissfully babble on.

"My mother always told me that mankind isn't as far removed from the primitive as we would like to believe," Meadow said. "That when we take the time, we respond just as our ancestors did to moonlight and springtime and nature. I think tonight we proved she was right."

He thought about cornering Meadow, asking her how, when she had amnesia, she remembered what her mother said, but Meadow grinned at him so mischievously he couldn't.

He'd made her sparkle. He'd given her satisfaction. For some ridiculous reason, tonight she trusted him. With her joy and easy acceptance of their relationship, she made him feel like Scrooge—armored against the good things in life, suspicious . . . old.

And horny. She made him horny.

It was damned embarrassing, walking around like some bull moose following a female in heat.

She'd been so small and tight. For a horrified, exultant moment he'd been afraid she was a virgin.

But no, only seldom touched, and not for a long time. And he, who had intended to take his pleasure of her—but on his terms and in his own time—had put his heart and soul into claiming her.

Without protection.

She could be pregnant right now.

"Watch your step." He led her up onto Waldemar's wide porch and opened the door.

Inside, moonlight streamed through the windows and lurked in square patches on the carpet, and, suddenly superstitious, he avoided walking through the white light. What if her mother was right? What if it was the moonlight that had caused his madness? He certainly had no other explanation.

Meadow showed no such care. She skipped along, apparently energized by sex with him.

Great, fabulous, wonderful, earthshaking, marvelous, dick-building sex.

"Be careful," he called. "Don't run into anything."

"I won't!"

If she was going to race around in the moonlight every night, he would have to order the lights turned on. Or perhaps he should keep her in bed at night through whatever means he had at hand.

He shook his head. He had to stop thinking of sex or he'd knock that vase off that table and lift her up there and—

Did he have no sense of propriety? Was he like his father after all? He'd worked so hard to develop the moral character that his parent had so obviously lacked. Now he'd broken every rule he'd set himself about women and about life. He could have created a baby with her, and he remembered all too well how miserable his childhood had been as the one bastard offspring of the Fitzwilliams.

Which brought him to Bradley Benjamin—what had happened to his plan to use her for revenge against Bradley?

He had, of course, and thoroughly enjoyed Bradley's attack of angina.

But now Devlin had spent an hour ardently enjoying her body to the point of madness. He slept with a liar, and one of the hated Benjamin clan.

Worse, he wanted to do it again.

Meadow got ahead of him. He heard her feet patter up the stairs, and like some creaky old man chasing a two-year-old, he pursued her, calling, "Don't trip."

She turned the corner at the top of the stairs. "I won't!" Her voice floated back, full of devilry.

Shit. What was she up to now? By the time he reached the top of the stairs, she'd disappeared.

"This way," she called.

Shit. He ran down the corridor toward their room. The door was closed. The light shone beneath it. He flung it open, fully expecting the sitting room to be empty. And it was. Except for her bathrobe pooled on the Oriental rug.

In the bedroom, he could see her nightgown tossed on the floor.

Did the woman ever keep her clothes on?

But it wasn't annoyance that made his blood surge and his subsiding erection stir.

She was naked again.

He shut the door behind him. He locked it. He walked into the bedroom—and through the open bathroom door he heard the shower running.

For a long moment he shut his eyes. Water . . . sluicing down her body. Her copper red hair . . . getting wet and turning auburn. Her hands . . . caressing her breasts, her arms, her stomach, between her legs, leaving a soapy trail of bubbles.

He found himself standing in the doorway, staring at the glass shower enclosure.

The view was even better than he imagined. She stood with her head tilted back, her arms up, rinsing the shampoo from her hair. Dense white bubbles slid off her shoulders and down her chest, and one small batch broke away to perch on her nipple. She was pale and starkly bare against the claret tile, and so beautiful his eyes blurred, probably because all his blood had left his head and rushed to his dick.

As if she sensed his heated stare, her eyes popped open. In a laughing voice, she asked, "What took you so long?"

22

"And I was afraid I would be too quick," Devlin said ironically.

Meadow's grin disappeared. Just like that, with a few words, he turned her from a merry water nymph into a woman who hungered . . . for him.

She popped the door open and gestured invitingly. "Let's test you out."

He glanced at the drawer by the sink. He kept condoms in there. There were condoms by the bed. Just in case, he needed to put some in the desk drawer in the sitting room. . . . Then somehow he found he had his clothes off. He stepped into the shower.

The multiheaded Hydra of a shower shot water onto their heads, into their backs, and vibrated their buttocks.

He told himself he was in here to do the responsible thing. He squirted shower gel on his hands and rubbed them together. "We have to talk. What we did in the garden was reckless." He rubbed her shoulders, and the combination of water and bubbles made her slickly erotic. "We can't allow passion to sweep us off our feet and onto whatever horizontal surface is available."

"Why not?"

"We're going to get caught." His hands trailed down her arms.

His fingers entwined with hers, and he slid up and down each finger, then stroked the palm of her hand.

She leaned against the wall. "By who?"

"By security personnel. By one of the maids." He watched Meadow draw short, shallow breaths, then used another splash of shower gel on her chest. "By your ob-gyn, who will announce you're pregnant." He rubbed the soap into a lather, then used it to wash her breasts.

"W-wrong time of the month." Each word sounded like a moan.

"If I had a nickel for every kid conceived at the wrong time of the month, I'd be rolling nickels for the rest of my life." Was he trying to convince her or himself?

She slid her feet apart, put her hands against the wall, braced herself as if he were trying to knock her down, when all he was doing was washing her. "Nickels or nipples?"

"What?" He loved the texture of her boobs—the dense, warm, heavy flesh, the soft skin, the responsive tips.

"I'm trying to ask if you're planning to wash anything but my boobs."

"They can never be too clean." And he supposed he was acting like an obsessive tit man, when actually he was more of a butt man. It was just that *Meadow's* tits were so fine.

He slid his hands around her and rubbed her back with the lather, then moved closer and rubbed her body with his. She clutched his shoulders while they slipped across each other in a slow, warm, slithering ballet.

Gradually the soap washed down the drain.

With his lips, he followed the bubbles on their descent. He kissed her shoulder, her breast, her stomach, her hip. . . . She moaned as he pressed his mouth to the small froth of hair over her pubis. He was on his knees now, and the scent of her—lavender soap and clean woman—made him hungry for more.

With his fingers, he parted her nether lips and tasted her with a long, slow stroke of the tongue.

She whimpered, and when he glanced up, she had her fist pressed against her mouth and her head back.

Because she screamed when she came. He knew that now. And she wanted to muffle the sound.

Good luck to her. He intended to make her scream again.

He wrapped his hands around her bottom to hold her still, and licked her again. The flavor of Meadow imprinted on his senses, and he knew no matter how hard he tried, he would never forget this night. With his lips he found her clit and carefully drew it into his mouth.

"Devlin!" She jerked as if he'd given her an electric shock.

He sucked on her, used his tongue to drive her over the edge, and in only a few moments she arched—and screamed. He fed her sensations, reveling in her pleasure, until her knees collapsed and her cries died down to whimpers.

He drew away, intent on standing, sweeping her into his arms, and taking her to bed.

Instead she shoved him down to the floor of the shower. She followed him down. She straddled his chest.

The showerheads splashed down on them. The tile was hard as hell. But one glance at her face revealed a woman intent on getting exactly what she wanted from him.

"Wait—" He wanted that condom.

She took his very, very erect dick in her hands and rubbed it up and down.

"My God!" All the synapses in his brain exploded like popcorn.

She took him in her mouth.

His muscles gave way. He fell back against the floor.

She sucked hard.

He shuddered, so close to climax he was willing to promise anything, reveal any secret, for one more stroke.

She had different ideas. "No, you don't." She sat up on his groin and adjusted his dick and her vagina until they met, and then performed the kind of wiggling, panting, forceful ravishment he'd always imagined being forced to endure.

But he'd never met a woman who shared his dreams—until now.

He'd never met a woman whom he trusted to take charge—until now.

Until Meadow.

She took him inside her inch by inch, rising and falling as she pulled him in, and the sweet, hot friction broke his will. "Please. Meadow. Please." He didn't care that he sounded like a boy, that he'd lost his control as well as his mind, as long as she gave him the kind of pleasure that made him die and resurrected him, all at the same time.

She braced her hands against his shoulders and rode him with an expression of furious need, her lips open, water trickling into her mouth and eyes.

The shower rained down on them, drowning him, pushing her sopping hair into her eyes. Her desire burned his skin, his heart. Need, desperation, put him in pain . . . or was it pleasure? He was lost in the labyrinth of time. He braced his feet against the floor and thrust as hard as he could, meeting her, trying to reach the center of her being, as if that would somehow make her his.

And he did it.

Or rather, she did it. She drove herself onto him, a wild girl obsessed with her needs, and at some white point of fusion, their passions melded and became one. He came so violently he lifted her with his body, while inside her he felt the spasms of her orgasm sucking him dry.

Finally he *was* dry. Empty. At last he came to rest.

She withered down on top of him, and he experienced a savage gratification that she was as replete, as exhausted as he was.

He wrapped his arms around her and held her. Just held her. Opening his mouth, he let the water flow in, trying to replenish himself for the next bout—which his every instinct told him would be soon.

Very soon—or at least, as soon as he could guarantee that, out of pure repletion, he wouldn't flow down the drain. As soon as he could lift himself off the floor and somehow resume the character of the man he had been . . . only a few hours ago.

He felt her chest rise and fall in a sigh. Bit by bit she inched into the sitting position. She looked down at him and smiled, a wobbly smile quite unlike her usual impish grin. She lifted herself off him and sat on the floor, her knees raised, her hands resting limply on them. "That was wonderful," she whispered.

"Yes." He knew he should say something meaningful. Something that expressed how earthshaking the night had been. But he didn't know what to say.

From the moment they'd met they'd been lying to each other, playing games as each sought some unknown goal. He didn't know how to tell her the truth—or even what the truth was. Somehow, tonight, the truth as he knew it had changed.

He didn't know what he wanted anymore.

But he did know they'd once again had sex—without protection.

"Son of a bitch!" Devlin surged to his feet.

Meadow looked up curiously. "What?"

"We did it again!"

"I noticed." Her voice was mellow, exhausted, pleased. "Do you want to lodge a complaint?"

"We did it without protection."

"I don't have any diseases. I swear to you I don't."

His mind, once so sharp, veered away from the subject at hand and onto the obvious track. "You're not active."

"You could make that sound a little more like a question."

Then the charade they were playing caught up with him, and he snapped, "How can you swear that when you don't remember your past?"

"Do *you* have a disease?"

A smooth counterattack. He appreciated her cleverness even as he answered, "No. But I am fertile, and I can hardly claim it was the moonlight again. What excuse can I use in the shower? It's the *soap?*"

She lowered her head and bit her lip to subdue a smile.

And with that smile, so beautifully provocative, he remembered the feel of her beneath his palms, her skin slick with bubbles. . . . Temptation struck him like a blow between the eyes. Not the temptation to take her again, although the urge hovered close. He actually wanted to admit that he knew she was lying about her amnesia, ask her her real name, beg her . . . beg her for *what*?

Kicking open the door, he stepped out.

He had come *this* close to saying, *You're not my wife.*

But damn it. No!

He wasn't the one who should step forward. Let her tell the truth. Let Meadow reveal herself, and then he would see if she was worth taking a chance on.

Meadow woke slowly and, without opening her eyes, inhaled deeply.

Devlin smelled so good. Like that peculiar man scent composed of strength and stubbornness, and with a hint of girlie lavender soap— or maybe Meadow was smelling herself with his scent on her.

Because she'd slept deeply last night, exhausted from her midnight adventures, but always she had been aware that Devlin held her as he held her now—tucked tightly against his body, her back against his chest, her butt in the cradle of his hips.

Devlin.

She hadn't believed a man could be what he was. A challenge. A lover. An enemy.

It was the stupidest thing she'd ever done in her life, wanting him, taking him. Yet she wanted to roll onto her back and wiggle like a puppy when she remembered the raw, wild passion between them.

Groping behind her, she slid her hand along his flank. He was tall, and each part of him was long and muscled. Last night he'd ridden her hard, and she'd returned the favor.

This morning she ached between her legs. In her life she'd been with one man, and maybe he'd been a peewee. She didn't know. She knew only that the length and breadth of Devlin was echoed in the size of his penis. Last night had taken its toll. Her body couldn't easily accept him again.

But knowing he would cause her discomfort didn't stop the wanting.

If she had the choice between forgetting last night and saving herself the inevitable pain, and reliving it, she would relive it.

His breathing was slow and easy, and with great care she turned in his arms.

His eyes were closed, his face lax. He looked like a man worn to exhaustion by too little sleep . . . and unexpected pleasure.

She believed that all things happened for the good, and surely he had come into her life now for a reason. And how could that reason be anything but good? He was, after all, Devlin.

Never mind that he made her feel restless. Panicky. Unlike the Meadow she had always been. Something in him called to her, and she responded with such lust. . . .

She stroked his chest, then pressed against one shoulder and pushed him onto his back. Sliding her hand down across the taut skin on his belly, she reached his groin and closed her hand on his erection.

His temperature went up five degrees.

She smiled. Maybe he was asleep. Maybe he wasn't. But either way she made him wild with greed.

He was so afraid of raw, brazen sex—unprotected sex, he called it. He wanted that rubber as a barrier between them during their most intimate moments. Grudgingly she admitted the good sense of his precautions, for all the reasons, but at the same time she liked to feel his flesh in her flesh, his come in her womb.

Probably she'd be a lot more perturbed if she thought there were a danger of repercussions, but they were safe. Last night was time out of mind.

More important, the time of the month would keep her safe.

Leaning over him, she lightly kissed his mouth. Then his shoulder. His nipple. His stomach.

He was definitely awake now.

His hip . . . she slid beneath the blanket. Under here the sunlight was muted and the air was warm and dense with their mingled scents. She teased him with tiny kisses down one thigh. She circled to his other leg, his other hip. Deliberately she allowed the ends of her hair to trail across his groin, and chuckled when his whole body went rigid.

He clamped a hand on her head, holding her in place.

From the end of the bed, a woman's soft Southern voice asked, "Darling boy, what's this I hear about your marriage?"

A woman was in their bedroom? A woman had violated the sanctity of their privacy? A woman asked about their marriage as if she had the right?

And he dared to indicate he wanted Meadow to remain hidden?

She sank her teeth into his thigh.

He flinched. His fingers tightened on Meadow's neck. In a loud, emphatic voice he said, "How good to see you, *Mother.*"

23

The ringing phone made Four jackknife up in bed. He stared at that instrument of torture, then at the clock.

Nine in the morning—again.

Was it *him*?

Of course it was him. Mr. Hopkins. Who else could it be?

Four didn't want to answer. He felt ill with whiskey . . . and fear. But the ringing kept on and on, as if the man knew for sure that Four was in his room. And that was just what Four feared.

Cautiously, Four hit talk. "Hello?"

"Four. I'm very disappointed in you." That familiar, gentle, demonic voice made Four want to retch. "You've been drinking when you should be searching."

"No, I haven't."

"Four, lying won't get you out of trouble. Not this time."

"I'm not lying!" *Down, boy. Don't snap at Mr. Hopkins; you might piss him off.* "I drink a little, then pretend I'm drunk. But can you think of a better ploy to search this place than to stagger around every night like I'm lost?"

The short silence that followed made Four break a sweat. Then Mr. Hopkins said, "Why, Four, I'm impressed with your ingenuity.

My kudos on taking one of your many failings and putting it to good use."

Even his compliments were carefully designed to make Four grovel. And Four could grovel with the best of them.

"Yet still, you've completely failed me, and after I did you the favor of buying stock in your company," Mr. Hopkins said. "Remember that company? The company you embezzled from?"

Four sat on the edge of the bed, his throbbing head in his hands. "I remember."

"Do you remember also that I didn't prosecute you when the theft was discovered?"

Neither had Devlin.

This was all Four's fault. He knew that. He was a screwup, always had been. But when he'd falsified those books in his father's corporation, he hadn't realized Devlin would get so pissed off. Sure, Four had personally convinced him to buy stock, but what was a couple of million bucks to a guy like Devlin?

But when he'd said that to Devlin, Devlin had looked at him, and Four had taken about five steps back. Even now he shuddered at the memory of Devlin's bitter dark eyes. Devlin had taken Four's little embezzlement as a betrayal, and no one betrayed Devlin without suffering repercussions.

So Bradley Benjamin the third had had to choose—sell Waldemar to the bastard son of the upstart Fitzwilliams, or let his son go to prison. It had been close, but now Devlin owned a new hotel, and Four's father's enmity toward his only son had deepened.

"Four, when I speak to you, I like to know that you heard me." Like a bulldog, Mr. Hopkins had his teeth sunk into Four's flesh, and he wouldn't give up.

"I remember everything," Four said.

After Waldemar's sale, Four had thought the worst was over.

But no. Because some guy he'd never heard of had bought a bunch of stock, too, and Mr. Hopkins didn't possess Devlin's kind, gentle soul.

Four's mouth dried as he remembered the warehouse where Mr. Hopkins and his men had taken him. He hadn't believed their threats at first. Stuff like breaking fingers and slicing off ears happened in the movies, not to the son of a distinguished Southern family. But those guys had done both, and all the time he'd screamed, Mr. Hopkins had been talking, talking, talking.

All too soon, it was clear to Four he'd been played for a fool. Mr. Hopkins had known the stock was no good. He'd bought it to put Four into his debt, so he could send Four into the house where he'd once lived to retrieve a painting unlike any Four had ever seen there.

"How much more of the house do you have to search?" Mr. Hopkins asked.

"I've worked my way through all the rooms on the first two floors and the basement. I've been in all the closets. I've searched the pantry. No luck so far." Four hesitated, but what had he to lose by telling the truth? "You know, that painting you described—it's not even Isabelle's style."

"Please. Four. Don't tell me my *business.*" Mr. Hopkins's voice sharpened.

For an instant Four thought he heard something—some tone, some accent—that sounded familiar.

But Mr. Hopkins's next words drove the thought from his mind. "Do you remember in that warehouse when one of my men held a knife to your . . . what's the anatomical name? Ah, yes. Scrotum."

Four swallowed.

"With one word from me, you could find another knife pointing at your scrotum. And with one word from me, you could find it cut off."

Four breathed heavily, trying to subdue his nausea.

"It's an unpleasant operation. There's a lot of blood. The victim screams a lot. And if he recovers, which is not guaranteed, he wishes he had died. Please keep that in mind as you search for the painting I described." The click as Mr. Hopkins hung up was almost inaudible.

Four headed for the bathroom. Holding himself over the toilet, he retched until tears came to his eyes.

The goddamned picture wasn't here. How could he find something that wasn't here?

And how much more time did he have before Mr. Hopkins took matters in his own hands, and sent his goons to kill them all?

How much time?

⌒

"Do you think she knew I was under the covers?" Meadow shimmied into her jeans.

"I'd wear a sundress." Devlin zipped up his beige linen slacks.

"A sundress? To meet your mother?" *Wait a minute.* He was distracting her. "So you *do* think she knew I was under the covers?"

"My mother will never acknowledge it if she did." The short sleeves of his polo shirt cut across his biceps in a most spectacular manner, and the dark blue made his eyes gleam when he looked at her undressed from the waist up. "And yes, when it comes to clothes, my mother's quite the fashion maven."

"But she should meet me as I really am." Meadow grabbed a cap-sleeved pink T-shirt and pulled it over her head.

He walked over to her and pulled the shirt back off.

"This is no time for that." The man was insatiable. She liked that.

He handed her a bra. "I've found, in dealing with my mother, that the less she knows, the better. She's like a steamroller, and once she starts rolling there's no escaping her. She'll flatten you unless you get out of the way."

Meadow looked at the bra, shrugged, and clipped it on. "You make her sound awful."

"She's not awful. She's a woman of power. She gets things done. *You'll* see." He tugged the shirt over her head and handed her a pair of sandals.

"That sounds ominous." She shoved her feet into the shoes.

"Ominous. Good choice of words." He took her arm and led her down the stairs to the elegant room where she'd hidden her key among the couch cushions. Eyeing the couch, she wondered if it was still there.

The room where the painting was supposed to hang on the wall over the fireplace, but didn't.

She flicked a resentful glance at the pompous old gentleman who hung there instead.

The room where she'd first seen Devlin Fitzwilliam.

Well. So the place wasn't all bad.

She straightened when a dainty, elegant woman rose from behind the dainty, elegant desk in the corner.

Devlin's mother was absolutely the right weight for her height; her blond hair was carefully colored and highlighted; she wore a lightweight pink wool suit with a skirt; and her skin had the sheen and texture of porcelain. Yet for all that she appeared to be every inch a Southern lady, she projected the kind of authority Meadow saw in her son.

When she stepped forward to hug him, she projected a stiff affection.

He pecked her cheek. "Mother, what a pleasant surprise. What brings you to the Secret Garden?"

"You can imagine my surprise when I met Scrubby Gallagher in Atlanta and he told me he'd met my new daughter-in-law." Her blue eyes were cool as she observed Meadow, from her unpedicured toes to her unaccessorized top. Her glance at Meadow's hair was a critique, and Meadow realized Devlin's mother had most definitely known she was under the covers—and she did not approve.

She did not approve of any such ill-advised and passionate behavior. She did not approve of Meadow's attire or grooming. She most certainly did not approve of her son's marriage to a hooligan, and she was plain ol' pissed about being left out of the loop.

And obviously everything was Meadow's fault.

So Meadow responded in the best way she knew how. She opened her arms wide, said, "Grace, dearest!" and headed for Devlin's mother.

Meadow caught Grace on the first pass and gave her a hug that rumpled her jacket and disarrayed her careful coiffure. She caught a glimpse of Devlin's amused, appalled expression.

"Mother, this is Meadow. Meadow, please meet my mother, Grace Fitzwilliam."

"I'm so glad to meet you, Grace, so I can thank you for raising my wonderful husband." Meadow beamed at her. "I just knew we would get along!"

Grace winced and rather forcefully disengaged herself. "Yes. Well. Yes. Lovely. So glad . . . But to not tell me!"

"It's a long story, Mother." Before Meadow could hug her again, Devlin pulled her close to his side—and no matter how hard she squirmed, he wouldn't loosen his grip.

"I suppose *your* parents know, er, Meadow." Grace tidied her suit.

"Not . . . exactly." Meadow shifted her feet and hoped Grace wouldn't pursue that line of questioning. Based on nothing more than a pair of jeans and a T-shirt, the woman clearly considered her a misfit. If—when—she heard the story of Meadow's amnesia, she could consider her a head case.

"If you're trying to keep this union a secret," Grace said, "there are better ways to do it than to parade around Amelia Shores causing Bradley Benjamin a heart attack."

"She didn't cause him a heart attack," Devlin said frostily. "He suffered angina, and I hear he's perfectly healthy again."

"Although if he did have a heart, it would certainly attack him," Meadow said.

"Bradley Benjamin is one of our leading citizens," Grace answered.

Meadow couldn't believe Grace was defending him. "He was mean to Devlin."

"But he's older and in ill health, so we allow him his foibles." Grace sounded calm, smooth, and so civilized.

Sort of like Devlin sounded when he was angry.

Fascinating.

Seating herself at the desk once more, Grace sorted through the papers stacked there, found one she wanted, and extended it to Devlin. "There's the guest list. I'll need Meadow's list before I order the invitations."

Devlin glanced at the sheet and shrugged. "Invite whomever you like, Mother."

Meadow felt as if she'd missed part of the conversation. "What list? For what?"

Devlin continued as if Meadow had never spoken. "Perhaps we could combine that party with the grand opening of the Secret Garden."

"What party?" Meadow asked.

Grace handed her the list. "That's rather impersonal."

"Not at all. Having two parties in a row would dilute them both," he said.

"Hmm. Yes, that's a point." Grace brightened. "Plus, I'd have a bigger budget for both."

"What party?" Meadow was considerably louder this time.

"My goodness, Meadow." Grace blinked as if shocked at Meadow's tone. "The party where we officially announce and celebrate your marriage to Devlin, of course!"

Not a good idea. It was one thing to flirt with him. To tease him into enjoying life. To have a small fling with him.

But a party? Where Meadow met not just Four, but all Devlin's friends and business associates? How dumb would that be? It seemed every time she took a step on the way to finding the painting, the shit got piled higher and deeper.

"I think we're ready to meet people, darling." Devlin looked into her eyes.

She saw the mockery there, brought her foot down on his, and ground it into his instep. "I think I need time to get used to my new home before we make an official announcement."

He bore the pain stoically. "Let me do the thinking. You don't need to worry your pretty little head about a thing."

Using all her teeth, she smiled into his face. "I can't help but worry, *darling*, knowing how much this grand opening means to you."

"To us. To our future." How he enjoyed testing her! Would she break and tell the truth rather than suffer the ordeal of a party feting their union?

His mother, of course, was impervious to the undercurrents. "Since you two aren't agreeing about this, we'll do it my way." Going to the table, she opened the boxes and pulled out a froth of packing paper. "I brought some things to use as decoration. Just some small things, Devlin; I know how much you hate my taste."

"I don't hate your taste, Mother. But I have my own decorators."

"And they've done such a quaint job." Grace waved a hand around at the exquisitely old-fashioned room.

"Quaint or not, I can't afford your idea of decorating. It's expensive, and I need things done when I need them done, not when you get the time in your schedule." They'd had this discussion before, and he was tired of it.

"I know that. I'm not reproaching you." At the point of losing, Grace abandoned the argument and pulled out a piece of china. "I found this for your display case."

"Oh." Meadow went to the box as if she couldn't resist. "This is wonderful. It's nineteenth-century Chinese cloisonné, isn't it?"

Grace looked at her as if she'd suddenly sprouted horns. "Yes, a footed bowl."

"Gorgeous! What else do you have?" Meadow carefully removed some of the cardboard packing and found a covered casserole. "English, of course. Portmeirion, Botanic Gardens?"

"That's right," Grace said.

"A good pattern for a party. Expensive but not precious." Meadow put it aside.

At his mother's indignant sputter, Devlin subdued a grin.

"Well, of course, it's very nice." Meadow didn't seem to realize

how deeply she was wounding his mother, who so despised *nice*.
"You don't want to spend a whole party terrified that someone's
going to break your precious antiques, do you?"

Devlin leaned a hip against the couch and settled down to enjoy
himself. "Mother likes to spend her time torn between terror and
triumph."

Grace glared at her son. "I simply don't believe Portmeirion is
ordinary."

"I didn't say ordinary," Meadow protested. "I said it was nice."

She'd just condemned the Portmeirion to perdition.

Delving farther into the box, she brought up another, smaller
box.

"Be careful!" Grace said sharply.

But Meadow unwrapped the tall vase inside with reverent hands.
"A Steuben. I love their work. Look at the iridescence!" She held it
in the sunshine and it flashed with purple, blue, and gold. Running
her fingers around the rim, she said, "It's in good condition, too—no
chips, only a few minor scratches."

The interaction between his mother and his lover fascinated him,
but more than that, Meadow's knowledge and the way she handled
the bowl made Devlin remember the night she'd arrived, and how
indignantly she'd refused to throw up in the precious Honesdale
vase.

His mother hated one-upmanship—if she was the one being one-
upped. With a flourish she unwrapped a wide-lipped glass bowl with
swirls of red and pink and orange and jagged hints of purple. "I'll bet
you don't know this one." Before Meadow could identify the artist,
Grace hastily added, "It's a River Szarvas."

"River Szarvas. Really?" Meadow pinned Grace with a look.

Grace actually squirmed. "It's reputed to be a Natalie Szarvas. But
the dealer who sold it to me didn't believe it, and neither do I. Natalie is River's daughter, so he has reason to build her reputation, but
the girl's only twenty. She couldn't make such a mature piece at that
age."

"Of course not." Meadow cradled the bowl.

"It's like holding a drop of sunset," Grace said.

"Exactly." Meadow smiled.

Every day since Meadow had landed on the floor of his library, Devlin had carefully observed her. He couldn't quite read her thoughts yet, but he was getting there . . . and she had some interesting thoughts. "So this River fellow is setting up an art dynasty."

"He runs an artists' colony in the mountains in Washington," Grace said. "Very large, very well respected, and apparently quite . . . bohemian."

A grin broke across Meadow's face.

"Bohemian?" His suspicions were rapidly becoming certainties.

"I believe your mother is trying to say they're a bunch of old hippies," Meadow informed him.

"Well, yes. So I've heard." Grace grimaced. "Their home in the mountains of Washington was a lodestone for artists, glassblowers, and, for God's sake, environmentalists."

"Heaven forbid!" To his ear, Meadow sounded phonily incredulous.

"According to my art dealer, everyone is welcome, and there's scarcely a night when they don't have guests 'sacked out' "—Grace made quotation marks with her fingers—"on the floor in the studio."

"That *is* bohemian," Meadow said.

Devlin could almost see her hidden amusement.

"But they're artists." Grace lifted an elegant shoulder. "What can you expect?"

"Exactly." Meadow handed her the bowl. "That's quite a find."

"If you ladies will excuse me, I'll leave you to your decorating. I have some work to catch up on." As he left Meadow alone with his mother, he heard Grace grilling Meadow about her family, where she'd gone to school, and what she did for a living. Glancing back, he saw Meadow's deer-in-the-headlights expression, and he enjoyed himself far more than he should.

When he reached his office, he was surprised to see that Sam wasn't anywhere to be found. Poor guy, he'd been working full-tilt for days. Maybe he'd finally crashed.

Devlin went to his desk. He didn't even sit down, but typed in *Natalie Szarvas,* and after Google had chided him for spelling it wrong, it took him to her home page—and he found himself looking at a picture of Meadow, hair up, sweat sheening her face as she worked the glass.

Natalie Meadow Szarvas.

He'd discovered who she was. Now only two questions remained. Exactly why was she here—and how long could he keep her?

24

$\mathcal{M}$eadow walked out of the library at a sedate, reasonable pace, and as soon as she was out of sight she broke and ran up the stairs.

She could kill Devlin for leaving her alone with that woman.

Shallow, self-important, domineering—every one of those words fit Grace Fitzwilliam to a T. Not to mention that she'd interrogated Meadow about her family, her background, her talents, her disposition, and her fertility. Grace was absolutely ferocious in her defense of her son. In fact, that was the only thing Meadow liked about Grace, or would have liked if that scariness hadn't been turned on *her*.

Rounding a corner toward their bedroom, Meadow ran into smack into Sam.

He rocked back on his heels, but he was sturdy and muscular and took the hit well. "Mrs. Fitzwilliam, is there a problem?" As always, he didn't look as if he really cared; it was a polite question only.

"Yes. I mean, no." She flapped a feeble hand back down the stairs. "I just left Grace Fitzwilliam in the library."

"Ah, yes." Sam nodded as if he understood.

"Is she always like that? Because she's the only person I've seen who could make Devlin back off." Meadow smiled to show she meant no harm.

As usual, Sam didn't smile back. "It's easy to see where Mr. Fitzwilliam gets his strength of character."

"What a good way of looking at it! I'll remember that." She glanced behind her. "Is Devlin in his office?"

"I believe so. After he left the library, he went right there."

"How do you know that?"

"I watch the monitors."

"I thought the monitors were in his office."

"There are monitors on every level—if one knows where to look for them. Every inch of the hotel is kept under constant surveillance." He sounded as if he were issuing a warning.

"Except for the rooms."

"Except for the rooms," he agreed. "Did you wish to go to Mr. Fitzwilliam's office?" Sam asked.

"No, I think I'll wander around the hotel a little more." With an irony she enjoyed, she said, "It's really a work of art, don't you think?"

"It is quite lovely." Sam watched her walk away, then called, "Mrs. Fitzwilliam, be careful where you go. The hotel isn't as secure as one might like to think."

She turned back and stared at him.

He stared back, his eyes flat, black, soulless.

Apprehension chilled her. "Are you . . . threatening me?"

"Warning you." He walked away.

She looked around. What was he doing in this corridor? Devlin's suite was here. Her suite. The suite they shared.

And their door was open. Had he been in there looking for . . . for what?

She walked into the sitting room. It looked fine. Nothing out of place.

Sam was an odd man. He didn't seem to have friends. He wouldn't talk about his background. He said threatening things to her. Maybe he really was a serial killer. Maybe she should say something to Devlin.

But what would she say? *You know your secretary? The one you trust? He says sort of hostile things, and the way he looks at me makes me think he doesn't like me.*

She walked to the bedroom. Nothing out of place here, either. Devlin's slacks, shirts, and jeans hung in the closet with her sundresses. His underwear was in a drawer next to her panties. He'd ordered enough clothes—clothes befitting every occasion—to keep her here through the month.

Maybe she should stop worrying about Sam and concentrate on Devlin. A month's worth of clothes? Why would he want to keep her here so long? And . . . married? Sure, men lied all the time, but they didn't claim happily-ever-after. If he suspected she was lying about the amnesia and he was trying to smoke her out, that was one thing, but he was telling *everybody.* Didn't he worry about what was going to happen when this was all over and he had to explain what they'd been doing?

Even she didn't know what they were doing.

Again the question skittered across her mind.

What game was Devlin playing? Perhaps she should be a little more cautious. . . .

She irritably shrugged her shoulders, trying to release some tension. She wasn't afraid of Devlin. They'd made love so wantonly, so sweetly, and never once had she felt a niggling of anything but joy.

She needed to find that painting so she could tell him the truth . . . yet what did she think he would do? *Give* it to her? He wasn't crazy. The painting was worth a fortune, and it was legally his. When she started the search, she'd believed it was rightfully, if not legally, her grandmother's, and her grandmother had said it was her inheritance. Taking it from Bradley Benjamin had been one thing. Taking from Devlin Fitzwilliam was another.

Meadow put her hand to her head. What had started out as an easily justified action had become confusing, and no matter how much she loved being in Devlin's arms, no matter how fondly she recalled his kindness to Mia and Mia's son, she had also heard him talk about Waldemar, and possessiveness rang in every tone. She'd listened to his fury.

A footstep. In the bathroom.

Who was hiding in there?

With her gaze fixed on the door, she started backing up.

Then a maid walked out, carrying a wilted bouquet.

Meadow collapsed against the wall. All this subterfuge was getting to her. She was imagining threats where none existed.

"Mrs. Fitzwilliam!" The maid bustled toward her. She was probably sixty years old, short, plump, with curly gray hair and a sweet, rounded face. She looked like somebody's grandmother.

But Meadow couldn't remember her name. Or anything about her. She was usually pretty good at this stuff, but with this woman she drew a blank.

Should she confess her ignorance, or try to fake it?

While she hung on the horns of dilemma, the maid said in a lowered voice, "I think I found your painting."

Meadow caught her breath. "Really? Where?"

"In one of the rooms. C'mon; I'll show you." She set off at a great rate, her short legs moving so quickly Meadow huffed to keep up with her. For an older lady, she was in good shape.

Meadow caught up just as the maid took a sharp left turn. She used her key card to unlock the door, turned the handle, and flipped on the light. "The painting's in here."

Meadow peered into the depths of a narrow storage closet. She could see a linen cart, a bucket, a broom, and a long shelf piled with pristine white linens. "I thought you said it was in a room."

"I took it out and hid it. It's leaning against the back wall."

"Really?" Meadow stepped inside and shoved at the cart. "I don't see anything back there that could be a—"

She turned in time to see the door closing.

"Hey!" As the latch clicked, Meadow flung her weight at the door.

It was solid.

She groped for the handle.

There wasn't one.

She stood staring at the plate with the slot for a key card. "Hey!" She slammed her hand on the door. "Hey, let me out!"

The insulated metal door remained closed, and it muffled the sound.

She didn't understand. Why would one of the maids shut her in a closet?

She dug through her pocket. Her key card, of course, wasn't there. She'd slapped on her clothes so quickly she hadn't even brushed her teeth.

Ew.

She yelled and pounded on the door for another few minutes, then backed away and took a deep breath.

She wasn't claustrophobic, so she didn't mind the closet. Really, it wasn't the closet that bothered her.

It was the malice behind the act of locking her in. What had she ever done to that woman?

She looked around. The closet was really pretty big. Sort of overcrowded with the laundry cart and the shelf sticking into the room, and when she went to the back and dug around, she found no painting.

Wow, big surprise.

She sat back on her heels and stared at the door.

Why had that maid done it? Was she even a maid?

She had to be. She knew about the painting, and Meadow had told only the maids . . . but maybe one of them had talked. Or maybe someone else knew about the painting. Or maybe the maid had heard Meadow was searching for it and thought it must be valuable and wanted it for herself.

But she had such a sweet face!

Meadow wrapped her arms around herself.

Her mother would tell her she had reaped what she sowed, that stealing the painting for even the best of reasons was immoral, and that art as valuable as that painting would of course lead to crime, even violence.

But Meadow had come so far. She couldn't quit now. And Grandmother Isabelle said she had saved the painting for an emergency.

This was an emergency.

For all the cheer Meadow had heard in her mother's voice, she knew only too well the ups and downs of cancer treatment. She'd known far too many patients, only to see them leave the cancer ward in body bags.

The trouble was, she was enjoying herself here at the Secret Garden. With no regard for the truth, to creating good karma, to what might be happening in a little town in Washington, she was falling in love with Devlin Fitzwilliam.

25

Oh, no. Natalie Meadow Szarvas, artist and wannabe thief, was falling in love with Devlin Fitzwilliam.

How could she be so stupid? He didn't even know who she really was. And she knew *he* was lying through his teeth.

But he was so good at it. Every time he told her a story about their affair in Majorca, she slipped a little deeper into enchantment.

She didn't think he kept her here for any good reason. She wasn't that far gone.

Still, her heart thrilled when she saw him. She wanted to stand at his side and be what he said she was—his wife. And how stupid was that?

But it didn't matter.

Did it?

She was doing the right thing.

Wasn't she?

As if in answer, the lights clicked off.

It took a minute of shock and fear before Meadow realized it was nothing dire. The lights were on a timer; that was all. Having them go off right now was not an omen.

But it was dark in here. Really, really dark.

She blundered toward the exit, guided by the thin line of light under the door. She banged her shins on the laundry cart. She kicked the mop. She got to the door and groped for the light switch.

And someone yanked the door open.

"What are you doing in here?" Devlin's dark eyes blazed with fury, and his feet were firmly planted at shoulder width.

"Devlin! Thank God. This maid shut me in." Meadow fell into his arms, embarrassed by her panic, guilty about the painting, and grappling with the discovery that she loved him.

He didn't hug her back; he only repeated, "A maid shut you in." He sounded unconvinced.

She didn't care. Closing her eyes, she inhaled his scent.

Yep. She was in love. His scent was ambrosia. Touching him made her melt all over him. And at the bedrock of her soul, she believed he would always be there to save her.

"Devlin," she whispered. "I knew you'd find me."

"You are so . . . ." For one moment he shook violently, as if he fought his instincts. Then his arms came around her almost ferociously. He backed her into the closet. The door slammed behind him, and when she lifted her head to ask what he was doing, he kissed her—kissed her as if this kiss were as necessary as breathing.

The darkness wrapped them in intimacy. The odor of clean, bleached sheets mixed with the potent scent of Devlin's sexuality.

She loved him. She needed him—now.

And he needed her.

He held her head in his hands and held her still, and each stroke of his tongue called to a primal part of her no one had ever touched. She let him take her breath, then took his in return. Frantic desire swept them along, melding them together in the darkness. She grew damp with longing, and she felt him against her, erect, hard as one of the marble pillars that surrounded the Secret Garden.

She pushed him away, tugged at his shirt, heard a ripping sound.

Briefly the little noise brought her back to sanity, but only enough to make her realize she was in too much of a hurry to care whether he was completely naked. She wanted him—now.

She reached for his belt.

He unzipped her jeans.

Together they struggled against the fastenings, stripping each other with speed and urgency.

She kicked off her sandals, her jeans, and her panties, and reached for his penis. He was so hard, so hot.

He handed her a foil pack.

She ripped it open and rolled it down the length of his penis.

He groped behind her, shoved stuff aside, lifted her, and placed her on the shelf.

The painted board was rough under her bare skin. He tilted her backward, pressed her shoulders back until they rested on the wall. Sliding his hands up her thighs, he spread her legs wide, exposing her. The cool air shocked her; the fire of his body promised her pleasure. He stepped between her legs and pressed the heel of his hand over her clit.

She pressed back, started to shudder with climax.

"No." He pulled back. "Not yet."

She whimpered, in such need she ached.

But he waited, although she could feel the tremors of passion that shook him. Then he explored her, and when he discovered the dampness that awaited him, he muttered, "Perfect." He positioned himself. The head of his penis felt impossibly large, searing her flesh. With tiny rocking motions, he pressed inside.

She moaned, taking him into her body, growing so full she couldn't imagine a moment when he wasn't with her. She sank her nails into his shoulders, and the small pain sent him surging forward.

For a brief moment he pressed close. Outside, his groin ground against her clit. Inside, the tip of him incited the deepest part of her. She couldn't see him, couldn't see a thing, but she felt surrounded, inside and out, by him—by his scent, his passion, his caress, his breath on her hair.

When he withdrew, a slow and torturous process, she wanted only one thing—to have him return deep inside her. With her feet behind his back, she pulled him close.

They grappled with each other, both reckless with the need for satisfaction.

The darkness intensified each sensation. Nothing he did could stop her. Her breath grew constricted. The dark flashed with colored lights. She sobbed softly, needing everything he had to give, reaching but not quite able to release. She needed . . . something . . .

"Come now." His voice told her clearly that he wasn't asking—he was commanding. "Come now." He thrust hard.

She screamed. In an agony of rapture she curled toward him.

He drove into her, taking her, his hips coiling and striking over and over, and the motion carried her into another climax, and another, until she couldn't tell where one ended and another began.

Between her legs and beneath her hands, she felt him tense. Every muscle went rigid, and he climaxed so hard her fingers slipped as sweat sheened his skin.

As suddenly as they'd started, they stopped. She breathed so harshly her lungs hurt. She trembled from the effort she'd put out, and she couldn't understand what had happened.

One minute he'd been opening the door. The next, they'd fallen on each other with a violence of lust. She'd never imagined such a mating—no tenderness, only heat and desperation.

Then his hand found her face, and he pushed her hair off her forehead. "Are you all right?"

"Yes." She was wicked and wanton, desperate for him, in love with him, wanting what she couldn't have . . . but she was all right.

"Are you sure? I didn't hurt you?"

"No. You didn't hurt me." She would walk like a rodeo barrel racer for the rest of the day, but he hadn't done anything to her she hadn't demanded.

Slowly he withdrew.

She bit her lip against a protest. Their relationship was so easy here in the dark. So basic. No lies, no deception, only two bodies straining together, searching for, achieving one goal.

If only love were so easy.

He lifted her off the shelf and steadied her while she found her feet. He pulled up his pants, zipped up, buckled his belt.

"Ready?" He didn't wait for an answer; he turned on the lights.

She flinched, shielded her eyes. When she looked up at him, her expression could not have been more embarrassed, more guilty.

What the hell was he doing? When had he lost all pretense at civilization and started fucking without restraint, without control, behaving like a sailor on shore leave?

But that wasn't fair; he didn't slam every woman into a closet, rip off her jeans, and thrust himself inside her.

Only Meadow.

"I, um, can't find my panties." She stood bare from the waist down, her jeans in her hand, looking helplessly around at the jumble of linens he'd shoved off the shelf and onto the floor.

He knelt, looking for her underwear, distracted by the length of her legs, which ended in the small, trimmed froth of copper curls over her slit. He wanted to spread her legs again, to taste himself on her, in her, until she once again cried out.

She filled his mind. She filled his senses. It didn't matter how many times he screwed her; he always wanted to do it again, and as soon as possible. He'd managed to wait long enough to get a condom on—yay, him—but only because he'd had to clear a space on the shelf to fornicate. If she had not been so efficient at rolling it onto him, he would have dispensed with safety and taken the chance of making her pregnant—again.

He was not like his father. He was not.

At least, he never had been before.

"Here." He handed her the tiny lacy thong and tried not to watch her pull it on.

Damn it. What the hell was he going to do about her? About the little liar who lived under his roof?

Because that was what had triggered his aggression.

She had lied to him. She had lied to him *again.*

Somewhere along the line he'd lost sight of his original goal—to use Isabelle's granddaughter to stick it to Bradley Benjamin.

Instead he'd been doing everything he could to make Meadow trust him. He'd given her every opportunity to tell him the truth about who she was and what she was doing here.

Instead she'd fed him some garbage about some maid shutting her in the closet, when in fact, she'd been looking for the painting and shut herself in.

He knew it because Sam had watched her every move on the security monitor. Sam had reported her movements to Devlin. And Sam never lied, and Sam never made a mistake.

26

$\mathcal{D}$evlin walked Meadow to their bedroom, then paused at the door. "Are you sure you're all right?"

He sounded so courteous, Meadow wanted to fling herself off the cupola. She was in love, and he was . . . remote. "I'm fine. Are you?"

"How could I not be?" He brushed his knuckles across her cheek. "But I'm very busy."

"Do you want a description of the maid who shut me in the closet?"

The motion of his hand stopped. "Of course. Tell me what she looked like."

She told him about the sweet-faced grandmother in the uniform.

"She doesn't sound like anyone who works here." His voice was very even, very calm.

"I didn't recognize her."

"I'll look into it." He didn't sound worried.

But he wasn't really the kind of guy who showed his worries. "Why do you suppose she did it?" That bothered Meadow more than anything.

"I don't know. Why do *you* suppose she did it?"

"Maybe I offended this woman somehow? Or she's some kind of psychopath who sneaks into hotels and locks people in linen closets?" Even Meadow thought that sounded stupid, but, *Maybe it's someone after the painting,* seemed an answer fraught with peril.

If only he were less aloof . . . If only she trusted him a little more . . .

"I'll look into it," he said again. "Will you forgive me for leaving you here, now?"

"Sure, but . . ." *Are you embarrassed by what happened in the closet? What can I do to make you stay?*

Do you love me?

"What is it? Are you scared?"

"No. No, I'm not scared." *Confused, uncertain, worried, yes. Scared, no.* "I need to shower. I'll see you later?" *Needy, Meadow. And clingy.*

"Of course." One corner of his mouth crooked up in what might pass for amusement. "When Mother's with me, we dine in manorial splendor."

"Oh, nooo." Meadow leaned against the door frame and looked up at him in despair. "Will she interrogate me some more?"

"I believe she'll call it conversation." He sounded almost normal now.

Her anxiety eased. She felt a little more like Meadow and less like a woman facing a disaster of mammoth proportions. "You should have heard her in the library after you left. That was *not* conversation."

Abruptly his half smile disappeared. "She doesn't understand what got into me, marrying so swiftly and without warning."

The tension returned, thicker and more oppressive than ever.

She straightened. "But we aren't really married."

Stepping close, he crowded her against the wall and leaned close enough that his breath brushed her ear, that his heat seared her flesh. "We married in Majorca. Unless you remember differently?"

She loved him. She ought to be able to tell him the truth. He seemed to want her to tell him the truth. So she would. "I . . . I should. I . . . It seems wrong, like we're not married." *The truth, Meadow. Tell him the truth.*

But when he looked so cool, like a quarterback planning a new play, like the big, ruthless developer his reputation claimed, she choked up. Would he throw her out? Maybe she was betraying him by lying, but what other choice did she have? Betray her grandmother? Leave her mother to die?

He flashed her one of those sharklike smiles that expressed no amusement. "Until you say different, we were married in Majorca, and I intend to remind you every chance I get."

He was bullying her, and any sensible woman would shrink away.

Not Meadow. Her stupid body yearned for his, her blood surging in her veins. She leaned her head away from him, giving him access to her throat, wanting his kisses on her skin. . . .

He stepped away. Briefly, gently, he caressed her cheek with his knuckles. "Try not to get into trouble."

She watched him leave, his long legs eating up the distance, his hips rolling with that assurance that told a woman he knew how to give her pleasure.

He must have transferred his heat to her, for her cheeks grew warm. Flinging herself into their suite, she locked the door and fell back on the small sofa in the sitting room. She would have never considered Devlin Fitzwilliam someone she could love.

He was a developer, a guy who created hotels that attracted people to the wild places in the world, where they could ruin them with sewage and sunscreen.

Yet at the same time, he saved old buildings, bringing them back to life instead of tearing them down.

And clearly he didn't comprehend the advantages of viewing life as a positive experience. In college they'd called her a Pollyanna, and he was the exact polar opposite—whatever that was.

Yet when she thought of what they shared, she wanted to share it some more. Her eyes closed. Her hand crept to the seam of her jeans, and she rubbed herself between her legs, imagining he was here, watching, helping—

The shrill ring of the hotel phone brought her to her feet, wild-eyed and mortified.

All these damned security cameras had made her paranoid. She felt as if she'd been caught in the act.

But by who? Who was calling her here?

Devlin. Who else?

Snatching up the receiver, she put all her longing into her tone. "Hello?"

"Meadow? Is that you?" Judith's voice, sharp, nasal, anxious.

"Judith!" Immediately Meadow's mind leaped to the worst. "Is it Mom?"

"No, she's fine. Just fine."

"Then what are you doing calling me here?" Meadow lowered her voice as if someone could hear her. And that was impossible—obviously the doors were soundproof. But somehow the security in the hotel felt as if it were turned against her, and she wouldn't put it past Sam to have planted a microphone in their rooms.

"I had to take a chance. I've been so worried about you."

"How did you get through to me?" Meadow had visions of Judith asking for her at the switchboard, and whoever worked the desk running right to Devlin with the information.

"I called and got a maid. She told me your room number, and after that I could direct-dial." Judith's voice lowered, too. "Have you had any luck finding it?"

The painting, she meant. "None."

"Are you looking hard? All the time?"

"No. I search when I can, but I have to act normal." Meadow paced toward the window and gazed out on the estate. It was all so peaceful out there, and such turmoil inside.

"Is Fitzwilliam giving you trouble?" Judith sounded fretful.

"Not trouble exactly. He sort of wants me to stay here, and I don't know why."

"You know why," Judith said.

Meadow didn't like Judith's tone. "No. Why?"

"He wants to sleep with you."

Meadow didn't know what to say.

Her hesitation must have been telling, for Judith asked, "*Have* you slept with him?"

"Judith!" Meadow hoped her horror sounded genuine enough.

"I went on the Web and read about him. I saw the pictures. He gets around." Judith made it sound like the ultimate sin, and for her perhaps it was. Certainly never in all the years Meadow had known her had she seemed interested in a man. Or a woman, for that matter—art was Judith's obsession.

"Really?" Nothing could have surprised Meadow more. Going to the desk, she brought up the computer and typed his name into a search engine. "I thought he seemed too calculating to be indiscriminate."

"Some women worship football players, and he's handsome."

His photo popped up right away, a youthful one of him in his football uniform, a later, unposed picture of him in a hard hat. "Not handsome. Not really. But a mesmerizing juxtaposition of gorgeous and rugged." Meadow wished she could paint him, but that gift had been given to Isabelle and Sharon, and not to her. She touched the cool, smooth screen, outlining his jaw with her fingertips. "I can see why women would chase him, but it's not just for his looks."

"What do you mean? What else is there?" Judith asked sharply.

"When he talks to me . . . he concentrates on *me*." Meadow's eyes half closed as she remembered. "No one else exists. It's . . . intoxicating."

Judith took a ragged breath. "While you're flirting with this man, the painting goes undiscovered and your poor mother is *dying*—"

Abruptly furious, Meadow came to her feet. "She is *not* dying.

Don't you dare put that out into the universe. My mother is recovering!"

"You're right. I know. I know." At least Judith had the good sense to back right off. "I'm sorry, I just . . . I'm so worried."

"All right." With an effort, Meadow controlled her temper. "Just . . . please don't say that. Don't even think it. And give Mom my love. Tell her I'll be home soon."

"With good news," Judith said heartily.

"Yes. With good news."

"Don't stop looking. Figure out a plan and stick with it. Everything's depending on you, Meadow! Everything's depending on *you.*"

Meadow hung up and sat down, limp with the flash flood of rage Judith's blunder had caused.

Meadow thought that Judith had always wanted to be Sharon's dearest friend, but because of these kinds of slips, she'd never managed to get close.

Judith said she believed what Sharon believed. She acted happy, said the right stuff, ate the right things. But she would barely discuss her background, and as Sharon told her daughter, "I'm afraid she's hiding some trying times and struggles to maintain a good public attitude. She needs to believe from the heart, poor thing, and I wish I could help her do that."

But Judith was right about one thing: Meadow had to figure out her next move. She was here in the hotel, and she was solid—solid because Devlin claimed she was his wife and because—Meadow didn't think she flattered herself—because he was infatuated with her body. Possibly as infatuated as she was with his body, and that fascinating, intelligent, guileful mind. He saw life as a chess game, black-and-white, and a series of premeditated moves that ended in one of two ways—winning or losing.

But she wasn't playing a game.

Last night and today had been genuine for both of them.

So how would this end?

The man Judith described as nobody's fool accepted Meadow's story of amnesia, then claimed she was his wife.

What piece did that make Meadow on his chessboard?

Black . . . or white?

Pawn . . . or queen?

Winner . . . or loser?

27

That evening, before they walked into the dining room, Meadow stopped Devlin by digging her fingers into his arm. "Promise you won't leave me alone with that woman again."

"Four's in there. He'll protect you." Devlin was in no mood to make promises to Meadow. Not after this afternoon. Not after she had lied about the maid, and lied again about her silly amnesia.

"Four is a very nice man, but he's no match for your mother."

"I thought all women worshipped at his feet." Today Sam had pressed to send Meadow away. Devlin had refused, but if there were very many more incidents like this one, he'd be forced to act.

"I only worship at *your* feet."

She was so good with the flattery. But in a few weeks he was opening a hotel. He knew from experience that a grand opening took all his concentration. He didn't have time to get Meadow out of a closet every time she screwed up and locked herself in. He really didn't have time to step inside and take her clothes off, or chase her through the garden in the moonlight, or fall in love . . .

She tugged him around to face her. "Promise me you won't leave me alone with her," she said.

Fall in love? With *Meadow*? That was impossible. She wasn't at all the kind of woman he admired. She was a liar, potentially a thief, a wild child without any sense of how to dress or how to keep her distance from the servants. If he got involved with her, really involved with her, he'd find himself rescuing stray dogs and eating tofu.

He didn't want that. That wouldn't work for him. He was a bastard, and his wife had to be like Caesar's—above reproach.

All of that was true. He knew it. So why, at this moment, was he thinking of their night together and how he'd been so enraptured by Meadow's passion and joy that he'd taken her without a single precaution?

"Devlin!" She tugged him around to face her. "*Promise* me you won't leave me alone with her."

Damn. He hated that, with one simple phrase, she slipped under his guard. "I'll stick like glue."

"All right, then." She straightened her shoulders. "I'm ready."

She wore a simple, off-the-shoulder shirt in a flattering chocolate brown and a soft, swirling flowered skirt. Her shining copper hair hung loose around her neck, a beaded bracelet one of the maids had worked for her wrapped her wrist, and she wore sandals again—sandals with a heel, but sandals nevertheless.

She was in no way ready to face his mother, but he wasn't going to tell her that.

The shock of Meadow would be good for Grace Fitzwilliam.

He offered Meadow his arm, and together they walked into the grand dining room.

Actually, it had been converted into a conference room for their corporate guests. The long table seated twenty, and Devlin had brought in a smaller round table and placed it in the alcove. Two broad side tables held computer setups, making the room multipurpose, yet elegant.

Grace leaned against the marble-faced fireplace, adjusting the swirling glass bowl created by Natalie Meadow Szarvas.

Four, of course, stood by the liquor decanter holding two cocktails.

"That's one way to get a head start," Devlin said.

Four grimaced, walked to Grace, and handed her a drink.

Four didn't look well. He was pale, his beige linen pants were rumpled, and his loafers were scuffed. Devlin shouldn't give a damn—Four had cheated him, then made the mistake of thinking it was okay because they were friends.

Yeah. Like it was okay for Devlin's father to screw Grace, get her pregnant, show up a couple of times a year and lavish attention on Devlin, then abandon Devlin to the troubles his occasional appearance created. Like it was okay for Nathan to ruin his own business, take the money, walk away from his legitimate family and his illegitimate son, and never look back. Devlin had had enough of getting screwed by people who were supposed to care.

Yet long ago, when they were kids, Devlin had developed the habit of worrying about weak-willed, likable Four. No matter how hard Devlin tried, he couldn't seem to break that tradition.

Taking Meadow over to Four, he handed her over, and spoke in his ear. "Please, Four. Keep your wits about you tonight, or my mother will have Meadow flayed for dinner."

Four brightened, always pleased to be handed a job he knew he could manage. "Sure. I'll keep an eye on her." He asked Meadow, "Can I fix you a drink?"

Devlin went to Grace and kissed her cool cheek. "You look marvelous, Mother."

"Thank you, dear. So do you." She wore a knee-length black sheath with a red silk paisley scarf draped over her shoulders and diamond studs in her ears. Her blond hair was dressed in some swirly thing at the back of her head, and he could almost feel her exerting her will on the room. "Shall we sit down to dinner?"

"Let's. I'm starving!" Meadow viewed the long table with dismay. "But we're not sitting there, are we?"

"We'll use the round table," Grace announced.

That surprised Devlin; he would have guessed Grace wanted the length of the polished wood to properly intimidate Meadow. As it was, sitting at the round table meant no one took the head. He wondered what Grace intended by such a democratic maneuver.

As soon as the servers had changed the settings and presented the little group with the first course, he found out.

"I've decided you two should remarry in a little more . . . proper . . . circumstances." Grace's tone made it clear a runaway wedding in Majorca was the height of immaturity. "With a little concentration and planning, we could pull it off by September."

To Devlin's surprise, Meadow shook out her napkin and shrugged. "Sure."

His eyes narrowed on her. She didn't care if his mother planned a wedding.

Why?

Because she didn't intend to be here for it.

Because she would be in the Cascade Mountains, blowing glass— or if she stole a valuable painting from him, in jail. "Excellent idea, Mother, but surely the maven of Southern planning and propriety could accomplish a wedding in less time than that. I hear June is an excellent month to get married."

"Pushing. Pushing," Meadow muttered into her water glass.

"I never thought I'd see the day that you'd get married not once, but twice, in a scandalous hurry." Four buttered a slice of his bread.

"What do you mean, in a *scandalous* hurry?" Meadow asked.

"Devlin's *so* concerned with appearances," Four said, "and this will look like he *had* to marry you—not once, but twice."

"I'm not amused," Devlin said. Not amused because perhaps, if the gods of fertility were against them, Four was right.

"Because I got pregnant, do you mean?" Meadow laughed. "Does anyone get married for that reason anymore?"

Devlin looked directly at her. "I do."

"But that's a recipe for failure. People marry because they have interests in common and because they're in love, not because they accidentally"—Meadow made quotation marks with her fingers— "made a baby."

"It's not easy for a child to be illegitimate," Grace said.

The intensity of her voice surprised Devlin. He hadn't realized his mother had even noticed.

Meadow looked at the three of them as if they were speaking a different language. "Is it easy for a child to have parents who don't care for each other? Or who divorce? I don't think so."

"Knowing my son, I'm sure it's a moot point." Grace utilized her society smile. "And it's not as if you two are hippies running around the woods like free-range chickens, having sex willy-nilly and without protection."

Meadow snorted into her napkin. "No, heaven forbid we should behave like free-range chickens."

In his lap, Devlin twisted his napkin into a knot. And heaven forbid that he should have knocked Meadow up.

Before Meadow regaled them with the assurance that moonlight really did act as an aphrodisiac, Devlin said, "Perhaps, Mother, we should ask Meadow how *she* wants to celebrate her wedding."

28

"*I* am sure, given Meadow's indifference to the niceties of society"—Grace coolly viewed Meadow's skirt and blouse—"she's happy to leave the details to me."

Until that moment, Meadow hadn't realized she'd fallen into a BBC costume drama. Yet here she was, the upstart who married the prince—that part was played by Devlin—and now had to prove herself worthy of her new role.

She only wished she could take it half as seriously as did Grace Fitzwilliam.

Free-range chickens, indeed.

She considered how best to express her sentiments in a way Grace would understand. "As long as my friends and family are around me, the details are immaterial."

"See?" Grace gloated at Devlin.

Meadow gave in to her spirit of mischief. "But we can't have the ceremony until Eddy returns from Europe."

"Is Eddy your uncle?" Grace asked.

"No, Eddy's one of my dear friends—and my maid of honor." Meadow beamed at Grace.

"Tell me Eddy is a variation of Edie?" Grace's fixed smile expressed pain and hopelessness at the same time.

"I think it stands for Edmund." Meadow frowned in overdramatic fretfulness. "But he hates that, so everybody calls him Eddy."

Four looked between Meadow and Grace, then lifted his glass and drained it.

Devlin rose from his chair and walked to the window. He stared out into the garden.

But his shoulders were shaking. Meadow had wanted to see him laugh for a long time, so she piled it higher and deeper. "I've known Eddy since grade school, and we promised we would be each other's maid of honor."

"You promised." Grace sounded faint.

"We used to imagine what our weddings would be like." Meadow relished Grace's horror. "We always knew he would be a lovelier bride than me—he's awfully pretty—and I made him promise he wouldn't overshadow me when I got married."

Grace fanned herself with her hand.

"Hot flash?" Meadow asked cheerfully.

A chortle escaped Devlin.

Four covered his ears.

"I don't have anything as vulgar as a hot flash, and if I did, it wouldn't be proper to mention it." Irritation tinged Grace's cultivated tone. Leaning back, she closed her eyes. "I feel faint."

"Only one thing to do for that." Meadow pushed back from the table, pulled Grace's chair out, grabbed her by the back of the neck, and pressed her head down between her knees.

Grace shrieked.

Devlin turned and stared.

"Sorry, old man." Four threw his napkin on the table. "I'm out of here." He left in such a hurry he almost burned a trail in the carpet.

"Best treatment for faintness." Meadow grinned when Devlin

covered his eyes with his hand. "Nothing to worry about. She'll be fine in a minute."

"I'm fine now." Grace's voice was muffled.

"You shouldn't come up too soon. You don't want to faint again," Meadow said.

Grace struggled, but Meadow held her in an untenable position. She could have wrestled her way free, but dignified Grace wouldn't lower herself to physically fight.

At least . . . not until she was desperate. Then she shoved Meadow back and sat up, brushing at her hair with her hands. "That is quite enough of that. We'll return to the wedding plans when you two are feeling more reasonable." She stood.

"Don't forget we need to discuss the party, too!" Meadow said.

Grace started to close her eyes and put her hand to her forehead in another pretended faint. Then she remembered, shot Meadow a wary look, and made quite a dignified exit, considering the fact that the back of her dress had hitched up to show an incongruously silky pink undergarment.

Devlin waited until her footsteps had faded before he burst into laughter. He laughed so hard he collapsed into a chair and held his sides.

Meadow watched him in satisfaction.

Laughter.

She'd bet he couldn't remember the last time he'd laughed like that, with all his heart and soul and body.

And amusement had a way of making him look . . . not softer, but more dashing, like a man who understood what it was to live life to the fullest without the suspicion and wariness that dogged his footsteps. When he stopped, he still grinned at her. "Do you really have a transvestite friend named Eddy that you've known since grade school?"

"Of course. Eddy's a great guy. I remember . . ." But she was supposed to have amnesia.

"What else do you remember?" Like a cat viewing a mouse that was struggling beneath its paw, Devlin watched her.

He'd caught her in her lie again. He looked remote again. He'd made her feel . . . uncomfortable again. "It's odd the things I remember and the things I don't. I guess I never mentioned Eddy to you before?" She held her breath and waited to see if he'd let her go . . . again.

"No. You never mentioned Eddy before."

She released her breath. For some reason he still wanted her here. She was safe for another day. "I seem to be distressing your mother."

"As if you care." He grinned again.

"I care enough to wonder why she's so . . . so . . ."

"Judgmental? Overweening? Concerned with appearances?" With his hands on his hips, he looked Meadow over from head to toe, and she realized that Grace might find her lacking, but Devlin appreciated every last inch. "She's not used to girls who aren't in awe of her."

"In awe?" Meadow strolled over, taking her time, letting her hips roll and her legs flex. "Why?"

"Because she's so good at everything. Don't you watch television?" He gathered her close.

"Not much." She didn't really remember what they were talking about—or care. All she knew was that he held her in his arms, and the warmth they created between the two of them could illuminate Seattle in December. She unbuttoned his shirt and slid her hand inside, loving the texture of hair over his soft skin. Standing on tiptoe, she kissed his jaw on one side, then the other.

He stood still, eyes half closed, allowing her the freedom of his body.

She zoomed in on his lips and—

"Dears, I have an idea for the party. . . . Oh, my God, are you at it again?" Grace stood in the doorway, her hands over her eyes.

Meadow exhaled in frustration.

Devlin buttoned his shirt. "You should knock before you enter."

"It's only evening. This is the dining room. The door is open. The waiters could walk in at any minute!" Grace peeked between her fingers, and when she saw they had separated, she marched right in. "Listen for one second, and then you can go back to doing"—she waved a slender, expressive hand—"whatever it was you were doing."

"So it's been a while for her?" Meadow said out of the corner of her mouth.

Devlin jerked with suppressed amusement.

Grace glared at Meadow, then at Devlin.

Then her gaze lingered on Devlin, her blue eyes thoughtful, and Meadow wondered what was going through her mind.

Devlin seemed puzzled, too. "Mother?"

"All right, here's my idea. See if you don't like *this*, Meadow." Grace panned the room with her hands. "I see the whole party taking place outside. We'll turn the estate into a carnival. We'll have games—not electronic games, but games like, oh, knock down the pins with a ball and, er . . ."

She waved her hand at Meadow.

"Break the balloons with the dart," Meadow supplied.

"Exactly." Grace nodded with satisfaction. "I knew you would know what kind of games they played at *those* places."

"She's good with an insult." Again Meadow spoke out of the side of her mouth.

"The best," he answered.

"I can hear you!" Grace tapped her toe.

"I know, Mother, and it would be best if you didn't listen," he said. "If we hold the party outdoors, it might rain."

"It won't," Grace said. "The elements don't have the nerve to mess with my plans."

"Wow." Meadow was impressed. "You could teach a class in positive thinking."

"Mother, who will we get for the freaks?"

Grace waved him away. "Those will be the guests, dear."

Meadow blinked. Who knew? Grace never cracked a smile, but she had a keen sense of humor.

"We'll have cotton candy and those red apples, and the waiters will be dressed like carnival barkers."

Devlin viewed her cautiously. "Mother, this doesn't sound at all like your kind of party."

"Dear, the party has to fit the people it honors, and in this case . . ." Grace gestured eloquently at Meadow.

Meadow contemplated blacking her front tooth and painting big red freckles on her nose.

Grace continued. "The waiters will circulate with trays. They'll have tokens to play the games, and champagne and hors d'oeurves."

"Champagne and hors d'oeuvres. That's more like it," Devlin said.

"In honor of Meadow, the decorations should be natural— flowers, flowers, flowers! And, as the centerpiece"—Grace flung her arms dramatically upward—"a Ferris wheel!"

In that instant, Meadow forgave her the insults and for barging in at the wrong moment—twice. "A Ferris wheel would be fabu!"

"Exactly!" Grace's lips puckered as if she had bitten into a lemon. "*Fabu* was the precise word I was looking for."

Devlin began, "It's not the word I—"

"A real full-sized Ferris wheel?" Meadow asked.

"But of course! It wouldn't do to skimp," Grace said.

Devlin tried again. "A Ferris wheel is not—"

"With lights and music! How about a roller coaster?" Meadow bounced on the couch.

"No. That would be overdoing it." When Meadow tried to protest, Grace pointed a finger at her. "We're going to invite all the best people in the South, and newspeople, too. It will be an event, and we don't want to be perceived as vulgar."

"Or free-range chickens." Then Meadow perked back up again. "I bet we could get Dead Bob. He performs at the Renaissance festivals. Oh, and the Fantastic Juggling Oxenberries."

"Very clever! A few shows would add to the ambience."

Devlin could hardly contain his exasperation. "Mother, I appreciate the thought you put into this, but—"

"Listen, Meadow." Grace's eyes gleamed. "The Ferris wheel will be the visual centerpiece of the party, and you and Devlin will announce your marriage from the top of the wheel."

"That's sick!" Meadow said.

"Sick?" Grace was taken aback.

"You know—awesome!" Meadow explained.

"Ah. *Awesome.*" That pucker was back. "Another word I was looking for."

"Ladies!" Devlin's single snapped word finally got their attention. "There will be no cotton candy. There will be no carnival barkers. And make no mistake, there will be no Ferris wheel." He stopped their outcry with a firm gesture. "That is my final word."

29

*D*evlin couldn't believe he had a Ferris wheel spinning in his yard, or that it released a shower of flower petals every time it reached the top, filling the air with a whirling, scented snowstorm. He couldn't believe he had carnival barkers and games, and, providing the music for the afternoon, an antique steam calliope painted blue, red, and yellow, and decorated with liberal amounts of gilding. He couldn't believe that Dead Bob was doing his act on the stage in the walled garden.

What Devlin really couldn't believe was that people, adult people, his distinguished guests, were eating and playing and riding the riding the Ferris wheel while shrieking like children.

This grand opening may have been his mother's concept—but it was Meadow's fault. Without Meadow's influence, Grace would have never thought up such an outrageous extravaganza.

Of course . . . the two women were right. He'd already seen three camera crews covering the event, and recognized at least five travel writers taking notes—and grinning. It was a huge success, but damned if he would admit it to Grace and Meadow.

Hands on hips, he stood on Waldemar's wraparound porch and surveyed the scene.

The waiters circulated through the crowd. Gregory Madison, federal judge, sat at one of the red-stripe-covered tables, eating from a pewter bowl full of cotton candy. Mr. Volchock, owner of last year's winning Derby horse, threw baseballs at stuffed clowns, while Mrs. Volchock clutched a teddy bear he'd won her. Jessica Stillman-Williams, Grace's boss, owner of two hundred cable stations across the United States and a ballbuster if ever there was one, wore a balloon animal hat while she stood in line for the Ferris wheel.

Four slouched against the trunk of the great live oak, drink and cigarette in hand, conversing with that girl, what-was-her-name. The cute one from the hospital.

She wore a shirt cut so low she was in imminent danger of fallout, and she was blatantly using her chest as an enticement.

It was working. Four hadn't once glanced at her face.

When he finished the cigarette, he ground it under his heel, then glared down at it. With great and obvious irritation, he picked it up and threw it in the garbage. Meadow had cured Four of his habit of tossing out his cigarette and leaving it. When she was finished with him, he'd be cured of his cigarette habit altogether.

If she stayed.

Like the call of a siren, the sound of her laughter drew his gaze toward her. He saw her at once, of course. She wore a wide, floppy straw hat decorated with a huge blue flower—his mother said it was so vulgar she might as well leave the price tag attached—a long-sleeved blue T-shirt, shorts that displayed smooth legs, and a liberal application of sunscreen. *Complete coverage is the price of fair skin,* she'd said, laughing up at him.

Hell, he'd be aroused if she wore a nun's habit.

There were better-looking women here—two rock stars who'd made it on their bodies, not their voices, three gorgeous models, and at least seven trophy wives—but the guys all stared at Meadow. She had a way about her; when she was around, it seemed the world was brighter, kinder, more joyous, and men, all men, wanted her to light their fire.

The lecherous sons of bitches. She was *his* fire.

The last two weeks had been marvelous and horrible. Marvelous because they'd been together every day and every night, because she looked at him as if he were the moon and the stars.

Horrible because he'd been working at a madman's pace, and while he did, she made a methodical search of the mansion and each of its rooms. She tried to disguise it as casual wandering, as visiting with the maids, as approving the decorations, but Sam kept track on the blueprints. She never returned to the same room, and once Devlin had caught her scowling at her map.

He felt almost sorry enough for her to tell her what she needed to know—but she kept her silence. She pretended to be an amnesiac.

And he refused to make himself a fool over a woman. He refused to find himself abandoned, scorned, and betrayed like Bradley Benjamin.

Devlin would not be the one to give his trust—and it really pissed him off that she made him want to.

Off to his left, the Amelia Shores Society of Old Farts sat on the porch, observing the proceedings with varying reactions.

Scrubby Gallagher sat with his feet propped on the rail, nursing an iced tea and watching the women. He couldn't have looked more content.

Penn Sample rocked a little too fast to be anything but annoyed by the hubbub.

Begum, one of the world's top models, sauntered by, and Wilfred Kistard adjusted his toupee, unbuttoned the top button of his tropical-print shirt, and went after her. Good luck to the old fool.

H. Edwin Osgood wore his trademark bow tie and thick glasses, and as he watched the frivolity it seemed the stoop in his shoulders became more pronounced. Probably the carnival made him feel old.

Bradley Benjamin sat stiffly on a straight-backed chair beside Osgood. He wore a summer-weight wool suit, a white shirt, a tie, and a straw hat. All he needed was a slave boy fanning him with a frond to be the picture of a wealthy nineteenth-century Southern planter. His posture, his scowl, everything about him was a criticism of the Secret Garden and the party.

His glower, and the opportunity to needle him, almost resigned Devlin to the cost of that antique calliope.

Devlin strolled over. "Enjoying yourselves, gentlemen?"

"This display of tastelessness"—Bradley Benjamin gestured at the party—"is a disgrace to a fine old estate."

"But really, you didn't expect any different from a common bastard like me." Devlin enjoyed delivering the line before Benjamin could.

"You don't show Mr. Benjamin the respect due him for his advanced age and noble position." Osgood's mouth puckered, and his skinny lips wrinkled.

"Oh, be quiet," Bradley snapped. He did not like having his age called into play.

Penn Sample's blue eyes twinkled with that artificial kindness he played so well, and which Devlin had learned meant trouble. "It would be a shame if something happened here before you could open your hotel."

"Such as?"

"We saw a cell tower had been erected." Benjamin never bothered to hide his hostility, but today he visibly bristled.

"Yes, it's hard to miss, isn't it?" Devlin leaned down to Benjamin's eye level. "See the people mingling with the crowd? The ones in black and white with headsets and mouthpieces? Those are my security force. They're on top alert."

"You had security before." Benjamin's papery lids drooped over eyes heavy with malice.

"Gabriel Prescott, the national head of the firm, is here and mingling with the guests. There won't be any incidents—or rather, any more accidents." Devlin straightened. "I declare that from this moment, the hotel is officially open."

Benjamin glared in helpless fury.

Devlin looked around at all of them. "Trust me, gentlemen, before the decade is out, you'll see three more hotels along this strip. But then, that's what you're afraid of, isn't it?"

It was. He could almost see them shivering in their fine leather shoes.

"Hey, Mr. Fitzwilliam!" Christian, the pastry chef, held up a football. "Look what I won!"

"Cool!" Devlin clapped his hands.

Christian launched the football at him. His aim was off, and Devlin had to dive to keep it from hitting Bradley Benjamin right in his pompous, offended old schnoz.

"Sorry, Mr. Benjamin!" Christian waved apologetically, and grimaced at Devlin.

Devlin shrugged in response and shouted, "Go long."

Christian backed up and up and up, and Devlin shot the football right into his arms.

The crowd around the porch applauded—Southerners loved football, and they really loved having their own winning quarterback right in their backyard. He was pretty sure it was the only reason they still had electricity—the head of the local power company was a fan.

Devlin waved, and dusted his fingertips.

Grace stalked up the stairs and toward the house, her arms straight at her sides, the picture of offended dignity.

Devlin hurried toward her. "Everything all right, Mother?"

She showed him the lapel of her white jacket. "Frank Peterson was waving a pimento-cheese sandwich and hit me with it. Ill-bred lout. He's the handyman. I don't know why you invited him."

"I didn't invite him."

"Then what is he doing here? Did he crash the party?"

Meadow walked up licking a three-scoop cone. "Who?"

"Frank Peterson," Grace snapped.

"*I* invited him." Meadow's tongue massaged the ice cream. Her hat brim bobbed. "You couldn't expect him to stay home while his wife was here."

Grace waited for Devlin to speak, but he was busy watching Meadow catch a creamy drop before it trickled onto her hand. So, with a resigned sigh, Grace asked, "His wife? Who is . . . ?"

"His wife is Jazmin, who works at the hospital." Meadow sounded patient, as if she were reciting information they all should know.

"And you invited her because . . . ?" Grace lifted a perfectly tweezed eyebrow.

"She was nice to me after the wreck." Meadow's cheeks were flushed with pleasure as she looked out at the carnival.

"I'll bet you invited Miss I-Have-Perky-Breasts-and-I-Know-How-to-Use-Them." Devlin indicated Four and the young girl.

"Weezy!" Meadow said.

"God bless you." Grace brimmed over with irritation.

"Her name is Weezy," Meadow said patiently, "and I invited her because I couldn't invite Jazmin without hurting Weezy's feelings. Besides, Weezy's keeping Four entertained."

Devlin noticed that Meadow's tongue had turned bright pink from the red sprinkles. He broke a sweat.

Weezy tucked her hand into Four's arm. As they strolled past, the silence on the porch varied from freezing disapproval from Grace to wide-eyed lecherousness from Penn Sample.

"He's taking me on a personalized tour of the house," Weezy called to them.

"I'll bet," Devlin said.

Meadow grinned and tugged at his arm. "Down, boy. You're married now. All you get to do is run to the end of your leash and bark."

From the direction of the old men, Devlin heard a series of horrified gasps and choking laughs.

She glanced at them. "Hi, Mr. Gallagher, Mr. Sample, Mr. Osgood, Mr. Benjamin. Got your hearing aids turned up?"

Scrubby Gallagher laughed. "And loving to hear you jerk that leash. Keep it up! You'll get him trained!"

Meadow gave him a thumbs-up, then went back to work on her cone.

As he viewed Isabelle's granddaughter, Bradley Benjamin's faded gray eyes blazed with irritation—and something Devlin had never seen there before.

Maybe the emptiness of a life badly lived?

God, Devlin hoped so. That would make this whole farce well worthwhile.

That, and the pleasure of getting into Meadow's pants every night.

"I suppose you invited the whole hospital staff so no one got their feelings hurt," Grace said.

Meadow looked down at her feet as she scuffed them. Her hat brim hid her face, but everyone knew the answer.

"Oh, for God's sake!" In a dramatic, exasperated gesture, Grace put her hand on her forehead.

"You told me I could invite my friends!" Meadow used her tongue to push the ice cream down into the cone.

Devlin wondered how long he could keep his erection below half-mast.

"Your *friends*, not the people who are in service to you," Grace said.

Devlin slid his arm around Meadow's waist. "Meadow makes everyone a friend."

Meadow shoved her hat brim back and looked up at him, and he saw the mischief in her face. "I suppose I shouldn't tell her I invited the rest of the household staff, huh?"

The expression on Grace's face was worth the price of the Ferris wheel. She stammered, "You . . . you invited the staff. The staff of the Secret Garden?"

"Well, sure. I told them to drop in when they weren't working. Look! They're having a marvelous time." Meadow gestured widely. The cone went flying and landed splat on the handrail.

Grace flinched and tried to protect her still-pristine white slacks.

In a voice that insulted and sneered, Bradley Benjamin said, "Mrs. Fitzwilliam, it might help if you maintained enough sobriety to hold on to your food."

"I haven't had a drink. I'm always this way!" She smiled at him with that special edge she maintained for Bradley Benjamin. "But it's okay. I'm an artist. We get to be eccentric."

Benjamin's gray eyes would have frozen bourbon in the glass. His lips moved soundlessly, but he wasn't swearing. Devlin saw it. The old guy said, "Isabelle."

Meadow saw it, too, because she removed her hat and inclined her head at him.

All Devlin's suspicions shifted, changed, became certainties. Meadow knew—had always known—about Bradley Benjamin and his position in her grandmother's life. And Meadow, who liked everybody, didn't like Bradley Benjamin.

"An artist?" Grace said. "I didn't know you were an artist."

"Oops," Meadow said softly. Wheeling on her, she said, "Grace, you've got something on your lapel."

Grace gave an exasperated huff. "If Meadow noticed, then I've *got* to go change. But I'll be back. Don't make your announcement until I am!"

"We wouldn't dream of it." Meadow watched her leave; then, the picture of guilt, she waited.

Waited for Devlin to question her about her art, he supposed. But he wasn't disposed to be an asshole today.

They had Bradley Benjamin for that.

Instead Devlin lifted her chin and kissed the corner of her mouth. "Ice cream," he said.

"Right." Scrubby put all his disbelief, all his envy, into that one word.

Devlin didn't care. All he cared about was having Meadow gaze at him as if she adored him.

The raucous music from the calliope, the clamor of the crowd, the smell of food and sunscreen—they all faded away. He was aware of nothing but Meadow's delightful smile, her warmth as she leaned into him, the scent of the lemon rinse she used in her hair.

"Mr. Fitzwilliam, if I could speak to you in your office?"

Sam startled Devlin out of his reverie.

When Devlin glared at him, Sam added, "It's important."

"Of course." Reluctantly, Devlin allowed Meadow to slip out of his grasp.

She stepped away from Sam. Looked at him *very* oddly. It was as if she knew Sam had been watching her when she'd shut herself into that closet, and blamed him for telling Devlin the truth.

"Don't be too long." She replaced her hat and skipped down the steps.

Devlin glanced over at the old guys. All of them watched her go, and all of them had that wistful, walking-down-memory-lane gleam in their eyes.

All of them except Bradley Benjamin. He looked furious—and old.

The fool. Did his pride keep him company when he sat alone every night?

Or had it occurred to him that if he'd kept Isabelle, he could have had Meadow for his granddaughter?

30

Sam indicated the bank of monitors in Devlin's office. "Usually while Mr. Four wanders the halls, he's reeling drunk. But today . . ."

Four walked along the corridor on the third floor, Weezy on his arm.

"He's probably looking for somewhere new to get laid," Devlin said. *Like the linen closet.*

"I wouldn't have come to get you if that was the case," Sam said. "Watch him."

Four was wild-eyed, his motions jerky, as he stared at each painting. Once he stopped before a landscape, leaned in, and looked at the signature in the corner. Weezy looked bored to death, and when she tugged on his arm, Four turned on her. It was obvious that he snapped, for she flounced off.

"He's looking for a painting, too?" Devlin couldn't believe it. It was too odd. Too similar to Meadow's behavior to be a coincidence. "What the hell do they think they're going to get out of the damned thing?"

"Sir?" Sam frowned at Devlin.

"Nothing." Devlin waved the question aside.

"Sir, do you think perhaps it might be a wise idea to send Mrs.

Fitzwilliam and Mr. Four away until it's ascertained that this painting isn't on the premises?"

"But it *is* on the premises."

Sam stepped forward, and he projected a surprising menace. "Would you explain yourself, sir?"

Devlin considered what to say, how much to say. "The painting is not what everyone hopes. It's not an important lost masterpiece. It's an early work, and a hurried work. I like it, but I have my reasons. Why?" Why, of all the people in the world, did Sam care so much?

"When Mrs. Fitzwilliam started searching, I took the liberty of looking over the appraisals of all the art in the house." Sam went to the file cabinet and pulled out the file. "There's nothing here that would indicate the kind of interest Mrs. Fitzwilliam and Mr. Four are displaying."

"Exactly." Devlin noted that Sam hadn't answered the question, but before he could ask, his walkie-talkie beeped. He glanced down and saw his mother framed in the small screen.

"I'm ready, and if you don't hurry, Meadow will go off and jump in the large"—Grace waved her arms—"blow-up clown thing."

Meadow thrust her head in front of the camera and rolled her eyes.

"I'll be there in a minute." Devlin clicked the off button and said to Sam, "Is there anything else before I go back?"

"I have the report on Mrs. Fitzwilliam from the detective."

"About damned time." Nothing else could have held Devlin in place. Nothing else.

"It took him a while to sift through and find the right information." Sam handed him a manila folder filled with papers and photos. His cool, dark eyes met Devlin's. "Mrs. Fitzwilliam has never visited Majorca."

"Let's keep that our secret."

But Sam still stood there, balanced between what he wanted to say and what he should say. He must have decided they were one and the same, because at last he used a low, slow voice to ask, "Have you thought that perhaps she's sleeping with you just so she can stay here and search for this . . . painting?"

When had Sam become so interested in all this? When had he started looking and sounding like the man in authority? "Of course I've thought it. How could I not? But if that's the case, it's worth it— and I'll bear up and suffer through."

"Yes, sir. Do you want me to do anything about Mr. Four?"

"No. Let him search. It won't hurt, and maybe it'll keep him away from the booze."

"Yes, sir." Sam turned away to his office.

Devlin stared at the folder, at Sam's neat printing on the tab. *Natalie Meadow Szarvas.*

He should go back to the party. He was the host. But Meadow hid too many secrets, and he'd not had time to search them out. He wanted to know everything about her, about her family, about her art, about her background. He held the answers in his hand, and he couldn't wait any longer.

Sitting down at his desk, he opened the folder and started reading.

When he was finished, he stood up.

Everything had changed. Everything.

He had to find Meadow. This time they would work this thing out.

Instead, when he stepped onto the porch, his mother saluted him with a glass of champagne and called, "It's the bridegroom! Come on, Devlin; we've cleared the Ferris wheel. It's time for you and Meadow to make your announcement!"

———⌒———

The day had been long and exhausting.

Devlin and Meadow had ridden the Ferris wheel to the top and made the announcement of their marriage to the cheering crowd.

No one had left until after ten, and then only the local half had driven away. The rest of the party had retired to the bar. It was after two by the time the last of the guests had staggered off to their rooms at the Secret Garden, sending the staff into a frenzy of work as they delivered extra towels, antacids, and bottles of water.

By the time Devlin came to bed, Meadow was asleep.

As he climbed under the covers with her, he resolved that he would talk to her in the morning.

But the second Meadow stepped out of bed, Devlin woke up. He lay there for a moment, waiting to see if she turned on the bathroom light.

But no. She slipped into her robe—and left the room.

Perhaps he was a fool, but he knew she wasn't sneaking off to visit another man. And the moon wasn't full, so she wasn't off to dance naked in the garden.

This was about her mother. That single sentence in the detective's report had explained everything.

Meadow wanted that painting to pay for her mother's treatment.

And how deeply Devlin resented the fact that she hadn't told him her troubles. Told him the truth. He'd given her so many chances, yet it seemed that while she trusted him enough to sleep with him, she didn't trust him with her secrets.

He got up and pulled on his jeans and a T-shirt. Going to the closet, he dug out his Reeboks.

All right, maybe some of the things he'd done, and some of the things he'd said, and some of the things he'd encouraged others to say about him, led her to believe he was a ruthless, unyielding jerk.

But didn't she know? Didn't she realize?

With her, he was different. He felt . . . young. He believed in possibilities. In wiggly puppies and in spring showers that brought May flowers. In miracles.

The idea of Devlin Fitzwilliam being silly in love seemed absurd—except that he was in love with Meadow.

He tied his shoes.

Well. Tonight he would teach her to trust him. He would do what he had sworn he would not—he'd confess the truth, all the truth. Kind, generous Meadow would realize the error of her ways, and she'd stay with him.

He headed out, figuring he could check the monitors across the dimly lit corridor, see where she'd headed off to search, and find her.

But when he accessed the room, the security panel was black.

He stared in horror.

Had Meadow turned off the whole system to look for her painting?

Because with the hotel full of guests, including the Godfather of Amelia Shores, Bradley Benjamin, the chances for undetected sabotage, for theft and disaster, had radically increased.

Devlin tore down the hall and toward his office on the main floor. He hit the landing at the top.

Someone was going into his office.

He shouted.

Gabriel shouted back, "I'm on it!" and disappeared inside.

Devlin took the steps two at a time.

As he neared the first floor, he realized someone had dropped a bundle of towels at the bottom of the stairs.

But as he got closer, he realized that it wasn't towels or rags or someone's clothes. It had a head of copper hair that shone dully, limbs arranged at an awkward angle, and it lay unmoving. Unconscious.

Meadow.

Dear God. Dear God. Please, no, God . . .

He knelt beside her. His hands trembled as he touched her face. Still warm. He pressed his fingers to the artery in her neck. Her heart beat. He called her name. "Meadow?"

But she didn't respond.

She'd fallen down the stairs.

A small trickle of blood stained the carpet beneath her head.

But he didn't dare move her, because this time . . . this time she might have broken her neck. This time . . . she was really hurt.

He leaned down close. "Meadow. For the love of God. Don't die. Please, don't die. I love you."

And he stayed there until the ambulance took her away.

But she never moved. She never answered him at all.

31

*D*awn was lightening the sky when Devlin quietly let himself in the front door of the Secret Garden.

"How is she?" Grace stood silhouetted in the entrance to the library, her hands tucked into the wide sleeves of her robe, her eyes worried.

"She has a hell of a gash on the back of her head and a lot of bruises on her arms and legs. They say she's fine, but they kept her overnight for observation. Dr. Apps says Meadow's been hit on the head too many times in the last month." He tried to grin. "So why do *I* feel punchy?"

"I knew it. That girl wouldn't let a fall down the stairs faze her. She could probably fall out of an airplane and bounce."

He only wished Meadow had looked a little less pale, and been a little less confused by where she was now and how she'd gotten there. "Yes. She is indomitable, isn't she?"

"Rather like me."

He was very tired, and it took him a minute to process her observation. Grace had paid Meadow the ultimate compliment. He almost staggered from the shock. "My God, Mother. You like her!"

"I don't like her. I think she's lying about half the things she says.

She dresses horribly. She's impertinent. She doesn't comprehend the most basic of proprieties. Neither of you has given me the slightest clue about her background, by which I must assume both parents are serial killers. And she's a Yankee." Grace's voice got sharper with each complaint. Then her face softened. "But she makes you happy, so that impertinent, unsuitable child of Yankee convicts . . . is fine."

"Thank you, Mother. That's very . . ." He started to say *sweet*.

She shot him a glare.

". . . open-minded of you." He laughed a little and rubbed his head. When he'd gotten out of bed and gone after Meadow, he'd been irked as hell that she hadn't confided in him, yet prepared to make the grandiose gesture of paying for her mother's cancer treatment.

What a great guy he was.

Yet Meadow seemed to think he was wonderful, and, even more amazing, so did his mother.

"Meadow told you she's an artist," he said. "I believe you know her. She made that glass bowl you placed on the mantelpiece in the dining room."

"No, she didn't. That bowl was created by River Szar—" Grace stopped in midsentence. She looked at him. She walked to the dining room. She looked toward the fireplace. She turned back. "Meadow is Natalie Szarvas?"

"Natalie Meadow Szarvas."

"She told me she was an artist, but I thought . . . Well! That explains everything. No wonder she's so eccentric. This will be so much easier to explain to my friends." Grace's eyes gleamed with satisfaction.

"And we all know how important that is." His mockery hid his real pleasure in her approval.

"I am friends with important people!"

"They're only important because they're your friends."

"As Meadow is important because she's your wife." In her peculiarly inept way of comfort, Grace came to him and hugged him. "It's late. You're tired. You've had a shock. Go to bed."

"Yeah." He was well aware that his confession of love to Meadow had been unheard—and unanswered.

Worse, he was relieved. He was a stinking coward—he didn't want to be the one who took the chance and offered his love, only to have the new, fresh, never-before-experienced emotion rejected.

He wasn't the kind of man who imagined Meadow had never danced naked in the moonlight, or that her open affection for him might just be . . . Meadow's affection for all of mankind. He was certainly one of her only lovers, but when it came to love . . . he might be one of the crowd.

Grace walked with him toward the stairs. "What does Meadow say happened tonight?"

"She says she doesn't remember." He grimaced. *Yeah, right.* More amnesia. But this time . . . he believed her.

After he'd gotten Meadow settled in a room, Dr. Apps had called him aside. "I see this kind of injury far more than I like to. A blunt object inflicted the wound on Mrs. Fitzwilliam's head."

He had stared at the doctor, his worst fears confirmed. "You're saying someone hit Meadow and pushed her down the stairs?"

"Actually, Mr. Fitzwilliam, in cases like this, that someone is almost always the husband." Maybe Dr. Apps didn't flirt with other women's husbands. Maybe she didn't flirt with wife beaters. But at that moment, she sure as hell hadn't been flirting with him. She had stared at him, arms crossed, eyes hostile.

"In this case, it isn't. But I will find out who it was." He had walked away, knowing full well that Dr. Apps believed in his innocence about as much as she believed O. J. Simpson's.

But the fact remained that someone had struck Meadow and pushed her down the stairs, and he intended to discover who—and make that person suffer.

It was because of that person that Devlin had had to face a horrible fact: He loved Meadow, and that love had the power to make him suffer.

He didn't want to suffer.

He didn't want someone else to hold power over him.

He had, in the space of only a few hours, been proven a coward and a weakling.

How had he come to such a pass?

But his mother stared at him as she always had, as if she didn't know what to do with him, so he knew his vulnerabilities remained hidden. At the foot of the stairs, he patted her on the back. "It's late. You need to get some sleep."

"I'm fine. I'm putting off the first day of filming for the new season. I must see Meadow with my own eyes, and really know she's well." Grace stood there, waiting for . . . what?

Oh. "That's great, Mother. I appreciate it, especially since I know how important the show is to your fans."

"Anything for my son and his wife." She presented her cheek.

He kissed it and watched her make her way upstairs.

Then he headed for his office.

There he found Sam and Gabriel reviewing the security tapes.

He seated himself behind his desk. He placed his hands flat on the cool surface, and coolly considered them both. "Well?"

Gabriel began. "The security system was off five minutes before my personal alarm sounded."

"Why so long?" Devlin asked.

"Because it was shut off by someone who knew what he was doing, and it was done remotely. The only reason he didn't circumvent my alarm was because I installed it right before the party. New technology. And I wouldn't have done that if you hadn't had the break-in three weeks ago. Stuff like that makes me twitchy." Actually, Gabriel didn't look twitchy. He looked furious.

Devlin switched his attention to Sam.

"I reviewed the tapes at the time the cameras went off, and again right after they came on. The only people in the corridors or on the perimeter were security personnel, Mia from the kitchen, who had

finished cleaning up and was heading home, Miss Weezy Woodward, who was leaving Judge Gregory Madison's room, and near the
top of the staircase . . . Mr. Bradley Benjamin the fourth."

Devlin found himself on his feet, and in a voice hoarse with rage
he said, "Four? Four did this?"

"Sir, Four does not have the technical skill to shut off the security
system," Sam said.

"Who else could it be? Do you have another suspect?" Devlin
demanded.

"Perhaps one of my security people." Gabriel made his suggestion
steadily. "They all have good references. Some have worked for me
for years. I pay them well. But security guards are always a prime
target for corruption."

Devlin paced out from behind his desk. "Have any of *them* been
sneaking around my hotel after a painting?"

Sam shook his head. "But sir, Four isn't violent. I can't imagine he
would strike Mrs. Fitzwilliam."

"Let's find out." At a deliberate pace, with Sam and Gabriel on his
heels, Devlin walked up the stairs and down the corridor to Four's
room. Just as deliberately, he slid his master key card into the lock.
And even more deliberately, with all his force, he slammed the door
open against the wall.

"Shit," Gabriel muttered.

Devlin flipped on the overhead light.

Four catapulted out of the bed.

"Four, you son of a bitch, is there something you want to tell me?"
Devlin used to be a football player. He knew how to make himself
look bulky and menacing.

He did it now.

His technique worked, because Four gave a sob and cringed back
against the bed. "Please, Devlin, don't kill me."

Guilty. Devlin could scarcely stand it. That feeble little asshole
was guilty.

He took a step inside. One step only. If he took any more, he'd go and wring Four's skinny little neck. "Give me one reason why not."

"It's not my fault! He's making me do it. It's Mr. Hopkins."

"Mr. . . . Hopkins?" Gabriel asked.

Four's attention switched to Gabriel. "He's this silver-haired devil with a smooth voice. So smooth. He calls me and he says . . . he says . . ." The pansy-ass wore a pair of silk pajama bottoms, and the knocking of his knees made the fine material shiver. "He says he's going to geld me! Or worse."

"Have you seen him?" Sam asked.

"Yes. I didn't see him well—he sat there in shadow—but he did this." Four pinched his ear.

Gabe turned to Devlin. "Remember, I told you about Mr. Hopkins. If he's got his finger in this pie, we're in deep trouble."

"We are. We are!" Four said.

"I've hired a couple of his people. My security's been compromised." Gabriel looked at Sam. "Can you handle this?"

Sam nodded.

Gabriel walked back down the corridor.

Four watched the interplay with feverish eyes. "He knows everything that's going on here. He's watching me. He's watching the house. You do understand, Devlin?"

"I understand. You're working for him." Devlin waited for Four to deny it.

But he didn't. All he did was confirm his own cowardice. "I had to! He's going to hurt me if I don't get that painting. He's going to kill me!"

So Four had pushed Meadow down the stairs. He'd tried to break her neck to save his own. The lying little weasel. "You should stop worrying about *Mr. Hopkins* killing you."

"Man. Please. You're going to help me, aren't you?" Four had the guts to look hopeful.

"You hurt my wife." Remembering how Meadow had appeared, crumpled at the bottom of the stairs, made Devlin want to sob, too.

Instead, he promised, "Now I'm going to kill you myself." He started after Four.

Four tried to back up. Fell on the bed. Scrambled backward.

Sam grabbed Devlin and planted his feet.

"Kill your wife? Kill Meadow? When? What are you talking about? I never hurt her. I never hurt anybody!" Four's blond, gelled hair stood up like an exclamation point.

Devlin strained against the restraint. "What a pile of crap. You charmed her. You made her like you. Then when you figured out she was looking for the same painting as you, you cut that steering fluid line."

"I didn't do that. He did. He did!"

"And when you saw her on the stairs, you smacked her on the head."

"I never touched her. Devlin, I swear to God"—like a goddamn Boy Scout, Four held up one trembling hand—"I would rather go up against Mr. Hopkins by myself than hurt Meadow."

"Get out." Devlin could scarcely speak for rage. "Get . . . out . . . now."

Four listened. He listened well, because he raced to the closet, pulled out his clothes, and flung them on the bed.

But he kept talking. He babbled as fast as he could. "Listen to me. I didn't hurt Meadow. If someone smacked her on the head, you'd better take good care of her, because if Mr. Hopkins knows she's after that painting, he'll take her out. No kidding, Devlin. Mr. Hopkins is going to kill me for failing." Four paused in the process of unzipping his suitcase.

He looked right at Devlin, and if Devlin didn't know better, he would have sworn Four was telling the truth.

"Devlin, honest. Mr. Hopkins will kill Meadow . . . just for trying."

32

$\mathcal{T}$he next morning, as Devlin stepped inside his office, the clouds had closed in and the gray day echoed his mood. He hated that Gabriel had spent the night firing some of his security staff and trying to track down one who'd gone missing. He hated that Four had betrayed him. He hated more that his tolerance for an old friend had led to Meadow's injury.

Worse, now he saw traitors everywhere. When Sam looked up from his desk, all Devlin could remember was his unusual interest in that painting. There was something damned odd about his attention to *that* detail.

"I hope Mrs. Fitzwilliam is doing well today, sir." Sam looked the same as he always did—a mix of Asian and Hispanic, calm, unflappable, efficient.

But when Devlin got back from the hospital and settled Meadow into her bed, he was going to do some research on good old Sam. "I spoke with the hospital this morning. They tell me she's resting comfortably and, other than bruises, has no residual trauma. I pick her up at eleven."

"Good news, sir." Sam rose to his feet. He squared his shoulders. "Mr. Fitzwilliam, I refused to wake you, but you have a visitor. He didn't want to be seen by your departing guests, so I put him in the dining room."

Devlin was in no mood to play games. "Who is he?"

"His name is Carrick Manly."

"Carrick Manly. Well. Daddy's *legitimate* son." No wonder Sam had made such a big deal of this announcement. He didn't know how Devlin would react.

Hell, Devlin didn't know how Devlin should react.

Nathan Manly had had one wife, and among his other breeding activities, he'd managed to father one son with her, making Carrick the anointed heir to his father's industrial kingdom. Only Nathan had ruined his business, taken the money, and run out on everyone, including Melinda and Carrick Manly.

In all the years since his father had disappeared, Devlin had never heard from any paternal relative.

Well . . . he hadn't gone looking for them, either. With a parent like Nathan, who knew what his offspring would be? Devlin had enough problems with friends like Four.

Four. Devlin had thrown him out, then almost sent someone after him. Because . . . what if Four was telling the truth?

But Sam had talked him out of it. "Sir, if this Mr. Hopkins really is searching for the painting, then Four is better off away from the action." Then he'd tried to pry more information about the painting out of Devlin.

Sam was definitely due for an investigation.

"Did Carrick say what he wanted?"

"He refused to speak to me," Sam said, "but I thought you'd wish to see him regardless."

"You thought right."

"I also thought you'd like information before you spoke with him, so I took the liberty of researching him and making up a file." Sam handed Devlin a manila folder full of information he'd gathered off the Internet: press clippings describing Carrick's privileged child-hood in Maine among American aristocrats, many more news stories from the time of Nathan's disappearance, and a mention of Carrick's graduation from college with a brief recap of the disgrace. The newest pictures were not clear; Carrick had clearly developed a talent for avoiding the photographers.

And finally, from January, the news that the U.S. government had filed charges against Melinda Manly, accusing her of collusion in the defrauding of the Manly Corporation's stockholders.

Devlin had heard about that, of course. He simply hadn't given a rat's ass. "Why did the government wait so many years?" he asked rhetorically.

Sam answered just as vaguely. "It's the government."

Devlin handed the file back. "You put him in the dining room, you say? Good choice. He can entertain himself in there." With the computers. With the books. With stealing the antiques, if he took after their father.

Devlin strode toward the dining room.

He opened the double doors, half hoping to catch Carrick pilfering the silver.

Instead he was sitting by the window, reading a well-worn paperback—one of his own, by the looks of it. He put down the book, rose, and extended his hand. "My name's Carrick Manly. I'm your half brother—and that's a phrase I've been using a little more often than I am used to."

Those recent, blurred photos didn't do him justice. He was approximately twenty-four, tall and broad-shouldered. His hair was dark, like Devlin's, and his brown eyes were intelligent.

Devlin thought they probably looked alike, and as he shook Carrick's hand, he said, "The apple doesn't fall far from the tree."

"So I see." Carrick checked him out as carefully as Devlin had him. "You look completely different from the last half brother I met." Clearly Carrick had been raised among the finest old families on the East Coast; his voice had a patrician accent, and although the clothes he wore weren't expensive, he wore them well.

"Who would that be?"

"His name is Roberto Bartolini. He's Italian."

"No more than half Italian, surely." Devlin gestured Carrick back into his seat.

Carrick corrected himself. "Italian-American."

"I believe I've heard of him. Saw his photo in the paper. " Devlin remembered the *USA Today* story he'd read at the airport last month. "Didn't he marry that famous crime-fighting lawyer in Chicago?"

"I was at the wedding." While Devlin seated himself, Carrick sank back and waited.

He showed an unusual amount of self-possession for a young man, and Devlin had to admire his handling of the situation. The other man didn't know if he would face overt hostility, amusement, or evasion, so he lingered in silence.

"Did you find him?" Devlin could think of no other reason Carrick would have appeared out of the blue.

"Our father? No. He's gone; the money's gone. Nobody knows anything. But perhaps you've heard—the government has accused my mother of collusion in Nathan's destruction of his industry and the disappearance of the money. I'm looking for any information he might have told you or your mother."

Devlin's ire rose. "After all this time, you come and ask a question like that?"

"Mr. . . . . Fitzwilliam. After my father left, times were difficult for my mother and me. Nathan absconded not only with the money from the company, but also with most of my mother's family fortune. The part of her fortune she managed to preserve she's used to maintain the estate, but other than that, we lost everything." Carrick held up his hand. "We had a lot, more than most people, certainly more than the rest of my half brothers. Nevertheless, my mother is ill suited for economizing, and times were difficult. Tracking down my brothers—a difficult business because, like so many things, my father took care to obscure his indiscretions—took a backseat to simply dealing with our circumstances."

"Yes. I see." Devlin did—reluctantly.

"After so many years, this indictment has caught us by surprise. My mother is not well, and she . . . considers this another disgrace visited on us by my father. She refuses to defend herself, and it's up to me to clear her. The only legacy my father left me was my brothers. Through them I hope to discover what a family truly is."

He was very good, this brother of Devlin's. Carrick sketched his circumstances, he stated his case clearly, and his appeal was both unsentimental and brief. In the past, Devlin had heard enough to know that Melinda and Carrick Manly had been abandoned as surely as Devlin had been; his only thought, if he had one, had been a brief, *Good.* But that had been years ago, immediately after his father walked out; he'd been very young then, and hurt by the knowledge that he'd been nothing more than another notch on a very scarred bedpost.

Now Devlin had other interests, and none of them concerned Nathan Manly.

Instead, they concerned Meadow. Meadow and her quest for a painting that would pay enough for her mother to have all the treatments she needed to be cured of her cancer. Meadow, who would do anything for family.

Devlin had worked so hard to avoid having anything to do with his half brothers; maybe he should take a lesson from Meadow. Maybe it was time to forgive.

So he would give Carrick what information he sought, move on with his life, and perhaps someday he would host a reunion of the Manly sons at one of his hotels. "On his last visit," Devlin said, "a few weeks before he pulled his disappearing act, Nathan gave me a ledger and asked me to keep it until he returned."

Carrick sat forward. "A ledger? That's more than I would have ever hoped."

"I looked at it then—believe me, I wanted to think it was a treasure map or a secret message telling me where to find him."

Carrick laughed, a brief, harsh laugh. "Oh, yeah. I did that, too. I kept thinking that he would . . . walk back through the door. . . ."

The two brothers looked at each other, united by the bitter memories left by a father's cruel abandonment.

They had more in common than Devlin realized, and perhaps Carrick's life as a disgraced son had been as difficult as Devlin's as a bastard—certainly Carrick had suffered a shock when his social standing and income suddenly dropped, and Devlin had not. Maybe being tough right from the start was an advantage he hadn't imagined.

"Have you thought that he may have left no trail that would lead to the fortune?" A likely state of affairs, in Devlin's view.

"My father—our father—did everything in his power to make himself and his fortune disappear, and he's been a rousing success. But I have to try," Carrick said simply.

With that, Carrick convinced Devlin. "The ledger is yours."

33

$\mathcal{D}$r. Apps finished the exam and put her stethoscope in her jacket. "You're going to be stiff for a few days, and you can't wash your hair until the sutures come out, but all in all you came through a tumble down the stairs very well."

Meadow sat up in her hospital bed and grinned at Devlin standing guard by the door. "Plus I managed to get out of the party cleanup today."

"We'll put you on the riding vacuum cleaner," he said dryly.

"Really?" Her eyes sparkled.

"No." He crossed his arms over his chest, stood with his feet apart, and exerted his authority. He was good at exerting his authority.

"But that would be fun!"

Either he'd lost his touch, or his authority didn't exert in her direction. "We do *not* have a riding vacuum cleaner."

"Oh." She looked crestfallen—and so much better than she had last night.

He hated that he wanted to kiss her, to hug her, to hold her until he was assured of her health, of her happiness, of her safety.

"Do you remember any more about what preceded the fall?" Dr.

Apps didn't look at him as she asked. Obviously, in her eyes, he was still a wife beater.

"I got up to . . ." Meadow glanced at him, then said, ". . . to look for a painting I want to locate—"

He took a long, deep breath. She had at least begun to trust him.

"And when I got to the top of the stairs, someone was there. I started to turn and . . ." She shook her head. "That's all. I don't really remember much until this morning." She put her head down and shivered.

Coming to the bed, he sat on the side and put his arm around her.

She put her head on his shoulder and leaned into him.

Yes. Trust. At last. "If you hadn't turned off the security system, we would know who hit you," he said softly.

She lifted her head. "I didn't!"

"Are you sure?"

"I would surely remember that."

"Okay."

"Really. I didn't do it!"

"I believe you."

"Just like that?"

"Just like that." He didn't intend to tell her the truth about Four. Not yet. He knew her well enough to realize Four's treachery would break her heart.

Then she smiled at him so sweetly, he felt like the bastard he was. Because she thought he believed her because he had faith in her word.

And he did. But proof helped.

"We're going to have to talk about this painting," he said.

"I know. But you'll understand."

Dr. Apps cleared her throat. "I have some news about your condition, Mrs. Fitzwilliam, which I think might be a surprise."

What the hell . . . ? Devlin's arm tightened around Meadow.

"Last night, among the other tests we ran, we ran a pregnancy test."

He couldn't move.

Meadow didn't move.

"It was positive." Their stunned silence spoke volumes to Dr. Apps, and she added hastily, "But you don't need to be concerned about the effects of the fall. The baby is fine, you're in good health, and it should be a successful pregnancy. As soon as you're home, call my office and I'll give you a recommendation for a good ob-gyn. You should make your first appointment immediately, and the doctor will figure out your due date. Do you have any questions?"

Meadow shook her head no.

Devlin still couldn't move, couldn't speak, couldn't think.

"Then I'll give you a few minutes to get yourself together. Just let them know at the nurses' station when you're ready for a wheelchair to take you down to the entrance." Dr. Apps backed out of a room so thick with atmosphere she almost choked.

"A baby," Meadow whispered, and pressed her hand to her stomach.

They'd made a baby. They'd made a miracle.

"I'll bet it happened that night in the moonlight. Don't you think it had to be that night?" Devlin didn't answer, but Meadow was thinking out loud, thinking of herself and how this affected her. "I know you don't know this, but my mother has cancer."

"What happened to your amnesia? Did you *forget* about your mother?" His sarcasm cut right through her reverie.

"What?" She blinked at him.

His face was blank, his eyes impassive. He was in shock, poor guy.

Taking his hand, she smiled. "I sort of lied about having amnesia. Don't tell me you didn't know."

"I knew. That's why I *sort of* lied when I said we were married." His voice had an edge she couldn't define.

But remembering that moment when they met, when their false-hoods had topped each other, made her chuckle. "When you said we were married, I didn't know what to do. I thought the situation would be temporary, that I could find the painting, take it out of the house, and you'd never know. Then I found out about your security and all the people working at the hotel, and things got more and more difficult."

"You were going to steal from me."

"Not really *steal*. My grandmother left it in the house in case of an emergency, like my mom's illness. So it was my legacy, but I had the bad luck to arrive about a year too late. You already owned Waldemar. I walked into a secure place, fell and hit my head, saw stars . . . and haven't been the same since." She placed her hand on his. "Because I've gotten to know you. Being with you has been wonderful, an experience like no other in my life. So like so many things, what looked like bad luck actually became good luck."

"By what stretch of the imagination do you think this is good luck?"

"What do you mean? Haven't you *enjoyed* our time together?" He had. She knew it.

"Yes. But we're having a baby." Abruptly she remembered his panic when they'd failed to use protection. She remembered his illegitimacy and the taunting he'd had to face as a child, and from people—like Bradley Benjamin—who should know better.

"I know we didn't plan it, and you don't like it because you've got these archaic notions about what it means to be illegitimate—"

"Archaic notions? Lady, I have walked the walk and talked the talk."

"I know," she said hastily. *He's sensitive, Meadow. You be sensitive, too.* "That was patronizing. But what I mean is, a baby always brings such joy. And when you think about how many blessings we have in our lives—the grand opening was a huge success, my mom's in remission, . . ."

He stirred beside her, looked at her hard.

Meadow kept talking. "It makes me realize why our baby came along now. If Mom gets sick again, a baby will give her something to live for."

"What an *incredibly* stupid reason to have a baby."

His words, his tone, slapped her across the face. Still, she tried to be upbeat. "You're right. I didn't set out to do this on purpose—neither of us did—but since it's happened, shouldn't we find every reason to rejoice?"

He stood up and moved away from her touch. "Rejoice? About bringing a child into the world with a sometime father and a disgruntled mother?"

Obviously this was not a subject to be easily managed with compassionate words and a loving touch. "I am not disgruntled, and you have no reason to be a sometime father."

"Oh, really? Where are we going to live so that I can be a full-time father—*Natalie Meadow Szarvas?*" His eyes blazed with an eerie triumph as he produced her name and placed it between them like a hot coal.

He was really angry. At her? At him? At their baby? Whatever it was, she didn't like this side of him. He roiled with fury and old, dark, angry memories.

And she . . . she fought a feeling of betrayal. "How long have you known my name?"

"I learned it the day my mother came with those glass pieces. I realized you were an expert; then it didn't take much research to find out your name or where you lived—which is the issue here." He leaned toward her. "We live on different coasts. Unless you've got some brilliant solution, one of us is going to have to move. I've got a business that is centered here. You've got a mother who's critically ill. Which one of us do you think it'll be?"

"You know my name. You've known it for weeks." For some reason, that made her feel as if he'd been laughing at her. "You lied to me about . . . me."

"I wouldn't start flinging accusations around, Meadow, or Natalie, or whatever you like to be called." He mocked her with her own names. "There's plenty of reason for finger-pointing."

"You know what I do for a living. You know about my family."

Her breath came in uneven gasps and burned in her chest. There was an issue here, a bigger issue. She knew it, but she was afraid to look at it. But she had to.

"I know your age, your weight, your IQ."

"You knew about my *mother*?" And that was the real issue. He had known about her mother's illness, and he'd let the farce go on.

He lifted his chin. He stared down his nose.

"You did know. You knew and you didn't offer to help? You knew I was looking for the painting that would pay her bills—and you just let me look?"

In her eyes, Devlin subtly shifted shape. He was no longer the man who frolicked with her in the moonlight, who teased her at dinner, who watched her eat an ice cream cone with a hunger that had nothing to do with the ice cream and everything to do with her. He had become cruel, indifferent, unyielding in his determination to win.

They stood on the chessboard, and she was a pawn.

She had feared that, but she had imagined she could change him, teach him that life was more than winning or losing. She'd fallen in love with him; he was the father of her child—and he was a monster.

Suddenly she found herself reclining on the bed. A red mist swam before her eyes, and her stomach roiled, but as the buzzing in her ears cleared, she could hear him saying, "I found out about your mother yesterday. I was going to offer to help, but I never had the chance. Then *this* happened."

She turned away. She didn't want to hear his excuses. She didn't want to hear him talk about their baby as a *this*.

Maybe he'd been wounded by his father's indifference and his mother's coolness. Maybe he'd been wounded so much he was an emotional cripple. Maybe . . . maybe Meadow had made the ultimate bad choice in men.

"Look, the solution is clear." He walked away, but not far enough—she could still hear him talking.

"We'll sneak off and get married so no one knows we conceived this child out of wedlock."

"Out of wedlock?" She wanted to laugh. She wanted to cry. "I can't believe you care about such a minor matter."

"You wouldn't think it was a minor matter if you'd spent your childhood fighting little snots who called you a bastard." He ran water. "After we're married, I'll build you a studio. The child will have a home with two parents." His voice grew near. He placed a cold wet towel on Meadow's forehead, and directly above her he said, "We'll make the best of a bad situation."

She clenched her teeth against a wave of nausea. Her face flushed; sweat broke out on her forehead. She fought her way back from the brink. "I will not marry you."

"Don't be ridiculous."

"My marriage is not going to be 'making the best of a bad situation.'"

"Possibly I phrased that badly."

"Perhaps you did. And perhaps you meant it just the way you said it."

"Meadow . . ." He tried to take her hand.

She jerked it away. "It doesn't matter. I will never marry you. Not because you're illegitimate, but because what the gossips say about you is true. You really are a bastard."

34

*M*eadow stalked into the house ahead of Devlin. "I am not going to discuss it anymore."

"You haven't discussed it at all." He followed her in and slammed the door. "You simply keep saying no."

"Which part of *no* do you not understand?"

"You're not being logical." And that heated his temper to a simmer. She had to be logical. How else was he going to keep her?

"Logic is overrated," Meadow said coolly. "And superfluous when it comes to love. My grandmother taught me that, and she was the bravest woman I know."

"But not the smartest," he said in frustration.

"No. That would be my mother."

"What's going on?" Grace stood in the doorway of the library, looking from one to the other in alarm.

"Nothing, Mother."

"I'm leaving your son," Meadow said.

"Damn it!" He didn't need the whole household in on this fight.

"Leaving him?" Grace held out her hand to Meadow. "Why?"

"Because like a free-range chicken, I managed to get pregnant." But for all her ire, Meadow couldn't resist Grace's outstretched hand.

"A baby? You're going to have a baby?" Grace held Meadow's arm out and gazed at her midsection, searching for proof. "I'm going to be a . . ."

"A grandmother." From inside the library, Bradley Benjamin cackled. "Did you hear that, Osgood? Grace Fitzwilliam is going to be a grandmother, and to the child of someone named *Meadow*."

"That is too rich," Osgood said.

Great. Just what Devlin needed. The old farts were still here.

Grace walked back into the library, dragging Meadow with her. "You leave her alone, Bradley Benjamin. If you want to take out your nastiness on someone, you take it out on me. I'm not in a delicate condition!"

Devlin followed and found only two old farts—Bradley sitting in the alcove in a brown leather recliner, smoke curling up from the cigar in the ashtray, and Osgood, on Bradley's right, sitting on a straight-backed dining chair, shoulders slumped, hands folded in his lap, his brown eyes wide behind his heavy glass lenses.

Osgood didn't matter. He blended into the scenery. Always had. Always would.

But Bradley sat like a petty god in his own fine heaven, breathing fire as his pretended indifference crumbled one feeble brick at a time.

"Don't worry about him, Grace," Meadow dismissed Bradley. "I have to go pack, anyway."

"No, you don't," Devlin said.

"Please, no," Grace said.

"You don't understand, Grace," Meadow began.

"Make her understand, and maybe I'll get it then, too." Devlin's voice rose with his frustration. "Because right now, I sure as hell do not know why you insist on leaving me."

Meadow interrupted at full volume. "Because I am not raising my child with a man who doesn't understand the difference between right and wrong. You only understand winning and losing."

"But you can't leave him." Grace took Meadow by the shoulders and shook her. "He's worth saving!"

"I don't need to be saved." Devlin couldn't believe his mother thought such a thing.

"I'm not in the salvation business," Meadow said flatly.

"Look, I know he has issues with . . . with intimacy and all that junk, but that's my fault. I'm his mother, and when he was a kid I was so busy trying to get my business going I didn't take the time to show him how to . . . love." Grace rubbed her forehead fretfully. "I don't think I'm very good at it anyway."

"Our relationship, Mother, has nothing to do with this," Devlin said.

The women looked at each other, then at him, and dismissed him with identical shrugs.

"He's an adult, and at some point everyone has to take responsibility for themselves. He's long past that point, so you can stop blaming yourself for your son's being a big, fat jerk." Meadow glared at him.

A cackle came from the chair in the alcove, and with a broad smile Bradley Benjamin rose to his feet. "I am so glad I stayed to look the old place over. I wouldn't miss this for the world!"

"Good! Yes!" Meadow flung an impatient hand out to indicate him. "Hang around and be exhibit A, the lonely, miserable old man Devlin is going to shrivel up and become."

Bradley's smile vanished, and his military posture became stiff and offended. "I am not lonely."

"Just miserable. You want to stay here and gloat over our troubles, because then you can go home to your lonely dinner with its place setting for one, and you can smoke your stinking cigars and no one will complain, and you can die alone and no one will discover you until the other tie-wearing old men notice that, for the third day in a row, you're not at lunch. And, of course, your funeral will be attended by all the right people, but who's going to cry, Bradley?" Meadow's voice shook with conviction. "Who is going to mourn?"

"Meadow." Devlin touched her arm. Later she would be ashamed of the things she'd said.

But not yet.

She jerked away. "Devlin is right. Someone will notice you're MIA before you've been dead for three days, because your little buddy H. Edwin Osgood sticks close, because somehow he gets his sense of importance from you."

"Well, really!" Osgood's lisp and his indignation were pronounced.

"Now I am going to call my mother"—Meadow flipped open her cell phone—"and tell her I'm coming home today. Because she loves me"—her voice thickened with tears—"just because I'm me."

She dialed the number and walked out of the room.

An uncomfortable silence fell.

Devlin looked at the other three.

They looked at him.

And he knew Meadow was right.

He was like his mother—stiff, uneasy with affection, and un-schooled in love. He *did* see everything in terms of winning and losing, but that didn't work with Meadow. Because it didn't matter if he held the power in their relationship—if he didn't have Meadow, he had lost everything.

He started out of the room after her.

"Are you going to crawl after that girl?" Bradley Benjamin couldn't have sounded more masculine and more offended.

Devlin stopped and looked back at him. At exhibit A.

Meadow was right. If he didn't stop worrying he would turn into his father, and brooding about the abuses of his childhood, and wor-rying that someone somehow would take advantage of him right now, he would become Bradley Benjamin, a man without real friends, a man without a family . . . a man without his love.

By God, Devlin was not going to replay Bradley's mistakes. "Am I going to crawl after that girl? On my belly." He turned to walk after Meadow.

"True love triumths," Osgood lisped.

"Shut up, Hop," Bradley said.

Devlin stopped in midstride. He turned to face the two old men. "Hop?"

"Hop. It's his old nickname. Hopkins. H. Edwin Osgood." Bradley sounded impatient, as if that were a fact everyone knew.

And maybe at some point Devlin had known it, but until last night when he heard Four's story about a behind-the-scenes murderer, Osgood's real name had meant nothing.

Of course, it could be a coincidence—but Devlin didn't believe in coincidence. He focused on Osgood. On his glasses, his dyed hair, his bow-tie. Was it possible? Could it all be a disguise?

Osgood came to his feet. As Devlin watched, the foolish, womanizing, Bradley-butt-kissing sycophant faded from view, leaving an old guy with sharp brown eyes that observed him coolly.

Like gunfighters, Osgood and Devlin squared off.

"*You* never have trouble with money." Devlin spoke slowly as he thought the matter through. "*You're* in a good position to know everything that goes on here. *You* live alone in your mansion . . . do you collect art, Mr. Hopkins?"

Grace moved closer to Bradley. "Do you know what he's talking about?"

Bradley looked from one to the other. His gaze lingered on Osgood. "No. What is it you think he's guilty of, Devlin?"

Both Devlin and Osgood ignored him.

Osgood inclined his head. "I have interests in a lot of fields, Mr. Fitzwilliam." He didn't lisp at all. In fact, his voice sounded completely different than Devlin had ever heard it.

"I'll just bet you do." This old fart had been searching the hotel for Isabelle's painting. This crony of Bradley Benjamin's had threatened to kill Bradley's only son, Four. This man whom no one really knew had ordered someone to hit Meadow and push her down the stairs. Devlin took one big step toward Osgood, wrapped his hands around that prissy bow tie, and lifted him up on his toes. "I ought to kill you."

"Devlin! He's an old man!" Grace wavered between horror and confusion. "He's one of us."

"Not unless you're a murderer, Mother. And he's not as infirm as he puts on." Devlin plucked the glasses off Osgood's face and looked through them. A minor correction only. He chunked them aside. "What about the hair?" he asked. "Is it shoe polish?"

"Nothing so crude." Osgood looked into Devlin's eyes, unafraid, slightly contemptuous. "Are you going to snap my neck? Because it's getting damned uncomfortable up here on my tippy toes."

Devlin jerked his hand away. "No. I'm not going to kill you." He went to the security alarm and pushed it.

Osgood massaged his throat. He put his hand to his mouth, held it there a moment, then cleared his throat. "Coward."

Two security guards appeared in the doorway.

"Take Mr. Hopkins into custody." Devlin hesitated, remembering Gabriel's doubts about his people, remembering, too, the reports about Hopkins's long reach and shadowy background. "We'll need more people." He picked up the house phone and dialed Gabriel. With a few brief words he filled him in on the situation. When he hung up, he said, "Gabe's going to call the police and the FBI."

"Do you think that will be enough firepower to keep me?" Mr. Hopkins mocked him, but the old guy looked a little pale and sweaty.

Good. He was worried.

"Osgood. What the hell is wrong with you?" Bradley snapped. "You're acting very oddly."

Osgood looked at Bradley. "Am I?"

"You sound peculiar." Bradley searched Osgood's face with his gaze. He took a step forward. "My God. Who are you?"

"'*What* are you?' would be a better question." Devlin glanced upstairs. He wanted to follow Meadow. He wanted to crawl, to explain that they would not be copies of Bradley and Isabelle. They would be themselves, Devlin and Meadow, in love forever.

But he wasn't going to leave Osgood until someone got here whom he completely trusted.

"Mr. Osgood, are you well?" Grace asked in alarm.

Osgood pulled at his bow tie. "Perhaps . . . not." The sweat was a slick sheen all over his face now, and when he shed his jacket, the armpits were stained.

Grace started toward him.

Devlin caught her arm. "No. Don't go near him. He's dangerous."

"Could I have a chair?" Osgood asked.

One of the security guards started forward, but before he could reach Osgood, Osgood groped behind him, then collapsed in a heap. He clawed at his arm, his chest.

"Heart attack." Bradley massaged his own chest.

"I don't believe it," Devlin said. The old guy was faking it.

"Honestly, Devlin. Look at him!" Grace said.

Osgood turned blue as he tried to get his breath.

So he wasn't faking it. But this was suspiciously convenient. "Are you okay, Mr. Benjamin?" Devlin asked. "Mother, help Mr. Benjamin to sit down."

Grace took Bradley's arm and took him back to his leather chair, then stood there and patted his hand until he snatched it back.

"I'll call an ambulance." One security guard headed for the phone.

The other guard shed his coat. "I'm CPR certified."

Gabriel walked in, took in the situation with one glance, and turned to Devlin. "What happened?"

"I think he took something. He put his hand up to his mouth, then cleared his throat." Devlin watched Osgood spasm.

Hands on hips, Gabriel nodded. "Good probability. That's pretty impressive, that he'd rather die than be arrested."

"Ambulance is on the way." The report from the guard was terse. "Everyone will hold their position until he's gone."

"You're seeing the hotel's emergency plan at work," Gabriel told Devlin. "In case there's a scheme to rescue him."

"Right." In the distance, Devlin heard the wail of sirens.

Emergency personnel poured into the hotel, took charge of Mr. Hopkins, stabilized him, and put him on a gurney.

Devlin and Gabriel followed them out of the library.

Sam stood by the open front door. "I'll ride with him."

Devlin lifted his eyebrows. *Interesting.* Apparently today was a day for all kinds of revelations. "Why should my secretary ride with such a dangerous man?"

"I'm federal agent Sam Mallery. Catching Mr. Hopkins is the reason I'm here." Sam walked out onto the porch, keeping the gurney in sight.

In key places around the yard, security personnel stood at the ready. Gabriel went to talk to the team leader.

Devlin wasn't letting Sam off with revealing so little information. "A federal agent? What is a federal agent doing working for me as my secretary?"

Sam pulled a small, efficient pistol from his holster inside his jacket and scanned the area. "We've known about Mr. Hopkins for years—he controls crime in Atlanta and most of the state of Georgia. We couldn't get a handle on who he was; talking to people in Atlanta got us a lot of information about his voice, about what they thought he might look like, but nothing concrete. He was a ghost. A very efficient, highly corrupt ghost. Then his influence started to edge north, toward South Carolina, and that gave me a lead." Sam never looked at Devlin; he kept his gaze on the emergency people, on the security guards, and most of all, on Mr. Hopkins. "I heard he collected art. He's one of those ubiquitous 'private collectors' you always hear about right after the museum loses a Picasso. That led me to a solid rumor that Waldemar hid an undiscovered masterpiece, and that led me to my career as your secretary."

"You're a damned good secretary for a federal agent." Devlin supposed this meant he didn't need to investigate Sam.

"Had to be. That's how I earned my way through school."

Fascinating. "Did you suspect Osgood?"

"I suspected everyone."

"Except me." Devlin enjoyed the irony of that.

The EMTs were loading Osgood into the ambulance.

"And then only because I knew what you were doing with your

544 · Christina Dodd

time." Sam walked down the stairs and waited for them to finish strapping Osgood and his gurney in place. "Also, Mrs. Fitzwilliam— or rather, Natalie Szarvas—was too young to be Mr. Hopkins. I did realize, though, that she was searching for the painting, and that put her in danger. That's why I had her locked in the closet by one of my agents."

"What?" *What?* What the hell kind of game had Sam been playing?

"I wanted her gone. I as good as told her to leave. I thought that if she told you what sounded like a crazy story about how *she* got locked in by a strange maid, and *I* told you she had locked herself in—and I had a tape to back up my accusations"—Sam grimaced like a man with resources—"you'd throw her out. But you never asked to see the tape. It was too late for me to step between you. You were already in love."

It was almost a knee-jerk reaction. "Not in love. Not then."

Sam climbed into the ambulance and perched on the seat beside Osgood's prone body. "From the first moment you looked into her eyes."

35

The ambulance hit potholes. Osgood felt like crap, but just as it was supposed to, the drug was wearing off. He jolted along. He stared at the ceiling, his eyes wide and unfocused. The federal agent sat beside the gurney, his pistol out, his expression still and tense.

Smart man.

Osgood waited . . . waited.

The wheels struck the pavement. The ride smoothed out.

And the ambulance slammed to a stop.

Before Sam had finished coming to his feet, the back doors whipped open. Two men stood pointing Uzis into the back.

Ah, it was good to have a contingency plan, as well as a contact with the local police who set that plan in motion.

Osgood freed himself from the restraints. He lifted himself up onto his elbows.

Sam looked to the front. The assistant driver had a pistol pointed at the driver.

The EMT on the other side of Osgood held a pistol on Sam, too, and handed Osgood a bottle of water—and the antidote.

Slowly Sam sat back, put his pistol down, and lifted his hands.

"Very wise, Mr. Mallery." Osgood swallowed the pill. He allowed the EMT to give him a hand onto the road. He dusted off his jacket, nodded to Sam, and walked to the waiting black car. Just before his men shut the door behind him, he heard the sound of the pistol as it fired.

He hoped it was one of his men killing the driver or Sam.

But he didn't really care.

~~~~~

When Devlin reentered the house, he saw Meadow.

Her tears had dried up. She held the phone as if it were a grenade. She was pale, but perfectly composed. She flicked a glance at Devlin, a glance that observed and dismissed him. She walked into the library.

Devlin followed.

Grace stood looking out the window.

Bradley Benjamin still sat in the chair, staring into space. He'd just been revealed as a fool, betrayed for years . . . by his old friend.

Meadow wobbled as she stood there, but her gaze steadied on Bradley Benjamin. "I talked to my father. My mother's back in the Hutchison Cancer Institute in Seattle."

Devlin put his arm around her, supporting her.

She didn't notice. All her attention was on Bradley. "She needs a bone-marrow transplant. I've already been tested. I don't match enough markers. But you might."

Bradley Benjamin stood. He looked around. "Me? Why would I match?"

"Because you're her father." Her tone was flat, no-nonsense.

"I am not her father." His faded eyes flashed. "In case you never heard the story—"

"*I* heard the real story." Meadow tapped her chest. "I know the truth. When I was eight and my grandmother got sick, she told me."

"That sounds just like Isabelle. Regale an eight-year-old with the story of her affairs, like they were something to be proud of." Bradley's voice shook with scorn.

"She didn't tell me about her affairs. She told me about *you.*" And obviously Isabelle had been none too kind. "She told me she loved you, but you made her miserable with your rules and your functions."

"She was inappropriate," Bradley said, as if that were a crime.

"She was real. When she had my mom, you and your dictates got worse—she was supposed to give up her art and become the right wife and the right kind of mother, as defined by *you.*" Meadow's scorn was as lively as Bradley's. "When you came to her and accused her of infidelity, she couldn't believe you would think such a thing."

"Her affairs were legion." Bradley's teeth barely separated, and his lips were stiff.

"*After* you divorced her!" Meadow took a breath, and with all the conviction in her slight body, said, "She was faithful to you. You're my grandfather. My biological grandfather. My mother is your daughter."

"Whoa," Devlin whispered. He had never imagined this.

Meadow swiveled. She looked him in the eye. "It's true."

"I don't doubt that for a minute, my love." How could he? The evidence stood before his eyes.

Meadow was a blend of grandmother and grandfather, mother and father, and an essence all her own.

Bradley trembled like a leaf in a gale. "That's twaddle. Isabelle told me she'd slept with that artist."

"No." Meadow walked to the couch. She bent, dug among the cushions, and pulled out a silver key, one to match the key that opened the secret garden. She lifted it, showed it to Bradley on her outstretched palm. "You had the garden cleaned up for her. You loved her. You'd had a child with her. She thought you trusted her. Then you accused her of sleeping with Bjorn Kelly. She agreed because she didn't want to live with a man who knew and valued her so little."

Bradley stood straight, his hands lax at his sides.

Devlin could see the thoughts racing across his mind, the incredulity, the possibility. . . . Devlin was willing to bet the old guy refused to believe Meadow, because if he did, his whole, bitter life was a waste.

Apparently Meadow thought the same thing, because she closed her hand over the key. She made a fist. "Look. It's a simple test. You provide a little DNA and you find out I'm telling the truth. Then you go to Seattle, donate the bone marrow, and save your daughter's life."

Bradley still didn't speak.

"You don't have to. But this is my mother we're talking about, so let me tell you what I'm willing to do to make you comply. I'll drag up the old scandal about Grandmother and you, and how you threw her and her child out without a dime. I'll sue you for what remains of your fortune, and I'll ruin what remains of your life." Meadow sounded cold. Meadow sounded ruthless. Meadow sounded like . . . Bradley.

"My God," Grace whispered. She looked between Bradley and Meadow. "My God."

"The alternative is a simple operation to harvest your bone marrow," Meadow said. "You'll be saving a life. Your daughter's life."

At last Bradley reacted. He staggered backward, fell into the chair.

"He's having a heart attack." *Two in one night!* Devlin leaped toward him.

Meadow followed. "He can't die now!"

But the old man put his head in his hands and gave a rasping sob.

Devlin stopped. He backed up.

The old son of a bitch was crying.

Meadow halted. She stuck the silver key in her jeans pocket. She shuffled her feet and, at last, knelt in front of Bradley. She touched his arm. "Are you okay?"

He took a few long breaths, then lifted his head. His papery cheeks were wet, and he looked at the tears in his hands as if he didn't know what they could be. Then he gazed at Meadow, and his eyes filled again. "My granddaughter?" He touched her cheek. "You're my granddaughter?"

"Yeah."

"She didn't betray me, then. When she said she slept with him, I just . . . just wanted to kill them both."

Meadow caught his hand and squeezed. "I know."

"Because I loved her. I loved her so much."

"She knew that. She told me she knew that."

"Did she? Did she really? Because I don't want to imagine she died thinking I didn't love her."

Meadow nodded.

"I've got to go. I've got to get a plane ticket." Bradley slapped at his pockets. "All right. I've got my wallet. All right." He started to walk away, then made an abrupt turn and came back to Meadow. He bent and kissed her forehead. "Thank you. Thank you."

Devlin sent his mother a speaking glance.

"I'll show you to a phone." Grace tucked her hand into Bradley's arm, and together they exited the room.

As soon as they were out of earshot, Devlin said, "Meadow, we need to talk."

Whatever compassion Meadow felt for Bradley Benjamin, she clearly didn't feel for Devlin. She walked toward the door. "We've already said it all."

"No, we haven't. Please, Meadow. I don't want you to go."

She didn't slow.

He went after her. "I want you to stay, to marry me."

She headed for the stairway.

"You're like her, and I'm like him, but we are not your grandparents."

She climbed the first steps.

He held on to the newel post and looked up at her. "Meadow. I love you."

She turned on him, her cheeks flushed, her blue eyes narrowed and furious. "You would say anything to win, wouldn't you?"

Of all the reactions he'd imagined, he'd never envisioned this one. "You think I'm lying? I've never said that to another woman."

"*Anything* to win," she repeated.

"I'm not saying that to win. I'm saying that . . . because it's true. I love you." How could he articulate it so she believed him?

With Meadow, one way always worked.

He ran up the stairs. He pulled her into his arms. He tried to hug her, to kiss her.

She held herself stiffly. She dodged his lips. In a voice rife with irritation, she said, "Look. Yesterday I was feted as your wife. Last night I was knocked unconscious. Today I found out I was pregnant, that my mother has come out of remission, told my grandfather the truth—and got my heart broken. Let's just drop this for right now, shall we?"

"No." She was slipping away even while he held her. "I can't let you leave me."

She looked up at him and spoke slowly and clearly. "Listen to me. I won't marry you."

36

$\mathcal{D}$evlin let her go. "Before you leave, don't you want to see how I recognized you?"

Meadow so badly wanted to walk away. But she couldn't. The clever bastard had said exactly the right thing to keep her here. "You always knew who I was?"

"From the first moment you opened your eyes."

Her heart took a hard thump. Her eyes. He'd recognized her eyes. "So tell me."

"I have to show you." He walked toward her, toward the door.

She stepped back. She didn't want him touching her. She might say she didn't want him, but that was only her mind and her good sense talking. Her body thought otherwise.

He didn't look at her or acknowledge her caution, although she never doubted that he noticed. He noticed everything, so he could win—by any means. With Devlin, it was victory at any cost.

But he walked past her and down the corridor, not looking back to see if she followed him.

At first she didn't. Stupid, but she suspected a trick.

"I found the proof in the attic," he called back.

That made her start walking, although she kept a safe distance. "What attic?"

"Did you think a great house like this would not have an attic?" He pressed the up button on the elevator. The doors opened at once.

She stopped a few feet away.

"Would you rather take the stairs?" he asked, and to his credit he used no mockery.

She thought about it before she answered. She didn't want to step into the small, confined space with him. She didn't want the discomfort of standing shoulder-to-shoulder with him, not speaking, pretending they were strangers while he sucked up all the oxygen. Or worse, having him talk to her about *whatever,* while she remembered the times, so numerous over the last weeks, when he'd taken a private moment in the elevator to kiss her silly.

"This is fine." She stepped in.

Fine. A tepid word indicating indifference—a false indifference, but he got the message. He didn't like it—his hands clenched— but he kept his voice low and soothing. "When this house was new, the servants lived in tiny rooms under the eaves, and one huge attic room was used for storage. It still is."

She'd seen the dormers sticking out of the roof, but . . . "There isn't any access."

He stared at her. "You looked."

"Of course I looked. I even asked the maids. They said there wasn't; they should know."

"Not this time."

The elevator doors opened on the third floor, and he led her down the corridor toward the blank outer wall paneled with dark wood. Leaning down, he reached into what looked like an outlet and popped a latch. He pressed on one side—and a five-foot section of wall swung on a pivot, revealing a dim, airless passage and, off to the left, narrow, steep stairs. He flicked on the light switch and gestured with an open hand. "You first."

The stairs had a worn carpet covering the treads, and ended in an open space—a corridor above, or perhaps the attic he'd talked about. The passage smelled old, closed up. She didn't like this place. The atmosphere felt . . . unhappy.

"Do you want me to go first?"

She didn't care that he sounded sardonic, as if he believed her vacillation had less to do with an impression of sorrow and had more to do with him. "Please."

"Then be careful. There's no rail." He started up, ducking his head to clear the low ceiling.

She followed. The walls on either side of the stairway weren't more than two feet apart, and she put her hands on them to balance herself.

One tread creaked. "I'm having that one replaced," Devlin said. "Step lightly."

She was glad to do as he instructed. The landing came none too soon, and she breathed a sigh of relief to be on level ground.

But the sensation of unhappiness increased as she stared down a corridor lined with closed doors.

"The servants' quarters." Devlin strode toward the great room at the end.

"What's in them?"

"Rusty iron bed frames. Battered cupboards. Trunks full of junk. When I bought the house I had everything appraised. Some of the better pieces were cleaned, and we're using them in the main part of the hotel. But most of the stuff up here is worthless." Entering the main part of the attic, he moved from one window to another, flinging them open. "Once the hotel is running smoothly, I'll get rid of it."

She followed him. The ceiling slanted from the peak at the middle down to the three-foot-high walls, with windows jutting out in dormers every twenty feet. The sunlight streamed in, and dust motes danced on the beams. The pine floor was unpolished, but in good condition. Scattered throughout the room was a jumble of shabby trunks, cracked vases, and wardrobes tilting drunkenly on three legs.

He stood with his hands on his hips and shook his head. "It's worse than I remember it."

"What a waste." She picked up a pottery bowl, and it fell into jagged halves.

The South Carolina spring made it warm up here. The open windows flushed the heat away, but by no means did they make it cool. She wanted to go hang out the window and pant like a dog in the car. Instead she loosened the top button on her shirt. "Where is this reason why you knew who I was?"

"Watch your step." He wove in and out of the wrecked furniture, making his way to the far wall.

"I will," she said, glaring at a spot right between his shoulder blades. Since he'd discovered she was pregnant, he acted as if she needed to be enclosed in bubble wrap. "I'm simply going to have a baby."

He glanced back.

She banged her knee on the corner of a steamer trunk. She cursed—quietly. That was going to leave a bruise.

Red and blue and yellow oil paints splattered the wall with color. A dusty wooden easel and a large framed canvas was turned backward and leaned against the wall.

Meadow's skin chilled, then heated.

Fifty-five years of accumulated junk had been piled into the room, but she had located the source of the unhappiness.

This was her grandmother's studio. Here Isabelle had painted her last painting. Here she had decided to walk away from Bradley Benjamin. Here her heart had broken.

Was the painting leaning against the wall *the* lost painting? Had she found it at last?

Devlin knelt on the floor before it. "Come and see."

She almost couldn't bear it. She so badly wanted it to be *that* painting, yet even if it was, even if Devlin allowed her to take it to pay for her mother's treatment, it wouldn't make any difference now.

The only thing that would save her mother was a match to her bone-marrow donor. To Sharon's father.

And the chances of a match were never great. Never.

Everything Meadow had done had been for nothing. She'd achieved none of her goals, and she'd had her heart broken.

She pressed her hand to her belly. At least she had her child.

Besides, the painting couldn't be the painting she sought, or Devlin wouldn't have recognized her eyes.

She shrugged off the hovering sense of defeat.

Perhaps the sorrow was not, after all, emanating from the attic, but from her.

Yet she had made the right decision for her and her baby. She didn't dare take the chance of having her child grow up with a father as sour and demanding as Bradley Benjamin. She only wished she were sure Sharon would be there to play the soothing chimes during Meadow's labor, and lift the newborn to the sky and offer it to the sun, and put its handprints in plaster and hang them beside Meadow's in her art studio.

Devlin watched Meadow without smiling, and in a soothing voice he said, "The bone marrow will be a match. Bradley Benjamin has to do one good thing in his life, and this is it."

Devlin's intuition about her thoughts gave her an uneasy feeling, as if she'd already allowed him too much familiarity with her mind to easily dislodge him.

"What is that?" She knelt beside him.

He turned the canvas—and she gazed into a face dominated by large blue eyes framed with sorrow. She saw the tanned skin, the jutting chin, the dark hair, so black there were blue highlights. The technique wasn't polished, and Meadow had never seen her look so young, but she recognized her anyway.

"Grandmother." She broke into a smile. "That's my grandmother."

37

Meadow examined the portrait from every angle. "It's a self-portrait. I'd recognize her style anywhere."

"I know. Look. She signed it, 'Isabelle Benjamin—*Herself.*'" Devlin pointed at the scrawl in the corner.

"She's so solemn!" Meadow touched the paint that formed her grandmother's cheek lightly with her fingertip. It felt dry and almost crumbly. "She must have painted it right before she left Bradley."

"I think so."

"But I don't look like her." She rubbed her fingertips together and frowned. A hint of rose pigment stained her skin.

"Your eyes are exactly like hers."

"Do you think so?" she asked, pleased to think she resembled the woman she had loved so much. Pleased that he thought her eyes were as expressive and beautiful as her grandmother's.

"You can't argue with me. This is how I knew who you are."

She didn't want to argue with him. She was already alone with him in a secluded spot—and considering the short time they'd been acquainted, she comprehended the workings of his mind far too well. He would try to convince her she wanted to stay with him. And she knew the danger there, for her body was a traitor to her mind.

So she ignored the remark and asked the next logical question. "Where did you find the painting?"

"Right here." He gestured at the wall. "After she left, Benjamin must have hidden it so he didn't have to look at the face of the woman he loved."

"Yes. Serves him right," she said. "Poor, stupid old man."

"What will *I* look at? I have nothing of you." He managed to look rugged and gloomy at the same time—an impressive feat.

"You have photos from our engagement party. You have the clothes you bought me hanging in your closet. And what the heck—as a memento, I'll make you a glass vase." When she realized his shoulder pressed against hers, she ruined her derisive effect by scuttling to the side, away from him.

"Will a glass vase contain your smile? The way you burst into the morning full of enthusiasm for the day? The way you dance in the moonlight, naked and glorious? Will it contain the love you've lavished on me without a single thought to how unworthy I am?"

"Right now, I'm thinking about how unworthy you are." She kept her gaze on the large painting, bordered by a wide frame of black enamel and gold leaf. "Look, I'm not going to let you seduce me again."

"I've never seduced you. Not once. You took me every time, took me on joyous trips into forgetfulness, into celebration. So no. I'm not trying to seduce you." His voice grew deep and smooth, as irresistible as heated glass and just as dangerous. "I want *you* to seduce *me.*"

It was true. Always she'd allowed her joy in him to carry her into intimacies. Stupid, ill-advised intimacies. Exasperated, forlorn, she faced him.

A mistake.

His rugged, Liam Neeson face hadn't changed; it was as striking and as manly as ever. But his eyes, his wide, dark eyes, humbly pleaded with her.

But she had learned her lesson. She didn't believe them. She would not believe him. And it infuriated her that she wanted to. "What do you want? Is this about *winning*? Before I walk out of your life, do you have to *win* one last time?"

"Yes. You're walking out of here, taking all the sunshine with you, taking my soul, taking my heart. You're going to go across the country, and I'll see you once a month when we fly to some airport to hand our baby to each other, and the best I can hope for is that she looks like you. I want you to stay here with me. I want to make you happy, and have you make me happy. I consider that winning." He sat down on the floor, crossed his legs, and looked at her. "So yeah. This is all about winning."

Clever, clever man. He'd managed to take a humble, supplicant posture—as if she believed he could ever be humble or a supplicant. "I'd be more impressed if you'd mentioned your heart and soul before you found out I was pregnant."

"I didn't even realize I had a heart until you said you were leaving me. Haven't you wondered why, once I knew who you really were, I didn't go to your family and demand an explanation? Why, once I learned of your mother's cancer, I didn't corner you? Threaten you to discover what you thought you could find? I didn't want to expose you. If I did that, I would have had no reason to keep you by my side." He took her hand. "Meadow, I love you."

She pulled it away. "You wanted to use me to get to my grandfather."

"Honey, I did that the first time he saw you. That angina he suffered was perfect. Not fatal, just painful."

"Typical." And very like Devlin. *Don't kill your enemies; hurt them so you can watch them suffer.*

The trouble was . . . she wanted to believe him so badly. She wanted to live with him, have him there while she delivered the baby, watch him carry their kid around in a little hard hat while he dealt with his construction projects. She wanted to dance in the moonlight with him, wake up at his side, make love until they were both exhausted.

But he'd proved she didn't know him at all.

She didn't know his mother, either. She had thought Grace would jump at the chance to get rid of her unconventional daughter-in-law. Instead she'd been upset, and her pleading stuck in Meadow's mind. *Please give him a chance. He's not bad—yet. You make him happy. You can save him.*

She didn't want a man she had to save. She wanted a man to stand at her side, solid and dependable, a man to be the father to her children, a man who supported her art . . . a man who loved her.

Devlin could be that man.

Or he could be a fraud, lying in every way about everything.

There was no in-between.

And in her heart of hearts, she didn't think he was a fraud.

"The baby . . ." she began.

"I like children. I've never had much to do with them, but no matter how this turns out between the two of us, I promise I'll be a good father to our child." He took her hand again.

Typical. Never give up.

He continued, "But the baby has nothing to do with this. I would still love you so much I'd make love to you without a thought to a condom, because whenever I'm with you, all the shields I've built over all the years disappear and I'm as open and as vulnerable as any fool in love." He tapped his chest. "You can refuse me now and know I'm bleeding."

She couldn't help it. She grinned at the way he phrased it. "So if I refuse you now, you'll bleed and never try to make me change my mind." She watched him struggle to find the best, most tactful way to explain he didn't give up.

She checked her watch.

He opened his mouth.

She interrupted him before he could get a single word out. "Never mind. I know you too well."

"I'll give up when I see you're sure."

He was pretty good at needling her with the truth, too. "We've got nothing in common," she burst out. "We come from different parts of the country. Our backgrounds couldn't be more dissimilar. You're in a cutthroat business with suits and wrecking balls. You read construction magazines, and I read—"

"*The Secret Garden.*"

"Yes! I'm an artist to the very roots of my soul."

"And yet we love each other."

"A shark may love a bumblebee, but where do they build a house?" she asked tartly.

"I would build my house anywhere you want if you would live in it with me." In a voice that enticed and beckoned, he said, "We could even live in Majorca."

"Really? I've always wanted to go there." *Focus, Meadow.* "I don't know if we can find a middle ground."

"We don't have to find a middle ground. If you want to live in a commune, I'll live there with you. I can't promise I won't improve the place. . . ." He searched her face. "This concern is so practical. So un–Meadow-who-dances-in-the-moonlight."

"I remember my grandmother very well." She looked at the painting, touched it again. The paint felt dried-up, bloodless. "She made her life. She painted. She raised Sharon. She walked. She took lovers. She was happy. But underneath . . . something was missing. She never loved another man after Bradley. She wanted him, and they couldn't live together. They were too different."

"The circumstances are similar, but not the same, because I'm not Bradley Benjamin, and you're not your grandmother. Look, Meadow, all I can promise is that you're the best thing that ever happened to me, and I'll love you forever. But if it makes you feel any better"—he pulled a paperback out of his jacket pocket and placed it on the floor between them—"things in common is a bridge that can be built."

38

The Secret Garden.

Meadow picked up the book.

It had been read. The spine was bent and a corner of the cover frayed.

"While you were in the hospital, I went to the gift shop—and found this. They'd received one copy that day. Now, I'm not a man who believes in signs"—Devlin had a talent for understatement—"but I couldn't ignore this one. So I bought it."

"And?"

"Read it in the waiting room." Her incredulous stare made him add hastily, "Not *all* of it. But I finished it before I went to sleep this morning."

"Weren't you afraid the other guys would think it was mushy?" She sounded snotty even to herself.

"When have I ever indicated I cared what the other guys thought?"

"All right." She couldn't stand to wait. She had to know. "What did you think?"

"Do you remember the miracle at the end, when Archie's dead

wife called him back to the garden?" Devlin leaned toward her, and his eyes glowed. "It sent chills up my spine."

She told herself she was inured to his charms, but she couldn't help herself. She had to respond with enthusiasm. "Wasn't that cool?"

"And proof that love never dies, but sometimes goes astray."

She should have known every word he said was to make his point.

But apparently he was finished talking, because he reached out and took her in his lap.

She tucked her head down to avoid his kiss.

He nipped at her ear.

With a gasp, she lifted her head to admonish him.

And the kiss he gave her made her forget how to scold, how to speak, how to breathe. Or perhaps he made her forget any reason to do anything except kiss him back.

When he lifted his head, she lay sprawled across his lap, eyes closed, a smile on her face. But she wanted him to know, without a doubt, that she hadn't been swayed by his kiss. Or at least . . . not only by his kiss. "I'm marrying you because of Mia," she informed him.

"Who?"

Her eyes popped open. "In Jordan's kitchen. Mia. The saucier."

He still appeared bewildered.

Yet she would bet he remembered. He recalled every person in his employ. "If you had never done a single noble thing before in your life, I'd know you were a hopeless case, but you helped that woman."

"I did?"

"You hired her when she desperately needed a job."

He stopped pretending he didn't know what she was talking about and gave her a cool, pragmatic response. "I needed someone local in the kitchen. I gave her the position because she fit the bill."

"You gave her a position and a decent wage. That's more than anyone else in this town was willing to do."

"She's doing a good job or I'd toss her out the door, divorce or no divorce, family or no family." The glint in his chocolate brown eyes was frosty, as if she'd accused him of nepotism.

"You gave her a chance, and then you gave her another chance. When most employers would have fired her, you helped her with her son." Meadow tapped his nose. "She worships you."

"Good God." His mouth, his wonderful mouth, turned down in dismay. "I can deal with only one woman who worships me at a time."

"Who do you have now?" She innocently blinked at him.

He kissed her again.

"Oh, yeah. I remember." She sat up and pushed her hair out of her eyes.

"So we'll get married right away." He was never a man to rest on his laurels. "In Majorca. On the beach where we first took our vows, with the breeze blowing softly over our flushed faces and—"

She interrupted before he could tempt her. "Nice try. We'll get married in Washington at my folks' place. Grandmother would like that." She glanced at Isabelle's portrait and saw a chunk of paint in the corner of the canvas that had crumbled. Leaning closer, she frowned. "Grandmother must not have known what she was doing. This is the wrong kind of paint. Look." She touched the chip—and a two-inch patch of pigment crumbled to dust.

She caught her breath in dismay. "Oh, no!" All around the hole the paint peeled back, begging to be removed. The canvas beneath glistened with golden light.

She stared at it, snared by an absurd thought. Excitement caught her by the throat. Was it possible . . . ? Could her grandmother have been so devious? With her middle finger she thumped the bare spot. More paint crumbled.

"What are you doing?" He caught her wrist. "Be careful. This is the art you've been searching for!"

"I think you're right. I think it might just be." In that corner, the other corner, her grandmother's forehead, all over, the paint was flaking off. Meadow leaned close, so close her nose was almost touching the canvas. "There's an oil painting underneath."

"An oil painting. Why would she paint over oil with water-based paints? That doesn't make sense."

"It does if she was trying to hide something very valuable . . . in plain sight." Gently Meadow removed his fingers from her wrist. As she picked at the chips, she revealed bits and pieces of the domestic scene—a Dutch mother holding a child, a father reading to his sons, a fire in the hearth, and steam rising from a kettle.

"But . . . Isabelle's self-portrait." He sounded appalled.

"She painted other self-portraits, and I promise they're better. She didn't waste time on this one. This one was not for posterity." Meadow held out her hand. "Give me your handkerchief."

Pulling it out of his pocket, he handed it over.

She used it to scrub at the painting until all of the overlay crumbled onto the floor.

Now every part of the scene shone. The oils looked as fresh and glorious as the day they'd been painted by a master hand.

"The Rembrandt," she whispered in awe.

"Rembrandt? It can't be a—" He stopped. Stared. Imitated her by leaning so close to the painting his nose almost touched.

She grinned as she watched amazement dawn on his face. He looked up at her. "It's a Rembrandt!"

"The lost Rembrandt. There have been rumors about it for years. My grandmother found it hanging in one of the guest bedrooms here at Waldemar. She tried to tell Bradley, but he laughed at her. She tried to tell Bjorn, but he laughed at her. She was on her way to fame in the art world, but this was the fifties. No one believed a mere woman could find the lost Rembrandt."

"Surely she could have convinced someone!"

"When she found it, she was in the last stages of pregnancy."

"Ladies don't put themselves forward while they're expecting." He understood.

She had thought he would, son of the South that he was.

"After my mother was born, Isabelle's unhappiness intensified. Her mother-in-law held sway in her house. Bradley didn't want her to paint anymore. They installed a horror of a nurse who barely let her near the baby." Suddenly nervous, Meadow rubbed her palms on her jeans.

"My mother wouldn't dream of interfering with our baby. We'll be lucky if she deigns to speak to it until it's eighteen." He put his arm around Meadow. "And I'll let you hold the baby when I'm not."

Meadow laughed and relaxed. Leaning her head against him again, she examined the painting once more. It was beautiful. It was a miracle. For the first time since she'd received her mother's call, she believed her mother would be cured, that Bradley Benjamin's bone marrow would match, that once again Sharon Szarvas would be healthy and vibrant.

Returning to the story, she said, "Grandmother knew she was going to leave Bradley. She couldn't stand to take anything of his, but she didn't want the painting to be thrown away, either. She considered it her daughter's heritage. When I was old enough she told me all about it. I was thrilled. I wanted to go and get it right away. But when I told my mother, she said no. She wanted nothing to do with her father, and considered that taking a painting out of his house would be stealing."

"Ah. That's why you didn't tell your mother where you were going."

"That's why."

"I wonder how she's going to greet Bradley Benjamin."

The answer was easy. "The universe sent me here, now, to get him for her. Why else would all this have happened?"

"That's coincidence. Actually, the universe sent you here, now, so I could get you." He kissed the top of her head, and when she looked up at him, he kissed her mouth. "What do you think the painting is worth?"

"At least twenty-five million," a strange woman's voice said.

They looked up, startled.

Judith stood beside a tall wardrobe near the entrance.

"Judith!" Meadow half stood. "I've been worried about you. I haven't heard from you since . . ." A recent memory, truly forgotten and now recalled, stirred in her mind, and horror chilled her.

Devlin put his hand on her thigh. "Meadow. Who is that?"

She didn't look down at him. Didn't take her gaze off Judith. "That's the woman who's an old family friend. That's the woman who's supposed to be with my mother." She locked eyes with Judith. "That's the woman who pushed me down the stairs."

39

When Devlin looked at the woman by the door, he saw a threat to be eliminated. He also saw the broad expanse of floor between them, the clutter of antique trunks, warped cabinets, and a myriad of broken appliances, vases—the clutter of bygone days—as well as Judith's cold, steady, calculating eyes.

He wasn't at all surprised when she pulled a pistol from the holster under her black jacket.

His gaze flicked around the huge room, seeing the chest, close to him but not much protection.

In a tone that mocked Meadow's chagrin, Judith said, "And I'm the woman who wants you to bring me the painting." She leveled the black eye of a pistol at Meadow. "Now."

Devlin remembered Judith's face. He'd seen her before. But where?

"Has my mother been alone the whole time I've been gone?"

As always, Meadow surprised him. This woman with the cold, flat eyes of a snake held a pistol on them, and Meadow asked questions about her mother.

Judith shrugged irritably.

Devlin diagnosed her reaction with surprise. She felt guilty.

"Your father was with her." Her husky, New York–accented voice tipped him off.

"You're a security guard here," he said. He'd seen her shadowed face on the tiny screen of his walkie-talkie. Now he could assess her. She was short and stout, and she wore the uniform all female security guards wore—a straight dark skirt, a plain white shirt, dark jacket, and sensible heels. She resembled a fifties housewife, if fifties housewives carried a Glock 26 made of superlight plastic polymer with a steel slide and sixteen rounds.

She wanted that painting, and she would kill Meadow and him, walk away, and never glance back.

Her gaze flicked to him. "I had the best references—from Mr. Hopkins."

"He just went to the hospital with a heart attack." And Devlin *had* done Four an injustice.

"So I'll get the credit *and* the painting." Judith smiled like a warped Mona Lisa.

He glanced again at the furniture. At the windows in their dormers. The night table with the cracked marble top. The tall antique wardrobe that staggered under the influence of a broken leg. The wardrobe held potential as a weapon. . . .

"Be quiet, Devlin!" Meadow said fiercely. She turned back to Judith. "My father can throw clay and blow glass, but he can't balance a checkbook, and you know it!" In an exasperated gesture, she pushed her hair off her forehead. "How could you leave them alone?"

"When you came out with the painting, I needed to be here to take it off your hands." Judith's voice was soft, emotionless. Her pupils swallowed the color from her eyes, giving them all the compassion of a snake's.

"You were going to steal the painting from me? The painting that would save my mother's life? Why? Why?" Meadow was almost stammering. "You have money. Why?"

"It's a *Rembrandt*," Judith said fiercely. "Do you know how much prestige goes to the person who discovers a lost Rembrandt? By God,

I may not be able to throw clay or blow glass like you or your father, or paint like your mother or your grandmother. But I'll go down in history as the woman who discovered the Rembrandt." She glanced at the painting, and her eyes gleamed avariciously. "Mr. Fitzwilliam, bring me the Rembrandt"—the gun focused on Meadow—"or I'll shoot her."

She'd been watching him, or listening to rumors, or both, for she knew exactly how to force his hand.

And he would give her the Rembrandt. The painting didn't matter to him—except that it was his, and what was his remained his—but he knew very well that once she had the painting, she could escape only if she killed him, and Meadow, and his child. That he would not allow. "Get behind the wardrobe," he said to Meadow.

He wasn't at all surprised to see her lift her chin at him. "What am I supposed to do, let her shoot you?"

"I can run and dodge." He used his eyes to reassure and command. "You . . . you are carrying my child." He waited until she nodded, reluctant but acknowledging. "Now . . . get behind the chest of drawers."

"It's not the chest of drawers that will protect me." She turned the large painting long side up and pulled it in front of her.

"What are you doing?" Judith's steady hand suddenly shook. "Meadow, what the hell are you doing?"

Genius. His little darling was a genius. Judith wouldn't shoot the painting, and Meadow had provided a distraction—for him.

He hit the floor and rolled behind a trunk.

A spray of bullets followed him. Splinters flew.

But he wasn't hit yet.

With the three-legged wardrobe as his goal, he dodged from the trunk to a cabinet.

The shooting stopped. Judith wasn't sure which way he'd gone.

"Judith, this isn't what we do." Meadow was moving.

Damn it. He could hear her shuffling to the side. Why couldn't she do as she was told? Why couldn't she just stay put?

But she used her words like poison darts. "I can't believe you're willing to kill for a *thing*. Possessions aren't art. It's the soul that matters—"

If she said, *What goes around, comes around*, he was going to kill her.

"—And you know what goes around, comes around."

"Shut up." Judith had probably never meant anything as sincerely in her life.

He heard her footsteps moving into the center of the room, away from obstructions . . . looking for him.

She shot as he dashed toward the entrance. Toward the three-legged wardrobe.

Bullets followed him, spraying wood chips in a path . . . toward his ass.

Agony ripped his calf.

He was hit. He was hit.

Goddamn it. Judith had put a bullet in his leg.

He stumbled. Made it to the buffet. The mirror shattered as the ammo smacked it. Glass pierced him. Shards pierced him. He didn't care. His leg hurt so fucking bad . . . in football, some big, stupid defensive tackle had broken his tibia, but the pain was nothing compared to this. This was agony. This was hell.

He glanced down. Saw the splash of crimson on his jeans, the shredded denim, the broken flesh.

He measured the distance to the wardrobe.

He wasn't going to have the speed he needed to knock over the wardrobe. Not and walk away alive.

Well.

So be it. He had experienced the greatest love a man could know, all in the space of three weeks. He had created a child . . . with Meadow. If he didn't survive . . . She would. She must.

If he threw himself across the open space, even if Judith shot him, his body would smack the wardrobe as a projectile.

He planned that it would strike Judith. He trusted Meadow to get out alive.

And he had to run before his leg was worthless.

Dimly he heard Meadow talking, talking. "The value of the painting is nothing if it's stained with blood—"

"Shut up," Judith said fiercely. "Just shut up and give me that painting."

"If I give it to you, you'll kill me," Meadow said, "and I carry the future within me. Don't you see, Judith—"

Devlin gathered himself to dash into the open.

As he did, the floorboards in the corridor creaked. He caught a flash of movement out of his peripheral vision.

Four, that damned fool of a Four, staggered out of the corridor and into the room, bottle in hand.

He spotted Devlin. He pointed—damn him, pointed right at Devlin—and in a slurred voice he yelled, "See, Devlin? I told you it wasn't me. I didn't push Meadow down the stairs."

"Go back," Meadow yelled.

"Fuck," Judith said, and blasted Four with a shot.

Four screamed, spun, and dropped like a rock.

Devlin didn't wait to see him hit the ground. Using his arms, he lunged up and over the buffet.

Judith reacted a second too late. She shot. She missed.

And he was still alive.

He smacked the wardrobe with all the force of a linebacker.

With a groan and in slow motion, the wardrobe tilted toward Judith. For a split second it hung in the air. The doors flew open. Books, dried tubes of paint, the bare ceramic base of a lamp fell out and rolled across the floor toward him.

Judith backed up, hands up to protect herself, eyes bright with fury, pistol pointed at the ceiling.

With a crash that shook the floor, the wardrobe slammed down. One door flew into the air. The cloud of dust blinded Devlin.

"Bastard!" The epithet exploded from Judith with force and virulence.

He hadn't killed her.

He couldn't stop yet.

But when he tried to take a step, pain ripped through him. His leg collapsed.

Through the settling dust he saw Judith. She sat on a rickety trunk, blood trickling from a gash on her cheek and soaking her sleeve. She held the pistol with both hands, and she pointed it right at Devlin.

He had nowhere to go.

His leg couldn't go there even if he did.

He was going to die—and he hadn't saved Meadow. She was going to die, too.

His gaze met hers.

No time for apologies. He was losing consciousness. He put his hand on his heart to indicate his love.

Meadow inclined her head and, in the most detached voice he'd ever heard her use, she said, "Judith, if you shoot him, I'm going to stab the Rembrandt."

He couldn't believe it. No matter how long he lived, he would never forget the sight that met his eyes.

Meadow held the painting at an angle in front of her, the large silver key poised, point down, above the canvas.

"What?" Judith whirled and stared at Meadow.

"You can try to shoot me. You might succeed. You might hit the Rembrandt or damage it." Meadow's amazing blue eyes narrowed until she looked . . . menacing. Very unlike Meadow. "But if you shoot Devlin, I guarantee you're going to end up with a painting so mutilated, the only thing you'll get credit for is screwing up a masterpiece."

He'd never seen Meadow sound so calm.

He'd never seen anyone look so cold as Judith.

Carefully she aimed the pistol at Meadow's head.

Meadow's cool look of menace was reflected on his face. Picking up the base of the lamp, he used all of his rusty football skills, aimed, and threw it at Judith's head. It hit with a resounding smack, knocking her off the trunk and out of sight.

He subsided, breathing harshly, pain-racked, covered with sweat.

He was done.

He had to trust Meadow to handle the rest.

He drifted on a sea of pain.

And when the pain turned into agony, he opened his eyes with a start.

Meadow sat beside him, eyes intent, ripping off his leg.

He was all for it if that would make the misery stop.

Dr. Apps materialized out of nowhere with a large, white-coated goon carrying two huge bags. She didn't even say hello. She merely took over the job of ripping off his leg.

"Hang on, Devlin." Meadow kissed a hand. His hand. "Just hang on."

Two of the security people walked past, holding handcuffs.

The pain in his leg eased. A little.

The security people walked past again, Judith staggering between them, a round, bloody circle in the shape of the lamp on her forehead.

"Nice throw, Devlin." The volume of Meadow's voice wavered as if someone were changing the volume.

Devlin tried to speak, but could only shape the word with his lips. *Four?*

"The emergency people say he'll be fine."

Devlin looked up at Meadow. He'd lost a lot of blood. He couldn't feel his fingers. The bullet had shredded his leg. The world was narrowing to the tiny pinprick of light that was Meadow. He was dying, and he didn't want to go. He wanted to stay here with her. He whispered, "Remember Majorca. Remember, you were walking down the beach in a sundress and you saw me and kissed me. . . ."

"Because I loved you the first time I saw you." She smiled at him, but her smile trembled as though she were scared. "Then I took your hand and led you down the beach to a secluded cove, where we made love."

He couldn't see her anymore, but he could still hear her. And in his mind he could see Majorca, and feel her hands on him, and remember falling in love with her for the first time all over again.

The story he'd made up wasn't a lie.

It just hadn't happened yet. . . .

40

At the sound of the scream, Devlin's head whipped around.

His gaze followed his mother's pointing finger. Then he ran past Eddy and Firebird, down the beach through the small, muttering crowd, and toward the waves.

"She's making a break for it."

"I knew she wouldn't make it through this wedding without trying to escape."

"Poor thing. All this trauma has been too much for her."

In a panic he plunged into the Mediterranean, ruining his leather shoes and soaking his Armani suit to the knees. Reaching down, he caught his nine-month-old daughter as she plunged under the surface. Lifting her out of the water, he held her to his chest and headed back for shore.

She squalled and kicked at being pulled out of the waves, while from under the flower-strewn arbor he heard Meadow laughing— laughing because she had taught Willow how to swim and was proud of their fearless daughter.

Sharon headed for him, her arms outstretched. "Aren't you a smart girl?" she cooed.

Willow wailed louder and tried to climb over his shoulder toward the sea.

"Don't encourage her." Devlin pulled out his handkerchief to wipe the sweat of fear off his face, and realized it was soaked with seawater.

"But of course we should encourage her," Sharon said. "She's learning her path, and as her guides, we should help her find her feet."

"Maybe she could find them somewhere besides underwater," Grace snapped. Then, in a mournful tone, she said, "Oh, look. She ruined her outfit."

At the sound of Grace's voice, Willow's crying cut off as if by a knife. Her bald head swiveled around, her big blue eyes fixed on Grace, and with a gurgle of delight, she held out her arms.

"No." Grace backed up, her hands fending Willow off.

Willow leaned forward, babbling her joy at seeing her grandmother.

"No, no." Grace wore a stylish hat, open sandals, and a beige linen suit, ironed within an inch of its life.

"Here. Let me take her." Sharon wore a yellow, off-the-shoulder cotton shirt and a gathered tie-dyed skirt and and she was barefoot.

Willow shook her head no at Sharon, and again reached for Grace.

"Come on, honey. Your *other* grandma loves you." Sharon also wore a scarf wrapped around her bare head, and a wide hat to protect skin made fragile by a massive dose of radiation and the subsequent bone-marrow transplant.

"Oh, for heaven's sake. Give her to me!" Grace took the dripping child and held her away from her pristine designer outfit.

Willow gave her a big, one-toothed grin.

"Oh, for heaven's sake," Grace said again, and cuddled his baby. Revulsion at the sopping diaper battled with delight at Willow's adoration. She smirked at Sharon.

Devlin exchanged a look with Meadow.

Their mothers were fighting again—what a surprise. Two more different women there could not be, and their rivalry was intense and focused—on Willow. Willow, who adored them, and had already learned to manipulate them both.

"Shall we start once more?" the minister asked.

Devlin's shoes squished with water and sand as he joined Meadow under the arbor and took her hand. He smiled into her eyes.

The minister began the ceremony all over again.

Meadow wore a simple white dress. She had flowers in her red hair, carried a bouquet of orange blossoms, and, like her mother's, her feet were bare. Her nose was freckled, she had a burn on her finger from her latest glass project, and she watched him as if everything he did and was amazed her.

Meadow was the bride of his dreams—and this was the wedding of his dreams.

Although the other weddings had been, each in its way, an experience he would treasure. The first wedding, occurring within two weeks of those traumatic events in the attic at Waldemar, took place in the cedar grove outside Meadow's home in Washington, and involved not one, but two invalids. Sharon refused to start her radiation and bone-marrow transplant until after the ceremony, but although she'd welcomed Devlin with open arms, she'd been wan and quiet, and leaned hard on the much-warier River.

Devlin's leg had supported him long enough for him to stand up with Meadow while the woo-woo holy woman (as his mother called her) had intoned a blessing and waved a crystal over the happy couple. Luckily, the pain helped him keep a straight face when he glanced at Grace, immaculate in her mother-of-the-groom dress with the matching pillbox hat, and standing lopsided with her Prada slingback heels sunk into the forest floor.

And at Four, equally immaculate in his idea of spring-wedding casual—a Dolce & Gabbana goatskin blazer and striped poplin pants.

And at Bradley Benjamin, dressed like a proper Southern gentleman and torn between horror at the other guests, who consisted of artists and distressingly casual locals, and worry and affection for a daughter he'd barely met and from whom he desperately wanted to win acceptance.

But his bone marrow had matched Sharon's on all six points, and his willingness—no, his need—to donate for Sharon and help her with her cure had begun the healing between father and daughter.

An interesting couple had crashed the wedding in Washington— a tall, broad-shouldered, Italian-looking man with a tall, gorgeous blonde on his arm. Devlin had recognized them right away; his brother Roberto Bartolini and his new wife, Brandi. That had been an interesting, potentially uncomfortable meeting made easy by Meadow's openhearted welcome and Roberto's Italian enthusiasm for family.

Now there were periodic phone calls and the occasional visits between the couples, and the idea of having brothers no longer seemed so alien to Devlin.

After that first wedding, Devlin and Meadow had lived in Washington. Meadow had cared for the artists' colony and grown ever more pregnant. While commuting between the two coasts, Devlin had gotten to know all her friends, especially the Hunters, the Russian grape-growing family up the road.

Sharon received her father's bone marrow—and damn near died. Devlin still broke a sweat when he remembered the look on Meadow's face the day he walked in to find Sharon had checked herself out of the hospital and gone home to live out her days.

She'd survived, but it had been a near thing, and Devlin didn't know whether Willow's birth or Sharon's stubborn determination to survive longer than Grace had contributed more to her continued existence.

A few months after Willow's birth, he and Meadow celebrated their wedding and Willow's christening at the Secret Garden *in* the secret garden by the waterfall. It had been, his mother announced with satisfaction, a real wedding with an ordained Methodist minister, Meadow trussed into a formal wedding gown, Devlin in a tux, and the guests, including Sharon and River, suitably if uncomfortably attired in dresses and suits.

Eddy hadn't been able to return from Europe in time for the first wedding in Washington, but this time he did indeed make a radiant maid of honor.

The first two weddings had been for their parents.

This wedding on the beach on Majorca at sunset was for them.

When Devlin and Meadow finished their vows and faced the smiling crowd, he knew he had truly given his heart and soul into Meadow's safekeeping.

And she knew he nurtured her heart and soul with equal care.

She looked around at her family and friends.

At her mother, cancer-free at last. At her father, quietly pleased for his daughter, but even more than that, ecstatic at the chance to visit the famous glassblowing centers of Europe. At Grace, wrinkled, disheveled, and thoroughly in love with her granddaughter. At Willow, wearing Grandmother's hat and teething on Grandmother's Christian Dior sunglasses. At Four, fidgeting because he'd given up his cigarettes. And at Bradley Benjamin, who, God help him, had tried for casual and managed old-guy absurd in a flowered shirt, shorts, and sandals with socks.

And at Devlin, still too rugged to be handsome, still tall and dark, still hers . . . and still alive. She had nightmares about that scene in the attic, about the amount of blood he'd lost before the paramedics got the bleeding stopped, about the damage done by the bullet to the muscle. He had survived both the hospital and rehab without incident, but when she woke at night and snuggled close and kissed him, he always kissed her back.

He'd been too close to death for her to take his existence for granted.

Now he lifted her hand in his and announced, "The party's set up in my yard right above the beach. Let's go up and celebrate our wedding!"

"Again!" Four raised his sweating glass to them.

"We're well married," Meadow answered.

"Third time's a charm," Devlin said cheerfully.

On the fringe of the crowd, an uninvited guest caught her eye. He removed his sunglasses and nodded once.

She gripped Devlin's arm. "Look. It's Sam!"

The day he rode away in the ambulance with Mr. Hopkins was the last time they'd seen him. The ambulance had been found empty except for the frightened driver and his dead assistant. Mr. Hopkins had disappeared completely. And repeated inquiries about Sam to the government and other officials had yielded no information.

The Rembrandt had gone to auction and brought in twenty-nine million American dollars. Judith had plea-bargained for a lesser sentence, and with her testimony and Four's, the feds had put a price on Mr. Hopkins's head.

The $29 million was rightfully Devlin's, but he had declared he was no fool. He'd turned the fortune over to Meadow, who had paid her mother's bills, given Bradley Benjamin a generous finder's fee, set up a small trust fund for Four—because, as she told Devlin, how else was he going to survive? He wasn't good for anything except entertainment—and used the rest for art scholarships in her grandmother's name.

Now Sam appeared, apparently hale and healthy. He watched their guests trudge up the path to Devlin's estate; then, as solemn as ever, he walked toward them. "Congratulations on your marriage."

"Oh, Sam!" Meadow threw her arms around him. "We hoped you were alive!"

Sam suffered her embrace without yielding an inch.

When she let him go, Devlin shook his hand. "Good to see you again, Sam."

"Good to see you, too, Mr. Fitzwilliam. And thank you for asking about me. At the time I wasn't able to respond to your inquiries."

"We suspected you were in deep cover." It was so good to see his pleasure at meeting them. At least, Meadow thought it was pleasure—with Sam, pleasure looked pretty much like indifference or anger or relaxation.

"I wanted to thank you both for your assistance with my investigation last year. In my line of employment I work for a lot of people, and Mr. Fitzwilliam, your organizational abilities and astute eye made my task easier." Sam replaced his sunglasses. "If you ever would like a job with the government—"

"What? No!" Indignant and incensed, Meadow stepped between Sam and Devlin. "He does *not* want a job with the government, and if I ever caught wind of him taking a job with the government—and I'm just as astute as he is—I would hunt you down and hurt you, Sam Whoever-you-are!"

Devlin caught her arm and pulled her toward him. "I believe I just declined, Sam."

"So I see." Something that might pass for a smile on anyone else tugged at Sam's lips.

"Would you like to come to the party?" Devlin gestured up the path.

"No, actually, I'm leaving the island as soon as possible." Yet Sam lingered, scrutinizing them as if looking for a flaw. Abruptly he said, "The investigation into your father and the disappearance of his fortune is reaching a climax, and soon there'll be closure for you and your brothers."

"How many brothers?" Meadow asked.

"What kind of closure?" Devlin took a step toward him.

"I can't say. I just wanted you to know." With a peculiarly Sam-like nod of farewell, he strode off down the beach until the setting sun swallowed him.

"That is a seriously weird guy," Meadow said. "I thought so the first time I opened my eyes and saw him, and I think so now."

"Hmm. Yes. I remember. You took one look at me and fell at my feet."

"Who has amnesia now?" *Smart-ass.*

Devlin tugged her toward him. "What did you think the first time you opened your eyes and saw me?"

She sniffed. "I thought you were rude and scary."

"And?"

"And sexy. And you smelled good."

"That's better."

From the party above them, the music started. People were laughing. Someone was singing. They heard the popping of corks and the clinking of glasses.

But here on the beach they were alone with the sea and the sunset—and each other.

He smiled down at her. "I thank God for the night you broke into my house and fell on your head hard enough to declare you had amnesia."

"And I thank God you saw my resemblance to Isabelle and said we were married."

"I don't know what wild hair got into me to make me say that." He shook his head, as if his own behavior bewildered him.

"I don't either, but every time you made up one of those fantasies about Majorca, I fell deeper under your spell." She kissed his chin.

"Have you ever wondered . . . ?" But it was such a silly thing to say.

"Have I ever wondered . . . what?"

He wanted to hold her, but he didn't want her looking at him while he offered his idea, so he wrapped his arms around her and brought her close, her back to his chest. "Have you ever wondered if your grandmother Isabelle sent you to Waldemar because she loved Bradley and wanted to give him another shot at happiness?"

"What a nice idea." Meadow leaned her head back against his chest. "You do realize my family's woo-woo quotient is rubbing off on you?"

"Don't be ridiculous." He looked over her head and across the water, where the last rays of the sun tipped the waves with gold. "I'm

Southern, and while Washington state was still primal forest, we had ghosts haunting our houses."

"You and I aren't so different after all."

He hooted. "Are you kidding? Did you see our guests? Our families? And look at us!" He indicated her bare feet and his ruined leather shoes. "We've got nothing in common."

She twisted in his arms. "What are we going to do about it?"

"Celebrate the difference, my dear." He gathered her close to kiss her. "Celebrate the difference."

About the Author

Christina Dodd is a *New York Times* bestselling author whose novels have been translated into twelve languages, featured by Doubleday Book Club®, recorded on books on tape for the blind, given Romance Writers of America's prestigious Golden Heart and RITA awards, called the year's best by *Library Journal* and, at the pinnacle of her illustrious career, used as a clue in the *Los Angeles Times* crossword puzzle. Christina Dodd lives in Washington with her husband and two dogs. Sign up for her newsletter at www.christinadodd.com.

Don't miss a brand-new historical romance

from *New York Times* bestselling author Christina Dodd

In Bed with the Duke

Coming from Signet in March 2010

Moricadia, 1849

The four-piece ensemble ceased playing, and with exquisite timing, Comte Cloutier delivered the line sure to command the attention of all the guests within earshot. "Have you heard, Lady Lettice,
of the ghost who rides in the night?"

Certainly, he commanded the attention of the Englishman Michael Durant, heir apparent to the duke of Nevitt. There had been
very little to interest him at Lord Thibault's exclusive ball. The musicians had played, the guests had danced, the food was exquisite,
and the gambling room was full. But of gossip, there had been
nothing . . . until now. And now, Michael knew, only because Cloutier failed to comprehend the seriousness of his faux pas. He failed to
comprehend that by tomorrow, he would be gone, traveling back to
France and cursing his penchant for gossip.

With every evidence of interest, Michael strolled closer, to stand
near the group of suitors surrounding Lady Lettice Surtees.

"A ghost?" Lady Lettice gave a high-pitched squeak, worthy of a
young girl's alarm. "No! Pray tell, what does this ghost do?" Before
Cloutier could answer she swung around to her paid companion, a

girl of perhaps twenty who stood at her left shoulder, and snapped, "Make yourself useful, girl! Fan me! Dancing with so many admirers is quite fatiguing."

The girl, a poor, downtrodden wisp of a thing, nodded mutely. From the large reticule she wore attached to her waist, she withdrew an ivory-and-lace fan to cool the abruptly flushed and sweating Lady Lettice.

Lord Escobar hovered at Lettice's left elbow. "Indeed, senorita, it is an unseasonably warm summer evening."

It was a gross flattery to call Lady Lettice "senorita"—she was a widow in her early forties, with the beginnings of the jowls that would plague her old age. But her bosom was impressive and displayed to advantage by her immodestly low-cut, ruffled bodice, and more important, she was wealthy, and the half dozen impoverished men around her wooed her for her fortune.

"So, Cloutier, tell me about this ghost." Lady Lettice withdrew a white cotton handkerchief from between her breasts and blotted her damp upper lip.

"This ghost—he rides at night, in utter silence, a massive white figure in fluttering rags atop a giant white horse. His skin is death, his clothes are rags, and where his eyes should be, there are only black holes. A terrifying apparition, yet the peasants whisper he is the specter of the last king of Moricadian blood."

"Peasants," Lady Lettice said contemptuously.

"Exactly." Cloutier's lip curled with a scorn that only a Frenchman could properly project. "But others who have come to this fair city to take the waters and enjoy the gaming tables have seen him, too, and if you are unlucky enough to see this fearsome ghoul, you should flee at once, for this fearsome phantom"—Cloutier lowered his voice in pitch and volume—"is a sign of impending death."

Michael snorted, the sound breaking the shocked silence.

At once, Lady Lettice fixed him with her gaze. "You're impertinent. Do you know who this man is?" She gestured to Cloutier.

Her mouse of a paid companion made a small warning noise and flapped the fan harder.

Lady Lettice paid no heed. "He is Comte Cloutier, of one of the finest noble families in France. One does not *snort* when he speaks."

"One does if one is Michael Durant, the heir to the Nevitt dukedom." Cloutier bowed to Michael.

"Oh." Lady Lettice extended her hand. "My lord. Your grace."

Cloutier did the honors. "Lady Lettice Surtees, this is Lord—"

"Please." Michael held up a hand. "In England, my name is old and honored. In Moricadia, I am nothing but a political prisoner, a nonentity, a man who has vanished from the world due to the oppression of the ruling family. Call me Durant. It is the only decent title for a disgrace such as me, and even my family name is too honorable." His voice was a low rasp, one that played into the tragedy he projected with a sure hand.

"A political prisoner?" Lady Lettice said. "I am shocked! How is this possible?"

"The only ghost in Moricadia is me, my lady, for until I was allowed out for this one night, my existence has been no more than a rumor." Michael bowed and strolled away.

"The poor man." Lady Lettice spoke in a whisper so high as to pierce ears. "What did he do?"

Michael paused behind a marble pillar to hear the answer.

No one replied at first; then Escobar reluctantly said, "Durant fell foul of the de Guignards. They accused him of assisting the rebels and undermining their position as rulers of Moricadia, and for these two years, he was believed dead. Only recently has it come to light that he is being held prisoner by Lord and Lady Fanchere, trusted allies of Prince Sandre."

"But I don't understand," Lady Lettice insisted. "How do the de Guignards dare to hold an English nobleman against his will?"

"In the case of Moricadia, the de Guignards overthrew King Reynaldo and won"—Escobar waved his hands toward the window, where brightly lit villas, gambling houses, and spas decorated the peaks of the Pyrenees—"all this. But we dare not talk of it. Prince Sandre has spies everywhere, and he does not tolerate dissension in his country." Escobar bowed. "Now, if you'll excuse me . . ."

Michael nodded to the man as he hurried past. Wise Escobar. He would seek another wealthy widow, one not at the epicenter of a possible upheaval.

A well-dressed youth of twenty-two stepped into Escobar's place. He paid no attention to the companion still vigorously fanning Lady Lettice's neck. Nor did any of the other suitors.

Fools. The girl was nervous as a rabbit. The drab gray wool of her plain dress did nothing to complement her pale complexion, and the cut completely obscured what appeared to be a shapely, if too thin, figure. She had typical English features, and might have been pretty, but she kept her eyes down and her shoulders hunched as if expecting at any moment a slap across the cheek.

In Michael's opinion, the lords and gentlemen who fought to capture Lady Lettice in wedded bliss would be well-advised to look to her cowed companion.

The young man jockeyed for position, and the result was disaster—for the companion. They bumped arms. The fan smacked the back of Lady Lettice's head, making the curls over her ears bounce. Turning on the girl, she bellowed, "You stupid thing, how *dare* you hit me?"

"I didn't mean—" The girl's voice matched her demeanor, low and timid, and it trembled.

In a flurry, Lady Lettice adjusted her hair pins. "I should throw you out on the street right now. I should!"

"No, ma'am, please. It won't happen again." The girl looked around at the men, seeking help where there was none. "I beg you. Let me stay in your service."

"She isn't really sorry," Lady Lettice told the others. "She only says that because she's an orphan, the daughter of a Yorkshire vicar who left her with nothing, and she would starve without my kindness. Wouldn't you, Emma?"

"Yes, ma'am." Emma adjusted Lady Lettice's shawl across her shoulders.

"All right, fine, stop." Lady Lettice pushed her away. "You're annoying me. I'll keep you on, but if you ever hit me again—"

"I won't! Thank you!" Emma curtsied, and curtsied again.

Poor Emma. If Michael weren't in such a mess himself, he would see what he could do for her. But as it was . . .

"Actually . . ." Lady Lettice stared at her handkerchief, and Michael could see the spark of some dreadful mischief start in her brain. "I'd like this dampened. Go to the ladies' convenience and do so."

"As you wish, Lady Lettice." Emma took the handkerchief and scurried away.

"Watch, gentlemen," Lady Lettice said. "The stupid girl has no sense of direction. She turns right when she should turn left, goes north when she should go south. The ladies' convenience is to the right, so she'll turn left."

Emma walked to the door, hesitated, and as promised, turned left.

Lady Lettice tittered. "Would you gentlemen care to wager how long it will take my stupid companion to find her way back to me?"

"Good sport," said Bedingfield. "I wager your handkerchief will still be dry!"

Michael, ever the fool for the underdog, quietly went to rescue the girl from her own folly.

⌐

Emma was lost. She stood in the garden and looked back at the château. From here, she could hear the music from the ballroom, see the light spilling from the windows. Surely, if she studied the location, she could find her way back.

But then what? She still wouldn't have accomplished her mission, and she knew very well the price of disobeying Lady Lettice's commands.

As she stood there under the stars, staring at the splashing fountain, she wished she was rich, noble, and beautiful instead of poor,
common, and well educated. What good did common sense and a
sharp intelligence do for a woman when her main duty was to fan
a perspiring beast? But as Emma's father had always said, she might
be a timid child, yet she had an analytical brain, and that was a gift
from God she should utilize to make her life, and the lives of others,
better and more fruitful.

So walking to the fountain, she dipped Lady Lettice's handkerchief into the pool—and heard a warm, rasping chuckle behind her.
Dropping the handkerchief, she turned to face Michael Durant.

"I came out to direct you to the ladies' convenience, but I see you
found a better solution." He nodded toward the fountain.

"It's not what you think." He would report her to the beast. She
was going to be thrown onto the street in a strange country with
nowhere to turn. She was going to die a slow death. "I didn't come
out here on purpose—"

He held up one hand. "Please. Lady Lettice made clear your amazing ability to get lost. She didn't realize your ability to improvise.
Miss . . . ?"

"Chegwidden." She curtsied. "Emma Chegwidden."

In the ballroom, she had watched him and thought him a handsome brute, big-boned, tall, and raw. His hair was red. His eyes were
bright, piercing blue. His black suit was well made, yet the clothes
didn't fit well: the formal black jacket was tight across his shoulders
and loose at this waist, and the ensemble gave him the appearance of
a warhorse dressed in gentleman's clothing.

"A pleasure, Miss Chegwidden." He bowed. "Shall I help you retrieve the handkerchief?"

In the ballroom, she had thought him a phony, another nobleman
flirting with tragedy for the outpouring of sympathy and the residual
gossip.

Out here, he seemed different, sympathetic to her plight. Yet he saw
too much, and he had a quality of stillness about him, like a tiger lying

in wait for its prey. So she must step carefully. Durant could be every bit as nasty as the other gentlemen, and a good deal more dangerous.

Glancing down into the clear water, she saw the white square floating just below the surface. "Thank you. I can do it." Without turning her back to him, she caught it in her fingertips, and wrung it out over the pool. "So she did this to humiliate me."

"She is not a gentlewoman, I believe. Nor a particularly pleasant woman." He walked up the steps and looked back at her. "Shall we go back in?"

By that, she assumed he meant to guide her to the ballroom, and cautiously she followed him.

"This way." He gestured down the corridor, and as they walked, he said, "I recall Lady Lettice was the only daughter of a manufacturing family, married for her fortune to Baron Surtees, and after a mere twenty-some years of hellish married life, Surtees escaped wedlock by dropping dead."

"You are uncharitable, my lord." Emma took a breath to avoid laughing while she spoke, and when she had herself under control, she said, "But yes. After his unfortunate death, Lady Lettice took his title and her fortune, and has lately been touring Europe in hopes of meeting her next, er, husband."

His height made her uncomfortable, and as they walked, she watched his hands. Big hands. Big bones. Big knuckles. Broad palms. Hands weathered by fighting experience. And she was walking alone with him. "Gentlemen of the Continent have a sophisticated attitude toward women of her age and wealth."

"I can imagine. This way." He took a twisting route leading down corridors lined with closed doors.

"Are you sure?" She could have sworn they were headed back to the garden.

"I never get lost." He sounded so sure of himself.

Irksome man. He might not get lost, but he was certainly in trouble. With more sharpness than she intended, she asked, "What did you do to get yourself arrested as a political prisoner?"

He stopped walking.

She stopped walking.

"In Moricadia, it doesn't do to poke your nose into local troubles." He tapped her nose with his finger. "Remember that."

Affronted by his presumption, she said, "I certainly would not do something so stupid."

His eyebrow lifted quizzically. "Of course not. You're supremely sensible."

The way he spoke made her realize—she'd just called him stupid. "My lord, I didn't mean—"

"Not at all. You're quite right. Now." He opened a door to his right.

At once, the sound of music and laughter filtered through, and peeking in, Emma saw the dining hall and, beyond that, the ballroom.

"Do you still have Lady Lettice's handkerchief?" he asked.

"I don't lose things, my lord." She showed it to him, still twisted between her palms. "I only lose myself."

"And now you are found. I'll leave you to make your own way to Lady Lettice's side." He bowed. "It's been a pleasure, Miss Chegwidden."

She curtsied. "My lord, my heartfelt thanks." She watched him walk away, then hurried past the long dining table and stepped into the ballroom.

She found herself standing behind Lady Lettice and her admirers, and opposite where she thought she should be. But she was back, the handkerchief was wet, and Lady Lettice and her nasty game had gone awry.

As Emma walked up behind the group of suitors, she heard Cloutier say, "She must arrive within the next minute, or I lose!"

"Lose what, my lord?" Emma stepped into the circle.

Lady Lettice jumped. Her skin turned ruddy with displeasure, all the way down to her amply displayed breasts, and she snapped, "Where did you come from, girl?"

"The ladies' convenience, as you commanded." Emma extended the handkerchief.

Lady Lettice plucked it out of her palm. "It's wadded up, and too wet. You stupid girl, can't you do anything right? Must I instruct you in every nuance? To think that you are the best the Distinguished Academy of Governesses had to offer is simply—" With a flip of the wrist, she opened the handkerchief.

And a tiny, still-wiggling goldfish slipped out and down her cleavage.

She screamed. Leaped to her feet, slapping at her chest. Screamed again.

The dancing stuttered to a stop.

The men around her backed away and burst into hearty laughter.

And a horrified Emma Chegwidden backed away, murmuring, "I am ruined."